P9-CUK-897

Also by Marie Harte

All I Want for Halloween
The Kissing Game

The McCauley Brothers
The Troublemaker Next Door
How to Handle a Heartbreaker
Ruining Mr. Perfect
What to Do with a Bad Boy

Body Shop Bad Boys
Test Drive
Roadside Assistance
Zero to Sixty
Collision Course

The Donnigans
A Sure Thing
Just the Thing
The Only Thing

Veteran Movers
The Whole Package
Smooth Moves
Handle with Care
Delivered with a Kiss

Turn Up the Heat
Make Me Burn
Burning Desire

HOT
FOR
YOU

MARIE HARTE

sourcebooks
casablanca

Published by Sourcebooks Casablanca, an imprint of Sourcebooks
P.O. Box 4410, Naperville, Illinois 60567-4410
(630) 961-3900
sourcebooks.com

Printed and bound in Canada.
MBP 10 9 8 7 6 5 4 3 2 1

Dedicated to D&R. I love you.
And to all the real romance lovers out there,
this is for you.

Chapter One

July in Seattle

"I HATE THESE THINGS," REGGIE MORGAN MUTTERED TO HIS partner as they readied to give a presentation to a full crowd of eager firefighting enthusiasts.

"Relax. You'll do fine." Mack ran a hand through his always perfect hair, the guy vain enough to constantly wear it styled. Then again, the new fire station *had* used Mack's chiseled chin, golden tan, and laughing, bright-blue eyes on a lot of the promotional material for Station 44.

"Why aren't *you* giving this ridiculous speech? You're on all the posters."

"You could have been." Mack grinned. "Your sister said you're no Idris Elba, but I disagree."

"Shut up."

"Well, maybe Morris Chestnut but with hair."

"Mack, come on. You're good at talking." He added under his breath, "You never shut up." When Mack frowned, he hurriedly tacked on, "*You* really represent Station 44."

"So do you and the rest of C shift. What's your point?"

Reggie had been stress sweating for the past half hour, thankful his dark-blue service uniform hid any unfortunate pit stains. Hell, put him in the middle of a roaring fire, in a submarine having technical difficulties eight hundred feet below the surface, or at a family dinner with his father and sisters giving him dating advice. All traumatic experiences.

But none of them could beat a Monday afternoon lecture at the local library in front of a ton of people, the majority under the age of ten.

Reggie tried again. "You're the station's wonder boy."

Mack smirked. "That's true. I am the most talented, best-looking, and—"

"Have the biggest mouth."

Mack shrugged. "And yet, the lieutenant wanted *you* to give the class. Go figure."

Reggie wished he'd never confessed to the LT how much he hated public speaking. Now the guy made it his mission in life to get Reggie over that nagging fear. "Yes, but he never said you couldn't help."

"And take any attention away from the great Reggie Morgan? No thanks. I'll just stand by, clicking slides and looking pretty while the *brains of the operation*—that's what you're always calling yourself, isn't it?—takes center stage."

Reggie did like to remind the rest of his four-man crew that he was the brains of their unit. And the brawn, come to think of it. Sure, the other two on duty had some muscle, but none of them could out-bench him. Mack might be faster on a distance run, but Reggie could break him in half without much effort. Of course, since his free time nowadays consisted of lifting weights when not hanging with the guys, that did explain—

"Quit stalling. You're up." Mack shoved him from behind the stacks where he'd been hiding, exposing him to a bazillion stares.

Reggie caught his balance, glared over his shoulder at Mack, then plastered a smile on his face and walked toward the large screen, which would display the slideshow presentation the station had put together for events such as these.

He looked out over the crowd of close to fifty—*hell*—children and a few parents, all waiting expectantly for Reggie to regale them with stories about firefighting and life in the station.

He cleared his throat and said, "Hello there," at the same time the librarian in charge of public events introduced him. Reggie ignored Mack's chuckle and watched his future ex-friend walk to the other side of the screen, pick up a remote for the slideshow, and wait.

The librarian was saying, "Reggie Morgan, one of our wonderful firefighters from the new station serving the Beacon Hill, New Holly, and South Beacon Hill neighborhoods. Reggie's here today to tell us what it's like to be a firefighter. He's got pictures too."

Mack waved at the crowd, at ease with being in front of people the way Reggie would never be.

"And I see that Firefighter Morgan's brought along an assistant," the librarian, old enough to be Reggie's grandmother, said with a smile.

"A handsome, *single* assistant," Mack said with a huge grin. "I'm Mack."

"Mack," Reggie said under his breath. "Behave."

Several of the parents with their children gave Mack a second look.

"I'll give you my number when we're through," the librarian teased and continued when the laughter had died down. "Welcome all, and let's get this show on the road." She turned to Reggie. "And thank you for agreeing to do this."

The lieutenant had carved out an hour for the lecture, part of the fire department's public relations and a way to engage the community. Reggie loved the idea of the station getting to know their neighbors, but not if he had to be the one doing the talking.

He gave Mack another look.

The bastard ignored him.

Reggie turned back to the crowd of eager faces and knew he might as well get started. "Hi, everyone. Thanks for coming out on a sunny summer day. I know you'd probably rather be swimming or playing than hearing me talk."

"Not me," one little girl said. "I have a lot of questions."

"Me too," a young boy agreed.

"Okay. Great." Reggie cleared his throat, not comfortable with such scrutiny. The little girl had dark eyes that seemed to look through him, not at him. She couldn't be more than five or six, dressed to look adorable in matching pink shorts and a T-shirt showing off her tan, holding a fuzzy grizzly bear.

But that cuteness packaged a small, intense, and scary kid.

He swallowed and pointed to the screen, now showing a picture of a fire truck and the number "44" emblazoned over it. "I'm Reggie. This is Mack." Mack nodded. "We're with Station 44, and we work C shift. Our station has four eight-person shifts—A, B, C, and D. And we have two lieutenants, who are our bosses. We—"

The little girl cut in, "How come you only have two lieutenants but you have four shifts? I know my math, and I think you're missing two."

Reggie contained a sigh. "Our lieutenants cover two shifts each."

"Oh." The little girl nodded.

"We have pretty much the best job in the world, because we get to help people when we can, and we get to meet new people all the time."

"But what if they're burned? That's not great." The little girl frowned.

Behind her, a well-dressed man, in slacks and a polo, rolled his eyes.

"That's a good point," Reggie agreed. "And maybe this job wouldn't be good for someone who hates fire or is afraid of blood. But we—"

"Blood?" The girl's eyes narrowed. "What blood? Do you make people bleed?"

Mack coughed but didn't quite muffle his laughter.

A few adults grinned.

The girl's father—uncle?—shushed her. "Emily, let him speak. Sorry."

"No problem." Reggie mentally thanked the guy. "Well, we as

firefighters in the awesome city of Seattle have to do a lot more than put out fires. As you probably know, there are thirty-four stations in the city, including Harbor View Medical Center. All of them run twenty-four hours a day, seven days a week."

Mack changed the slides, showing the layout.

"We have five battalions, and each battalion has a chief."

One boy raised his hand. Not the intense Emily, thank goodness.

"Yes?" Reggie said.

"Do you mean battalions like the Army? My dad is in the Army."

"Are you in the Army?" Emily asked. Without raising her hand.

"Actually, I was in the Navy. Mack was in the Air Force, and two of our crew who aren't here were in the Marines."

"Semper Fi," a woman said from the back of the room.

Semper Fi—always faithful, the Marine Corps motto.

Reggie grinned. "I'll tell them you said that. But you know, we live with an always-faithful mindset when we work too. Firefighting is a lot more than using a hose with water to put out a fire. Does anyone know what 'lifesaving' is?"

A little boy in the back answered, "Saving a person so he doesn't die."

"That's a great answer."

The boy beamed.

"Every firefighter in Seattle must first be an EMT—an emergency medical technician. We do something called basic life support. That's like taking your pulse or listening to your heart. We can splint your arm if it's broken and take you to the hospital to get fixed. Has anyone ever seen an ambulance?"

Mack clicked the slide to show them an ambulance, and everyone's hands raised.

"That's what we drive when we're not in the fire truck. Actually, most of what we do is help people get better. We help them in our ambulance, what we call an aid vehicle, and let them go see their own doctor when they want. But if they're really bad off, we might take them to the hospital."

"Do you wrap them like mummies?" a little boy wearing a superhero shirt and cape asked.

"No, not like mummies." Reggie wanted the kids to understand. "The ones who take the really hurt people to the hospital are called paramedics. They do advanced life support. So, if you had a heart attack or got shot or had a really bad break and were bleeding all over the place, the paramedic might treat you in the back of the ambulance. And you know what?"

"What?" asked a girl wearing blue frames with thick lenses. Her eyes looked huge behind them.

"We don't really have that many paramedics, which is kind of weird, if you think about it. We have paramedics in our fire stations, but we only have seven medic units in all of the city. The medic unit is what the paramedics drive. Remember, I said that we EMTs use aid vehicles, like the ambulances. The medic vehicles look like ours but inside, the paramedics do the fancy stuff, like give IVs, intubate, and handle acute sickness and trauma. They go to a special school for that."

"Did you go to school?" Emily asked, her powerful gaze burning a hole through him.

"I did."

"Do you shoot people?"

"Ah, no."

"Do you stab them?" a boy sitting next to her asked. "So, you make them bleed then you patch them up?"

"No." The boy's identical twin shook his head. "He doesn't make them bleed. The paramedic does."

Reggie bit back a groan. "No, the paramedic doesn't make anyone bleed."

"Does he stab them with a sword?" another child asked.

"No, we don't stab or shoot anyone."

"Do you have a gun?" another child asked.

Mack's face had turned red with his effort to hold back laughter. And the class went downhill from there.

By the end of the lecture, Reggie had regained control, only barely, but enough to answer questions from the adults as well. He and Mack showed everyone slides of the inside of an engine truck, explained how the different stations had different equipment, and how their SCBA (self-contained breathing apparatus) gear worked. They'd brought a clean one for a live demonstration, and the children had a lot of fun looking through the mask and trying on a helmet.

The class turned out to be informative and entertaining.

Even though Emily continued to try to stare into Reggie's soul.

She walked up to him at the very end despite her parent trying his best to get her to leave. The man held up his hands in defeat. "I give up."

Reggie noticed that she carried a stuffed brown bear, a cute and furry little grizzly with an ax strapped to its back. Apt that she carried a stuffed predator considering the girl's ferocity with questions.

She looked from her bear to him. "You use an ax like Brownie. And you're brown like Brownie."

Reggie nodded. "I am."

"I think you're pretty."

He blinked.

Mack guffawed behind him.

"Ah, thank you. I think you're pretty too."

"P-R-E-T-T-Y. I'm a good speller."

"I see that."

"I wish I had teeth and claws so when Marty Binker hits me, I could carve him up." She curled her fingers and pretended to claw his arm. "After the fight, you could heal me by doing BLS and I wouldn't have to go to the hospital." She leaned closer to whisper in a loud voice, "Uncle Doug had to go to the hospital because he was pooping a lot."

The man with Emily, Doug apparently, turned bright red. "Okay, Emily, we need to get you back to your mom." In a lower but still audible voice, Doug added, "She owes me big for this."

Emily continued, "But then they gave him ivy and he had more fluid and got better."

"Ivy?" Mack asked.

"I think she means an IV." Reggie stared at the little girl who said *ivy* and *fluid* in the same sentence. "It must have been pretty serious if Uncle Doug needed an IV. I'm glad he's better."

She nodded, solemn, and Reggie was struck by how cute she was when not grilling him. She reminded him of Rachel, a little girl he'd been doing his level best not to think about while surrounded by so many children. The sadness that had never left him returned, though he refused to let it show.

"I'm glad he's better too." Emily smiled. "I'm Emily." She held out her hand.

He shook it, conscious of how much larger than her he was. "I'm Reggie."

"I know. I was paying attention."

"Emily, we need to go," Doug reminded her.

"Okay. Thank you for the stories. Maybe you can come over for dinner with me and my mom. She's really nice and makes macaroni with hot dogs in it. And she hardly ever poops. Well, sometimes, but—"

"And we're done." Doug scooped Emily up in his arms and tickled her. As she laughed, he said to Reggie, "Thanks for the class. And really, you did great. Especially in front of the terror of John Muir Elementary." He nodded to Emily.

Reggie grinned. "Thanks. Today was harder than running the gauntlet when I was in the Navy."

Doug laughed. "I'll bet. Thanks for all you do. You too, Mack."

Mack nodded. "Anytime."

They left, and Reggie was sorry to see them go. Though the little girl had been a tough sell, he felt as if he'd won her over by the end.

"You know, you should have gotten Emily's mom's number." Mack rubbed his chin. "She doesn't poop a lot, apparently. That's pretty much your speed, right?"

"Shut up."

Mack laughed.

They drove back to work just as a call came in.

"Thank God." With any luck, they'd get someone they could help to take Reggie's mind from cute little girls he'd never see again. Adorable Emily and her brown bear, and Rachel, the daughter who might have been.

———————

When Doug handed Emily off to Maggie after her return from an excruciating visit to the dentist, Maggie thanked him, her lower lip still numb. "You're the best. Thanks for taking my tiny terror." She sank back on her couch in her semi-clean apartment while Emily raced to her room.

"Don't mention it." Doug, her neighbor, fellow teacher, and best friend, shook his head. "I mean it. I want to forget today as soon as possible."

She groaned.

He sighed, looking downtrodden. For a man of thirty-nine years, Doug looked much younger. He smiled and laughed a lot, living in the moment, something she'd been doing her best to emulate. So, for Doug to sigh like that...

Doug looked her right in the eye. "Just another day in the life of Emily Swanson. We went to the library. And Emily asked... questions."

Maggie cringed. "How bad was it?"

Doug started laughing.

Maggie's daughter was six going on thirty. A precocious little genius with lofty dreams of becoming the first-ever bear-princess-assassin. The idea being to gouge out the patient's heart with her bear claws, eat only a tiny bit of it as bear-payment, then kill her victims to save the bear kingdom from evil poachers.

And no, Maggie would never again allow her ex to read her daughter Grimm's fairy tales while binging on Animal Planet. Stephen knew better.

Doug caught his breath, finally. "I think she scared the firefighter giving the lecture. The guy was built like a tank and had to be over six feet tall. But he had the look of fear when your daughter asked him question after question. He did pretty well, overall. Then, of course, at the end, Emily told him he was pretty and mentioned I was once hospitalized because I pooped too much." Doug dragged a hand over his face. "It was really embarrassing. Not just because of the poop mention, but because both firemen there for the talk were drool-worthy."

Maggie grinned.

"I'm not kidding. We should take Emily on a tour of Station 44 when C shift is on duty."

Maggie laughed. "I'm telling Benny you said that."

"Please. Who do you think will be driving us to the station?"

"Good point." Maggie loved Doug and Benny. Her family, if not by blood, the married couple had been supportive and loving from the very first day Maggie had met Doug at school. He had been more than welcoming. Thanks to him, she'd found the apartment next door when she and Stephen had divorced.

"Have I ever told you how much I love you and Benny?"

"Not since yesterday. But go ahead and tell me again. I earned it."

Maggie reached up for a hug, and he leaned down to give her

one. "Wow," she exclaimed. "My hands are almost overlapping behind you! You've been losing weight!"

He pulled back with a huge smile. "I love you even more now. Make sure to say that again in front of Benny. We're having a competition. Winner gets an all-expense-paid dinner at Canliss."

"Isn't that contrary to losing all that weight? Rewarding yourself with food sends the wrong message, doesn't it?"

Doug glared. "Until you've had their caramelized mussels and dry-aged rib-eye, don't judge."

"And don't you guys have a joint bank account? What's the point of who pays?"

"Your daughter told centerfold hunks I pooped so much, I had to be hospitalized. Let me have this contest."

She bit back laughter. "Oh, er, right. I hope you win." She looked him over. "But you're one to talk, calling someone else a 'centerfold hunk.'" Doug had dark hair he kept constantly black thanks to a salon, a trim figure even when *not* dieting, and features she would have called pretty on a woman and oddly stunning on a man.

In contrast, Benny had height and mass, most of it muscle, though the slow-building tire around his middle attested to his love of good food. He had brutish features, full sleeves of tattoos over bronze skin, and wore his shaggy hair back in a ponytail. A retired semiprofessional wrestler who now taught piano and dabbled in painting, Benny loved nothing more than to gossip about the apartment complex and lament Maggie's lack of a love life.

The pair complemented each other, and Maggie had found in them real family.

"So how did you end up taking Emily to the library? I thought Benny volunteered."

Maggie had a summer job to make ends meet and often relied upon Emily's "uncles" to help with childcare.

"He was supposed to, but they needed his help at the community center since their piano player called in sick. And honestly, he's been dying to play something that doesn't involve scales."

"Oh. I'm happy he got to play today. And I'm sorry about your, ah, pooping problem."

Doug grimaced. "Oh, stop. It was one time when I had the flu, two years ago. I was dehydrated, is all. How the hell does she remember something from that long ago?"

Maggie had long ago stopped wondering how her daughter did half the things she did. "It's Emily."

"True." He shrugged.

"Was the library fun, at least?"

"The lecture was surprisingly good, considering the fireman looked like he was about to pass out when he started."

"I used to be that way. But after being traumatized by dealing with a classroom full of seven-year-olds, I got over public speaking fast."

"And then you had Emily."

"Yep. The cure for all that ails you."

The cure returned to the living room in last year's Halloween ninja costume, carrying her bear and throwing stars made of tinfoil.

"I need nunchucks, Mag-Mom."

Maggie refrained from rolling her eyes. At least Mag-Mom was better than Margaret-Mother—what Emily had taken to calling her last month. With any luck, Maggie would become "Mommy" once more. "Nunchucks? What for?"

"To hunt down the assassins after me and my new friend, Reggie."

"The scared, hunky fireman," Doug murmured.

"So Reggie was nice?"

Emily nodded. "And pretty. He thinks I'm pretty too. I bet if I asked nicely, he'd give me a baby brother."

Doug choked.

Maggie just stared at her daughter with wide eyes. "A baby brother? I thought you wanted a turtle."

"I did, but Sherry has a baby brother, and she said he smiles at her all the time."

"Probably just gas," Doug said.

"Maybe." Emily narrowed her eyes on her mother. "But Sherry said he looks like her mom and dad and kinda like her. My brother would be an EMT ninja who has fire dog stickers." That said, Emily did somersaults down the hallway with Brownie the bear, making explosion noises.

"EMT ninja? Stickers?"

Doug grinned. "Reggie, the hunky fireman, is an EMT, and he gave out stickers at the end of his speech. She's right. Any baby you had would be a ninja and fight boo-boos. A win-win. Let's schedule that tour of Station 44."

"Oh boy. Let's not. The last time Emily wanted to set me up with someone, Mr. Nelson's wife was not amused."

Doug laughed. "No, but Benny and I were. And hey, now you get extra fries with your order at the deli when Mr. Nelson waits on you."

They didn't eat there when she saw Mrs. Nelson at the counter, however.

Maggie sighed. "I'd better go make Emily some paper towel nunchucks before she orders the real thing off Amazon."

"Can I just say how happy I am to spend time with that beautiful child, watching her grow and learn? And that Benny and I can give her back at a moment's notice?"

"No, you can't say that."

"Die, evil fire lord," Emily screeched from her room and gave an almost maniacal laugh. "You are thwarted again. This time, my dagger will spear your heart."

Doug looked at Maggie. "Your six-year-old knows the word 'thwarted,' and her dagger is 'spearing' someone's heart. Yep, I'm ecstatic to leave that little girl with her mommy." He danced out the door with a wide grin.

"*Thwarted* by a six-year-old, her poopy uncle, and a pretty, if scared, fireman," Maggie muttered and went in search of her craft bin, praying she had something to satisfy her brainy, beautiful, tiny terror.

Chapter Two

REGGIE SPENT TUESDAY, THE FIRST DAY OFF IN HIS TWO-SET cycle, exercising at the station. He had two days off, one on again, then four days off before the cycle restarted. His crew of four had decided to join him at the station.

Though they all worked together, they liked to play together as well. He and his buddies found time at the gym both therapeutic and needful. Besides, nowhere could Reggie get better equipment and a decent facility with showers for *free*.

Mack grinned while Reggie deadlifted, embellishing yesterday's class at the library to anyone who would listen. The dick. "So Reggie's got that nervous sweat going on, his bald head dripping with nerves, when—"

"I'm not bald. It's a close cut, but I've got hair." He ran his hand over his head, pleased with his barber.

"—the kids were brutal." Mack hooted, and Brad and Tex hung on his every word.

Like Reggie, the rest of his team had bonded over shared prior military experiences in addition to being Seattle firefighters. While Reggie had served in the Navy, the best of the armed services, Brad and Tex had been Marines and Mack, Air Force. They still liked to razz one another, but in a good, brotherly way. Having grown up with two older sisters a rabid bear would know better than to mess with, Reggie knew the difference between brotherly teasing and being plain mean.

At the thought of a "rabid bear," memories of the adorable kid from the previous day came back.

Mack was saying, "They kept asking Reggie about blood and guts since he made the mistake of trying to explain basic life support and advanced life support to them."

Feeling the need to defend himself, Reggie spoke up. "I only told them that if someone got knifed or shot, they would need paramedics, not an EMT."

Tex nodded and, in his slow, drawly Texan accent, said, "Probably not the smartest thing to say to little kids. Might scare 'em, hoss."

"Everyone's a critic."

Mack continued to give the team the rundown, ending with, "Then the girl tells Reggie she wishes she was brown and pretty like him and her bear. It was adorable."

"Well, he *is* pretty," Brad said with a large smile. "So, so pretty."

"Like a beauty queen," Tex agreed.

Reggie glared at Mack, imagining the ribbing in his future once everyone knew what had happened. "I hate you."

"Who, me?" Mac tossed a small, stuffed bear at him with an *I'm Pretty* sash across its chest.

The guys cracked up.

Damn. Part and parcel of being a firefighter—being able to dish it out and take it. The ribbing, teasing, and the laughter. They'd been making fun of Brad forever. The guy looked like a buffer version of a Ken doll, and Ken had been fooling around with a bunch of Barbies and other toys all over the station, doing perverted things to poor Barbie.

Tex had seen his life upended when he'd started dating the battalion chief's daughter. Now cowboy figures and blond dolls were up to no good all over the place. And since the other lieutenant in the station, who worked with B and D shifts, resembled the cartoon character Dora the Explorer, she'd been finding Dora stickers on her notebooks and tons of action figures on or near her desk.

Reggie used to find their situations funny as hell. But he had a feeling life was about to get a lot less funny if fuzzy brown bears started humping My Little Pony.

"Look, it wasn't that funny."

Tex wore a large grin. "No, it really was. And is." He high-fived Mack. "Reg, you have a real way with words."

Mack grinned. "Funny, but little kids understand him no problem. Grown folks? Not so much. I'm thinking he's at a social level of about first grade. Maybe second."

Brad snickered. "Come on, Mack. Reggie's at least as smart at a third grader."

"Shut up, all of you." Reggie lifted to muscle fatigue, trying to ignore Brad's grin as the big guy spotted for him. "So what's up with tonight? You guys busy with your girls or are we on for bowling?"

Brad nodded. "Avery and Bree are hanging out for a girls' night. So I'm free."

Mack smirked. "He means he's *allowed* to go out." He shot Tex a look. "And since Bree has allowed Tex some alone time, I guess that means he can play with the other kids too."

"Got you by the nads, eh, Tex?" Hernandez laughed as he entered with the other four members of C shift, the guys of the *second-best* crew.

Tex flipped Mack, Hernandez, and the rest of their shift off, to much laughter.

The others returned hand gestures and started teasing Reggie about his drama at the library. Reggie threw the stuffed bear at them, which caused no end of entertainment.

"I think I'm done working out," he muttered.

Mack groaned. "Me too. I need food. So tonight? Eight o'clock for bowling? I'll reserve a lane."

Tex frowned. "You can't reserve lanes there."

"You can when you know the manager." Mack winked. "Later, losers."

Reggie watched him go. "Sometimes I want to pound on that guy."

Brad wrapped an arm around his shoulders. "Same."

"No kidding," Tex teased. "Too bad he's family, eh?"

Reggie sighed. "The little brother I never wanted."

"Well, with your sisters, it's no wonder. Lisa and Nadia scare me." Brad shivered, which had Tex and Reggie laughing.

Reggie knew the guys loved his sisters. Heck, he did too. But yeah, they could be scary when someone threatened their baby brother.

Tex shook his head. "See you slackers tonight. I have a few errands to run." Tex left with a wave.

Brad groaned. "Me too. I tried telling Avery she should be doing the grocery shopping since we've moved in together. I mean, women are into shopping, right?"

"How'd that go for you?" Reggie already knew the answer.

Brad grimaced. "I clipped coupons last night after apologizing several times on the phone. And in person this morning." That brought a twinkle to Brad's eye. "And I'm leaving right now to buy groceries. How do you think my suggestion worked for me?"

Reggie shook his head. "I could have told you that."

"Well, where were you when I was being less than smart?"

"I'm here now, dumbass."

Brad laughed and left, Reggie following.

Filling his day off with several errands of his own, Reggie picked up a few things, cleaned his house, and did laundry. He also talked to his dad, a mistake he'd known he'd made as soon as he'd heard his father's upbeat attitude.

Which of course he shared with the guys when bowling later that night. On their second pitcher of beer, Reggie lamented his family's new lease on life.

"So my dad is telling me all about how he's charming his new girlfriend. I swear, the guy has love advice for me way too much. I think he needs a hobby."

Mack guffawed and placed Reggie's stuffed bear with that stupid sash in front of him. "That's because your dad is popular with the ladies. Like father like son, eh?"

"Keep it up, dead guy walking," Reggie growled.

"Oh, my bowl." Mack darted away from the table and bowled a strike. The bastard.

Reggie sipped his beer, doing his best not to laugh. It never helped to encourage the guys.

Brad grinned. "I have to say, your dad is an inspiration. Women love him. Men love him. He's a terrific guy."

"Yeah, yeah." Reggie groaned. "I love the guy. Don't get me wrong. But just because he's in love doesn't mean I have to be." Not again, at least, not so soon. "I mean, he's been happily single for years. But suddenly he's out to find a wife?"

Tex goggled. "Harry Morgan wants to get married? *Your* dad?"

"I know, right?" Reggie frowned. "Maybe he's doing it to get me back out there, in some weird, father-does-it-best kind of example."

Brad, Tex, and Mack, who'd returned to the table, wore identical expressions. *Thoughtful* expressions.

Brad said, slowly, "We know a few ladies who—"

"No."

Brad gave him a coaxing smile. "Come on, Reggie. We've been cutting you a lot of slack, but it's time."

"I've dated. Heck, I went out last week."

"On a call," Tex reminded him. "Flirting when on a call doesn't count."

"Besides, *she* was flirting with *you*," Mack corrected. "That really doesn't count."

"I flirted back," Reggie said, knowing he had weak support.

"Nope." Mack shook his head. "It's time."

Reggie didn't like to think about why he'd been so slow about dating again.

"Amy's gone, right?" Brad reminded him. As if Reggie needed to be reminded about getting his heart ripped out. "She and Rachel are back with her ex, and they're happy. That's a good thing."

"It is." It really wasn't, because Amy's ex was a huge douche, and

Reggie had no doubt the guy would dump them. Again. But there was nothing he could say about it. Not when Amy had been so insistent that Rachel needed her father back in her life. No matter that the guy hadn't been there while Reggie had been raising his kid for two years. Oh no.

"He looks pissed," Mack murmured.

"Yep, there it is." Tex slapped Reggie on the back. "The way I see it, you need to move on. It's been what? Seven months now?"

"I guess." Seven months and two weeks, actually.

Mack and Brad nodded.

"More than time to get back in the saddle."

"I know. I, ah, I actually have a blind date tomorrow night." That he'd been dreading.

The group as one stared openmouthed at Reggie.

He scowled. "What? You wanted me to go on a date. I'm going on one tomorrow."

They all started talking at the same time. "With who?" "How did you meet her?" "Prove she's real or I'm calling your sisters."

Reggie held up his hands in surrender. "Whoa. Hold on. The woman is real. She's a friend of my sister's. She works at one of the colleges and is single."

"How old?" Tex asked. "Sixty? Seventy? Older?"

"Ass. She's close to my age, I think." He hoped. Reggie didn't mind an older woman, but he didn't think he was ready to date a grandma yet. With his sisters' views on dating younger women, he knew his date would be nowhere near her teenage years.

"Which sister set you up?" Mack asked. "Because if it's Lisa, you're probably okay. But if it's Nadia…" Mack cringed.

"He has a point." Tex nodded. "I love your sisters, but Nadia had a warped sense of humor." He grinned. "Love that gal."

"It was Lisa. Trust me, I thought about that," Reggie said. Mack had the right of it about Lisa being the safer bet. "You guys aren't helping, you know. Hell, maybe I should cancel."

"No, you should go." Brad nodded. "Look, how bad can it be? You go to dinner with a lovely woman even your sister approves of, you eat, enjoy the company, and if you're lucky, you connect and meet up for a second date."

Mack frowned. "Huh. I thought you were going to say, 'If you're lucky, you don't go home alone.'"

Tex nodded. "Or: 'If you're lucky, you find a few hours in the sack with someone special.' A second date?" Tex rolled his eyes at Brad. "Nice, choir boy."

Mack snickered, and even Reggie couldn't hold back a smile at Brad's blush.

"Dickheads," Brad muttered. "It's not wrong to like the one you're with."

"We know that, Brad. But seeing you in touch with your emotional side is just… It's beautiful." Tex wiped fake tears, which had Mack laughing even harder.

Brad sighed. "It's Avery's fault. She keeps making me watch these fix-my-life reality shows."

"I love those." Mack nodded. "Iyanla really knows what she's talking about." He paused as everyone looked at him. "What? I'm serious."

Reggie laughed, needing this time with his friends. Because who knew what tomorrow would bring? Then again, Brad had a point. How bad could it be?

━━━━━━━━━━

It was beyond awful. His date was pretty, pleasant, and funny. Or she had been until she'd jumped him when they'd settled inside his car after dinner. Reggie had turned to thank her for the night and been kissed, groped, and straddled for dear life.

It had been a while since he'd had sex, and having a gorgeous woman rub all over him had caused an erection to pop in seconds. But damn, he didn't want any of it.

The date had reminded him of how much heartbreak would come at the end of it all. All the smiles and laughter couldn't make up for the tears later. And the sex, while relieving, would only complicate matters with a woman Reggie wasn't sure he liked that much. Funny and pleasant sure the hell weren't the same as hilarious and captivating.

He'd nicely but firmly told her no, having to grasp her wrists to stop her from fondling him.

Since he'd driven them both—*huge* mistake—he had to take her home. So he got to experience her mortified tears, self-loathing, and venom for his leading her on by telling her she'd looked pretty.

By the time he'd dropped her off, he was ready to drink.

And then his sisters and father texted to remind him about Sunday morning breakfast. Where they'd proceed to grill him on the date, that was, if the woman didn't confess what a poor companion Reggie had been before then.

Shoot me now.

———————————

Maggie politely declined an invitation to dinner from one of the new guys, for the third time this week, at the law firm where she worked part-time, filing. On the plus side, he looked close to her own age, was single, and didn't live with his parents.

But shouldn't the lawyers know better than to try interoffice relationships? She'd been down this same road before. At her last summer job, in fact, in a different office. If this one happened like the last one, she could envision the future. They'd go out, he'd offer to buy dinner. Then he'd expect her to sleep with him. If he didn't and actually turned out to be a nice guy, he'd want to continue dating, not understanding when she needed to take time to be with Emily or Doug and Benny.

And this new guy would definitely be offended when she didn't drop everything to see him through some drama or other. She's already gotten the sense he was high-maintenance from his paralegal, who had a habit of rolling her eyes anytime she left his office.

Maggie needed this job to enjoy a pleasant summer before school started again in the fall. Though on a teacher's salary, Maggie lived well within her means and could technically afford not to work a summer job. But a part-time job did wonders for her budget.

Smiling, she bumped into one of the senior partners and earned a frown. First time since she'd been working there that she'd seen that happen. Normally he was all smiles.

"Ms. Swanson, it's come to my attention that there's been some inappropriate behavior with you and one of our lawyers. We should discuss this in my office."

She looked beyond him at the new guy sitting in front of the boss's desk. Jeez, had he even waited ten seconds before telling on her for not being nice?

With a sigh, she said, "Is this where you warn me to be nicer to the new guy, or where you try to fire me for some type of relationship New Guy invented?"

The senior partner frowned. "Please, come into my office, Ms. Swanson."

The latter then.

She followed him but didn't bother to sit. "I've been working here for a month. In that time, I have been nothing but on time and professional. I do my job, and I do it well. I offer to cover for those who are late or need help."

"But—"

"I'm talking," she said to shut down the new guy. To the senior partner, she continued, "Now, because I told our newest partner that I didn't think going out on a date would be a good idea, I'm in here to get a lecture about office policies. And note, I have told him no not once, but *three* times."

New guy flushed bright red.

The boss looked from the new guy to her, and his tension eased. "I'm sorry, Ms. Swanson. I was under the impression something else had occurred."

"I'm sure you were. I'm here for the next month and a half because I need this job. But I don't need it bad enough to put up with sexual harassment from New Guy."

"My name is Trent," New Guy said through gritted teeth. "And it wasn't sexual harassment. This is a big misunderstanding."

"You'll be hearing from my attorney." She nodded at the boss. "Good day."

Before she could leave, the partner tossed Trent out on his ass and did his best to keep Maggie at the office. But she didn't want to spend the rest of her summer uncomfortable and on edge working a job she didn't love for so-so pay. She was better off working elsewhere or just enjoying her summer with Emily. They'd have to scrimp to get by, but Maggie could make fun day trips for them both that cost nothing.

The partner, eager to make it all go away, offered her a month and half's salary if she'd just leave, no lawsuit and no bad talk about the company.

Knowing she didn't have the money for a lawyer and had no intention of finding one, Maggie pretended to dither before accepting his terms. Now she had the income without having to do the work. Win-win.

"You have a deal. But I'd advise you to take a hard look at Trent, because I can guarantee he's going to cause you problems."

And so, one and a half month's salary richer, one asshole poorer, she returned home.

The next morning, she drove Emily out to a friend's house in South Beacon Hill for a playdate. Since the other girl's mom had things well in hand, Maggie took the time to do a little grocery shopping. After buying enough to last them the week, she picked up a chattering Emily.

As they started to leave the parking lot, Emily squealed, "Stop! Stop, Mag-Mom!"

Maggie slammed on her brakes, only to hear several people behind her honk their horns.

"Emily, don't do that! What's wrong?" Maggie's heart wouldn't stop racing.

Emily pointed out her window. "That puppy's in trouble."

Maggie looked out only to see a puppy on South Othello, in the middle of the road. The poor thing looked as if it had already been hit and was limping in one direction, then a car would roar by, beeping, and the dog crawled the other way.

"What the heck? Fudge this!" Proud for calling on the right F word with Emily in the car, she made a right turn and parked on the side of the road without blocking traffic. Maggie turned off the car and left the windows partially down due to the heat. Her heart racing, she said to Emily, "Stay here while I rescue the dog. You don't leave the car or unlock the doors. Do you hear me?"

Emily nodded, her eyes wide.

Maggie locked the vehicle and rushed to the puppy. She waved at traffic to slow down and grabbed the dog, running back to her car. The poor thing was shaking, its back leg stiff. It looked...well, to be honest, the little pit mix was so ugly, he was cute. He had scars and bruising and was bleeding from a few cuts. Yet when she opened her hatchback and settled him in the trunk, he remained still and quiet, just looking up at her with sad eyes.

Her heart melted. "You poor thing."

"Mag-Mom, we have a dog!"

"Don't get ahead of yourself, Emily. He might have run away from someone who's upset and missing him." Though Maggie didn't see a collar on the little guy.

She rounded the front of her car to get back in. "Don't be disappointed if we can't—"

Then something big hit her. And she saw black.

———————

"Ma'am? Ma'am? Are you with me?" A deep voice rocked her back to consciousness.

Maggie had no idea where she was or what had happened. "Emily? Where's Emily?" Wow. She sounded terrible, and her throat hurt.

"Emily's right here with me. She's sitting right next to us. No, don't turn your head. You're fine, and Emily's fine."

"I'm here, Mommy." Emily cried and sniffed and cried some more. "Reggie's here. And Frank's here too."

"Frank?" Reggie? She blinked up at a very muscular man wearing a navy-blue shirt with an EMT logo on it. A glance behind him told her they were inside a vehicle of some kind. An ambulance? "Are you Frank?"

The man smiled, and Maggie distantly noted that his dark-brown eyes seemed full of compassion, his hands gentle as he moved them over her face and looked into her eyes. He shone a light, and she flinched.

"Hmm. I'd say you have a slight concussion, but we'll get you all checked out, so don't worry. No, Ma'am. I'm Reggie. Frank would be the puppy your daughter found."

"Huh?"

Reggie, he'd said his name was, scooted down her body, looking her over, then focused on her right arm. "Do you remember what happened to you?"

Emily remained by her side.

Maggie tried to recall, and it came back in pieces. "Emily had a playdate. I went shopping. On our way home, she screamed at me to stop because a poor puppy was stranded in the road." Maggie frowned, and the motion caused to her moan.

"Mommy!"

Emily's shriek didn't help her headache.

"I'm fine, sweetie." She looked to Reggie. "Just a little headache."

"Mm-hmm. I'd imagine you'll have a big one."

"Yeah, well, I got the dog back into the car. But when I went to get back inside, on the driver's side, I think…" She paused. "Did someone hit me?"

He touched her arm, and her breath caught, the pain more than she could stand.

"Sorry. Yes, you were clipped by someone speeding by and not paying attention to the road. The police talked to him. But your forearm… You might have a break. My guess, radial fracture. An X-ray will tell us more. In any case, it's not an open break, so that's good. But you're going to hurt until we can get you some pain meds."

"Oh, yeah."

"Reggie will make you better," Emily said. "Brownie likes him."

Maggie looked from Reggie to Emily, who stood without her bear.

Reggie looked back at her. "I was lucky enough to teach your daughter and some other smart kids about fire safety and being an EMT at the library. Remember, Emily?"

"Is this BLS?" she asked.

Reggie nodded. "Man, are you smart."

Emily beamed. Then her little face closed in on itself, and she scowled. "You're not going to stab my mom, are you?"

Reggie coughed, but Maggie saw his smile. "Um, no. We don't stab people, remember? We fix them up. In fact, we're going to give your mom a ride to the hospital. You and your Uncle Doug will meet her there, okay?"

Emily nodded.

"Where's the puppy?" Maggie asked.

Reggie answered, "He's with a clerk at the grocery store. She's going to hold him until you or your brother can swing by to get him."

"I don't have a brother." She blinked. "How did you get Doug's information?"

"Emily handed me your phone. She told me Uncle Doug is your emergency contact. I just assumed 'uncle' meant brother."

Her head hurt, her arm throbbed, and she ached all over. "Why can't I move my head too much?" she asked when she realized she had little movement there.

"We put you in a brace. You might have taken more damage from that hit than we can see. So we're going to take you to the hospital and get you all checked out before you move and possibly injure yourself." He glanced at her daughter. "Emily, how about you go with Uncle Doug while Mack drives me and your mom to the hospital? I promise to take very good care of her."

Emily nodded. "Will you make Mommy better?"

Reggie gave her a kind smile. "I'll do my best."

"Okay."

A man in uniform appeared at the back and looked inside. "We ready to go?"

"Emily said it's okay. She's ready to go with her uncle now."

The man smiled. "Then let's get going." He helped Emily get down and handed her off to Doug, who looked worried. Then Mack said, "Buckle in and hold on. We're rolling."

The doors closed, and Reggie sat close.

Maggie started to feel tired again but didn't want to scare Emily. "Reggie?" she croaked. Wait. Emily had left with Doug. Or was she still sitting next to Reggie out of sight?

He leaned close.

"Am I really okay?" she asked in a low voice, tears leaking down her cheeks, the fear of leaving Emily finally impressing on her.

Reggie grasped her good hand and squeezed. "I promise. You'll be okay. You're injured and you're hurting, but you look pretty darn good for someone who was hit by a car. Trust me, I've seen a lot worse."

She would have nodded, but the brace held her still. "Thank you."

"Anytime." He smiled again.

She looked into his eyes and saw what she needed.

Maggie closed her eyes and slept.

Chapter Three

MAGGIE STARED AT THE BOUQUET OF FLOWERS ON HER nightstand, eager to get home. The flowers were beautiful and bursting with color, a gift from Doug and Benny, but she could feel each second in the hospital costing her money.

The guys had been a godsend. With Stephen out of the country, unable to care for Emily, Maggie would have been hard-pressed to find help.

She still had no idea what Doug and Benny had done with the dog Emily had spotted. She wasn't sure that she could afford to keep a puppy, with the pet deposit and additional monthly pet fee likely more than she could handle. Especially now, Maggie thought, glaring at her arm in a splint, held in place by a sling.

Her head hurt, but painkillers made the pain tolerable. According to the doctor, she'd been *fortunate* that she'd had a stable, closed fracture. No need for pins or plates. No surgery. Just a splint until the swelling went down. Then she'd get a cast. But she couldn't use her arm for a while. At the least, she was looking at a solid six to eight weeks of downtime, having broken her dominant arm, and seven to fourteen days to recover from her concussion.

Maggie's eyes welled. So much for a fun-filled summer spent with her daughter.

Someone knocked at the door, and she hastily wiped her eyes. "Yes?"

The door opened. In walked a familiar face. The EMT from the ambulance ride, the man Emily talked about every time she visited. Reggie this, Reggie that.

He saw her and hesitated by the doorway.

"Please, come in." Maggie pushed a button on her bed to sit up more.

The sight of Reggie in the clear light of day, looking both larger than life and better-looking than any man had a right to be, was the icing on the cake that was her life. Maggie no doubt looked like the scruffy *before* picture of the worst sort of makeover while this guy should have been posing on a man-of-the-month calendar.

"Reggie, right?"

He smiled. "Yeah. I hope it's okay I stopped by. I was thinking about you and Emily and wanted to check in."

"That's so sweet of you."

He stuffed his hands in the pockets of his jeans and looked away, taking in her room and centering on her flowers. "Pretty."

"From my best friends." She smiled. "Please, have a seat."

He sat and seemed even taller while sitting down. Well, maybe not taller. But now not dazed and so lost she couldn't see straight, Maggie looked at the man and saw everything.

Behind the short-sleeve Mariners T-shirt and jeans, he had huge muscles under medium-brown skin. He was clean-shaven, his hair cropped short, his brown eyes dark and soothing.

"Emily was right. You are pretty."

He rolled his eyes, and she laughed.

At the sound, he smiled back. "I see where she gets it from."

"That's right. You had the pleasure of my daughter's inquisitive nature at the library. Doug told me you did great. Emily's a huge fan."

He looked relieved. "Oh, good. I have to tell you, your daughter's a hard sell. But I think I finally convinced her I'm not out stabbing people to take them away in my murder bus."

Maggie laughed again, pleased her head no longer pounded anytime she so much as moved. "She has a vivid imagination. And she's on a predator kick after watching too much Animal Planet. Forgive her."

"Nah. She's a cutie. I like smart girls."

Well, then you're not going to like me much. She bit back a sigh and swallowed her disappointment. Not that she had any energy to date or could conceive of Reggie wanting to go out with a woman he'd seen at her worst.

Which made her think… *Oh God.* She'd been passed out for a time. Had she drooled? Had her shirt ridden up, showing her flab to the world?

"What's that face for?" he asked.

"I just realized I was passed out in the street and have no idea what I looked like while unconscious."

He grinned. "Aside from that busted arm, you looked pretty enough to me." He blinked, as if thinking maybe he shouldn't have said that. "Ah, I mean, you were fine."

"No, no. Stick with 'pretty enough to me.' I'll take that." She stuck her good hand in her greasy hair, knowing it stood on end when she took her hand away. "See this?" She pointed at her hair. "Yeah, I need help."

He chuckled. "So, how are you, Maggie?"

"Oh, I just realized I haven't introduced myself or thanked you." Maggie wiped her hand on her shirt and held it out, pleased when he wrapped a callused palm around hers and gave it a gentle squeeze. "I'm Maggie Swanson. You met Emily, my daughter, already. I can't thank you enough for taking care of me when I was down. And you were so sweet in the ambulance." She felt herself tearing up.

"Aw, hey now. Don't cry. It's all part of the job." He grabbed her a box of tissues and set it by her side.

"Thanks." She blew her nose, sounding awful. "Between the hair, my bloodshot eyes, stuffed nose, and scars, I must look like I belong in the morgue."

He chuckled. "But hey, that bruise on your forehead doesn't look like it'll scar. So you have that going for you."

"Yay."

He gave her a thumbs-up and a superbright grin.

She had to laugh. She liked him. Reggie was funny and kind. And Emily loved him. Big marks for the guy.

They smiled at each other in silence until Reggie cleared his throat and said, "Huh. I guess I should introduce myself better. I'm Reggie Morgan, firefighter and EMT for the city of Seattle." Reggie nodded to her. "Ma'am."

"Please. It's bad enough I have bedhead, a knot I hadn't realized I had on my forehead—but thanks for saying it won't scar—and hairy legs." *Did I really mention my unshaven legs in front of this sexy guy? Shut up, Maggie!* "Er, ah, ignore the legs comment."

"Ignored."

"You were really sweet to come down here and check in."

He shrugged. "It's no biggie. Emily's worry stayed with me. Thought I'd make sure her mom was okay." He made no move to leave, so she hurried to ask another question.

Benny and Doug hadn't mentioned the puppy, and not wanting to alarm Emily, Maggie hadn't said anything to her daughter about the dog either. "Say, do you have any idea what happened to that dog?"

"To Frankenstein?"

"Huh?"

"That's what Emily named the puppy. Because he was scarred and all. Frank's a rough little guy. Been through a lot."

The poor dog.

"I, ah, that's another thing I wanted to talk to you about. When you're better, I mean."

"Huh?"

"Well, your friends went back to get the puppy from that woman at the market. She gave it to them, but according to them, they can't have the puppy in their place. And Emily insists she can keep it once you're better." He watched her expression, but she was still processing the name Frankenstein, trying to remember the dog, which remained a blur.

"My friends and I foster animals sometimes. There's a pet charity that holds adoptions around town. Pets Fur Life. We help them."

"I think I've heard of them."

"Well, I kind of told Emily I'd watch Frank for her while you're recovering. I hope that's all right."

Maggie sighed. "It's super nice of you to do that for us. But I'm not sure we'll be able to keep him."

"Oh." Reggie sounded disappointed. "Can't keep animals at your place?"

"We can, but it's an added cost." Maggie blushed. "I don't want to break Emily's heart, but we've never mentioned getting a pet. Now she's talking about Frank while I'm not sure what's going on." She put a hand to her throbbing head.

Reggie stood, looking concerned. "You okay?"

"Sure. Just tired."

"I should go."

"*No.*" She swallowed. "I mean, could you stay a little longer? I like visitors."

"Sure." He sat again.

Relieved he wouldn't be leaving, she searched for something to say. "How long have you been with Station 44?"

"Since it opened a few months ago."

"Oh, right. Do you like what you do?"

"I love it." He smiled. "Especially when we get to help people like you. Knowing you're okay makes everything better. Sometimes we're not so lucky. It's hard."

"It would be for someone who cares."

He blinked and looked down again before meeting her gaze. "So, ah, what do you do?"

"Me? I teach second graders. I was working part time for a law firm this summer, but I recently gave my notice. Jerky boss."

He nodded in sympathy.

"I had planned to spend the summer with Emily, maybe get a smaller part-time job until school starts again." She forced a smile. "But obviously this is for the best." She thought about going home, how tough it would be even trying to put on a bra. And wanted to cry all over again.

"What's wrong?"

"I just realized working with my left hand is going to be a problem. I'm right-handed." She glanced at her splinted arm. "Plus, I had plans for Emily and me. Ceramics. Rock climbing. Painting." She groaned. "Oh man. This sucks!"

———

Reggie pretended he felt nothing for the charming woman in the hospital gown, her arm in a sling, her hand swollen, her forearm wrapped. She hadn't been kidding about her hair sticking up. Since she'd let it go, a clump remained pointed at the ceiling. To his bemusement, her daughter looked a lot like her. Cute where Maggie was beautiful. Funny where Maggie had him choking back laughter.

She seemed so down-to-earth and laid-back despite her injury.

Damn, she was pretty. Smaller than the women he typically found himself attracted to, but her personality sparkled. Even under the bruising, she shone with life.

He found himself fascinated and had no idea why. Everything about her was wrong. A woman he'd helped while on duty. She had a kid—just what Reggie didn't need. Another woman with a child. He hadn't spotted a ring on her finger, and her emergency contact was her friend, not her husband.

How to ask if she had a boyfriend or fiancé he didn't know about?

And this is your business why?

He coughed, an odd case of nerves making him feel weird while he stared into brown eyes a shade darker than his own, surrounded by thick lashes. Her shoulder-length, mink-brown hair framed a thin face, made more dramatic by her pale complexion and full, rosy lips.

"I'm, um, not taking you away from anything, am I?" Maggie asked, hesitant. "I mean, you're probably busy. Kids, wife, girl-friend. Boyfriend?" She blushed. "*So* not my business. I just wanted you to know how much I appreciate you coming by."

His cue to leave, obviously. Reggie stood. "Oh, nah. I have off until Tuesday. Only real thing on my calendar this weekend is breakfast with family." He sighed. "My dad and my sisters are going to grill me about a blind date—with a woman—that went very wrong."

Maggie chuckled, though her cheeks remained pink. "Better you than me. I'm happily divorced and happily single. The last time Doug tried to set me up with a friend, I threatened to sock him in the eye. He's not the best when it comes to hooking up his friends. Ugh. What a worm." She looked at Reggie, her blush intensifying. "Not Doug, that last blind date was the worm."

"Ah, gotcha." He loved how unkempt and uncaring she seemed to be. No fussing with herself, no odd flirting or grabbing at him. Of course, she was laid up in a hospital with a busted arm, but Reggie had no shortage of women cozying up to him. No matter what the guys thought of his stale love life, it wasn't for lack of offers.

"Well, I guess I should get going."

"I don't want to keep you." She bit her lip. "Just one thing though. You said you're watching Frank for Emily?"

"Oh, yeah. He's at my place. But if you're not going to keep him, I can try to get him a good home through Pets Fur Life."

"Would you, I mean, I shouldn't ask, not after everything you've done, but…"

"Hey, ask me anything," he said with a smile. *And I'll do it. Right now. Whatever it is.* He wanted to smack himself. *And there I go again, being a woman's doormat because she's pretty and has a cute kid.* He could almost hear his sisters lecturing him on having a backbone.

"Would you mind holding on to Frank until I can come by to get him? I think they're letting me out tomorrow, just as soon as the doctor okays my scrambled brains as normal." She winked at him. "Little does he know I'm always like this."

Reggie laughed, relieved to be able to stay in contact with her. "Sure. No problem."

She looked around, found a pen and pad of paper by her bed, and slowly wrote something down. "My number for you. I'm happy to come get the dog at your house, or we could meet somewhere. You're doing us a huge favor. I'm really grateful for all your help."

"It's not that big a deal. Frank's a cutie, and to be honest, he's still at the vets healing up from his accident."

"Oh wow. I totally forgot to ask." Maggie shook her head. "That poor thing. Is he okay?"

"Believe it or not, no breaks in the little guy. Just a strained back leg, contusions, and a few cuts on the mend. He'll be just fine."

She let out a sigh. "Good. Bad enough Emily's dealing with me in here. I don't want her to fret about the dog."

"I told your friends to let her know he'd be okay."

Her warm smile made him feel ten feet tall. "Thanks, Reggie."

"No problem."

"Feel free to text or call when you're ready. And I swear I won't share the number with Emily. If she sees it, she'll be texting you at all hours. She's addicted to texting, to prove she can spell." Maggie made a face. "And the scary thing is, she can."

He felt his phone vibrate in his back pocket and wondered if he should tell Maggie he'd already been communicating with Emily through her friend Doug. "Well, you see, when I talked to Doug about the dog, I kind of gave him my number."

"And Emily's latched on to it. Oh no. I'm sorry. I know my daughter. How many times has she interrogated you about life in general?"

Reggie couldn't hold back a smile. "Maybe fifty?"

Maggie groaned.

He laughed. "It's all good. I told her when I'm working, I can't always talk, and Doug took the phone from her when she got too gabby."

"God bless Doug."

Oh, hell. He had to know for sure. "So, not your brother, you said?"

"Nope. He's my neighbor and is happily married to Benny. They're Emily's pseudo-adopted uncles. My ex travels a lot, and he and I are only cordial because of my daughter. Not to give you the rundown of my life, but there's not much to it."

"So, ah, no boyfriend?"

She looked at him. "Nope. No blind dates or boyfriends for me. And no girlfriends for you, huh? Not after that blind date."

"No way." He forced a laugh, feeling stupid for being so blatant about her status. "Wish me luck with my family. And call me if you need anything."

"Anything?" She grinned. "What if I need my toes scratched? I mean, with the cast on, I might not be able to reach a lot."

"Sorry, Maggie. You're on your own when it comes to feet."

"And here I thought all firefighters had to protect and serve."

"Well, there's serve, and then there's *serve*."

They both laughed, and their close connection settled over Reggie like a warm, comfy blanket.

He waved. "I'll talk to you soon."

"Yeah." She kept smiling.

"I guess I should go."

"Okay."

"Bye."

"Bye."

They stared at each other some more until Reggie took his dopey ass into the hallway, her door closing behind him. There, he leaned against the wall and sagged, feeling excited, nervous, and stupid for no reason.

But he didn't have time to lollygag. He had to hit the vet then the pet store to grab some food, bedding, and treats for Frank. Just in case Maggie decided to keep him. If not, Frank would have some things to take to his forever home.

And speaking of Frank…did that give him a great idea for tomorrow.

———

Sunday morning, at ten on the dot, Reggie showed up at his father's place, just a few blocks from his, carrying a wounded puppy and a bag full of puppy necessities.

Lisa opened the door looking summery in a tank, shorts, and her hair in a neat twist. Cool and comfortable, Lisa could give lessons on how to survive the heat. His sister never seemed to sweat. A real feat considering she engaged in high-level business dealings worth megabucks. Her job could make or break million-dollar companies.

Nadia, the eldest, could be heard chatting with their dad, probably in the kitchen. No matter what they gathered for, the family always ended up in the kitchen around Dad's large island, where the big guy liked to bake.

With any luck, he'd serve that peach cobbler he'd been bragging about.

Lisa looked from him to the puppy, and her mouth dropped open. "What is that you have there, Reginald?"

He bit back a sigh, hating when she used his full name but used to her teasing. "A rescue puppy I'm watching for a friend."

A friend. To his astonishment, he found himself wanting to be a lot more than friendly with Maggie Swanson, a woman all wrong for him.

"Oh, what a sweetie." Lisa cooed over the injured pup, who promptly cuddled into her warm arms and licked her cheek. "You sure we can't keep him?"

"Actually, I'm not so sure. The woman and little girl who want to adopt him don't know if they can keep animals in their apartment. I'm helping out because—"

Nadia suddenly appeared next to Lisa, her expression suspicious. "Woman and a kid, huh? It's not Amy and Rachel, is it?"

"Nadia, hush." Lisa blocked their older sister and stepped back for Reggie to enter. "It's not Amy." She leaned closer and whispered, "It's not, is it?"

Reggie's cheeks felt hot as he closed the door behind him. "No, it's not, damn it."

"Good." Nadia stomped back to their father. "Reggie's here!"

"I think Portland heard that," Lisa muttered and snuggled with Frank. "What's the deal with this little guy?"

"Yesterday I had a call to the scene of an accident, where a woman rescued Frank—that's short for Frankenstein, by the way—from being hit in the street. After she secured him in her car, someone sideswiped her. She suffered a broken arm, a concussion, and bruising. She also had a six-year-old daughter watching it all from the back seat."

"Oh, Reggie. That's awful." Lisa walked with him into the kitchen, where he paused to give his dad a big hug.

"Heard what you said. That's terrible. Is the woman okay?"

"She's fine. Better than Frank, here."

"Frankenstein? Nice name." Nadia huffed.

So annoying. "I didn't name him. The six-year-old did. Her name is Emily." He told them how he'd first met the little girl, to much laughter.

"I want to meet this kid." Nadia grinned. "She sounds like my kind of girl. Feisty."

"More like scary," Reggie muttered. When his sister shot him a look, he hurriedly continued, "I figured I'd help them out since I help with Pets Fur Life, just until the woman is back on her feet. I hate to disappoint her daughter. They don't have anyone to help." He didn't mention her best friend neighbors.

"So sweet." Lisa nodded at the dog.

Nadia didn't look so convinced but said nothing about the puppy. She took him from Lisa with gentle care and soon fell in love. Reggie could tell. He'd seen the signs before with a calico that was *still* living with his sister, despite the six years she'd spent supposedly trying to find him a good home.

He snorted. Soft-hearted and stubborn.

"So, little bro, tell us about your date," Lisa said before he could quickly turn the subject toward his father and cooking.

"It was awful," he said with enough force that the guys at the station would have left him alone.

Not Nadia and Lisa.

"Why? What did she do?" Lisa looked baffled. "Regina is so nice and sweet."

"And grabby," he added under his breath.

"What?"

His father snorted and turned away.

"We didn't connect. It's not meant to be."

Nadia didn't look convinced. "Why not? Was she not smart? We know you have a type. Pretty, built, and kid-friendly. You want to be a dad. It's in your genes."

"Blame him," Reggie said with a nod to his father. "If Harry Morgan weren't such a great guy, I wouldn't want to father my own kids."

"Aw, that's nice, son."

"Stop deflecting," Lisa ordered. "What happened?"

Reggie hated the inquisition. He loved his sisters, but because they happened to be a few years older and stepped in once their mom died, they'd forgotten he was a grown man who owed nothing to anyone so...

His ire faded under the glare of two Amazons.

"She was too pushy, okay?" he blurted. "One minute we were having a nice—not great or spectacular, but nice—time at dinner. Then on the drive home, she was all over me. Like a damn octopus."

His dad gave him a wide smile. "That's because you're a chip off the old block. Women know a good man when they see one."

"Uh, thanks." Now if only his dad would stop the conversation right there. Harry Morgan, unfortunately, liked oversharing. Reggie still had nightmares about his dad trying to teach him about the birds and the bees so long ago.

"You know, if you decide you like her, I can help you in the romance department. I know all about how to charm a lady. I did manage to snag your mom, remember."

Reggie cringed. "No thanks, Dad." Discussing dating tips with his father was something he never, ever, wanted to do.

Nadia nodded. "Good point. Reggie, Dad knows how to treat a lady. You should listen to him." She turned to her sister. "But next time, Lisa, let me find him a girl."

Lisa glared. "What? So I made one mistake with Regina. She's sweet, and they have similar names." Lisa paused. "Hmm. That would have been a problem at some point, wouldn't it? Reggie and Regina. Ugh. Like twins at a slumber party."

Nadia nodded. "Wearing the same pigtails and pajamas."

"I have no idea what they're talking about, but you and I should skedaddle while they're chatting." His father nodded to the backyard.

Nadia put down Frank, who hobbled outside with the men.

"Bad date, eh?" his dad asked.

"Not until the end, really. It was okay before that," Reggie admitted. "That's part of the problem, I guess. I'm over Amy, Dad. I swear." Most days, Reggie knew that. But he missed being a part of his own family. Not that he didn't love his dad and sisters, but he wanted a woman and child to call his own. "If Amy couldn't see me for what an amazing guy I am, she's not worth it." He kept telling himself that.

His dad smacked him on the back. Reggie winced.

"That's right. So this Regina was boring."

"Pretty much. And after dinner, well, I didn't want to upset her, but if all I'd wanted was a hookup, I would have gone elsewhere." *And I wouldn't have had to do dinner first,* he thought but didn't say, hearing how obnoxious that sounded in his head. "But I don't want that."

"Too bad. Can I have her number?"

"Dad."

"Kidding. I have a girlfriend of my own now." His dad chuckled and brought them to his tomatoes. "Gonna be a nice crop of Stupice and a new bunch of Matina. Look at that fruit."

"Nice, Dad." Reggie appreciated his father's skill with vegetables. Guy had a green thumb that continued to get greener as he aged.

"Reggie, I'm not one to give advice."

Reggie raise his brow. Seriously?

"But you're a keeper. You have a job you love, own your own home, do charity work, and hell, boy, you're almost as strong as your dad." Harry made a muscle impressive in size. Still not as large as Reggie's arm, but then, lately Reggie put in a lot of time at the gym, while his father had a life. "My point is, love will find you when it finds you. And with you, it'll smack you upside the head. Hard. I know you thought Amy was it for you, but I have to say, I didn't see it. She used you. Not on purpose. She was a nice girl. But so damn needy. And all you did was give."

Reggie could see that now. And it still hurt.

"When you find the next woman who gives you hives and makes you think so hard, your head and heart hurt in equal measure, make sure she gives as much as she receives. You deserve that."

"Thanks, Dad."

"You're just like your mother. That woman was always there for me and you kids. Stubborn as a mule, but she had the biggest heart." Harry smiled warmly before his grin turned wicked. "And I know when I get up there next to her—"

"Up there, hmm? Been going to church a lot lately, have we?"

Harry ignored him. "—she'll scold me for taking so long to fall in love again. She'd never begrudge an old man finding some happiness before he rejoined the love of his life."

Reggie sighed. "No one wants you to be unhappy, Dad. Just maybe don't share so much."

"Ha! What's life without conversation and laughter? And music." He left Reggie behind to shout, "Lisa, turn on my jazz before Nadia turns on that crap music those schoolkids of hers listen to."

"Jeez, Dad. Not this again." Nadia groaned.

Reggie looked down at Frank, who sat at his feet and stared at the tomatoes and fresh dirt just begging for some digging.

The dog looked up at him, back at the tomatoes, and up again.

"I wouldn't. Dad is pretty easygoing. But mess with one tomato plant and he'll never let you hear the end of it."

Just then, his father started reaming Nadia for a garden offense she'd committed back in high school.

"See what I'm saying?"

Reggie swore the dog sighed before turning and walking back inside.

He followed with a smile, wondering what Emily would think when he shared that nugget with her.

Chapter Four

EMILY WATCHED HER MOM WALK SLOWLY INTO THEIR apartment with Uncle Benny half carrying her. Mommy had hurt her arm, and she said each step felt like the arm was breaking all over again, so Uncle Benny helped her walk while Uncle Doug carried her bag.

It looked kind of funny, because Uncle Benny was so much bigger than Uncle Doug and Mag-Mom. If he fell, he'd probably smush everyone. Then Emily would have to get Brownie to help carry them all. Or maybe Reggie.

She really needed to talk to him again. She just had to get Uncle Doug's phone.

She smiled, remembering how funny Frank had looked when Reggie had sent his picture earlier. He'd put a hat on Frank and some doggie sunglasses while Frank shared a breakfast with Reggie and his family.

Emily wondered when they could visit Reggie and if her mom would finally make her that brother she wanted. For a long time, Emily had liked being the center of attention. Her dad and mom had divorced a few years ago. Emily hadn't understood much, but not a lot had changed except she got a new place to live and found more family. Uncle Doug and Uncle Benny were the best uncles she'd ever had.

She saw her dad a little, just like before, so that felt normal. But her mom seemed happier, and now when Emily *did* see her dad, he always had a smile for her and time to play.

But Sherry kept talking about her baby brother. And she said all kids should live with two parents. Either a mom and a dad, two dads, or two moms. But there had to be two in there somewhere.

Personally, Emily wasn't convinced. Her mom liked to say Emily had four parents, with her mom, her dad, and her uncles. But that didn't help Emily get any closer to a new baby brother, so Sherry had to be right.

Except now Emily kind of, almost, had a dog. And she had a new friend in Reggie, who was babysitting that dog. Frank might just be better than a turtle. But better than a brother?

She glanced at Brownie, who growled back at her, still waiting on a new set of nunchucks since he'd accidentally crushed the last set. *When are we getting our magical puppy?* he asked in bear talk. *I made him armor, but I need him to fit it properly. How will we fight the evil king if I can't ride into battle?*

Emily sighed. "I don't know, Brownie." She *really* needed to talk to Reggie.

Mag-Mom settled onto the couch, and Uncle Doug put a pillow under her arm.

"Thanks, Doug. That's better." Mag-Mom sighed.

"How's the head?"

"Pounding."

Emily frowned. "Is your head going to explode? Won't that make a mess?" Mag-Mom didn't like messes. An exploding head might be a problem. Emily didn't think anything but a magic wand and wizardry could put a head back together. *I mean, it works when I cast spells for Mrs. Potato Head.*

"Um, no. My head is okay. Just a little sore."

Uncle Benny chuckled. "You want to see a head explode, you should see when I make your Uncle Doug my famous lasagna." In a low whisper, he confided, "I use extra pots and pans so his face turns real red before his head pops clean off. But it grows back, so he's okay after."

Emily stared, wide-eyed. "Awesome."

"I know."

"Benny," Uncle Doug warned. Then he pointed a finger at

Emily. "And you. Go get that thing you made." He nodded toward the hallway.

Emily hurried to her room and returned with a homemade *Get Better* card. She handed it to her mom, who though tired, still looked prettier than any princess Emily had ever seen. "For you, Mag-Mom." At a look from Doug, she corrected, "I mean, Mommy."

Her mom grinned and read the card, decorated with not only macaroni pasta but with glitter, fuzzy eyeballs, and patches of brown felt—Brownie's idea. "I love it!" Mag-Mom put one arm around Emily and hugged her.

Emily sighed. Mommy had the best hugs. The secret, protective magic inside Queen Mag-Mom swelled around Emily like a giant bubble. Emily couldn't see it, but she knew it was there.

Not everyone had a magic bubble. Mommy had it. Uncle Benny and Uncle Doug had it too. Daddy's bubble was kind of weak, probably because she didn't see him that much. But Reggie had a bubble almost as big as Mommy's. Emily really needed to talk to him again. He'd been so nice explaining about BLS. And he'd taken care of Mommy and been really gentle.

Once at the hospital, where she'd seen him with her mom, he'd answered all of Emily's questions. He told her about the differences in kinds of breaks and how good it was that Mommy's hadn't broken the skin on her arm. He showed her a cart in the hallway, where they kept bandages and medications, as well as a zapper thing that could start a person's heart if it stopped.

He never talked down to Emily, the way a lot of grown-ups did. But he also didn't let her mess with the zapper thing or give him a needle. Reggie had "boundaries"—what Mommy insisted a smart person had to have to handle her princess.

Emily thought Reggie had the stuff to handle her. The way Uncle Benny did, and the way Uncle Doug mostly did. Not like her dad.

Part of her missed Stephen Swanson, but a bigger part of her liked her new family just fine. Mag-Mom, Uncle Doug, and Uncle Benny played with her. They liked her being so smart. Uncle Doug taught her multiplication and division. Uncle Benny taught her the scales and how to play piano. He called her a little genius, which she liked.

Even Reggie had told her how cool it was that she asked questions, and in the hospital, he'd insisted she ask him anything she wanted, and he'd tell her the truth.

And she believed him.

Daddy and some of her teachers didn't like her "brain that never turned off," even though she knew her dad loved her. Maybe she kind of annoyed him though. He always asked her how old she was and how she knew what she knew. Lots of times, he'd ask if her mommy made her say things to sound superintelligent, which Mag-Mom never did. She only wanted Emily to be herself. But sometimes it seemed like her dad wanted her to ask a lot less questions and be less smart. She'd have to ask him the next time he came to visit.

"Emily, honey, go grab your mom a blanket, would you?" Uncle Doug said as he and Benny settled in chairs near Mag-Mom.

She nodded and put Brownie next to her mom. "Guard her, Brownie. Don't leave the queen."

He looked at her and nodded. *Yes, Lady Emily.*

"Whew, I was scared for a minute there." Her mom kissed her on the cheek. "Thanks, honey."

"It's okay, Mommy. Brownie and Uncle Benny will protect you and Uncle Doug."

Uncle Doug sighed. "Why do I feel so emasculated around the Swanson women?"

She didn't know what that meant, but Mommy laughed, and Uncle Benny grinned, so she hurried to her mom's room, grabbed the green blanket, and hurried back to toss it over her mom's waist. "Now can I use your phone, Uncle Doug? Pleeaasse?"

He sighed. "Fine. But this is the last time today. If you bug Reggie too much, he might block me."

"Not that he doesn't want to talk to you," Benny cut in. "But he's a firefighter, and they have busy hours."

Emily nodded. "I know. I promise. Just one more time."

Doug handed her his phone. She thanked him and raced down the hallway to call her new favorite hero once she'd settled in the closet with some privacy. She pulled on the light switch, made sure she was alone without any spiders or monsters, and clicked on Reggie's number.

"Hello?" Reggie answered, his voice deep but gentle. He didn't roar like a bear, but heroes didn't have to roar. They beat up bad guys and always acted with polite manners. Kind of like a bear-ninja-king.

"Hi, Reggie. It's me." After a pause, she added, "Emily."

"Hi, Emily." He sounded happy to talk to her.

"I'm not supposed to bug you, but I need to talk to Frank."

He chuckled. "Hold on."

Except instead of the dog, a lady asked, "Who's this?"

In the background, Emily heard Reggie say, "Nadia, gimme back my phone."

"Who's *this?*" Emily asked instead, worried for her new hero. Had an evil witch trapped him?

"I'm Nadia, Reggie's big sister. Who is this?"

"Oh, I'm Emily." Relieved to know she wouldn't have to battle Nadia to save Reggie, Emily shared, "Reggie's watching my dog. Do you know Frank?"

"He's yours?" Nadia sounded nice. "He's really cute. But he's still healing."

"So is my mom."

"Is she now?"

"Yep. Reggie saved her. He didn't shoot her or stab her in the leg or anything. Instead he did BLS and saved my mom's head from exploding."

"My brother, the hero."

"He is." Emily nodded, her voice still low. "Can I talk to Frank now?"

"To the dog? Um, sure." The phone rustled. "Hold on."

She heard Reggie say, "I'm going to hang up and call you back with FaceTime. Okay?"

Emily nodded. She did FaceTime with her dad sometimes.

"Emily?"

"Oh, okay."

He called back and she answered, seeing his face, which was so neat. "Look at the picture," he said.

Emily watched as the phone moved away from Reggie to center on Frank, whose nose kept getting bigger the closer he moved to the phone. Then he licked it with a giant tongue before barking and looking away.

"Frank, gross," Reggie complained. He turned the phone so she could see him with Frank. "He says hi."

She waved. "Hi, Frank."

"I want to see her," another lady said.

Reggie sighed, then leaned closer to whisper, "Sisters can be such a pain."

Emily nodded, though she had no idea if that might be true. "Yep."

Reggie chuckled and turned the phone so she could see three more people. An older man who looked kind of like Reggie and two pretty ladies stared back at her. One had really neat braids and muscles; the other lady had a neat hairdo, a fancy shirt, and red lips. Painted on? Lipstick, maybe, she thought, remembering her mom's makeup.

She waved. "Hi. I'm Emily. Frank is my dog," she said as a reminder.

The ladies grinned, and the older man laughed. They all yelled, "Hi, Emily."

Reggie moved back into view. "My family makes me eat with them on Sundays."

"Oh. My mom makes me eat with her all the time." She heard more laughter. "I'm not supposed to call you too much, or Uncle Doug said you'd block him."

"I won't block you, but on days when I'm working, I won't be able to talk, or I'll get in trouble."

She understood that. "Okay." After a pause, she said, "When can I see Frank again?"

"I tell you what, Frank is still needing some time to heal, and I know your mom needs time to heal too. But what if I brought him over in a few days? I have to work on Tuesday, but I could bring him Wednesday, if that's okay with your mom."

"Okay."

Reggie paused. "Are you going to ask her?"

"She said yes for a day this week." Or she *would* say yes. Emily knew that Mag-Mom was worried about Frank. She just needed a little time to relax and rest at home before she could see the puppy. And Emily figured Wednesday would give her mom a few days to rest up and get happy again.

"Sounds good. Have your mom send me your address and a good time to come over, and I'll see you guys Wednesday."

Excited as much to see Reggie as to see Frank, Emily said, "I can't wait. Will you tell me some more stories about fixing people?"

"I will. Bye now."

"Bye, Reggie."

She stared down at Uncle Doug's phone, thrilled to be seeing her new hero again. And Frank! They'd need to get some toys and a doggie bed. She raced out of the closet to her bedroom to make plans...

Reggie turned to his sisters and dad, cringing inside at the interest he saw.

"So, Emily, huh? She sounds a little young for you, bro." Nadia smirked.

Reggie groaned. "Save it. I've heard it all from the guys. Trust me."

Lisa laughed. "She's a cutie. But I can't tell if she's more excited about seeing you or the dog." Frank sighed into Lisa's arms, tucked against her chest, in heaven.

"The dog, no question," Reggie said. "And before you say what's worrying you, Dad, no, I'm not interested in getting to know this little girl and her mom any better. I did a nice thing taking the dog, but that was a Pets Fur Life decision. We can help home him if they can't take him."

"Okay, if you're sure." His dad frowned.

"I'm sure."

Crap. Even Nadia looked suspicious.

Lisa frowned. "I said I liked Frank. Why do you need to take him to Pets Fur Life?"

At that, Nadia turned to her with a scowl. "Hold on. You're at work all day. I could take Frank. Porkchop needs a friend."

"Porkchop, the cat you named that you're still trying to give away?" Lisa snorted. "Yeah, right."

"I am not."

"Oh, please. You mention that anytime we come over. As if we believe you're heartless enough to give up your cat."

"Heartless?"

Reggie shared an eye roll with his father. "So, Dad, about that peach cobbler you've been bragging about?"

"Great minds think alike, son." Harry removed a tray from the oven, and the entire kitchen smelled like home-baked goodness.

"Since you're being good *by not arguing*," he said in a raised voice, "you get the first piece."

Nadia and Lisa snapped their mouths closed.

Reggie motioned for his father to give him a huge helping and ate it with a side of ice cream. He sighed with pleasure. "Ah, now this made coming to breakfast worth it."

"Nice to know it's not for my stellar company," his dad complained. "But then, maybe you've been avoiding me because you're having woman problems." He talked over Reggie's groan. "Reggie, I don't think you understand. I can help you."

His sisters exchanged an amused glance.

Their dad ignored them. "You're apparently unaware of how dashing I can be. Last night, when I was out with Layla, we ran into Chrissy. And it was obvious that she misses me."

"Jeez, Dad. Try dating women from different nursing homes," Nadia said under her breath.

Their father heard her and glared. "Girl, you are not too old to spank."

Nadia coughed. "Um, er, yes, sir."

He continued, "First of all, Chrissy never lived in a nursing home. It was an *assisted living* space. And Layla lives in her own home, thank you very much."

Reggie sighed.

His dad wasn't done and turned back to Reggie. "Son, romance is about love and respect. I loved your mother like crazy. About broke me when she passed. But I think she'd understand my need to find someone new."

"Of course she would." And especially after so much time. *But we don't have to talk about it.*

"Chrissy was a lovely lady, but she didn't want anything serious, and I respected that. Layla though, she's a sweetheart." Harry's eyes glowed. "Turns out her dad was in the Navy back in the day, so we have the Navy in common. But even better, that woman can *dance*. And she likes my kind of music." He looked to be in heaven.

Reggie was glad his father had found a new lease on life. And that turned his thoughts to Maggie and Emily and what the hell he thought he was doing even thinking about dating a woman with a kid again. Which he totally wasn't. Mostly.

"Is that how you know, Dad?" Lisa teased. "When you find that other person who likes your kind of music? Is that true love?"

"No, but it's a beginning." Harry turned a keen eye on Reggie. "And it helps if she shares your same interests."

"Jazz and *romance*?" Nadia said, wiggling her brows.

At their father's wide grin, the siblings groaned.

"You just had to ruin my appetite, Nadia," Lisa complained.

Reggie agreed…in theory. His father's cobbler was too good to pass up.

––––––––––

Hours later, Reggie sat with Frank in his backyard, enjoying a beer while the puppy trotted carefully, mindful of his back leg, checking out the freshly mowed grass.

Life was good. Reggie knew that. He had a house, a garden with potential, great friends, and now a cute little dog needing his help. He loved his family, though he could do with fewer details from his dad and less dating help from his bossy older sisters. They did make him laugh though.

His dating life might be nonexistent, but his sisters were no better. Nadia could barely commit to a cat, and Lisa hadn't yet found a man good enough for her, despite everyone in the family crying over her ex, a guy Reggie had loved and of whom even Nadia had approved. The guy liked kung fu movies, pop culture references, and disco. But he'd wanted to marry Lisa, so of course Reggie's commitment-phobe of a sister had dumped him.

And they said he had problems.

"I'm telling you, Frank. Women aren't any easier than men at finding love."

The dog looked over at him before sitting under the maple tree in Reggie's yard, enjoying the shade. The weather continued to be a lovely seventy-four, and Reggie had done some much-needed landscaping.

After finishing off his beer and watching the dog and the tree while feeling like he should be doing something other than lazing around, Reggie headed back inside and tore into a project he'd been putting off.

Decluttering his guest room.

For months after his breakup with Amy, he'd put off the chore of cleaning up all evidence of his relationship, storing it in the guest room no one ever used. His house in North Beacon Hill was a work in progress, but he'd bought at the right time, seeing the potential in the space.

An older home, its rooms were larger and had wood floors that had seen better days. But as Nadia would say, it had great bones. His bedroom had an attached bath, with another bathroom in the hallway for visitors. Two extra bedrooms, a large living area, dining room, and kitchen big enough for a table and chairs took up the first floor, with a roomy basement that could be turned into a man cave or finished entertainment area, if Reggie decided to do anything with it except store extra crap.

The one-car garage typically housed his car, not because he worried about leaving it in the driveway to get stolen, but because he didn't like cleaning it, and keeping it in the garage kept the bugs and dirt away.

Reggie lived by the phrase "work smarter, not harder." Unlike Mack, who lived and breathed to clean his car, Reggie considered his vehicle nothing more than a conveyance. His house was for living in, eventually, with his family.

A family he no longer had a right to.

With a sigh, he emptied the first box containing a few of Rachel's forgotten toys, items Amy had told him to throw away. A few dolls and a blanket he'd once bought for the little girl he'd considered his own.

Pictures of Amy, Rachel, and Reggie filled the second box, and though he told himself he didn't care, it hurt to see what could have been.

He'd been genuinely in love with Amy, a lovely woman with bright, hazel eyes and an infectious smile. Gorgeous and vulnerable, she'd called to the protector in him, and they'd had two years of togetherness that made him feel good, like a man should. Her daughter, Rachel, had been a blessing, a beautiful girl whose smile made the world brighter. Giving, sweet, and funny, she'd been the best part of Amy, bringing out a love Amy sometimes had trouble expressing.

Unfortunately, Rachel's father had problems. He'd left Amy destitute, and Reggie had helped her pick up the pieces. Just when he thought they'd finally gotten past their troubles, her ex had come back into her life, claiming he'd missed her and their little girl. Two fucking years after having been a ghost while Reggie had been the one to help take Rachel to dance class and ceramics class and school. While Reggie had been there for Amy, helping her with everything from rent money to community college tuition and a place to live.

But it had never been about money or helping Amy out. Reggie had done for her because he'd loved her. So much. It physically pained him to remember all their good times, and there had been many.

But in the end, he had to admit his friends and family had been right. Amy had been a taker, and she cared more for herself than for Reggie. He didn't begrudge Amy or her daughter a relationship with Rachel's father, but he knew it would be at their expense sooner or later. Just a few weeks into rekindling things with her ex, Amy had confided that she thought he might be stepping out on her again.

Too hurt to be of any help, Reggie had said nothing. Not taking her back when he had a shot at doing so.

I missed that opportunity. But was I right to keep the door closed?

He stared at a picture of Amy laughing while Rachel made a face, the pair standing with Reggie's arms around them both.

Happier times.

Or was that all in his head?

A vision of cute Emily and her mom struck him, familiar patterns forming when he knew better. Had he really seen Maggie's blushes as interest? As potential attraction and a beginning?

A beginning of what? The end?

Reggie snorted and packed up all the photos but the one he held in his hands, the fake perfection he'd imagined a harsh contrast to his reality.

He took the boxes out to the trash, determined this time to really get rid of them. But that one picture of the three of them he'd keep.

He went back inside and found Frank out back, looking pitiful while whining to come inside.

"Come on, Frank. Just a few steps, little guy."

Frank blinked up at him, unmoving. Reggie sighed and lifted the tiny pit into his arms before taking him back inside. They watched TV later in the evening. But before Reggie turned in for the night, he had to take out the recyclables.

He set the bin next to the trash can, the boxes of neglected toys and pictures among the refuse. He wanted to go back inside. Reggie *tried* to go back inside, but something in him refused to go without once more looking through the photos.

It was close to two hours later before he went back inside with two more pictures. One of Amy, and the other of her and Rachel. But at least he'd let most of the memories go. If not the pain and tears that went with them.

Chapter Five

TUESDAY MORNING AT WORK, REGGIE TRIED TO EXPLAIN TO A dizzy octogenarian why she really needed to get to the hospital. Then Mack stepped close, and the woman on the gurney froze, staring at him.

"Mrs. Parson? I really think you need to get seen by a doctor," Reggie was saying.

"Oh, my Lord, it's really you." She continued to stare at Mack, her grin turning to a leer.

"Um, Mrs. Parson?" Reggie tried again.

"I stuffed twenty dollars down your shorts, and you never did give me that show you promised," she accused Mack, who just stood there with the woman's husband, looking shell-shocked.

"Well, then. I'll drive," Reggie said, gleefully helping Mack lift her into the aid vehicle. He couldn't *wait* to tell the others about this. "Mack, you and Mrs. Parsons can sit in the back on the way to the hospital."

Her husband narrowed his gaze at Mack. "Hmmph. You better keep your hands to yourself on the way, buddy." He walked off to his Cadillac, ready to follow them.

Reggie watched Mack get in the cab and saw the older lady pinch his butt when he passed her. The poor guy banged his head on a cabinet.

Reggie couldn't help laughing, especially when Mack glared at him.

"Now, now. Hands to yourself, Mrs. Parson." Mack leaned closer to the older woman and in a loud whisper, said, "Be nice and you just might get that dance you wanted."

She tittered and leaned back on the gurney.

Not wanting to see any more, Reggie closed the doors behind him.

He delivered the woman to the hospital after calling in her details, and once he and Mack handed her over to a waiting nurse, they left in silence, driving back to the station.

Mack kept watching him. Waiting. Finally, he blurted, "Just say what's on your mind, already!"

Reggie burst out laughing. "Really? What exactly did you promise her for twenty bucks?"

Mack sighed. "This is not going to go well for me, is it?"

"No, it isn't."

The rest of their day passed in a wild litany of cases, no doubt due to the promise of a full moon. In between a few bouts of allergic reactions gone bad and two cardiac arrests, they had a young boy with a Lego stuck in his ear—in an effort to block out his father's snoring—and a man in his twenties who'd broken his ankle while falling, having tried to jump from his roof to the next-door neighbor's roof, just for something fun to do.

But none of that beat the old man who'd broken both of his legs while falling down a flight of stairs, drunk. They'd had to cut his pants off him to assess his injuries and found a large zucchini strapped to his thigh.

"I'm so trying that before I go out on my next date," Mack was saying as the gang sat around the living area in the station, all of them recovering from the craziness at three a.m. on Wednesday morning.

Tex snorted. "A zucchini, huh? Better than a carrot, I guess."

Reggie tried to quell more laughter, but he couldn't help it. The affront on the drunk guy wouldn't leave him. "Oh man. That guy was cracking me up. He insisted that we swear not to share his secret. Apparently the key to finessing women is a garden vegetable. I don't think I stopped laughing through the drive and even after we dropped him off."

Mack agreed, his grin wide. "It was brutal. The dude was drunk out of his mind, strapped in on the way to the hospital, and telling me all about his love life. Guy had some kind of game. The things he told me about his lady friends have scarred me for life."

Reggie snickered. "Talk about a wild night."

"Oh, we can top that." Brad laughed.

"Bring it," Mack ordered.

Tex shook his head. "You think you guys got the wacky ones, Brad and I helped a woman who drank a whole gallon of laundry detergent to try to kill the alien baby that she'd been carrying for fourteen months. Now, normally I'd feel bad for a woman that out of it, but every time she complained about her baby daddy from outer space, she'd foam at the mouth. Like, bubbles came out."

Brad had to wipe tears of mirth from his eyes. "Tex is trying to keep it together, but I can hear him talking to her, and he's asking what exactly she drank, because it smells Downy fresh. So, while discussing an impending alien invasion and her mutant offspring, they start comparing laundry soaps."

Reggie and Mack died laughing.

Tex cleared his throat, trying to get a handle on his amusement. "Then she vomited, and swear to God, it smelled like the Tide Clean Breeze my momma uses. I complimented her on it, and she just smiled and blew a few bubbles at me." He shook his head. "Definitely the effects of a full moon."

Reggie stretched. "You know what? You guys win." Even Mack agreed. "I'm beat. I'm going to try to catch some z's before we head home in a few hours."

"Me too," Mack said. "Anyone have plans before we're on again Friday?"

"Avery and I have dinner with her folks." Brad made a face. "Her dad's still an ass. But man, her mom can cook. And she's such a sweetheart."

Tex grinned. "Bree and I are going to a concert tonight. Anyone up for some alternative rock?"

"I'm in." Mack nodded.

"Not me," Reggie said, reluctant to bring up his plans with Maggie. *No, with Emily. The kid, not the mom.* "I'm due for a break, even from exercise."

Brad muttered, "About time, Mr. Universe."

Reggie opened his mouth to argue and yawned instead. "I'm focused on puppy training. Furry Frank's on the mend. Nadia and my dad keep taking turns watching him. I'm afraid if I'm not careful, I might not be able to free the little guy from my family."

Brad grinned. "If I had to bet between you or Nadia winning, I'll probably go with your sister."

The others nodded.

"Way to have my back."

Brad looked wounded. "Hey, she's meaner than you. I mean, er, more aggressive."

"Assertive," Mack murmured.

Brad nodded. "What I said. Assertive."

Reggie chuckled. "I'm telling her you said that."

"Please don't."

"So we're agreed we're on our own this break," Tex recapped. "That means this weekend, when we're off, barbecue at my place."

Mack nodded. "Deal."

Reggie agreed, still relieved that his newly coupled-up buddies continued to make time with the single guys in the group. He and Mack exchanged a nod, knowing the truth of the matter. That things had changed. Never before had Brad or Tex been so committed to women. Both had found life partners, Reggie knew. But what did that mean for the odd men out?

Apparently not much. Though the guys spent a good bit of their time off with their ladies, they still maintained their important friendships outside of work. Reggie prayed that would never change.

"Later, guys." He stood and left for his bed.

When he woke a few hours later, he learned Brad and Tex had taken the call that had come in after Reggie had gone to sleep. He'd been so tired, he'd dreamed of bubbles and dancing bears. Yeah, he owed them.

At changeover, they went over the previous events with their lieutenant and the oncoming crews, everyone amused at the chaos they'd experienced.

The gang said their goodbyes, and Reggie left for home, wondering why he hadn't mentioned his plans to see Maggie and Emily. After all, his purpose in visiting them was to return the puppy.

Reggie felt funny, as if by hiding his date that wasn't a date, he was maybe lying to himself.

But hey, he could feel attracted to a woman and not act on it. Just because he found Maggie more than appealing didn't mean anything would happen between them. Bringing Frank to his forever home was part of the fostering process, nothing more.

Satisfied with his less than lame excuse, Reggie went home to get some much-needed sleep. Hours later, after packing up all of Frank's toys and food, he picked up the puppy from his father.

"Good luck, son. Just know Frank has a home if your friends can't keep him."

Reggie smiled and cuddled the dog in his arms. "I take it he left your tomatoes alone."

Harry nodded, serious about his gardening. "We had a talk when he looked a little too interested in my dirt. But we came to an agreement. I gave him a bone to chew on; he left my tomatoes be."

"You're spoiling him."

"It's good for his teeth," his father said. "And before you go lecturing me again, I know he's a puppy." His dad huffed and handed Reggie the chew, which was shaped like a piece of bacon. "You'll note that his treat is bacon-flavored and rubber. Now get out of here before Nadia comes over to say goodbye. She might wrestle you for him, and we both know she fights dirty." His father chuckled.

Reggie took the advice and left in a hurry. Once in the car, he programmed the address Maggie had texted him.

Full of nerves and wishing he weren't, he forced himself to go less than the speed limit, taking his good old time, as he drove to Maggie's apartment complex bordering North Beacon Hill and Mt. Baker, not too far from his own house, he thought with pleasure.

He parked along the street in front of her building and brought only the puppy, dressed in his harness, leash attached, and a small bag of toys and treats. After letting Frank do some business on a strip of grass nearby, he carried the puppy up the stairs and headed for Maggie's apartment.

Instead of an indoor apartment area, all the units faced the outdoors. From the ground, a wide common stairway led up to a large landing. From there, the stairs split to direct people to one of two units—large, twin buildings that looked well-maintained and fairly new, painted an inviting yellow. The complex appeared to have four stories, with possibly a rooftop area, though Reggie couldn't tell from the ground.

Light and airy, the open walkway—especially in view of the blue skies and overhead sun despite the hour—felt joyful, the red, orange, and indigo clouds offering a cheerful palette of early evening.

On his way to Maggie's door, Reggie passed a tall guy covered in tattoos, his wild hair pulled back in a loose ponytail, and thought he looked familiar. The man grunted a hello and moved past him, entering an apartment one door down from unit 204—Reggie's destination.

Reggie wiped a sweaty palm on his jeans, wondering what the hell was wrong with him, and pressed the doorbell, telling himself to relax. In his arms, Frank fidgeted, so Reggie put him down and waited maybe five seconds.

Emily opened the door and stared from Frank to Reggie. Her smile so bright, it blinded, she cried, "You brought Frank!" She hugged the puppy, who licked her back with enthusiasm. After a few moments, she added, "I missed you too, Reggie."

"Aw, aren't you cute."

"Emily?" her mother called from the apartment.

"They're here!"

"They?" Maggie's voice grew louder as she approached the door. "What have I told you about opening the door without looking through the peephole first? I—Reggie?"

Emily took the leash from Reggie and urged Frank inside. She unclipped the leash and handed it to Reggie before disappearing down the hallway with the puppy.

Leaving Reggie alone with Maggie.

Maggie looked confused.

Reggie wondered if he'd gotten the wrong day to visit. "Hi."

"Hi." She blinked at him then moved back. "Sorry. Please, come in."

He entered, and she closed the door behind him. He noted a step stool next to the door, presumably for Emily and the peephole. "Good safety measure."

Maggie sighed. "I try, but it feels like a losing battle." She wore a long skirt and a T-shirt, her feet bare, her toes painted a pretty pink. Her arm remained in a sling, wrapped in bandages, but she looked much better than she had in the hospital. Well-rested with shiny, neat hair and eyes that clearly focused, Maggie looked beautiful. And baffled as she stared at him.

Reggie gripped the leash. "So, um, you seem surprised to see me."

"I thought you were Sherry."

"Who?"

"A six-year-old friend of Emily's who was supposed to come over for macaroni and hot dogs." Maggie's mouth firmed. "Wait here."

"Hey, I can go—"

"*No*. Please, just hold on a minute," she insisted in a voice that commanded obedience.

Reggie blinked, not having seen this side of her. So different from the funny, vulnerable woman laid up in a hospital bed.

As he tucked the leash back into Frank's bag, he heard her clearly from down the hall. "Did you lie to me, young lady?"

"Nopers."

"Try again."

"Sherry *is* coming over for macaroni and hot dogs."

"Tonight?"

"Yeppers." Emily sounded too perky for someone about to land in hot water. Reggie couldn't help grinning. "But Reggie got here first."

"Emily, why didn't you tell me he was coming?"

"I did."

"When?"

"I said Reggie and Frank were coming over."

"You never mentioned it would be tonight."

"So?"

Silence.

He imagined a whispered tongue-lashing.

Maggie reappeared with a chagrined expression.

Reggie felt like a heel for barging in when he hadn't been invited. At least, not by the woman in charge. "Hey, it's no biggie. I can go—"

Before he could take a step back, she latched on to his hand with her good one. Her touch both soothed and excited him, and his stomach felt tight. Her hand was small, her hold surprisingly firm. "Not one step, buddy."

He froze a moment before letting her tug him toward her kitchen.

The apartment seemed roomier inside than he might have expected. A bold royal blue painted one accent wall in the living area, surrounded by cream-colored walls decorated with pictures of flowers, some professionally done, others clearly drawn by a child. He found the artwork charming, especially because all the pictures had been framed and matted with care.

The furniture looked comfortable yet stylish, nothing too formal, but what he might have expected of someone with Maggie's warmth. As they passed the living room and a seating area comprised of a rectangular table, two chairs, and a bench, they entered the kitchen. On the raised counter separating the kitchen from the dining area, he noticed bottles of ginger ale and grenadine, as well as maraschino cherries. A bucket of ice and glasses sat on a floral tray next to the ingredients.

"Would you like a drink? Something posh, like, say, a Shirley Temple?" Maggie's lips quirked. "I prepared a fancy dinner with drinks for Emily and her friend, Sherry. But there's plenty for *all* her friends." She smiled. "I am happy to see you again, Reggie, honestly. I just wasn't expecting you *tonight*. And no, you can't go. You're here now. You have to stay."

"Ah, okay then." He bit back a smile. "I'd love a Shirley Temple, but only if I can make it."

She nodded. "Please do."

"One for you too?"

"Yes, please."

He fixed them both drinks, giving her extra cherries.

Maggie sighed with pleasure. "You read my mind. I love the cherries."

He sipped, watching as she did the same. "I wasn't expected at all? I thought you sent the directions."

"Emily must have. Doug showed her how to use the map app." Maggie shook her head. "I've been meaning to call you but frankly lost track of everything. I know it's only been five days, but I've been having to adjust thanks to this stupid arm." She nodded to her sling. "How's Frank been?"

"Terrific. The vet called to confirm Frank doesn't have a chip and is free for adoption, by the way."

"Good."

"Frank's such a great puppy. He and my dad have bonded since Frank didn't touch Dad's precious tomatoes. But I think Emily might have to fight my oldest sister for him. Nadia's become attached."

The dimple in Maggie's cheek made him smile.

Silence settled between them, and he realized he'd been staring. Then again, so had she.

She hurriedly sipped more of her drink. "You think these drinks are awesome, you should see what I can do with hot dogs and macaroni and cheese."

"I can't wait." Amused at the idea of sharing a meal he hadn't had in ages, he leaned against the counter while Maggie took a seat by him. "So how's the arm?"

"Good. The swelling has been going down. I get the cast on tomorrow. Oddly enough, I can't wait. I keep banging into things, and it hurts."

"You mind if I take a look?"

"Sure."

He carefully eased her arm out of the sling, pleased she didn't appear pained. The swelling had gone down a good bit, as expected. "Can you move your fingers or hand without pain?"

"No."

"Hmm."

"What? What does that mean?"

"Nothing, just checking. You know you broke it. The X-rays told you that. But you should be icing your arm if you can."

"I tried, but it hurts."

"You taking anything for the pain?"

"Just Tylenol. I don't want to be groggy or out of it with my crafty six-year-old close by. She's sweet but a handful. Don't get me started on the credit card phone mischief that happened a few months ago."

He chuckled. "You said you get the cast put on tomorrow?"

"Yeah. Doug is going to watch Emily for me."

Reggie frowned. "You're not driving yourself to the hospital, are you?"

"No. I plan to grab a Lyft or Uber."

"I can take you."

She stared at him.

"What?"

She blushed, which he found fascinating. What did she have to be shy about? This same woman who'd worried she might have drooled when unconscious and mentioned her unshaved legs in the hospital was shy about accepting a ride?

"I, ah, you don't have to do that. I'm sure you're busy."

"Actually, I have to head to the hospital tomorrow, so it's no bother. And you live pretty close."

"Oh?"

"Yeah. I'm in the neighborhood."

"That's nice." She smiled again. "I would love a ride, but I really don't want to be a burden."

"Nah. I wouldn't offer if I had plans. But I'd intended to see a friend tomorrow at the hospital. He's a nurse, not sick or anything." He'd call Neal tonight and set something up. He wasn't lying, exactly. Neal *had* been nagging him to hang out more. "What time's your appointment? Or do you just show up and take a number?"

"It's at ten thirty."

"Perfect. I can drop you off then catch my buddy for an early lunch. And I can drive you home. It shouldn't take long."

"You're sure?"

He nodded. "It's really no trouble unless you'd rather go by yourself. You might have errands or something after." Okay, he was good, giving her an out. Not sounding as if he was desperate to spend more time with her.

"No, no. I'd love a ride." She looked relieved.

Before Reggie could say more, the doorbell rang. Emily yelled, and the dog barked, both racing for the door at the same speed, though Reggie saw Frank, sans harness, still limping a little.

"I'll use the peeper, Mag-Mom," Emily said.

Reggie blinked. "Mag-Mom?"

"It's a phase." Maggie rolled her eyes. "Maggie-Mother was last month. Now I'm Mag-Mom. Hopefully, I'll be back to Mom or Mommy again soon."

He chuckled and peeked out of the kitchen to see Emily on the small stepladder looking through the peephole.

"It's Sherry!"

Reggie winced. "She's pretty excited, eh?"

"You mean she's loud." Maggie stepped next to him to watch her daughter, still sipping her drink. "It's like she thinks I can't hear since I broke my arm, which I know makes no sense. She's always shouting." To Emily, Maggie said, "Stop yelling and let Sherry in, you little goofball."

Sherry and her mom soon entered and exchanged pleasantries, though the mom gave Reggie a thorough once-over that made him a little uncomfortable. Sherry's mom departed, and Sherry, after shaking his hand with wide eyes, went with Emily and Frank to play in Emily's room.

He saw Maggie watching him. "What?"

"I'm surprised you're not running for cover after Dina's once-over." She shook her head. "I love her, and Sherry's a great kid, but Dina's not what you'd call subtle."

A long silence made him wonder exactly *why* Dina might object to him being there.

Maggie added after a pause, "Any good-looking man and it's like Dina forgets to blink and breathe. I apologize for her." She moved back to the counter and sat, and he followed.

He ignored the warmth in his cheeks and teased, "Good-looking? I think you mean divine. Handsome. Gorgeous, maybe. Those fit." *Ha.* And the guys called him a terrible conversationalist.

She laughed. "Sorry, Adonis. My mistake."

He loved her sense of humor. "Macaroni and hot dogs and Shirley Temples. Man, did I luck out tonight or what?"

Maggie's smile faded. "Yes to all that. But Reggie. I need to talk to you about Frank." She cleared her throat. "I kind of have a plan, but it'll involve your help. And you've been so helpful already with everything. I hate to ask."

"Ply me with enough nonalcoholic drinks and I'll say yes to anything."

She smiled again. "You're too easy."

"That's what they all say." He grinned. Her blush made him laugh.

"Fair enough. Oh, and I almost forgot. I have whipped cream for the drinks."

"Well, hell. Now I definitely can't say no." *To* anything *you might want, Maggie.*

Chapter Six

THEN GET NAKED AND WAIT FOR ME ON MY BED.

Maggie cleared her throat, reminding herself there were minors present. Jumping the man who'd been so sweet to her would just be wrong. "Great. So, well, before we discuss Frank, I'll only let you take me to the hospital tomorrow if you let me make it up to you. Let me make you dinner. A *real* dinner, no hot dogs involved."

"Hmm. You seem to have me pegged. I like to eat."

"Whew. I was worried because you're so small and skinny."

He grinned.

Her temperature rose by several degrees. Good Lord, the man was sexy. "Right. So, um, Emily really wants Frank. And I think a dog would be a good way to teach her responsibility. But with my arm busted, and with the summer kind of on hold, I just need a little more time to get us ready for Frank."

"So you want me to keep him for you?"

"If it's at all possible. I know it's a lot to ask," she said in a rush, not sure what to make of his expression. "But I'll pay for his food and care. I can reimburse you too." She'd do whatever she could to make this easier for him. "I need to talk to my landlord to okay it before Frank comes to stay, in any case. Then I need to make sure we have a good potty route and to figure out how we'll keep him once I go back to work." She bit her lip, wishing she'd have thought the dog idea through before agreeing to home him. Cripes, why did wanting to impress Reggie take precedence over logic and sensibility? "Well, shoot. That might prove a problem."

"A dog is a big responsibility," he said. "But maybe we can work something out. I know the puppy was sprung on you pretty suddenly." His voice gentled. "And you know, it's okay if you can't take him, Maggie. That doesn't make you a monster."

Then why did she feel like one at the thought of disappointing her daughter and letting poor little Frank down? She would not cry. "Thanks." She coughed to cover her emotion. "It's just that this means so much to Emily, and after all that poor little puppy has gone through, I'd feel guilty knowing he didn't have a good home."

"I wasn't lying when I said my sister is in love with him. Heck, my dad is too. Trust me, no matter what, Frank will find a loving place to live."

"Thank you." She blew out a relieved breath and reached for his hand again. She squeezed it, aware of his immense strength. "You're a good man, Reggie."

"Aw, stop." He sounded embarrassed, but he squeezed back.

She let him go, not wanting to dwell on how much she liked touching him. "So tell me about your dad and sister."

"Sisters. I have two."

"Oh, right. You did mention them in the hospital. How did your Sunday brunch go, anyway?" Was it wrong that she loved the fact his blind date had gone terribly? Or that she couldn't stop thinking about the man who'd been so nice to her—because it was *his job* to take care of people?

Talk about a bad time for her to start noticing men again. But something about Reggie had stayed with her since first meeting him. And that had nothing to do with the trauma she'd suffered, with Reggie's astonishingly good looks, or with his strength. She saw something in his eyes when he looked at her. When he looked at Emily and even Frank. The tenderness there, and that strong wit and warmth, had her wanting to know all about him. For some odd reason, she just knew they'd have a lot in common.

"Oh man. I told you I had a blind date that didn't go well. My dad and sisters tried grilling me."

"Tried?"

He sighed. "They're brutal."

"So, if you don't mind me asking, what didn't work?"

He shrugged. "Look, I'm not too proud to say my dating history isn't the best. I broke up eight months ago with someone I'd been with pretty seriously. It's been tough for me to get back into dating." He grimaced. "I hate games."

She nodded. "Tell me about it. When my ex and I divorced three years ago, I felt like my world had ended. Was I making a mistake taking Emily away from her dad? Did I expect too much? Was I...?" She trailed off, aware she'd totally taken over the conversation. "Sorry. There I go, rambling."

He smiled. "I'd much rather hear about you."

"Ha. My house, my rules."

"Oh, please, now you sound like my dad."

She laughed. "He sounds like my kind of guy. Come on, Reggie. You're among friends. Spill. What happened on your date?" She cupped her chin on her palm and blinked up at him.

He tried not to laugh, but she'd perfected her pretty-please-with-puppy-dog-eyes expression years ago. "Fine. You win. But stop batting your lashes at me. You're making me dizzy."

She chuckled.

"If you must know..."

"I must."

"Regina was very nice. Intelligent, pretty, well-mannered."

Maggie hated her already.

"But...?" she prodded.

"I'm not someone to gossip or speak ill about someone behind their back."

"Please. I barely know you and I can tell you're a good guy. But we're sharing dating horror stories. You have to tell me."

"Sharing?" He raised a brow. "So you're going to give me a story if I tell you one?"

"Yep." She crossed her heart. "Swear."

"Fine. Regina was grabby." He blew out a breath. "I admit it. I don't like being pawed. My father tried giving me advice on dating and romance like I'm sixteen again. As if jazz and dancing will solve all my problems." He frowned. "Are you laughing at me?"

She coughed. "No, I'm not." She was *dying*. Reggie getting dating advice from his dad? She could just imagine that conversation and Reggie trying to avoid it. "I feel for you. I do. I've had the same reaction on many dates." But she had a tough time envisioning Reggie trying to avoid a human female octopus. And she shouldn't. Except he was huge and strong and...helpless? She coughed louder, struggling to hold in her amusement.

"Ha. I heard that." He bit his lip, but she saw his smile.

The oven beeped. "Saved by the casserole."

"This isn't over." He shook a finger at her. "And I thought we were having macaroni and cheese?"

"With hot dogs, in a casserole." She grabbed an oven mitt and went to remove the pan from the oven, but Reggie beat her to it.

"What are you thinking?" He glared and took the mitt from her hand. "Here. Let me get that." He expertly retrieved the casserole from the oven and set it on top of the stove. Then he removed the mitt and turned off the oven. "Please don't tell me you'd have done that if I wasn't here."

"I'm pretty strong." She'd one-armed the thing into the oven, after all.

Reggie looked skyward. "So smart and pretty. And so senseless."

Her initial pleasure from his compliment faded. "Hey."

"Don't 'hey' me." He mock glared at her, then ran a finger along her cheek.

She froze, battling sensations of desire, pleasure, and mortification he might see how attracted she was.

"Yes, yes, you're a strong, independent, single woman. But dang it, don't hurt yourself on my account." He darted back to finish his drink. "Now, how about we get back to sharing stories? Your turn."

It took a moment for her brain to fire up once more. Then she frowned. "Hold on, buddy. I want to know details. Like, what did you like about your date before she turned all grabby?"

"Seriously?"

"Hey, I like dissecting things to death. Just ask my ex." She smiled through her teeth. "Besides, you owe me." *For frazzling me with a touch.* "I could totally have lifted that hot pan with one hand."

He gave her arm a dubious look. "Ah, okay. Sure. I believe you." He clearly didn't. "Regina was nice enough, but she was kind of boring. She agreed with everything I said. I guess… It was more about me than her. Sometimes you connect with people." He stared into her eyes as he said that, and she wanted to believe he meant that about *her.* "Sometimes you don't."

Shoot, he's still looking at me. Does he mean he's not connecting with me? Or he is? He touched my cheek! "Right." She had no idea what to make of him, so she grabbed some plates and silverware to set the table for four. Reggie took the plates from her but let her set the napkins and forks. At her direction, he moved the pan to the table with some hot pads.

She asked him, "Would you mind making two fancy drinks in those plastic wine glasses for Emily and Sherry?"

"Sure."

"And if you'd like something a little harder than fruity ginger ale, I think I have a beer or two in the fridge. Maybe a hard cider. Or milk or lemonade."

"Lemonade for me. What would you like?"

"Honestly? Another Shirley Temple."

He grinned. "Coming right up."

To Reggie's surprise, dinner felt comfortable, fun, and had him laughing more than not. Emily proved an impeccable host, taking over for Maggie. The little dictator placed him on the bench next to her mom and seated Sherry next to herself in the chair across from them.

After rearranging drinks, she scooped everyone some dinner. Of course, Maggie then scooped them all real-size servings instead of the tablespoon of food Emily had offered.

Sherry, a cute little blond girl with big, brown eyes, stared at him a lot through the meal. Low chattering accompanied the staring, with her and Emily nodding or giggling while watching him.

"Okay, Emily, that's enough of that," Maggie said calmly after the little girls whispered and giggled again. "We don't whisper in front of people because that makes others feel excluded. If you can't share it with everyone, you can't say it, period."

Sherry frowned. "I'm not supposed to talk about bad things at the table though, Ms. Maggie."

"Why don't you tell me what's on your mind, Sherry?"

Sherry bit her lip, looked at Emily, who nodded, then said, "Emily told me Mr. Reggie stopped your head from blowing up. But we're not sure if he has medicine for babies."

Reggie paused with his fork before his mouth. He lowered the food to the plate. "Babies?"

Emily explained, "Sherry just got a baby brother. But her mom was in the hospital when she had it. And she had it in her belly for a long time before that. So do you have medicine for it in Aid 45?" She turned to Sherry. "That's the name of his ambulance."

That she remembered the name of the vehicle impressed him. But the baby medicine confused him. "What?"

Emily sighed. "Reggie, Sherry's mom got medicine to have a baby. Her dad said he got a special pill for her. So can you get that kind of pill for my mom? Or do you have to cut her open and plant it in her? Like a seed, which is what I think her dad really did. He planted a seed in her mom's belly then had to clean up all the blood after he cut her open. And that would be neat but gross, so Sherry didn't want to say that."

Sherry nodded, waiting expectantly for his answer.

He turned wide eyes to Maggie, who looked equally surprised. "Ah, er, you want a baby?" he asked Emily. That seemed safe enough.

Sherry answered for her, talking a mile a minute, "Emily wanted a turtle. But I got a baby brother. And he's cute and laughs a lot when he's not crying. But then he drinks milk from mom's booby, and that's okay because that's how he eats. Emily thinks a brother might be better than a turtle. I'm not sure about that. But now she has Frank. And he isn't a brother or a turtle. But he's neat and licks a lot. So can you give Ms. Maggie a baby or not?"

"I, ah, huh?"

Maggie took a long drink and turned to him with a huge question on her face. "That's a terrific question, Sherry. You don't plant babies in Aid 45, do you, Reggie?"

Emily looked intrigued. "Do you?"

Reggie paused, not sure how to answer, and both annoyed and amused Maggie was letting him handle a baby discussion in her own home. "I thought the stork brought babies."

"Hmm. I don't know." Emily frowned. "Frogs have babies called tadpoles, but tadpoles come from eggs. And the stork doesn't bring them. So who brings frog babies?"

Totally random question. He latched on to it and didn't let go.

After the girls continued to plague him for answers on all sorts of baby reptiles, baby mammals, and baby birds, they asked to be excused and left the table after clearing their plates.

Reggie returned to his cold casserole, only to have Maggie take his plate away. "Hey, I was still eating." And it was surprisingly great food. The macaroni and cheese had been homemade, and the smokiness and salt of the hot dogs made the meal delicious.

"It's cold, answer man." Maggie chuckled. "That was mean of me, but you're so good at answering questions from little girls. Doug told me you did great at the library. I wanted to see for myself." She hefted the plate with one hand. "Let me warm you up some more." She scooped him more food, heated it in the microwave, and returned a minute later. "There. Eat."

He hoped he wasn't making a pig of himself, but he was hungry. "This is delicious, you know. I had no idea six-year-olds had it so good."

She winked. "I'm not bad with simple foods. I like comfort over cuisine."

"Me too." He liked that she took the seat across from him so he could see her. Dinner with her at his side had been tough. He'd been distracted by her all night, annoyed he couldn't see her yet glad he hadn't appeared besotted with her in front of her keen-eyed daughter. "You know, this has been a terrific dinner. The conversation was stimulating, the meal delightful, and the drinks not too shabby either."

Maggie laughed. "You were so good with the girls. Do you have any? Are you an uncle?"

The hurt returned, as it normally did, at thoughts of Rachel. As if he'd been masking it with dinner and laughter, hiding his pain behind a veil of normalcy. And damn, but he didn't like feeling that way. Weak. Vulnerable.

After a moment, Maggie said, "I'm sorry. I shouldn't have asked. But you were so great at discussing frog babies. You're a natural."

He gave her a smile, hoping it didn't seem as sickly as it felt.

Conversation turned to foods they liked and disliked, and gradually his discomfort over the past faded.

But long after he'd cleared his plate, he felt the need to explain. "So, um, about having kids… My ex-girlfriend had a daughter. *Has* a daughter. I was in her life for two years. Then they left." He stood to clear his place and put the dish in the sink.

Before he could clean it, she stopped him. "I'm sorry, Reggie."

He shrugged. "It was a while ago. I'm over it."

She nodded, watching him.

Now, feeling embarrassed and not sure why, he tried to focus on the dishes.

"No dishwashing for you. You're a guest. One who makes a killer cocktail."

Relieved she'd ignored his emotional weirdness, he smiled. "Don't say I didn't try to help clean up."

"You can talk to me while I put them in the dishwasher."

He watched her for a few seconds as she tried not to struggle to get everything in the dishwasher using her left hand. "Just stop. I can't handle this."

He gently urged her aside and filled the dishwasher in no time. There wasn't that much to do, after all. But he saw her smirking as she leaned against the counter next to him. "Was I just set up?"

"What? Who? By me?"

He frowned to hide the smile curling his lips. "You don't fool me."

She raised a brow.

He turned to talk to her and somehow had her caged between his arms, his hands clutching the counter on either side of her.

Damn. The woman was staring at his mouth.

"Reggie?"

"Yeah?" He sounded hoarse.

"I just wanted to thank you for everything. And for tonight." Her dimple flashed. "Now that I know where baby robins come from, my life is complete."

"You may be cute, but that was a jackass move on your part," he murmured, captivated by her smile.

Her low chuckle bewitched him, was all he could think, as he let her draw him down for a kiss that struck him to the core.

Chapter Seven

MAGGIE DIDN'T KNOW WHAT HAD COME OVER HER, BUT SHE *had* to taste Reggie. And dear Lord, he was so much more than she'd imagined. Talk about hot.

The feel of his warm, soft mouth had her gasping, her entire body alive like it hadn't been in forever. She'd never been so in tune with a man before, so automatically dialed in to his taste, scent, and touch. Reggie smelled like the subtle spice of cologne mixed with sex. He knew how to kiss, clearly, but he let her take the lead. Giddy, Maggie knew nothing but how much she wanted him. *Needed* him. But the kiss, so soft and gentle, wasn't nearly enough.

She put more pressure on his neck, dragging him closer. And then, damn it, she pressed for more. Sliding her tongue into his mouth set off the fireworks inside her body. Between her legs, she ached, and her nipples felt like hard points demanding attention.

Except instead of moving his hands where they could do her the most good, Reggie froze.

Oh no!

Shaken and embarrassed that she'd been just as grabby as his disastrous blind date, she pulled back and stared up into wide, brown eyes. "I'm *so* sorry. I—"

"No." He lifted her to sit on the kitchen counter and just looked at her, probably trying to decide how to nicely reject the bruised idiot.

Mortified, she tried to apologize. "Reggie, I—"

"Stop talking."

She shut up, knowing she deserved whatever he had to say.

Reggie watched her with intense eyes. Their heights more

aligned with her sitting on the counter, he leaned closer, not having to bend.

Then he *kissed her back.*

His large hands cupped her cheeks, holding her steady while he moved closer. Her legs automatically parted, gripping him with her thighs.

Reggie's mouth led to all manner of naughty thoughts. First and foremost, he wore too many clothes. She edged her good hand over his biceps, taken with his strength, and moved to his shoulder, his chest. Oh wow, was he solid. Like a freaking rock. And he burned, his skin hot beneath the material of his shirt.

He moaned and stroked his tongue against hers, lighting her up like the damn Fourth of July. His lips caressed and devoured, making her feel both cared for and lusted after, his need as pressing as hers.

He shifted between her legs, and she would have given anything to run her hand down his front, wanting to feel him against her as intimately as possible.

As if he felt what she did, he put a hand on her leg, rubbing her through her skirt. His thumb edged her inner thigh. She tried to shout a "hell yes" into his mouth, sucking his tongue the way she wanted to suck other parts of his body.

He shuddered and pulled away to catch a breath then dove back, both hands on her thighs, edging the material of her skirt higher.

She wished she'd worn a shorter skirt, but at least this one had plenty of material, proving easy enough to move.

And then Reggie's hands were on her bare knees.

He pulled back to stare at her, his eyes narrowed and dark, his breath coming as fast as hers.

"Damn, Maggie," he said and pushed those hands higher.

"Yes," she whispered, lost in his gaze, and licked her lips.

He leaned in again, his thumbs nearly where she wanted them, right at the apex of her hot, wet—

"Mag-Mom!"

They both froze.

"Mag-Mom! Reggie! Come see this!" Emily yelled from her room.

Reggie quickly moved her skirt back in place and helped her to her feet on the floor.

Maggie had to grab his arm to stop from stumbling, her body unsure as to what had just happened. "I…I…ah…"

"Yeah," he sounded strangled. "I'll join you guys in a just a second. Might want to get back there and see what she did with Frank."

"Frank. Right. Yes." Maggie hurried away from Reggie, fanning her cheeks and telling herself to cool it. To douse the raging lust bomb just waiting to go off inside her with a blast of reason. She'd been a hairsbreadth from an orgasm on her kitchen counter from some heavy petting. How sad was that?

And how glorious would it have been if Reggie had ignored their interruption and finally reached his target?

She crossed her eyes, feeling like an idiot for being so easy on the trigger. But with Reggie for a kissing partner, who could blame her?

Which made her stop in her tracks outside Emily's door.

Would Reggie blame her? Would they be awkward after this? *What did I just do?*

―――――――――

Reggie tried to catch his breath, willing away an erection that threatened to erupt like Mt. Vesuvius. *Fuck.* He'd never, ever, been so hot for a woman so fast. And what made it all worse was that she'd started it, and he'd been helpless to keep himself from finishing it. Had her daughter not yelled from the other room, he feared he would have taken Maggie right there on the counter, in the kitchen, in full view of anyone happening by. Like, say, two six-year-old kids!

Taking deep breaths and forcing himself to think of puppies and kittens to will away his desire, he managed a passable feeling of calm and walked slowly down the hall, hearing laughter, barking, and Maggie's smooth voice as she chatted with the girls.

That kiss had been bad enough, but pulling back to see her aroused expression, reading her embarrassment that she thought she might be the only one feeling so passionate? The woman wanted him. Badly. How could Reggie not respond? Especially when it was Maggie, her beautiful face and body reacting to *him*.

He stopped at the doorway. Poor Frank was dressed in a camouflage hat while Emily's bear rode in a puppy-size saddle on top of him, a handmade throwing star tied to one paw, and a small bag of jelly beans tied to the other. Near them, Emily and Sherry held two Barbies, making them fight.

"I want the baby beans!" Emily roared. "It's my kingdom, and I will have dominion!"

"No, they are mine, evil princess!" Sherry shot back between giggles. "What's dominion?"

Maggie tried to cover her laughter, rubbing her chin. "Ah, dominion is being in charge of everything, Sherry. Like, taking over."

"Oh." Sherry's doll slapped down Emily's. "No. It's my dominion. My baby beans! And I get to keep the Frank pony too."

Emily's eyes narrowed. She gave an evil laugh and held her doll over her head. "I will slaughter your—"

Maggie grabbed the doll before it could descend. "Okay, you two," she quickly cut in, clearing her throat. "Let's get the peace talks going."

Reggie stared at her six-year-old, looking cute as could be, talking about dominion and slaughter. He met Maggie's gaze. "I'm officially scared."

"And this is just a declaration of war." She turned to the girls. "No more talk about violence. What if you guys *share* the knight and Frank pony and become twin princesses with baby beans? If you still want to pretend fight, you can duke it out with a dance battle." Maggie pressed play on a nearby tablet, and pop music spilled from a Bluetooth speaker on the dresser.

"Yay!" Emily cheered. "Dance battle!"

The girls giggled and danced around with their dolls, eating jelly beans while Frank shrugged off Brownie and tried to get out of his saddle.

Reggie couldn't help laughing as he got the puppy out of the saddle and hat. He left the three behind, rejoining Maggie in the living room.

"Nice job avoiding a slaughter in there," he said to her, still grinning.

Her eyes sparkled. "I try to keep the peace around here."

He loved seeing that joy, and the kernel of happiness normally buried under stoicism and duty sprang to light inside him.

Her eyes remained warm, but her smile faded as she watched him.

As if the time with the children hadn't happened, his mind immediately recalled the feel of Maggie in his arms. Her mouth, her smooth skin under his palms…

"Um, er, about before…" She blew out a breath. "I, ah…"

"Yeah." He sighed. "We really need to do that again."

She blinked at him and slowly smiled, her grin dazzling. "We do, don't we?"

He nodded and rubbed his head, doing his damnedest to will away his growing arousal.

"So, I wasn't too grabby or anything?" Maggie's cheeks turned pink. "I want to say I'm sorry for dragging you down for a kiss. But I'm not." She paused, watching him. "Should I be?"

"Hell no." Reggie knew if he kissed her again, he'd want more. So, instead, he drew her into his arms and carefully hugged her, conscious of her hurt arm. He pulled back to look down at her. "But maybe the next time we kiss, we do it where there aren't any kids around."

Her eyes widened.

He realized she might think he only wanted to get together again for sex and said, "I mean, I want to kiss you. But we could slow down, have dinner, talk. Then, well, you know..." *Making a mess of it here, dude.* "When you're ready," he added.

She nodded. "And when you're ready."

"Hell, I'm ready now," he muttered.

She glanced down at his fly and gaped. "I'll say."

"Damn, Maggie."

She surprised him by laughing so hard, she started crying. "I'm sorry. It's just... The girls have the worst timing. But I guess it wasn't so bad. I mean, I shouldn't be jumping the guests." She wiped her eyes. "Heck. I'm sorry, Reggie. Not for the kiss, but for my timing. You poor thing."

He saw the humor in it, but fuck, he wanted her right now. *Bad.* Hearing her laugh turned him on. *I'm such a weirdo.* "Yeah, talk about getting grabby...with one hand." They shared more laughter and teasing.

"I'd better go." He took her hand in his and kissed the back of it.

Her eyes darkened as she looked up at him. "You should go. You're not safe here." She tugged him toward her, and he leaned closer. She gave him a quick peck on the lips. "If you stay any longer, you might not leave. Ever." She gave an evil laugh.

Not leaving sounded just fine to him.

"Why? Do you have a bunch of bodies under your bed?"

"Yes. And a bunch of etchings you really need to see. Come back with me to my bedroom," she teased. She couldn't know how much he wanted to take her up on her offer.

"I would, but then the girls might get an X-rated introduction to magic baby beans."

Maggie cracked up. "You really got put through the ringer tonight. The girls, me. I'm going to start calling you Saint Reggie."

"Please, don't." He brushed a lock of her hair behind her ears, loving the fact she tensed when he touched her. He tried not to look but couldn't help noticing the hard points of her nipples beneath her T-shirt. "I'll pick you up tomorrow morning at nine thirty, okay?"

"Sure." She nodded. "What?"

"For your appointment to get a cast."

"Okay. Yes, thanks." She walked with him to the door. "I really appreciate it." She glanced away then back, looking surprisingly shy. "And I really liked kissing you."

His heart hammered in his chest. "Not nearly as much as I liked kissing you. And no, you weren't too grabby." Not grabby enough. He inwardly groaned at thoughts of her hand grabbing him between his legs. "I'd better go."

"I—"

The dog barked. Hell. Reggie had forgotten Frank.

"I should probably take him with me."

"For now." Maggie put her hand on his arm, and the contact heated him all over. "Thanks for everything. But not the kiss. You don't get thanked for that."

"What do I get then?"

"If you're lucky, a repeat." She winked.

Reggie left with Frank, his dreams filled with Maggie, that damn kitchen counter, and a never-ending dress that stopped him just short of reaching heaven.

———

When Maggie finished her appointment the next day, Reggie was there waiting. Her cast felt heavy, but the sling helped.

"Nice." He nodded at her arm. "Do I get to sign it?"

She handed him a Sharpie she'd brought with her just for that purpose. "Go for it."

He wrote his name and, next to it, drew what looked like a circle with eight wavy lines dangling underneath it. Then he added googly eyes.

"What is that?" she asked, confused.

"An octopus, Ms. Grabby." He grinned.

She blushed. "Oh, stop. It's not my fault you're irresistible."

"That's my line."

She smiled and let him lead her back to his car. "Thanks again for taking me. How was lunch with your friend?"

Reggie had spent the time waiting for her since Neal was out of town on vacation. "Oh, uh, fine. He's a great guy. I met him through work."

"You must meet all kinds of people."

They reached the car, and Reggie unlocked it and held the door open for her. She got in, and he realized taking care of her, even doing something small, made him feel good. *Easy, let's not go down the caregiver path again.*

He forced himself to relax and got in with her. But their proximity in the car gave him a heady dose of her delicate, floral perfume. The scent went straight to his head...and other parts. He glanced over to see her fiddling with her purse and noticed her lovely breasts. Though not overly large, they were handfuls he'd love to cup. To hold. To kiss. To... *Stop it. Take her home.*

"Heading back to your place," he announced, more to himself than her. "I—" Her hand on his thigh stopped him.

"Reggie, would you mind if we went somewhere else? Doug and Benny are taking Emily for me this morning. They're going to the zoo to give me a break. And, though Doug refuses to admit it, it's so he can see the alligators. He loves them." She paused. "Could you drop me off somewhere downtown? I can get a ride home, so you're not stuck with me."

"No way. I have the day off and would like nothing more than to chauffeur you around." He decided to be honest. "Let me do this, or I'll spend my day staring at my already-clean house. I even dropped Frank at Nadia's because she insisted. So no need to rush back to take care of the puppy. I'm embarrassed to say I have nothing else to do."

Instead of poking fun at him, Maggie commiserated. "You're as bad as I am. When Benny told me they had plans to keep Emily entertained, my first thought was, what will I do with myself?" She shook her head. "I mean, I can really use some me time, don't get me wrong. But I'm a boring person. What will I do? Heck, what would you do in my place?"

Something in her eyes told him she wanted exactly what he did but didn't want to admit it.

Her hand on his thigh felt heavy.

Reggie tried desperately to get his mind out of the gutter. "My friends are I are big into board games."

"Oh?"

"What would you say to coming back to my place"—*Don't do it, man, you know what will happen*—"and playing some games? We could hang out and be boring together."

She squeezed his leg. His dick twitched in response.

"That sounds like fun." She wet her lips, and he swallowed a groan. "Let's go."

They arrived too soon, the radio and light discussion about the downtown area keeping things easy between them. But as soon as they pulled into the driveway, Reggie felt the heaviness of anticipation clouding his thoughts.

"Want something to drink?" he asked as they entered the house.

"This is so cute. I can see you here." She smiled. "Sure. I'll have what you're having."

"Iced tea it is." He poured them both glasses while she looked around.

"This is beautiful."

"Believe it or not, this is all me. My sister, Lisa, tried to help decorate the place, but her taste isn't mine. She's into plain white and no clutter. She calls it being a minimalist. But I know better. She hides her crap better than anyone I know." He handed her the tea.

"Thanks." Maggie took a sip. "Nice. I love the mint."

"Me too. You know, I liked your place a lot."

"We have the same taste in style, I think. We like it to look nice but feel comfortable." She walked through his living area to the kitchen, looked around, then settled back in the living room on the couch. "Do you like to cook?"

"I do, actually."

"Wow. A nice house, it's neat, and you cook." She frowned. "Are you married to two other women or living with your parents? What gives? You can't be too perfect."

He chuckled and joined her on the sofa. "Can I record that and play it back for my friends and family? They all think I'm too serious. I mean, just because I like to be responsible, it's like I'm cursed with an incurable disease."

"Ha! I can top that. Because I wanted to make a five-year then a ten-year plan and figure out finances and vacations ahead of time, my ex called me inflexible and controlling. Me, controlling!"

He nodded. "Same. Just because I like to plan and have an emergency fund, I'm no fun and can't be spontaneous. I can be spontaneous. I just like to plan for my spontaneous time."

"Exactly."

They clinked glasses, drained them, then sat facing each other. Reggie tried to behave as he normally would with the guys over. He could almost believe that her breasts weren't moving faster with her rushing breaths or that she wasn't looking at him like she wanted him to get naked and do her right then and there.

"What games do you have?" she asked.

"I'll get them." He rushed off the couch, doing his best to stop being so sex-obsessed, and returned in control of himself, with several games.

She frowned. "Parcheesi?"

"It's one of my favorites. Like Trouble, where you try to get all your players to the end first. And you land on other players to send them back to start over."

"Hmm. I see. You like games where you make the other player angry."

Reggie shrugged. "If you're not playing to win, why play?"

"Right. Because second place is for losers."

They smiled through their teeth at each other then laughed.

"So are we betting anything?" Maggie asked.

Strip Parcheesi sounded good to him. "Ah, no. Let's just play one game, see if we still like each other after it, then we'll go from there."

"Seems fair. When I win, I'm going to tell everyone I know I beat you with one hand. See? One hand?" She gave him a goofy grin.

He sighed. "I can already tell this is going to be a long game."

"I slaughter all those who oppose my dominion!"

"I totally see where Emily gets her evil side."

She snickered.

The game took a long time, because both Reggie and Maggie thought nothing of taking cheap shots rather than going for a quick victory. She talked a lot of smack, so he felt okay to do the same. Not having to hold back was fun, and it made him realize he'd kept his competitive nature in check a lot when with Amy, letting her win or being gentle about a victory so as to not hurt her feelings.

With Maggie, he didn't even try. And she seemed to prefer it that way, gloating, smirking, and basically being a poor winner.

"Ha. Sucker."

He raised a brow. "You do realize this is my house and my car that brought you here?"

"Whatever. Two words for you Reggie—second place."

He couldn't help staring at her. She was so damn cute, and frankly, sexy, acting out like a punk.

"I'm sorry, remind me again of what you do for a living?" he asked, trying not to laugh.

"I teach second graders." She flipped him off. "Now you see why I need to let out my true self. Being nice and caring for a living takes its toll."

He laughed. "Oh man. Don't I know it."

She cleared the board and put it away.

To Reggie's surprise, an hour and a half had passed. "Hey, are you hungry for lunch?"

"I thought you already ate."

This is what you get for lying about Neal. He tried to play it off casually. "Neal didn't have time for a meal. We just hung out for a little. I have stuff for sandwiches."

"Oh, sure." She joined him, standing close enough he had to force himself not to reach out and caress her cheeks. He loved how soft she felt and how her eyes had melted when he'd cupped her face. "Can I help?"

Sure. Jerk me off while I fix you a ham sandwich. "No. Nope." He forced a smile. "Ham and cheese okay?"

"Great. I'll be right back." She left, and he soon heard the bathroom door close.

After fixing them sandwiches, adding chips and refills for their drinks, Reggie took the plates outside. The sun was high overhead, the day a perfect beginning to August. Butterflies visited the cosmos and lantana by the wooden fence in the back. And the maple gave the grass in the corner a nice bit of shade. When Maggie joined him, she sat next to him at the table, watching the butterflies flit in the warm summer sun.

"Wow. It's like a mini paradise back here. I'm jealous." She bit into her sandwich. "Yum," she said, her mouth full.

"Today is exceptionally nice. I'm glad I'm not working. Don't get me wrong. I love my job. But it's tough to be inside the engine, riding around in the heat with the uniform on, on a day like today."

"I'll bet." She looked around the garden, seeing the thriving plants he'd worked hard to seed. "Did you do all this?"

"Yep. Green thumb, like my dad."

"I'm terrible with plants. It's a flaw."

"Oh?"

"Sadly, though I love to eat, I've never grown my own veggies."

"Too bad. It's fun."

"For you. When you spend a ton of time trying to grow something from a seed and it dies, it's a bummer."

He nodded. "I get that."

"So what do you do when you're not firefighting or driving around broken women?"

"Broken. Ha. Right. Then who whooped me at Parcheesi?"

"Well, I might be broken, but I'm not a loser." She winked. "Tough to keep up, eh, old man?"

"Please. I'm only thirty-three."

"Yep, a good four years older than me." She sounded proud of that fact. "So, what do you do for fun?"

"Well, it's obvious I like gardening. I also work out." He flexed.

She swallowed. "I can tell."

"I wish I could say I do a lot more than that. I don't. Hence me being boring and playing games to inject fun into my life." He ate his sandwich then turned the tables. "What about you?"

"Wait. You forgot about the blind dates. You do that."

"For *fun,* you said."

She grinned. "You look like you ate a lemon."

"Ha ha." He felt so comfortable with her here. "What about you? Besides keeping the bloodshed to a minimum with your evil minion at home, what do you do for fun?"

"Not much." She sighed. "I was planning on some rock

climbing with Emily this month. Benny knows a guy who owns a rock-climbing gym. It would have been a blast. We might still do ceramics though. I like art." She faced him, her expression animated. "I was hoping to do some painting, believe it or not. I want to try watercolors, and I thought Emily and I could go take a day trip to Mt. Rainier, and I'd paint the mountain or something." She blushed. "Sounds silly, but the plan was to do it and come home with a masterpiece."

"I think it sounds fun."

"You like to camp?"

"I did as a kid. It was okay. But I'm more a bed guy than a ground-with-ants-and-bugs-walking-over-you guy."

"I get that." She shivered. "Truly. I like sleeping above the ground, not on the ground."

"Did you camp when you were a kid?"

She frowned. "No. I grew up in the boring suburbs out east. Dad was a teacher, mom a homemaker. We had a nice life, but it wasn't exciting."

"Do you get to see them often?" Reggie wondered. She hadn't mentioned her parents much, just her friends helping her.

"They died right after I graduated high school. It was rough. I loved them a lot, and I had no other family, well, none I'm close to."

"Ouch. That's hard."

"It was. But I got through college, married Stephen, moved out here, had Emily, divorced Stephen, and now have nothing better to do than harass the poor guy who saved me." She sighed. "Should I apologize now or later for how badly I'm going to continue to beat you at our next round of board games? Or should I just let you win because you did, technically, save my life?"

"That's true. I did save your life." Not at all. "Several times, in fact."

She was trying not to laugh. "Oh?"

"First, I saved you from your head exploding in the ambulance, you know, when Emily was screaming your name. Then, I saved you in the hospital from dying from embarrassment. I was nice, even when confronted with your hair that stood by itself. And you told me all about your unshaved legs."

Her cheeks were totally pink, but she laughed.

"And then last night, I saved you from burning up in the oven when you would have killed yourself pulling that pan from the flames."

"Now that's not true. I totally could have gotten that casserole out by myself."

"I'm sorry. Who's lying now?"

She poked him in the chest. "Hey, it's not my fault one of us is built like a tank. I exercise when I can. And with this broken arm, I can't lift weights the way I normally do." She flexed her good arm, showing a pretty skinny set of biceps.

"Gee, I'm impressed."

"Oh, screw off."

He chuckled, rose, then helped her to her feet. "Okay, Atilla. Let's go back for a second round of who's better at being a sore winner. You or me?"

"Me, of course. Because you have yet to win."

"Oh, those are fighting words." He grinned. "Let's make this serious. This time, the winner gets a prize."

"Bring it."

Chapter Eight

Unfortunately for Maggie, Reggie brought the win. And he rubbed her nose in it. Granted, finding out who killed Professor Plum hadn't been that tough a challenge. But the way Reggie gloated, one would think he'd just won an Olympic gold.

He congratulated himself, pumped his fists, and generally spoke in small words so she could "understand she'd just gotten herself a big, old second-place-is-for-losers trophy." He left the room and returned to hand her an actual plaque with the word *LOSER* engraved on it.

"My friends and I take our game nights seriously," he confessed, his eyes laughing.

God, she wanted to eat him up. Reggie was fun, funny, and treated her like an equal. Most of the men—though there hadn't been many lately—she'd dated tended to be larger than her, and they treated her like some fragile thing who could barely do for herself.

Reggie could easily bench her. The guy clearly worked out. But he challenged her and loved trash-talking. Man, she was crushing on the guy. Hard.

They hadn't discussed last night's kisses. Or about wanting to continue any kind of physical intimacy. But being with him today was so great. She didn't want it to end by bringing up any awkwardness between them.

Then she noticed the time. "Oh wow. It's three already. I can't believe it's so late."

Reggie's smile faded. "Huh. I hadn't either. I guess you need to get back."

She checked her phone only to find Benny's message that they were heading to the snakes and would swing back much later after feeding Emily dinner.

She looked up with a smile. "Nope. The guys are heading to the reptiles and don't intend to be back until later."

"Oh." Reggie relaxed. "Do you want me to take you back?"

"No. I mean, I'm in no rush. I just feel bad about monopolizing your free time."

They both looked at each other, then at the Monopoly board on the table.

"I guess I have the energy for a speed game," she offered. "I mean, it would be rude not to give you back your *LOSER* trophy."

He smiled, his teeth even, white, and straight. Oy. Now she found his teeth sexy. She needed help.

"Let's go, little girl."

"Little *girl*? I don't think so."

He sighed and gave her a thorough once-over that woke her body right up. "I don't think so either. At all." He grabbed the board and set up the game on the coffee table. They sat on the floor by it in the living room.

A half hour underway, Maggie owed Reggie a lot in rent. Damn it. As they continued to roll the dice, she noticed him checking her out. More and more of his gazes landed on her lips or her chest.

"You know, I owe you for that stupid railroad."

"Railroad*s*. As in, more than one." He smiled like the shark he was.

"But I was thinking, we might be able to make a deal. I do own all the green and yellow properties you keep landing on, after all." She deliberately toyed with her neckline and saw him latch on and not blink.

"A deal?" Did his voice sound deeper?

"Yep. How about a kiss from your tenant? Just a friendly peck on the cheek to defer my rent."

He stared at her lips. A small grin found his mouth before he gave her a scandalized look. "I don't know. Only if it's a friendly, nonsexual kiss. Because I don't want to come across as creepy, and I'd never take advantage of one of my tenants."

"You're such a good guy, Reggie," she said, breathless.

His stare grew more intense.

She leaned closer and planted a kiss on his rough cheek, feeling the start of stubble and wishing she could feel that between her legs.

He groaned. "Th—that's enough, Ms. Swanson. No need to linger."

She smiled and sat back, then rolled the dice again.

This time Reggie landed on her property. "I know I *seem* to have a lot of money." They both looked at the many fake bills collected in front of him. "But it's all actually sunk into investments. I'm cash poor."

She arched a brow. "Oh?"

"Yes. I think that maybe I could do you a service in return for your looking the other way on my rent."

"A service?" Her heart raced. "What kind?"

"Well, you appear to be injured. I'm not a doctor, but perhaps I could make you feel better."

"H-how?" She coughed, her mouth dry.

Wicked, Reggie smiled. "I'll show you."

He moved to settle in behind her, sandwiching her between the table and his big body, backed by the couch. She sat with her legs splayed, and he framed her legs with his own, his groin wedged against her lower back.

"There, that's better."

"What are you up to, rent-avoider?"

He chuckled and pushed her hair back, his fingers causing sparks of need to flare where they grazed her cheek and neck. Then he whispered, "I'm going to relax you."

"Bang-up job, so far," she muttered, feeling like a tensed coil about to spring.

She felt the vibration of his laughter through their connection. "Now lean forward a minute."

She did and let him ease the sling off her neck. He took it, so careful with her arm. "That's it, now relax and rest against me. You'll feel great in just a few minutes."

"Said the spider to the fly."

His lips curled against her ear. "Just a light massage." Reggie easily wrapped his arms around her and took her good hand in his.

He started rubbing her palm, rotating her fingers, and kneading the pad of her thumb.

"Oh wow. That feels amazing."

"Mm-hmm." He continued to ease the muscles of her left hand, then her forearm.

The touch felt fantastic, but she couldn't see him. She could, however, feel him. And she didn't think she'd imagined that pole in his pants rubbing against her backside.

She burned, feverish from the arousal building at his touch.

"Good?"

Damn him. "I think you missed a few spots," she said, sounding weak.

His deep laugh shot her libido into overdrive.

Reggie slid his hands over her arm to her stomach. "You seem tense."

"Oh, shut up."

He chuckled and slid his lips closer to her ear to whisper, "I'm tense too." He nibbled her earlobe, and her body shouted for him to stop teasing and touch her where she needed it.

The nibbling turned to kissing as Reggie ran his lips down her neck to her shoulder, then back up to her ear, her cheek. She turned, unable to wait, and met his mouth while his hands rubbed her stomach, grazing her ribs right under her breasts.

It should have been awkward in this position, nearly in his lap, having to turn her head to meet his mouth. And it was…but she didn't care.

He was kissing her, and it felt so damn good. His hands moved up, so that he cupped her breasts. And his clever fingers ran over her nipples, which had grown stiff and so sensitized, she swore he'd grazed between her legs with that touch.

"So sweet," he murmured and slowly shifted her body so that she was soon straddling his waist, on her knees, with them face-to-face.

Reggie stared at her. "You're so sexy. So pretty."

"Yeah? Well, you're slow." She moved his hand back to her breast. "Now kiss me, squatter. You owe me rent."

His slow smile was the most beautiful thing she'd ever seen.

And then her brain turned off.

Reggie's kiss fried her. His lips, his tongue. Teasing with the promise of so much pleasure. She could do nothing but follow his lead. Maggie lost control of her body and her awareness of anything not Reggie. He held her breasts, palming them before pinching her nipples with the right amount of pressure. Not too much, but just enough to keep her squirming on top of him.

"That's it." He sat her on top of him, that solid erection grinding between her legs. "Fuck, you feel good."

She kissed her way down his throat. "So do you."

He moaned and forced her to kiss him again, where she sucked his tongue and stroked him, licking deeper. His kisses grew more demanding.

He found the snap of her jeans and stayed there.

She let go of his neck to help him unfasten her pants, giving him the encouragement he needed.

And he took it from there.

His hand slid down her front, not stopping until his fingers met the wet desire between her legs.

She sucked in a breath, shocked at how much she needed this. Needed *him*.

He met her gaze, his satisfied, hungry, and he watched as he pushed a thick finger inside her.

"Reggie," she rasped.

"Maggie," he whispered back and thrust his finger deeper.

She rocked against him, dragging him close for a kiss, and instinctively sought more.

Reggie was happy to agree, grinding his hand against her clit while he thrust his finger in and out of her body, bringing her to a sharp, instant climax that rocked her existence.

While she clamped down on him, she pulled away from his mouth, moaning and shaking.

"Fuck, you're sweet," he rumbled, holding her while she came down, finally removing his hand.

After a few moments, she realized she felt tension in his big body and knew they hadn't finished.

"Wow. Consider yourself paid in full," she said and kissed him.

He pulled back, his eyes cloudy with lust, and smirked. "I know I'm good, but I don't think anyone's ever traded me kisses for Monopoly money before."

"Yeah? Well, it's time you got a bonus from your happy tenant."

"You don't have to…" He paused when her fingers pulled at his jeans.

"I can't unless you help. Unless you'd rather I didn't—"

He moved so fast, he nearly knocked her off him. "Oh, sorry."

She could see his desperation and gave him a sly smile. "You're going to be sorry."

"So are you when I make a huge mess." He bit his lip when she snaked a hand down his underwear and gripped him. "Fuck, Maggie. I'm so hard."

"And I'm so wet." She leaned close and nipped his earlobe. Pumping him up and down, she whispered, "Imagine how good it will feel inside me."

He moaned and stroked her back, his hands frantic.

"How wet and hot I am." She tongued his ear, and he jerked up, nearly unseating her. "You feel so good. So big." She wiped her palm over his slit, feeling the moisture there. "So wet yourself."

"I'm close." He pumped up into her hand, moving faster.

She wanted him inside her for real, but she couldn't stop to get him there. Instead, she moved her fist faster and kissed him.

He tensed and groaned into her mouth as he came, jetting into her hand as he continued to thrust.

She pulled back from the kiss to watch him, seeing him in the throes of something wonderful. *How can he look so sexy when coming?*

Not awkward or pained, but as if he'd been enlightened and had come to some higher place of pleasure. Wow, was he *sexy.*

Reggie finally stopped, and she let him go, wiping her hand against his belly. The guy had come. A lot. All because of her.

After a moment, he looked at her. She smiled, and he drew her close for a kiss.

She clenched his shoulder, loving how he held her close. In Reggie's arms, she felt sexy, desired, and safe.

They ended the kiss together.

Reggie stared. "Wow."

"I second that."

They continued to watch each other in wonder, until Reggie said, "So, um, should we talk about this?"

"This?"

"Us," he said and looked away before focusing on her once more. He seemed uncomfortable, and not just because he'd made a mess in his underwear. "This is awkward."

"Because of the mess or the situation?" she had to ask, conscious her smirk wasn't appropriate since he was trying to be serious.

Reggie kissed her again, until she couldn't see straight.

His slow grin turned into a smirk of his own, and they both laughed.

"Okay, you win." He hugged her before pulling back. "Let's talk about this, and *us*," he emphasized, "after I clean up."

"You made a big mess."

"No, *you* made a big mess. I was helpless while that firm hand made me see stars."

"This tiny thing?" She held her hand up. "Wow. And here I thought I was a weakling compared to you. Apparently, I've got a death grip."

"Smart-ass."

She scooted off him and stood. Reggie left and returned a few minutes later wearing a different T-shirt, having given her enough time to straighten herself and wash her hand.

"That was hot," she said, at the same time he said, "That was *so* hot."

"You're right. That needed an extra 'so.'"

He tried not to smile. "Maggie, be serious."

"Fine. I like you. A lot. I'm obviously attracted to you. And I'm not great at dating."

"Everything you said. Yeah." Reggie studied her. What did he see, exactly? Because when Maggie looked in the mirror, she saw a cute, nearly thirty, single mom. Not exactly gorgeous or swinging-from-the-chandelier sexy. "I know we just met, and neither of us seems to be actively looking to date."

"Nope."

"Yeah, nope. But we connect."

"Oh yes, we do." Maggie tried to stop ogling him, but he was so pretty.

"Maggie, focus."

"I'm sorry." She blushed. "Continue."

He opened his mouth and closed it. Looking like a fish.

"You want to ask me to chalk this up to something physical and not let it happen again." She sighed. She'd heard it before, but usually she was the one calling it quits.

Reggie frowned. "I was going to say I had a lot fun today, both before and after Monopoly. And I want us to start dating."

"Oh." She blinked and smiled. "Oh. Yeah. That sounds good."

"But I know it's tough with having a child, so I'd like it if we kept this just between us." He looked pensive. "I've been down this road before. My last breakup hurt a little girl. I don't want that for Emily."

Maggie loved that he cared. "I don't either. I agree. How about you and I go out a few times and have fun? We can see how things are between us, no pressure."

His shoulders relaxed, and his smile returned. "No pressure. Except of course for all the pressure trying to focus on anything not sex-related around you."

She blushed. "I thought that was just me. Good to know you feel it too."

"Oh, I do." He walked to her and cupped her chin to look up at him. "I like you, Maggie. A lot."

"Me too."

"But I know it's tough to be with an Adonis like myself. So, if you can't handle it, just let me know."

"Who's the *loser* who had to trade sex for rent, Adonis?"

"Hey, you started it." He kissed her.

"I was trying to cheat. You clearly have no idea how to invest your Monopoly money." She kissed him back. "I still owe you a dinner."

"You do." He seemed to like that fact.

"How about tomorrow night? My place. Emily is due for a sleepover at Sherry's."

"I'm on duty tomorrow. How about Saturday night?"

"Perfect."

Reggie treated her to a wide smile. "Sounds great. Although…" He cleared his throat. "We haven't talked about sex."

"Sure we have." Maggie brightened. "Remember when you told the girls all about tadpoles at dinner?"

He laughed. "You're a pain in the ass."

"But a cute one."

"You so are." He kissed her. "You and I are planners. And with the way things happen between us, eventually there will be sex."

"A lot of sex." *Eventually? If I had my way, in the next five seconds from now.*

"A lot." His eyes narrowed. "I've got stamina. Just warning you."

"So do I." Maggie licked her lips.

He groaned. "Stop it. I'm trying to cover an important topic."

"Safe sex. Yes. I do have a few condoms in the house. Somewhere." She frowned. "Maybe. It's been a while. I always use protection. I'm also on birth control."

"Good. I always use protection too. I'm safe and healthy."

"Me too."

"Great."

"Good."

They paused. Maggie admitted, "I really, really want to have sex with you."

"So do I," Reggie said, his voice hoarse. "I want to be inside you right now."

He was doing it again. Making her think sexy thoughts.

"But we should probably slow down." He cleared his throat. "And practice safe sex."

"Right. When it happens, we'll be safe."

"But it's good to know if we *did* have sex, without a condom, we'd be covered."

"Not literally covered, but protected from baby-making. Yes," she said.

Reggie covered his eyes. "You're making it so hard to have this conversation. And before you smirk and say, 'How hard?'—this hard." He took her hand and put it over the firm bulge in his jeans. "Now I think we should take you home before I come in my pants again."

"So we'll talk about blow jobs and oral sex later in our relationship?"

"*Fuck.* Go get in the car."

Maggie obeyed before she did something really stupid and pulled down his pants for round two.

———————

To Maggie's regret, they had to postpone their date. Sherry had come down with a summer cold, and Maggie didn't feel comfortable imposing on the guys next door yet again after the zoo trip.

Reggie completely understood. So they flirted on the phone Saturday night once Emily went to bed.

It constantly surprised Maggie how much she enjoyed talking to him. Reggie's deep laugh warmed her every time, and she liked that he appreciated her sense of humor and intelligence. Before she knew it, the hour had reached eleven. She only knew because a yawn took her by surprise.

"I guess I should let you go," Reggie said with regret.

Maggie couldn't believe they'd been talking for over an hour. It felt as if only a few minutes had passed. "Yes. But don't forget, we need to reschedule that dinner I owe you."

"About that…"

He's going to break it off but do it gently. Damn. I knew this was too good to last.

"How about you bring Emily over for brunch tomorrow? She can visit Frank, and you can see how masterful I am with eggs and bacon."

Relieved he hadn't broken things off, she teased, "You had me at bacon." She had to stop second-guessing him and herself. "Can I bring anything other than Emily?"

"No. Just you two. And, ah, this isn't a date. At least, not between you and me."

"It's not?" Ah, yes, their agreement to keep things strictly between them.

"Think of it as a friendly foster meeting for Frank. He's missing Emily. And I have a feeling she's probably missing him."

"You have no idea. She loves him." And wouldn't it be heart-breaking if they couldn't keep the puppy?

"Yeah, well, I just want you to know I'm sticking to the plan. We keep our new dating life to ourselves. Tomorrow's just a friendly brunch."

"Brunch. Sounds perfect. Emily will be so excited. But, sadly for you, you're second place in her affections to *a dog*."

He laughed, as she'd intended. She didn't want him feeling pressured to entertain her daughter, but Emily had been asking about the puppy.

"Touché. I'll see you two tomorrow morning. Say, ten o'clock?"

"Perfect. Thanks, Reggie. We'll see you then." Just after she disconnected, she received a text from Benny.

Got time to talk?

The guys normally didn't call so late. She hoped everything was okay. She texted back, Sure. Door's open.

Maggie unlocked the door and grabbed some water to drink. Benny entered after a brief knock.

Tall, gruff, and intimidating, even in plaid pajama pants and a Skynyrd T-shirt, Benny walked in carrying a bottle of beer. He closed the door behind him before walking toward her.

If she hadn't known him, she wouldn't want to cross him. Ever.

But his typical expression—menacing with a bite of I-dare-you-to-screw-with-me—turned into a wide smile upon seeing her. "My favorite short lady, not counting the tiny one sleeping in the back."

"My favorite giant. How's it going, Benny?"

She stood to hug him, and he lifted her in his arms, easily holding her off her feet as well as managing his beer.

She gasped. "Put me down, you big oaf."

He laughed and set her down before taking a seat on the couch. He lounged and sipped his beer.

Maggie sank into the plush cushion next to him. "Thanks again for taking Emily to the zoo the other day. She had so much fun."

"Us too." Benny smiled. But he seemed a little off.

"Are you okay? Where's Doug?"

"Sleeping."

She blinked. "This early on a Saturday night?" Doug became a night owl on the weekends.

Benny sighed. "We had a fight."

"Uh-oh. Lay it on me." They hadn't had one of these conversations in a while. Maggie was often a sounding board for the couple, and since she loved them both, she never took sides.

"It's not my fault," he said, defensive. "But I might have overreacted when some guy at the zoo started flirting with Doug."

"Tell me."

Benny groaned. A former semipro wrestler turned piano teacher, he'd lived a varied and exciting life. Not so popular as the wrestlers on television, but he'd traveled and performed all over the world, making a decent living achieving a low level of fame, especially in the Pacific Northwest. He'd had his share of groupies. But from the first moment he'd laid eyes on Doug, he'd fallen in love.

Maggie still thought their relationship one to aspire to. Despite their differences, they'd managed to find something special. They had committed to each other so fully, they gave her hope that someday she too might have a love as lasting as theirs.

"We had just taken a tour around the place and returned for the snakes. Emily's fascinated with them. And Doug wanted to see the alligators again."

"He's got a predatory kind of nature, you know?"

"I know." Benny sounded glum.

She patted his knee.

"Emily and I were checking out the salamanders, and the zoo guy came out and let her hold one. She was thrilled, let me tell you."

Maggie smiled.

"I realized Doug wasn't with us, and I saw him talking to some tall, good-looking blond. Just his type."

"I thought *you* were just his type."

"Nah. For some reason he and I clicked right away. But he typically likes the blond, streamlined ones. Not hulky bears." He sighed.

"You mean hunky beasts," she corrected. "Stop feeling sorry for yourself." She knew this song and dance, but considering how pathetic she'd been feeling with Reggie moments ago, she could give Benny his due. "If you weren't gay and happily in love with Doug, I'd have made a play for you the first time I saw you."

"Really?" Benny perked up, his dark-blue eyes hopeful.

"Of course. I like my men handsome, strong, and smart. And let's face it. You play the piano like you were born with ivory keys. You're huge, you still lift weights and keep trim just for fun, and you're gorgeous."

"Well, I don't know about gorgeous." He stroked his bristled chin. "And trim is way out." He slapped his belly, which, to her bemusement, seemed flatter than it had been the last time she'd given him a good look.

"You've lost weight."

"Not as much as Doug." He groaned. "Maggie, we've been married for four years now, together for six, technically. How am I still so neurotic about my relationship?"

"Because you're you?"

He glared. "I know I have a tendency to lean toward the dramatic. Why do you think I was so popular during my wrestling days?"

"I can only imagine."

"Doug has always been a catch. He's sophisticated and smart. He likes science and learning. He's great with kids."

"I know. We teach together."

Benny rambled on. "Men notice him. A lot. And Doug is always friendly, so sometimes I imagine he doesn't notice people flirting. But they do."

I bet he notices and likes it. Because who doesn't want to feel attractive? She loved Doug, but he liked the attention. And with his looks, who could blame him?

"Okay, you know this, Benny. What made yesterday different?"

"The guy gave Doug his number!"

"Oh."

"Yeah." Benny growled, "I can handle flirting, but a phone number?"

"Doug took it?" That she couldn't believe.

"No. I stormed over there and made sure the flirty guy noticed me. He took off like a shot. Afterward, Doug said I made a scene for no reason. He wasn't happy with me."

"Benny, you either trust Doug or you don't."

"That's what he said." Benny drank more. "I know I should trust him. But I'm starting to go gray and getting fat, and he's only getting more handsome. Honey, I'm almost ten years older than he is. Why wouldn't he want someone younger?"

"Because that someone isn't you." Maggie felt for him. "Benny, do you know how Doug describes you to his friends? As a big teddy bear who could snap a guy in two. He brags about how strong you are, how sexy his man is. And he's so proud of all you've accomplished. He's into you. Still, after six years. I know this because he's *always* talking about you. And no, not to complain about you leaving your shoes all over the house."

Benny flushed.

"He loves you so much. You don't know how lucky you are."

Chapter Nine

Just thinking about their relationship made Maggie tear up.

"Hey now, I didn't come over here to make you sad."

"I know. But you're so lucky, and you don't realize it. I would give anything to have the kind of relationship you guys do. You might argue, and you might fuss over who drives to dinner or who gets to pick your next vacation, but you have each other. I've watched you guys for years, and no matter how many spats you have—"

"I don't think I'd call them spats," Benny muttered. "Maybe fights, knock-down, drag-outs. Epic verbal throwdowns."

"—you always come back to each other. Sometimes I think I'll never have that." She huffed. "Oh, hell. This isn't about me. I want you to feel good about yourself, Benny. You're still hot and sexy. Doug is still over the moon for you. But when you act like you don't trust him, he hurts."

"Fuck. I know." Benny sighed. "It's my insecurity, my self-doubt. Normally I shrug it off, but yesterday it hit me. Here's this hot blond flirting with my guy, and the light is hitting them just so, and they look like the perfect couple. And there's me, no longer in my prime and looking like I just left a dumpster."

She raised a brow. "You're the one into grunge wear and garbage-casual chic, I think you called it. Let Doug dress you up."

"We argued about that too." He groaned. "I messed up, and I know it. How should I make it right?" He knew the answer. Benny was actually a kind, loving man. But he liked to talk things out. So she'd accommodate him, knowing Doug would appreciate what she had to say.

"First of all, apologize. Do it up big, and grovel."

Benny's lips quirked. "I can ham it up."

"I figured." She chuckled. "Then take him dancing or to the theater. Flatter him, get him flowers. When's the last time you got him flowers?"

Benny grimaced. "I can't remember."

"Benny."

"I know. Lately I've been going through a midlife crisis, wondering if I've made the right decisions in my life. Not about Doug," he said, waving away any such thoughts. "I mean, about leaving the ring when I did. I love teaching and playing piano, and I have a tidy nest egg put away for the future. Enough that we can live here and travel whenever we want and still be able to retire comfortably. But it's tough when people recognize me and talk about me being a has-been."

"*What?*" She sat up straight. "Who said that about you?"

Benny sank deeper into the couch. "No one. But I know they think that when they recognize me. I used to be Bear Destruction. Now I'm barely able to pin Emily."

"Oh, stop. First of all, I'm sure no one recognizes you without the goatee and that weird face tattoo. And of course, without your red tights with the bear paws."

"Hey, don't sound so judgy. The henna face tattoo was cool. It was a look."

A bad one. Fortunately, those face tattoos weren't permanent. "And second, who gives a crap what anyone thinks? You are the mighty Bear Destruction, and everyone else can go screw off. You're also able to walk without a limp or spinal injury because you quit when you did."

"Yeah, I know." He sighed. "I needed to hear it, I guess. I can only bitch about my problems that aren't problems to Doug so much. He gets tired of my complaining."

She leaned forward to kiss Benny on the cheek. "You can complain to me anytime. I love you."

He smiled. "I love you too." He took another sip of his beer, studying her. "So, why the whining, woman?"

"Whining?"

"About wanting what we have. From what a little birdie told me, you might just be having a baby soon."

Maggie choked on the water she was sipping. "*What?*"

He grinned. "No baby? So this Reggie guy doesn't have a 'special seed that makes babies'? I was told it probably looks like a jelly bean but isn't."

"Oh, that Emily." Maggie made a fist, and Benny laughed.

"I've been dying to come over and ask what's up with you and the big, rough-and-tumble type I spotted the other day. Is your Reggie perchance a tall, muscular hottie with a face to die for? Smooth brown skin, a mouth made for sin?"

Maggie sighed. "Yep." She blinked. "I mean, not that he's mine or anything. Or that I know how sinful his mouth is. Or, I, ah…"

Benny's grin grew way too wide.

"Oh man. You can't tell Doug."

"I thought he and I were supposed to share everything since we're in love."

"I mean, well, you can, I guess." She fumed. "Don't tell anyone else. *Especially* not Emily." She glanced over her shoulder at the edge of the hallway and softened her voice. "Reggie is the EMT who helped me when I found Frank."

"Yes, yes. Fast-forward past all that. I know who he is. I know what he looks like—*good, baby Jesus*—and I know all about him coming over for dinner with Sherry and Frank, and how you made gooey eyes at each other over macaroni and hot dogs."

"I did not make gooey eyes." Maggie glared at him. "We sat next to each other throughout the dinner. We didn't even look at each other then."

"Not then. But now?"

"Now, well… I just…"

Benny sat up straighter. "Oh, this sounds good."

"I can't help it. He's so sweet and nice."

"And sexy and built." Benny wiggled his brows.

"Yes to all that. We just happened to kiss the other night."

"Yes!"

"Benny, shh."

"Oh, sorry." He pumped his fist and whispered, "*Yes.*"

"I really like him. Reggie is the first guy in a long time who makes me feel special. And he's been a sweetheart, taking me to get my cast, helping with Frank."

"Honey, he digs you. Of course he's being nice."

"We spent the day together after that. When you guys were at the zoo."

Benny turned so that he faced her fully, his beer forgotten. "What did you do?"

"We played board games at his house, can you imagine that?" She laughed, remembering. "He was so much fun. He hates to lose. He has a beautiful yard. He made me sandwiches. We made out." She tacked that on quickly, waited two seconds, and saw Benny's jaw sag.

"You made out?" he whisper-shouted. "*Oh my God.* Tell me."

"He's such a great kisser." She sighed. "I mean, I forgot my name when he kissed me."

"And?" Benny leaned closer.

"And we might have fooled around…a little."

"I'm so proud of you!"

"Stop it." Her face felt hot, and she knew she probably looked like a human cherry.

"You finally found someone you like. He's single?"

"Yep."

"Doesn't live in his mother's basement?"

"No."

"Isn't indebted to the IRS for millions? Is still employed?"

"No and yes."

"Fuck me. You found a sexy, single fireman. And he's sweet on you. Maggie, your life is way more interesting than mine. Hold on." He drew out his phone and made a call.

"What are you doing?"

"Shh." He waited. "I was wrong. I'm sorry. I know. I owe you big. But Maggie got busy with the hottie from the library. She's telling me all about it right now."

Maggie sighed.

Not even a minute later, the door opened, and Doug stood there, his hair rumpled, in a T-shirt and shorts. "Well? Get the wine going. What did I miss?"

———————

Treats, wine, and an interrogation—the likes of which even the Spanish inquisitors might envy—later, Maggie had poured her soul out. "I keep thinking he's going to break up with me. And I feel like he can do so much better. Heck, you've both seen him."

"When did you see him?" Doug asked Benny. The pair sat next to each other on the couch. Maggie sat in the chair near the sofa. They'd spread out a few bottles of wine alongside a platter of goodies she had on hand—Nutter Butters, cubes of cheddar, and jelly beans. A feast of champions.

Benny answered, "I passed him in the hall the other day. I hadn't realized it was him until I saw him stop at Maggie's door. Then Emily kept going on and on about Reggie at the zoo. I put two and two together."

"I knew they had dinner together, but I thought it was all about Frank." Doug turned an accusatory stare on her. "Say it again."

She rolled her eyes. "I'm sorry I didn't tell you about him. I've been trying to wrap my mind around what he and I might be doing."

Benny reached across to pat her knee. "Been so long, you've forgotten how to spell it? S-E-X. I thought you were a teacher."

"Shut it."

Benny grinned, and Doug laughed. Then they smooched, and she sighed.

"See? That's what I want. What you have."

"I have a possessive husband who keeps testing me." Doug shot Benny a look. "He's a slob, he has trust issues, and he thinks I'd have been happier if he'd stayed in the spotlight and broken his back, his head, maybe his dick. I dunno. He thinks it's better to be popular than healthy and loved."

Benny, wisely, held his tongue.

"But if that's what you want, Maggie, more power to you."

Benny gave him a tentative smile. "I love you."

Doug sighed. "But he's cute, and I can't live without him."

"*That. That's* what I want. Eventually."

"You got a man, go for it, I say." Doug nodded.

"But I just met Reggie."

"So what?" Benny said and grabbed Doug's hand. "When you know, you know."

"I don't love him." She gaped. "I barely know him."

"Get to know him." Doug popped a jelly bean in his mouth. "Stop putting up roadblocks in your head every time the man talks. Just because he changes his plans doesn't mean he's getting ready to nicely ditch you. I never knew you were so phobic when it came to men."

"I'm usually not."

"Ah," both Doug and Benny said together.

"What?"

"He makes you nervous, right?" Benny asked. "Who's the last guy you got nervous about?"

She had to think. "Maybe Brent? But I dated him two years ago."

"And for maybe two weeks. He was hot but so stupid." Benny frowned. "You can do so much better than that."

"I know. You guys told me. Several times." Maggie took a cookie. "I want to be smart. I really like Reggie. And I know I need to stop second-guessing what he says. I also know that being a single mom isn't helping my case. Emily is great. I love her. But anyone I date has to love her too. That's why Reggie and I are keeping us—whatever the definition of us is—a secret."

Doug nodded. "That's smart. We won't say a word."

"Not a peep." Benny turned an invisible key over his lips. "So long as you keep us informed. I want to know how the dates go. Details. Everything."

"Especially the sex parts," Doug agreed with a grin. "Don't leave anything out."

She flushed.

"We seriously need to know, do firemen do it better?"

"Better than who?"

"I don't know. It's an expression." Doug shrugged. "When is Stephen coming back? We're happy to watch Emily whenever you want to go out, but if he had her for a while, you'd have a nice break to focus on your new man."

"Good point," Benny agreed. His phone beeped. He glanced down and sighed. "Oh man. It's late. We should let her get some sleep for tomorrow."

"Yeah." Doug pulled Benny to his feet. "Wear something cute and flirty, but not too sexy. Wow him with your girl-next-door prettiness."

"And do flip-flops. Guys dig pretty toes."

"They do?" Doug asked as they walked to the door.

"I like yours." Benny kissed him.

Doug blushed. "Yeah, but you're weird."

"Get out of here, lovebirds." She followed them to the front door and closed it behind them.

Seeing the pair gave her hope. Doug had told her about how

he and Benny had weathered many rough patches. No matter how hard things got though, they always came back to each other. Love and happiness were real. And it came when you least expected it.

Doug had broken off with a steady boyfriend of five years. He'd sworn off love, and on a whim, went with his brother to a wrestling match, something he'd never have done on his own. Then, bam, he'd seen Benny, who'd seen him right back. The pair fell instantly in love. Two years later, Benny left wrestling and settled in with Doug. And then they'd married.

Maggie wouldn't say she'd felt love at first sight with Reggie. After all, she'd been dazed from an accident. He'd been on a call. But seeing him in the hospital room, something in her knew he was special. And after just one kiss, she knew they had something rare between them. But it had all happened so fast. And sex, no matter how great, couldn't be the foundation to a relationship. Just look at her and Stephen.

She was silly to rush expectations with thoughts about tomorrow and forever. But some part of her did want to get married again. She did want a stable life for her and Emily, not for financial gain or because she felt her daughter needed a daddy. Emily had a father. But Maggie didn't like feeling lonely. Her daughter and good friends could only fill so much in her heart.

She still ached for that special someone, a man she could laugh with, confide in, and love to distraction.

Maggie sighed, drank down the last of her wine, and dragged herself off to bed. She'd stop worrying about tomorrow and try to get some sleep tonight.

Unfortunately, tomorrow came too soon.

———————

"Emily, hurry up!" she shouted from behind the shower curtain Sunday morning. Maggie had woken *two and a half hours* late.

Emily, who typically bounced up and awake at seven on the dot, had decided to play with her toys and watch cartoons, indulging in the cookies and candy Maggie had forgotten to put away last night.

So now, when Maggie had less than twenty minutes to get them out the door, her daughter was dawdling instead of getting her little tush in the shower. Normally, Maggie would have Emily shower by herself. But she didn't have time to let Emily play.

With her cast in a plastic bag to keep it dry, Maggie worked furiously with one hand. She'd finished with her hair and body, nicking her leg in two places with the razor, and was bleeding into the tub. "Emily Katherine Swanson, you get your butt in here, now!"

Emily dragged herself in the bathroom and undressed with the speed of a sloth. After yanking her in the shower, Maggie hurried her through the shampoo and conditioner, then soaped her up, rinsed her off, and tossed her out. "Dry off. We're leaving in ten minutes."

Emily complained, loudly, until Maggie reminded her just who they were going to see.

Then her daughter moved like a Tasmanian devil, whirling around, spraying water everywhere as she shook like Frank to get dry as she danced out of the bathroom.

"Dry off with the towel, please," Maggie reminded her. "All over, including your hair."

"I know, Mag-Mom," Emily yelled back from her room.

Maggie could only be glad for the generous soundproofing in the apartments of the complex. Otherwise, she had a feeling they'd have been kicked out ages ago.

Drying her hair proved a burden, so she left it somewhat damp while she hurried to dress. Keeping Doug and Benny's comments from the night before in mind, she threw on a pair of white khaki shorts that reached mid-thigh, a cute pink top, gold earrings, and a light dusting of makeup. *Girl-next-door cute coming right up.*

Emily saw her put on lipstick and demanded some for herself, so Maggie got out the kiddie lip gloss she'd bought for her daughter. A little brush over her mouth and Emily was ecstatic.

"I'm going to show Reggie my lips." She puckered, and Maggie tried to hold back laughter. "Just like this." Emily made fish faces at the mirror.

Maggie hurried them both, grabbed her phone to look over the directions to Reggie's, since she hadn't paid good enough attention the last time she'd been there, and drove them to brunch.

She felt a little nauseous on the way, both from nerves, the wine the night before, and excitement at seeing Reggie again. She couldn't get his smiling face out of her mind. The sex and the lusting were all well and good, but the sheer amount of affection she felt for him didn't seem normal.

It's just a brunch. Relax, she kept telling herself.

By the time they arrived at his house, she'd almost convinced herself that today would be no big deal.

Until Reggie's front door opened, and he stood there, waiting with one hand on his hip, holding Frank in the other.

Emily was smiling and bouncing in the back seat of the car.

"Hold on, Jumping Bean." Too much sugar this morning.

She parked. The minute Maggie opened her daughter's door, Emily tore up the sidewalk to Reggie. "Look! I have shiny lips, Reggie. Look, Frank." She made the fish face, causing him to laugh.

Slower to arrive, Maggie soon joined them.

"And look who else has shiny lips," he said, staring at her with an intensity that had her stomach aflutter.

She pursed her lips at him. "See? But mine don't have any glitter."

He grinned and stepped aside. "Please, come in, guys. After all, it's not every day I get to see pretty ladies with shiny lips." The door banged shut behind them, making Maggie jump. "You okay?" he asked as he set Frank down.

The puppy scampered after Emily, barking up a storm while Emily danced around him, twirling like a ballerina.

"Fine, thanks."

"Hey, Emily," Reggie said. "Play with Frank out back in the yard, would you? His ball is out there, and he likes to play keep-away."

"Oh. I will!" She ran outside with Frank in tow.

Before Maggie could take another step, Reggie dragged her with him into the hallway out of sight.

"What—?"

He kissed her, and her body fogged with lust. When he let her go, he hugged her to him, and she knew she wasn't the only one getting hot and bothered. It was nice to know she wasn't the only one with sex on the brain. "I can't help it. I had to do it. Blame your shiny lips and those shorts." He set her back and nudged her gently toward the kitchen.

"My shorts?"

"They show a lot of leg. Yum." As he looked her over, he seemed pensive. "You okay? You're beautiful, as always, but you seem a little…off. How about some coffee?"

Her stomach churned. "No thanks," she said.

"Orange juice?"

More acid for her stomach? "Um, do you have any tea?"

"I might." He rummaged and came up with a box of Earl Grey. "How about this?"

"Perfect." She watched him fix her a cup. "My stomach is a little queasy from last night."

"Oh?" He leaned on the counter, facing her. "Someone out partying?" He glanced at the little girl and dog racing for Frank's fuzzy frog. "Too many Shirley Temples? Don't tell me Emily drank you under the table?"

She chuckled. "I wouldn't put it past her. No, she was in bed. I had just hung up with you when Benny came over." She took the tea he offered and drank with appreciation. "Oh, that hits the spot."

"Benny?" he asked, his voice a little flat.

"He's one of my best friends. Doug's husband. Trust me, if you'd met him, you'd know him. He's six-six and scary-looking."

"I might have seen him outside of your place. Tattoos? Long, brown hair?"

"Yep. That's him."

"So what did he want? Or do you guys usually hang out?"

"We do sometimes. But last night he needed advice on how to make things right."

"Ah, man problems." Reggie grinned. "So what did you tell him?"

"Why should I give you advice on how to fix a mistake? Are you planning on making some with me?" She heard herself sounding flirty but didn't care.

"I am a planner. We both are." He sighed. "Plus, I'm a guy. We typically screw up a good thing without meaning to."

"Well, Benny got jealous and acted like he didn't trust Doug, which he does. He's just a little irrational sometimes."

"How long have they been married?" Reggie moved them outside so they could sit and watch Emily play with Frank.

For a stray still healing from a bum leg, he showed no sign of trauma and was wonderful with Emily. Not biting or nipping at all, only running around with a puppy smile on that homely little face.

"Doug and Benny have been married for four years. They usually get along. But Benny's doubting himself lately, and Doug is handsome and younger, and he likes being noticed."

"He seemed like a nice enough guy to me."

"That's right. You met him at the library." She sipped and smiled, recalling what Doug had said about Emily's questions. "He's a great guy, and so is Benny."

"But still prone to jealousy and arguments."

"Aren't all couples?"

"Were you and Stephen?" he asked.

She paused, surprised he knew her ex's name. She had mentioned him before, but Reggie had remembered. She stared at him, and he glanced away and drank his coffee.

"Forget it. None of my business, really."

"No, it's fine. Stephen and I had a good marriage. Until we didn't. We grew apart, unfortunately. I wanted a home and family. He wanted to travel the world and pretend Emily was an extension of us and not a real person. With him, it was all about building his business, not his family." She swallowed the rest of her anger at her ex, surprised it still burned. "He's a nice guy and a good"—*not great*—"dad. But we're both so much better off apart."

"Huh."

She watched him, waiting for more of a reaction. "What does 'huh' mean?"

"Nothing. I just thought there'd be more drama. Always seems to be that way with exes."

She sighed. "And that there is another sign. There should be more drama when people who love each other break up, shouldn't there?"

"I don't know. I don't like drama, as a rule."

"Me neither."

He smiled at her.

"What?"

"You're cute."

She frowned. "Now you're insulting."

"Cute is good." He glanced at her toes and smiled wider. "I love pink."

"Yeah? I love yellow." He wore a yellow T-shirt.

"Thanks."

"Now how would you like it if I said *you* looked cute?"

"I'd say thank you."

She scowled. "Fine. How about if I told my friends you were 'nice'?"

He straightened. "Nice?"

"Yep. A supersweet, nice guy. Polite too. Hmm, what else? Well-dressed?"

He shuddered. "All things you say about a guy you're dumping. Fine. I'm not nice, and you're not cute."

"Better."

He muttered, "You're more like a barracuda hiding behind the dimples of a perky brunette."

"Hey." She did her best not to smile.

Chapter Ten

"Reggie, you take that back. I'm not perky."

"Could have fooled me."

Maggie did a double take when she saw where his gaze had wandered, noting the smirk on those firm lips. She leaned closer to whisper, "Reggie Morgan. You did not just say perky and look at my breasts! My daughter is over there."

"What does that have to do with boobs? It's not like she's responsible for them, is she? Technically, that would be your bra." He sipped his coffee, his look sly. "Your face is really red."

"There had better be a big stack of bacon with my name on it, mister."

He bit back a grin, barely. "If I say how cute you are right now, will you hit me?"

"So hard, you won't stand for a week."

"You're a little scary, aren't you?"

"You have no idea." He watched her with caution, and she smiled at him through her teeth. "I *hate* perky."

"Fine, I'm sorry. You're limp, dull, and boring. So, so boring." He eyeballed her breasts then wisely said nothing more, drinking his coffee.

Not what she had been going for, but she'd won the argument. She thought. "Thanks."

"Mag-Mom, look! Frank can sit."

After the twelve times her daughter told the puppy to sit, he did.

"Er, nicely done, honey."

Reggie clapped, and Emily took a bow before returning to Frank and his mound of toys.

"Now that I have freely admitted you are anything but perky, let's get back to your discussion with Benny. What did you tell him? You never said."

"I told him to say he was sorry and to grovel. Oh, and it's not only men who like that. Women like it too when the people who've wronged them grovel." She gave him a look.

His eyes crinkled with amusement. "Duly noted."

"Good. I also told him that he either trusted Doug or he didn't. And he does, he's just going through some stuff that's making him doubt himself. It's more about Benny than Doug."

"It usually is when one part of a couple is distrustful."

"Have you had issues like that in your past?" She genuinely wanted to know. "I was married, and I've dated, but I've never gone out with a cheater. Well, that I knew of. That would really hurt, I think."

Reggie nodded. "Happened to me once, and only once. When I was a lot younger, I dated a woman for a while. I thought we were happy. I was in the military at the time."

"You were?" She hadn't realized that. "What service?"

"Navy. I was a sonar tech. Anyway, I thought things were good. Turned out she was screwing around on me when I was out training. Wanted to get married for military benefits, and apparently some side benefits with an ex-friend of mine who happened to be married at the time. We broke up soon as I found out."

"Good for you. I've never understood why people cheat. I'm not trying to be judgmental or anything, but if she was unhappy, why didn't she break up with you? You weren't married, no kids, nothing but feelings keeping you together, right?"

"That's what I said. I did everything for her. Helped her with bills, always paid when we went out. And she used me." He frowned. "I always play the role of caretaker in my relationships."

"Huh. Me too."

He watched her with interest. "Really?"

"Well, maybe not like you did. But it felt like it when I was married. Then again when I was dating. I always felt like I was catering to my partner. When I was married, we did everything Stephen's way. I like to keep the peace, so I didn't argue a lot, though I could have. And when I was dating, all the guys I was with always wanted to boss me around. I let them and eventually broke off with them. I couldn't handle always having to be the one to give in. Or worse, to give up my time, my plans. You name it, I did what they wanted to keep the peace."

"Same." Reggie looked bemused by her admission. Then he glanced at his cup. "I'm out. Hey, do you need more tea?"

"That would be nice."

"Let me get it for you."

"Ha. And have you accuse me of using you for Earl Grey? Forget it."

He smiled. "Now who's the bossy one?"

She flexed. "I am. Check out my amazing, though subtle, power."

He chuckled, especially when Emily joined her and starting flexing as well.

"Now you, Reggie. Now you," Emily pointed at his arms.

He flexed, no doubt preening when Emily's eyes bugged out and she gasped. Though Maggie felt the same awe when studying Reggie's finer than fine body.

"Have you ever competed?" she asked. "You know, in a bodybuilder competition or anything?"

She'd swear he flushed before he turned to go inside. She and Emily followed him.

"Nah. I work out because it makes me feel good. For fun, and well, for work. The fitter I am, the better I'm able to help someone who needs it."

"It's a hobby too?"

"Well, I'd be lying if I didn't say I liked it because it makes me feel strong. I like being bigger than most people. I look like I can handle myself, so they think twice before trying to jump me." He looked at her and winked. "Then again, some people are so bossy, they don't care how big I am and jump me anyway. I can totally respect that."

She blushed. Man, he had to stop teasing her like that. *Emily, remember Emily*.

The little girl smiled up at Reggie. "I want to be strong too. I want to get big muscles."

"Here we go," Maggie muttered.

But Reggie was thrilled to help and took Emily to a room down the hall. Maggie followed and watched him help Emily lift a small hand weight. The spare room was used as an exercise room, housing a stand of free weights, a weight bench, a medicine ball, and stacked metal plates and a bar in a vertical stand. One wall had been covered in mirrors.

Emily stood in front of it, grunting and puffing as she did bicep curls with Reggie's help. He had her use both hands for one weight.

"Man, I had no idea how strong you are," he said, sounding impressed. He winked up at Maggie. "This is five pounds, Emily. You're amazing." He helped her daughter lift the weight each time, grunting. "Yeah, like that. Each time you lift it, you grunt. You sound like a real man when you do that."

Emily sounded like a sick pig.

Reggie chuckled. "Okay, that's enough of that. I need to get our food going."

"Emily, go play with Frank, okay?"

"Yes!" She ran to the doorway but paused to thank Reggie. Then she hurried back and hugged his leg before taking off again.

He looked both scared and pleased.

Maggie thought his expression adorable. "Now who's cute?"

"Bite me," he said and stomped past her, only to pause and return to kiss her on the mouth. "Women."

She laughed at his back.

They spent time in the kitchen, him cooking, and her watching since he declined her every offer to help. Just as the bacon came out of the oven, the doorbell rang.

Reggie frowned.

"Want me to get it?"

"Yeah, would you?"

She hurried to the door and opened it. "Hello?"

An older man and two pretty women who all looked like Reggie stood at the door. The older woman, likely in her mid-thirties, wore braids in her hair and smiled widely at the sight of Maggie.

The man grinned, his gaze more appreciation than humor. "Hello there. Is Reggie in?"

"Sure. Um, hold on."

The woman wearing a cute skirt and floral tank top muttered, "That liar." She fluffed her hair, looking like a supermodel.

"I knew it. Not feeling good, my ass." The woman with braids had muscular arms and wore a pair of athletic shorts and a Nike shirt.

Maggie wanted to let them in but felt awkward since it was Reggie's place. "Reggie, you have visitors."

"I told the guys I'd see them…" He paused and stopped right behind her. "Oh, er, hi, Dad. Nadia, Lisa."

Everyone stared at one another, his sisters with glee as they looked from her to Reggie, and his father with clear amusement.

"Son, you think we might come in?" His dad held up the dish he'd been carrying. "I brought more cobbler for you, since you're not feeling so well."

Maggie frowned and turned to Reggie. "You're sick?"

"Sick of telling the truth, maybe," his buff sister said with a snicker.

"Nadia." Reggie wiped his hand over his face. "Hell. Come on in." He pulled Maggie back from the door and sighed. Loudly.

"Where's Frank?" Nadia asked. "I hear him, but I don't…" She saw Frank and Emily dash by the open back door, both girl and dog racing as if for a finish line. "Emily?"

Maggie blinked. "You know my daughter?"

"We video chatted." Nadia smiled, and Maggie saw Reggie in her grin. "Hi there. Since my little brother has forgotten his manners, I'm Nadia, his sister." They shook hands.

Lisa held hers out. "And I'm Lisa, his other sister. Nice to meet you."

"I'm Maggie. It's so nice to meet you too." Maggie smiled, not understanding why Reggie looked so ill at ease. She turned to his father. "And you must be the jazz man. Word has it you're quite a dancer and know all about romance."

His dad grinned, shoved the dish at Reggie, then took her hand between both of his. "You can call me Harry. It's lovely to meet you, Maggie."

She smiled. "You too. From what I've heard about you from Reggie, I like you already."

Harry wrapped an arm around her shoulders, and she felt at home with him immediately. Odd, because she normally didn't take to men she'd just met, but he had a way about him. A charisma now missing from his scowling son.

"Would you like to meet Emily, my daughter?"

"I surely would." Harry stopped at the back door and gestured for her to precede him.

Maggie called to Emily, who, upon seeing Harry and his daughters who followed, stopped playing with Frank and rushed over to meet the new adults in the yard.

"Hi." Emily smiled brightly. "I know you."

Harry bent low and held out a hand to Emily, who daintily shook it.

Hmm. Her daughter seemed awfully polite.

Harry smiled up at Maggie. "I had the pleasure of video chatting—briefly—with your daughter as well."

Behind him, Lisa smiled. "I'm Lisa. We met. This is Nadia, my big sister. You met her too."

Emily grinned. "Hi. This is neat. Are you here for brunch too?"

Everyone turned to Reggie, who looked a little ill. "Sure. The more, the merrier."

"Oh, good." Nadia moved back to her brother and slung an arm up and around her brother's shoulders. She squeezed him tightly. "I'll go in and help him in the kitchen while you guys stay out here. We'll be back." Nadia smiled, but Reggie didn't look so pleased.

Then Harry asked Maggie about her arm, and she turned her attention to the charming man by her side instead of the scared one walking with his sister as if about to face a firing squad.

———————————————

Reggie swore to himself. What had he been thinking to cancel brunch with the family? He should have gone, then come home and met with Maggie and Emily. Except he'd wanted to impress Maggie with his cooking skills.

Idiot.

"So." Nadia stood there, leaning against the counter while Reggie added more eggs to his scramble. "Sickie isn't too sick after all."

He fake coughed when he drew closer to her. "I think I'm allergic to *you.*"

"We were worried. You never miss brunch unless you're working."

"I tried today."

"Tried and failed." Nadia snorted. "Here we are, trying to do a good thing looking out for you, and you're here with a woman and her cute kid. And don't even try pretending you're nothing but friends. I can tell."

"I barely looked at her."

"Ha. My proof."

Reggie rolled his eyes. Nadia was weird.

"So, this is Maggie. The one-armed chick with the adorable daughter." Nadia frowned. "Are they taking Frank?"

"Maybe."

She sighed. "I guess that's okay." She watched him work, not offering to help. Nadia loathed kitchen duties. And chores. And baking. Basically, anything she considered "domestic." She'd instigated the be-my-butler game with him as a kid. He'd spent years thinking it normal to wait on his sister hand and foot until his father had caught on and fixed things.

Reggie smiled politely. "Please, don't help. Just watch me."

"Okay." She smiled. "Liar."

"Nadia…"

"Why didn't you tell anyone you had plans? That would have been much better to swallow than that you ditched us for your new honey."

"And her daughter." Not what he should have said, he realized, when her eyes narrowed. "I just meant I'm not here seducing anyone. I invited them over to see *the dog*. Period. But I knew if I mentioned it to you guys, you'd be all over me about an Amy do-over or that I'm repeating patterns." He groaned. "Can't I just make brunch for my new friends?"

"Sure you can." Her voice gentled. "But when you can't stop staring at her legs, or you keep glaring at Dad for getting too close to her, we can kind of tell you like her a lot more than in a friendly kind of way."

"*Damn it.*"

"And now, swearing like a sailor." She tsked, her stupid grin way too wide. "You're surely on the path to no good. Lying, swearing. What else have you been up to, little brother?"

"Sistercide, if you keep talking."

She snickered. "I think you mean sororicide."

"That you know the word for killing one's own sister is scary all by itself."

"Hey, do I smell bacon?"

"You have the attention span of a gnat."

"Flattery will get you nowhere. Now about that bacon. Is it almost done?"

He glared at her. "Didn't you eat at Dad's?"

"Yeah, but I'm training. I need the protein."

"Please. Bacon's more fat than protein. And I highly doubt you're hitting the right daily macronutrients."

"Eh. I just want bacon, okay?"

"Stop grilling me about Maggie and you might get a few strips."

"Fine." She huffed. "Can I have some coffee too?"

"Say the magic word."

Her eyes narrowed. "If you want me to leave you alone, get me a.damn cup."

He growled and grabbed her one, then shoved it into her hand. "Pot's over there."

She smiled prettily. "See? Manners are a good thing. Maybe if you showed them more to Maggie, you'd be happier about life."

"So, sororicide, you said?"

She laughed and laughed. But at least she went outside and gave him a break.

Except his father entered with Maggie, looking entirely too chummy. Maggie seemed enthralled. No surprise there. His father could charm the stripes off a tiger.

They sat at the counter, watching him and talking.

When he tuned in to what they were saying, he cringed.

Harry laughed. "So there he is, butt naked and running down the street after his sisters. Reggie's first attempt at streaking and only thirteen years old."

"Dad, stop."

Maggie grinned evilly. "So young to be an exhibitionist."

He scowled. "Lisa stole my clothes."

"Off your body?" his father asked, knowing full well what had happened.

Reggie flushed. "Look, we were kids trying to be cool. Cutting school and skinny-dipping in a friend's pool. Then my sister thinks it's funny to steal my clothes and run. Well, it wasn't funny."

"I think it's pretty funny." Maggie grinned.

"Me too." Harry's wide smile had her laughing.

"*Now* you do. Maggie, he grounded me for a month. And Tony Aldridge got the girl I was crushing on. So not cool, Dad."

"Poor Reggie."

"You don't sound all that sympathetic, I have to tell you." Reggie pointed the spatula at her. "Keep it up and I'm giving Emily all the bacon."

"I'll be good." She didn't sound convincing.

His dad said, "Me too." A pause. "And then there was the time I caught him in his room with a ruler, measuring—"

"*Dad.*"

"His biceps. What did you think I was going to say, son?"

Maggie choked on her tea.

Reggie finished cooking as fast as he could. Best to get his family out of here before his father started remembering all the other crap he'd done that was best forgotten. Or worse, somehow brought up Amy and Rachel in casual conversation.

That he could really do without.

———

Emily looked at Reggie's sisters and wished she had some. Jeezy-peezy, she really needed to get some magic seeds. But maybe she'd get some for sisters instead of brothers. Frank tugged on his rope, so she tugged back.

Nadia and Lisa looked at each other. Then they looked

back at the house. They nodded to each other and motioned for Emily to join them at the far side of the yard. The women crouched down, so Emily crouched as well, which caused them to laugh.

"Yeah?" Emily said.

Lisa put a finger to her lips. "Shh."

"Okay," Emily whispered. "Why are we whispering?"

"Because we have questions. And we don't want our brother to hear us."

"Oh." That made sense.

Nadia petted Frank, who rolled on his back, exposing his belly. "He is so flippin' cute."

"He is," Emily agreed, mentally adding "flippin'" to her vocabulary.

"Nadia, focus." Lisa looked at Emily. "So, kid, what do you think of Reggie?"

"He's awesome. He's my favorite person. Well, next to Frank."

"Frank's not a person," Nadia said.

"He is," Emily defended him. "He's just shaped like a dog."

"Nadia, hush." Lisa glared at her sister before smiling back at Emily. "We like Reggie too."

"He's fun. He showed me how to lift weights. And when he came for dinner, he made me a Shirley Temple."

The sisters exchanged a glance. Nadia's eyebrows rose. "Dinner?"

Emily told them all about her shared meal with Sherry and Reggie.

"Well, now. That sounds like it was fun." Nadia smiled.

"It was. A lot." Emily frowned. "But I really need those seeds. Or is it a pill? Sherry doesn't know. I don't think her dad does either. Babies don't come from pills." She snorted. "Pills make you feel better. But things grow from seeds."

"That's true." Lisa nodded. "I once tried to grow a watermelon from a seed. Didn't work. But my dad grows things from seeds all the time."

"Really?" Emily needed to talk to Mr. Harry.

"You should go ask him about baby seeds," Nadia suggested.

Her sister nodded, her smile wide. "Oh yeah. You really should."

"Okay."

They headed inside. Emily went to wash her hands and heard Reggie say, "What? Why are you two looking at me like that? Why are you smiling?"

Emily thought he had the best family. He had sisters and a dad, but his mommy had died. That's what Lisa told her. When Emily asked if she was still sad, Lisa had nodded, but she claimed it was a nice sad. Not so hurtful because her mom had died so long ago and now she only had good memories.

Emily didn't know. She loved Mag-Mom. Her mommy. If Mag-Mom left, Emily would be so alone and sad. All the time. She had no brother or sister to smile and tell jokes with.

Which made her more determined than ever to find out about the seeds.

She rejoined everyone in the kitchen. They were getting plates of food, like at a buffet restaurant, and Mag-Mom got Emily a plate with eggs, bacon, and some good-smelling peach cobbler.

They all sat and ate, talking about how great the food was.

Emily decided to ask the most important question of the day. "Mr. Harry?"

"Yes?"

"Nadia and Lisa said you make a lot of things grow."

"I do." He smiled at her.

She studied him. "You look a lot like Reggie."

"Or you could say he looks like me."

"Yeah." She frowned. "So did you plant a seed for him to grow? Or did his mom get a baby pill? Because I want a little brother, and maybe some sisters, and I think Reggie would be super nice if he'd plant a few in my mom's belly."

Reggie choked.

Mag-Mom gaped, her face turning red.

Lisa and Nadia coughed and laughed and coughed some more.

Mr. Harry bit his lip. "Well, now, this has got to be one of the best conversations over brunch we've ever had."

Emily grinned. "I'm smart."

"You are indeed." Harry laughed. And kept laughing.

Chapter Eleven

REGGIE DIDN'T UNDERSTAND WHY HIS FAMILY TOOK SO MUCH fun in torturing him.

After everyone but he and Maggie died laughing, he quickly changed the subject to Maggie's teaching career. She and Nadia discussed the effort it took to teach children and seemed to be getting along rather well.

Lisa chimed in here and there, while his father spoke in a hushed voice with Emily, who kept nodding, looking at Reggie, then nodding again.

Reggie didn't even want to know what the pair were discussing.

Seeds. He rubbed his eyes, not sure whether to laugh or cry.

He knew he'd never hear the end of this. But at least Maggie no longer looked so mortified.

They wrapped up brunch with some funny stories from his father's growing years, which never failed to amuse Reggie and his sisters.

Once the meal ended, everyone helped with the cleanup. He took pride in the fact that Emily helped without having to be asked. And then felt stupid for having any emotion at all since he'd had no part in instilling manners in the girl. She was his friend's child. Not his.

He had to remember that.

"Bye, son. Thanks for brunch, and so glad to see you on the mend."

Reggie refused to touch that one. He returned his dad's hug and whispered, "I'll get you back for this."

Harry grinned.

Reggie hugged his sisters goodbye, surprised to see them

treating Emily and Maggie so warmly. Normally, they treated any woman near their little brother with an aloof politeness.

"So nice meeting you," Lisa was saying.

Nadia rubbed Frank between the ears.

"You can keep him too if you want," Emily said. "We can share."

"Aw. You're such a cutie." Nadia rubbed Emily's head. Emily woofed, and Nadia laughed. "Wow. It's getting hard to tell you and Frank apart."

"Really?" Emily frowned. "I'm not that furry."

"Emily, she's teasing." Maggie chuckled. "Although when you don't brush your teeth, they get pretty furry."

"Yeah, but they aren't sharp like Frank's. Well, maybe this one." Emily started fiddling with her tooth.

"Let's go, Dad." Lisa gave her father a gentle nudge and pulled Nadia with her. "Talk to you soon, Reggie." She gave him *the look*.

He groaned silently, not wanting to get into that conversation with his family. They'd be all over his relationship with Maggie, and he had no idea what he was doing with her, so how could he tell them what he didn't know? "Can't wait," he lied.

"Ha." Nadia shook her head. "Sick. Sick in the head, more like," she muttered on her way out.

Finally, they left.

Maggie, Emily, and he looked at one another. Then Frank sat by his heels and stared up at them as well, which Reggie found adorable.

Maggie met his grin with one of her own. "Why do I feel like I just survived a storm and not brunch?"

"You mean barely survived."

"Your family is funny."

"And nice," Emily said. "Mag-Mom, did you see Lisa's toes? They were red. I want red toes."

"Maybe later, if you're good." Maggie put her hand on Emily's shoulder. "Now why don't you go finish playing with Frank? We need to leave soon so Reggie can get back to his day."

"Okay." Emily needed no further encouragement to be with the dog. She ran through the house to the backyard, calling him, and he ran after her with a bark.

Reggie felt as he if he'd just finished a race, exhausted.

"Sick, huh?" Maggie said.

"Dumb, I know. I just thought it would be nice for the three of us—you, me, and Emily—to spend the morning together with Frank without the third degree."

"They were nice to me. I didn't feel bothered by any of your family."

"That makes one of us."

She looked sympathetic. "Sorry. Was it bad?"

"Well, not so bad until Emily asked if I planned on planting seeds in your belly." The thought of doing so gave him an uncomfortable rush he ignored. "I thought my sisters would choke to death laughing."

"That was embarrassing, yes." She grinned. "And hilarious, to be honest. I'm sorry she embarrassed you."

"Oh, please. You were red too."

"Maybe a little."

"You looked like one of my dad's prized tomatoes."

"Stop."

"You did." He couldn't help grinning back at her. "Done in by a cute six-year-old. We're pathetic."

"We really are." She glanced outside at her daughter with Frank. "So, what do we do about the puppy, Reggie? Emily has her heart set on him. And honestly, I like him too. But we have no yard. And when I go back to work, how can I take care of him during the day?"

"That is an issue, isn't it?" He felt for her. Out in the yard, Emily was making Frank carry one of his plush toys on his back. It kept falling off, and she kept laughing. "I don't know what to tell you. My sister wants him, and she has a job teaching, like you. She also has a cat at home."

"But cats have litter boxes and don't mind when you're not around." Maggie sighed. "Dogs need a lot more attention."

"Are there pets in your apartment building?"

"Yes. I've seen plenty of people walking their dogs outside the complex. I would love a dog, to be honest. I just want to be fair to him."

"Your problem is you need someone there for him when you're at work and Emily's at school."

"Yeah."

"They have doggie daycares. Dog walkers."

"Which cost money. I'm not against paying someone, but if it's between getting Emily new shoes or making sure Frank has five walks a day, I'm choosing my daughter." She groaned. "Why couldn't she have tried to rescue a cat from the street?"

"Because cats are smart enough not to hang out by cars," he said. "Look, you aren't in a rush, right? Why not enjoy the summer while we try to think of some way to house him in the fall?"

"We?" She took a step in his direction.

"Well, I'm partly responsible."

"How's that?"

"I let Emily FaceTime the dog. They bonded. That's on me."

She huffed, her eyes bright with amusement. "How dare you. Yes, it is your fault. Now my daughter is hooked on the dog and on FaceTime."

He chuckled. "You know, there's another option."

"Oh?"

"We could ask my dad to dog-sit him during the day. He likes Frank. And it'll get Nadia to visit more. He's always complaining that his daughters ignore him."

"Don't you guys see him every Sunday for brunch?"

"Yes, we do." He sighed.

"Ah."

"Just something to think about." He studied her, wondering if he'd been obvious about how much he liked her at brunch. "I hope my family didn't scare you off."

"Nah. If I can handle Emily Swanson telling me I have boogers in a full, quiet auditorium, I can handle your family."

He blinked. "Oh."

"Yeah, oh." She blew out a breath. "It was last year at a Christmas concert. I had a slight cold. No big deal, until my daughter told over a hundred people in a hushed auditorium that I had something in my nose. The word she used was a 'booger.' At least the lights were dim."

He chuckled. "I really like your kid."

"Thanks. I do too."

They stood close, near but not touching. He forced himself to keep his hands in his jean pockets for fear he'd take her in his arms and kiss her in front of her daughter. "So, ah, you let me know about dinner."

"I will. I'm waiting for Sherry's mom to call me back." Her dimple flashed. "She owes me one."

"Well, I'm excited to eat anything you make me." He forced himself to stop thinking about eating *her* and cleared his throat. "What did you think of brunch? Was my cooking up to snuff?"

"You make a mean brunch, Reggie."

"I really do." He buffed his nails on his chest.

"So modest too." Her attention turned to Emily, shrieking with laughter while Frank licked her all over, the two of them rolling in the grass. "I hate to go, but we have a few things to do today. What are you up to?"

"Got a workout with the guys later."

"You hang out with them a lot, don't you? Even out of work?"

"Yep. They're my brothers from other mothers." He grinned. "You'll have to meet them sometime." As soon as he said it, he wanted to take the words back. Meeting the guys meant involvement, attachment, that she was much more than a friend. Instead, he kept his grin in place and his tone light. "But we don't meet as much as we used to now, with a couple of them finding women who can tolerate them."

"Must be tough." She agreed. "Hunky firemen are a hard sell."

"I know." He gave a sad sigh.

She punched him in the arm. "Ow. I think I just broke my good wrist," she complained, shaking her hand. Since she'd barely tapped him, he knew she hadn't done any damage. "I'll text you about dinner."

"Make it a call." When she moved to pass him, heading toward the back door, he stopped her with a hand on her shoulder. He leaned closer and whispered, "I like talking to you." He kissed the shell of her ear, felt her shiver, and let her go, conscious of his growing erection.

"I-I'll call." She let out a loud breath. "You're evil. And don't you dare look down at my shirt or you'll see just how perky I am." She hurried to the back. "Emily. Time to go."

After waiting forever for Emily to say goodbye to Frank, Reggie, his body now completely calm, walked them out to their car. Frank walked with him. The puppy, to his surprise, had turned out to be a shy little guy, no worry about him darting away. Hopefully, he'd learned his lesson from nearly being hit in the street.

Before Emily got in the car, the cute little girl walked up and gave Reggie a hug. And damn if her affection didn't create a huge surge of happy warmth. He wanted to kiss the top of her tiny head but refrained, telling himself he didn't have the right.

She pulled away, smiling. "I'll miss you, Reggie."

"You mean you'll miss Frank," he said drily, to which Maggie chuckled.

"Yeah. But maybe when I see you again, you can tell me BLS stories. You didn't say any today at brunch."

"Hmm. I think I can do that."

"And Mag-Mom can make homemade pizza, and you can eat

dinner with us again." She gave him a wide, calculating smile. "Just us. No Sherry this time. But bring Frank."

"Sure."

She looked back at her mom then leaned closer to him and whispered, "And the baby seeds. Bring them too." Before he could respond, though he had no clue what to say to that, she darted into the car.

Maggie frowned. "What did she say?"

"Ah, I think I was just ordered to a family dinner."

"I see." She moved closer to him and, in a low voice, said, "Well, you're more than invited. But remember, *my* invitation comes first." She winked, turned, and left.

He watched the car drive away. "What do you think, Frank? Am I an idiot for even thinking about accepting any kind of invite from those two? Or an idiot because I *can't* stop thinking about them?" He and the dog sighed, turned, and went back in the house.

━━━━━━━━━━

Maggie spent the rest of her day doing chores. Everything took longer with one hand. Fortunately, her broken arm no longer ached so much, and if it did start to twinge, taking Tylenol helped.

Emily did her part by cleaning her room. She dusted then vacuumed with a play vacuum Stephen had bought her last Christmas. It didn't do anything but make noise, but Emily loved it.

Benny and Doug popped over for dinner, and the four of them enjoyed Emily's recap of brunch. When Emily left to go play, her friends turned to her, doing their best not to laugh.

She groaned. "There's nothing more to add. Emily told you everything." Right down to asking Reggie to plant baby seeds.

The guys shared matching, shit-eating grins.

"Laugh it up until she starts asking when you two are having babies."

Doug snorted. "She can ask all she wants. While Benny and I have been known to have the occasional argument, we've never fought about that. We both love being honorary uncles. We don't need a child. We have Emily."

"What you're really saying is that my daughter has put you both off from ever having children," she deadpanned.

"Yes," they said as one.

She laughed, knowing they didn't mean it. They didn't want children because both had experienced issues with their parents when growing up. And while they loved other people's kids— Doug and Benny both taught after all—they were content to have only each other and close family to care for. *Me and Emily included*, she thought with warmth.

"You two look good. Everything settled now?" she asked them, looking pointedly at Benny.

He sighed. "Yes. I groveled."

"And bought me flowers." Doug beamed. "And we're going to dinner and a show on Wednesday."

"Oh, nice. What are you going to see?"

"A funny play about a lesbian librarian who falls in love with a gay janitor then kills her boss for having an affair with her wife. And yes, it's a comedy."

"Er, sounds like fun." She had no urge to see that show.

"You mean it sounds so horrible, it should be funny," Benny said drily.

"Yes, that."

"Want to go?" Doug asked.

"And ruin your date night? No way. I want you two to get lucky. You don't need me there to ruin it."

"Good point." Benny winked.

Doug blushed.

"And speaking of getting lucky…" Benny raised a brow. "How goes it with studly?"

She frowned.

"You know, Reggie?"

"Shh." She looked for Emily and, not seeing her, shook her finger at him. "What did I tell you about being quiet?"

"Which is why I called him studly. Duh."

"Real mature, Benny." Doug smacked him in the back of the head.

"Ow."

Doug watched her. "Well?"

"Well what?" she asked. "I went to brunch with Emily. We went so she could see the dog. It wasn't a date."

"Mm-hmm."

"It wasn't. And there was no action whatsoever."

"Pity." Benny shook his head.

"Yes, well, if Sherry's mom would call me back about a sleepover, I might be able to remedy that."

Her friends perked up.

"You don't have to wait for Sherry's mom. We can watch her," Benny offered.

"Yeah," Doug said. "She can sleep over at our place. We always love having her."

"Thanks, but I feel bad always relying on you two. Besides, Dina owes me."

Her phone pinged. Great timing. She looked down to see Dina's message confirming a sleepover at her house for Tuesday night. "Perfect. Tuesday night." She smiled wide. "Now I just need to get Studly to agree to come over."

"Oh, I'm sure that won't be a problem. Text him now." Doug motioned to her phone.

She felt like a teenager gossiping about boys with her friends, but she texted him anyway with a promise to call tomorrow, since he had asked her to.

Her phone chimed immediately. Reggie had sent her a thumbs-up.

"Did you get an eggplant?" Doug asked. "Because that's a little forward."

"Doug." She blushed. "Stop it. He said yes, is all."

"Nice. You're cooking dinner, hmm? What are you going to make?"

"I don't know. Maybe my famous chicken masala."

Benny gasped. "Oh, my favorite. Can we come over?"

"No."

The guys laughed. They spent the remainder of the evening playing cards, and Emily joined them for a game of Jenga.

After her friends left, Maggie waited for Emily to brush her teeth and wash her face. She joined Emily in her room, pleased with her daughter's cleanup effort. Emily had a tendency toward being disorganized and claimed she "needed the mess to stir her creative side." Benny had taught her that, for which Maggie had thoroughly chastised him. But the damage was done.

For Emily to have cleaned with such thoroughness meant the little imp wanted something.

"Wow. I'm so impressed with your room." Clothes in the hamper, dusted shelves, toys all put away, and even a few clothes messily folded and sitting on her chair in the corner. The plush mini armchair Maggie had reupholstered with a synthetic purple velvet had become Emily's favorite item next to Brownie. Emily liked to sit in and dictate orders from "her throne."

Emily got in bed and let Maggie tuck her in. Maggie kissed Emily and Brownie, the stuffed bear snuggled next to her daughter under the covers. She sat on the bed and stroked her daughter's hair. Sometimes it amazed her that she'd given birth to someone so wonderful. Love filled her to the brim, the feeling so visceral, it brought tears to her eyes. She'd been so lucky despite so many setbacks in her past. And she knew it.

"I love you, Ninja Princess."

"I love you, Mommy."

Ah, back to Mommy. Maggie swallowed a sigh of relief. "That's Queen Mommy, isn't it?"

Emily giggled. She clutched Brownie, and Maggie wished she'd brought in her phone to snap a quick picture. Before she could get up to leave, Emily grabbed her good hand.

"What's up, honey?"

"Mommy, are you mad because I invited Reggie to dinner?"

"No. But we did talk about you asking me before you invite anyone over, remember?"

"I know. I'm sorry."

"It's okay. I know you like Reggie."

Emily stared at her, intent. "Do *you* like Reggie?"

"I do. He's a very nice man."

"Is he your new friend?"

"You know, I think he is." *What a lovely thought. I've made a new friend.*

"Good." Emily looked relieved. "Mommy, when can Frank come live with us?"

Maggie had been anticipating the question. "Well, Reggie and I have been talking about how best to take care of Frank. Right now, because it's summer and you and I are both home, it's easy to take care of him. But when we go back to school, Frank will be sad all by himself if he's here alone. So we need to find a way to make sure he's not lonely when we're gone."

"He could come to school with me."

"I wish he could. But animals don't come to school unless they're service animals." She and Emily had discussed a service dog at school before. "Frank will be a fun family dog, not a service dog."

"Could he be a teacher dog and go to school with you?"

That was a clever thought. "I don't think so." But it wouldn't hurt to ask. She'd send her principal a note, though thoughts about allergies and school liability made her think not.

"Can Frank go to dog school?"

"I don't know. Reggie is helping me look into that. He knows a lot about animals because he helps them get adopted sometimes."

"I like Reggie a lot."

"I know." She smiled at her daughter, who had a heart that never stopped giving.

"And I really liked his sisters and daddy. They were so nice. Mommy, Nadia lifts weights too. She had big arms. Not as big as Reggie, but they were big. She was funny. And I liked her braids. Can I have braids like that?"

"How about we put your hair in a French braid tomorrow?" She paused, pleased her daughter had enjoyed herself with Reggie and his family. "Nadia and Lisa are smart and pretty, aren't they?" Beautiful women who looked like a feminized version of Reggie. And she considered him beautiful. She wondered what he'd think if she told him that, then knew she couldn't, because he'd realize how much she'd grown to like him and run *far* away.

"They are." Emily nodded. "Good night, Mommy."

"No more Mag-Mom, hmm?"

"No. I'm done with that now."

Maggie had no idea how her daughter's brain worked. "Funny kid. I love you. Good night." She kissed Emily's forehead, making a memory of her daughter's strawberry-scented shampoo, her bubblegum-flavored toothpaste, and soft, rosy cheeks. *My beautiful baby girl.*

She left a night-light on and the door cracked and went down the hall. Grabbing a book she'd been reading, she settled in for a relaxing night. But try as she might, she couldn't get Reggie out of her thoughts, and she daydreamed about what their next date might be like.

Then had to take a cold shower before she went to bed.

Chapter Twelve

Reggie spent Tuesday afternoon guarding his every word. The guys were on his ass about blowing them off so much, wanting to know exactly what he'd been doing while off duty.

What a crock. He'd spent his Sunday afternoon brooding at home, worrying about how attached he was growing to Maggie and Emily, so he'd missed playing softball with the rest of C shift and the knuckleheads on A shift. Apparently, they'd lost against the county behavioral health team, which happened to have a few ringers who'd played college ball.

Reggie was known as a home run hitter, and his presence had been sadly missed, according to Mack.

They sat at a table in the back of the Slow Boat Tavern in Hillman City, near Mack's place, drinking some phenomenal beer and eating shelled peanuts.

Mack complained, "I mean, Brad was up, and he was so focused on shaking his ass for Avery that he struck out. Twice."

"Asshole." Brad scowled. "The guy pitching struck out a ton of people."

"Not me," Tex said.

"Not me either." Mack shook his head. "We needed you, Reg. What the hell?"

Reggie did his best to pretend their curiosity wasn't making him damn uncomfortable. "I told you. I was helping my dad out with some stuff."

"Stuff? What stuff?"

Reggie glared at Mack, who glared back.

Tex and Brad shared a sly look.

"What?" Reggie asked them. "What's that about?"

"We know where you were." Tex nodded.

"At home," he immediately responded. "I mean, at my dad's." *Shit.*

"Uh-huh." Tex put his hand out, and Mack swore before slapping down a five-dollar bill on it.

"Hey." Reggie hated when they bet on him. Typically, in their group, they bet on the guy screwing up with women. Reggie bet on Brad, Tex, and Mack quite often. But as he rarely dated since his breakup, he wasn't used to being the center of attention.

"I'm surprised at you, Reggie." Brad shook his head. "So how is... What's her name, Mack?"

"Maggie," Mack grumbled. "Cost me five bucks."

"Look, you losers, I wasn't with Maggie." Not exactly. The morning, sure, but technically, he wasn't lying about the afternoon. "I wasn't in the mood for a game, okay? I lied about being at my dad's. Bam. You caught me."

Tex smirked. "You know who else caught you? Lisa, when she, Nadia, and your dad showed up to check on your supposedly sick ass for brunch, and guess who they found there, Brad?"

"I don't know, Tex. Who? Who did they find with Reggie?"

Reggie put his head down on the table. *Freakin' loudmouthed, can't-keep-a-secret Lisa.*

"Why, they found Maggie and her cute-as-a-button daughter, Emily!" Tex smiled, his voice super loud considering there wasn't too much of a crowd to talk over.

Mack punched Reggie on the shoulder. "How could you?"

Reggie groaned. "This is why I didn't want to tell you guys the truth. You fucking nag."

"Who's nagging? I'm clearly disappointed with you. That's not nagging."

Reggie sat up and wiped a hand over his face, not looking forward to the smug assholes watching him with overly dramatic disappointment.

"I heard brunch went well." Tex sipped an IPA.

"How the hell are you so tight with my sister? Does Bree know about this?" Reggie couldn't see Tex's girlfriend being okay with that.

Tex sighed. "Ah, Reggie. Bree loves and trusts me. My friendship with your sister is a thing of beauty. We like to look at each other, realizing how damn gorgeous we are. We stare for hours, then we go our separate ways."

Everyone stared at him.

"I exaggerate. We share texts, spying on you."

Mack burst out laughing.

"You son of a bitch." Reggie reached for him across the table, but Tex was too quick and scooted back out of harm's way.

Brad chuckled. "You should see your face, Reggie. But I get it. Such betrayal. Lisa should know better."

"Lisa?" He growled. "I know she's nosy. But Tex is my brother. He should have my back. Fuck it. *You all* should."

"Now, now." Mack patted him on said back and held up his hands in surrender when Reggie snarled. "Whoa. He's hulking out, guys! Run!"

Reggie tried to stay mad, but Mack pretending to be scared out of his mind, with that look on his face, was funny.

He fought laughing but ended up joining the others. When they'd finally settled down, he saw them waiting for him to explain. *Damn it.*

"I, ah, I didn't want to mention Maggie. Because you guys are going to tell me I'm repeating an ugly pattern."

"Which would be?" Brad prodded.

Reggie gritted his teeth.

"Sorry, can't hear you." Mack cupped his ear and leaned closer to Reggie.

Reggie shoved him back, and the goon laughed. "Getting in too deep with a woman and her kid."

"And?" Tex motioned for him to keep talking.

"And being with someone who's a taker. But I'm not, damn it. I just met her, she's not a taker, and I've been helping her with an injured puppy. This isn't a relationship thing."

They all just looked at him.

"Fuck you. She's hot. I like her. Leave me alone."

Brad grinned. "There we go. Now don't you feel better for being honest?"

Reggie flipped him off.

Tex laughed. "Relax, man. We're just giving you shit because you bailed on us."

"And *lied about it,*" Mack emphasized. "That's what's really annoying about what you did. And the fact we lost to a bunch of nerds."

"Nerds?"

"They work in behavioral health." Mack huffed.

Reggie snorted. "And?"

"We're firefighters." Mack looked confused.

"That has nothing to do with being a nerd."

Brad agreed. "He's right. Look at Reggie. He never loses a fight with those fists, and he's a huge nerd."

"Huge." Tex stood. "More beer?"

Reggie nodded. "Grab me one. Now hold on. I'm not a nerd."

"You totally are." Mack sighed. "Get me and Brad another too. He's almost empty."

Tex left.

Reggie cracked a peanut and tossed the shell onto the floor, where it joined thousands of others. "I guess I'm not seeing how you classify someone as a nerd."

"It's simple," Mack explained. "Your love of eighties pop culture and all things nerd-related."

Brad laughed. "Dude, relax. Nerd isn't an insult. Look at all the successful 'nerds' out there. Tech giants, corporate millionaires, you…"

Reggie reluctantly agreed. "Fine. But you know, if you really want to talk nerds, have you seen *Revenge of the Nerds?* Released in 1984. Classic movie."

Mack groaned. "I need more beer."

"What? You don't remember Ogre?" Brad grinned. "How about the Omega Mus?"

"You want to talk real movie magic, how about *Beverly Hills Cop?* Eddie Murphy is a genius. *Big? Back to the Future? Beetlejuice? Ghostbusters? E.T.?* I could go on."

"Please don't," Mack muttered.

"No, do." Brad leaned forward. "I know a lot of those. I didn't know they all came out in the eighties though."

"It's a little before my time, but I love that decade." Reggie beamed. Now *this* he could talk about. "And who could forget a classic Navy movie like *Top Gun?* Those are my peeps."

Mack huffed. "Who? Val Kilmer and Tom Cruise?"

"Ha! You know the actors. You saw it. Admit it."

"Of course I saw it. It had jets in it and takes place at Miramar. That's a Naval station and not an Air Force base, but jets, man. Who doesn't love jets?"

Tex had returned with four bottles and stood behind them, staring. "Tom Cruise? What the hell did I miss?"

"And then you have eighties TV," Reggie said, enthused. He could talk about this shit all day. "*ALF, Magnum P.I., Knight Rider.*"

Mack nodded. "Okay, I'm with you on *Knight Rider*. It's a car. *That talks*," he said to the guys.

Knowing his fascination with wheels, Reggie let him have that one. "*The A-Team*. You know you've all seen that."

"Well, yeah. Streaming the oldies," Tex said as he sat. "I notice you didn't mention *The Dukes of Hazard* though."

Mack shook his head. "You mean a series about Southern idiots who ride around in a hot rod with a cousin named Daisy who wore shorts up to her… Yeah, Reggie. You have to include that one."

The guys laughed.

But as they soon segued into the Mariners' chances for the playoffs if they continued the way they'd been playing, Reggie accepted that beyond his enjoyment in discussing '80s pop culture and hanging with the guys, he couldn't get Maggie and his upcoming date out of his mind.

His heart raced just thinking about it.

An hour later, they walked the seven plus blocks back to Mack's, where they'd parked. There, they downed water and had a pull-up contest in Mack's backyard.

Reggie and Brad were neck and neck, though Tex put in an impressive showing.

But to everyone's surprise, Mack ended up winning, the guy a bit leaner and, hell, strong enough to edge out Reggie, the previous champ.

"Damn, son, who knew you had it in you?" Reggie gave Mack a congratulatory pat.

Mack, for dramatic effect, acted as if Reggie had knocked him out instead of giving the light pat to his shoulder. He sprawled on the ground as if dead. Tex was laughing. Brad sighed and leaned down to flip Mack onto his back.

The faker gasped and groaned. "Laid out by a squid. I'm so embarrassed."

"And we're back to Naval insults." Reggie grimaced. How many years had they been friends? Yet the old service rivalries never faded. "Rich, coming from you."

"Wait for it…" Tex grinned.

"Chair force."

"Oh, I'm so wounded." Mack snickered. "That's so lame."

"Keyboard warrior? I know. Call Sign: Virgin."

Brad and Tex laughed at that one. Even Mack cracked a smile.

"Okay, time for me to quit while I'm ahead." Reggie stretched, feeling a good ache in his lats. "I'm out of here. See you guys tomorrow."

Brad stepped in front of him, moving pretty fast for a big guy. "Now hold on, Reggie. What are you up to tonight? How about we all hang at my place?"

Tex frowned. "I have plans."

"I don't." Mack held out his hand. "Hey, Lurch, help me out."

Tex sighed and extended a hand, yanking Mack to his feet.

Reggie started sweating. "Ah, I'm just going to head home and get some rest before tomorrow."

"Aw, hell." Tex slapped him on the back. "Big guy's got a date."

"Reggie. We don't blame you." Mack used his nice voice. "Maggie's pretty. Even with the broken arm, she had that helpless, vulnerable, save-me-Reggie look to her."

Reggie groaned.

The guys sneered at him.

"Just be careful man," Brad advised.

"No, I planned on giving her all my money and letting her rip my heart out," Reggie snapped.

"He just doesn't learn." Mack shook his head. "Maybe try for a relationship then sex. Buying love is just wrong. Not to mention illegal."

Mack narrowly dodged Reggie's fist.

Brad held him back with a laugh. "Easy. We're just teasing you. Enjoy your new 'friend.'" He used air quotes.

"Damn it. She *is* a friend."

"Yeah, that's all she is. Sure." Tex snorted. "That's why you're lyin' to your brothers. Fella, you need to relax and enjoy your lady. And quit fibbing to us and yourself. Just be careful."

Reggie felt like an ass. One, because he couldn't lie his way out of a paper bag. And two, because though the guys teased him, he knew they had his best interests at heart. "Okay, okay. No more lying."

"You suck at it," Mack added, so unhelpfully.

"Have fun tonight." Brad smiled. "You should ride with me tomorrow."

"I want him," Tex and Mack said at the same time.

"No way. You're always with him," Tex argued.

"Yeah, but now he has a story worth hearing," Mack argued back.

Reggie escaped while he had his chance.

And like clockwork, he grinned like a fool at thoughts of Maggie.

———————————

Maggie couldn't believe how nervous she felt. It was just dinner. Just Reggie, whom she knew and liked. Considered a friend.

Emily had been so excited to sleep at Sherry's, she hadn't done more than talk about it all day long. When Maggie dropped her off, she apologized in advance to Dina.

"I hope you don't mind her so excited. It's not sugar-related; it's Sherry-related."

Dina laughed and waved her away. "I'll drop her off at one tomorrow, if that's okay."

"*Okay?* I get to sleep in. I love you."

Smiling, she left, feeling light and bouncy and full of energy.

Now, two hours later, she had the chicken warming in the oven. A side of sweet potato casserole that Doug called her best side dish, a salad, and some fresh green beans from the farmer's market rounded out the meal. She'd also purchased a nice fresh bread and cooked up a strawberry cheesecake for dessert.

Heck, even if Reggie failed to show, she had a feast she couldn't wait to eat.

She went back to the bathroom to check her reflection. Clean, conditioned, shiny hair. Check. Great makeup that didn't look heavily applied. Check. Form-fitting red tank and white shorts— not too short but showing plenty of leg. Check. Toenails and fingernails red to match the shirt. And check.

After fiddling with the gold hoops in her ears that gave her confidence, she went back out and inspected her living room for the fifth time. Everything had been cleaned and freshened to death. She had nice little bouquet of carnations set on the coffee table next to a vanilla-scented candle.

All in all, her apartment looked dynamite. And, on the off chance they did make it back to her bedroom, she'd cleaned up in there as well, adding fresh sheets and a spring mix of daisies on her dresser.

Counting down the minutes to Reggie's arrival, she paced, clutching her phone.

It beeped and startled her. Calming herself and trying to be less of an idiot, she looked down to see a text from Benny. He there yet?

She chuckled, not sure who was more excited about this date—her or the guys.

At least they hadn't stuck around, out on their own date while she, hopefully, had hers.

Not yet. Go have fun.

He sent back a sighing emoji and a zombie.
Zombie? she texted.

B safe or this could hapn 2 u.

How lovely. A zombie to remind her to use protection. She rolled her eyes. Then sent him a rolling eye emoji.

The doorbell buzzed, and she jumped again and laughed at herself. A little hysterically. To say she was wound up for her date was understating it.

She sent Benny a quick text. He's here!

Benny sent her a four-leaf clover and two zombies in love.

Amused, she put her phone in her back pocket and went to the peephole. She looked and saw Reggie standing there.

Here goes nothing.

She opened the door with a smile that widened as she looked him over, conscious of him doing the same.

Just…wow. Reggie wore a pair of khaki shorts that reached mid-thigh. And holy hotness, the man had killer legs. Muscular thighs and calves, his feet tucked into canvas slip-ons. The lime-green, short-sleeve polo he wore emphasized the breadth of his chest and width of his biceps.

She had to work to process normal functions and forced herself to blink. Remembering her manners, she stepped back and asked him to come in.

He did and handed her a bouquet of flowers she hadn't noticed, too busy ogling the man.

It moved her that he'd brought her flowers. "Oh, wow. They're so pretty."

"They smell good too." He stared at her so long without saying anything, she wondered if she'd missed part of the conversation.

"Reggie?"

"You're beautiful."

She flushed. "Well, not half as much as you. Who knew you cleaned up so nice?"

He chuckled. Then he leaned close and kissed her softly on the cheek. The scent of his cologne made her dizzy. And hot. Very, very *hot.*

Maggie darted from him to the kitchen to find a vase for the flowers. "Come on back. What do you want to drink?"

"I'll get it. You look busy."

She smiled over her shoulder at him before turning back to the cabinets. Shoot. The vase wasn't on the lower shelf, as she'd assumed. She'd forgotten that she'd had Benny move it for her last week to make more room for things she actually used. She reached up on tiptoe but still couldn't reach it. Before she could turn to grab her step stool, a large body brushed against her back.

"That what you want? Way up top?"

She felt him everywhere. The press of him sent waves of desire crashing through her. "Um, yeah. The blue glass one."

He leaned closer, and she had to close her eyes to focus on not turning and just kissing him. Once again jumping the poor guy in the kitchen. *What is wrong with me?*

He eased back and placed the vase on the counter.

"Thanks." She sounded way too breathy.

His low chuckle told her he might have been teasing her on purpose. But when she turned around, she saw an innocent smile before he fetched himself a lemonade. "What do you want?"

You. Naked. Now.

"Lemonade works for me too."

He took their glasses to the table she'd set. After she put the flowers in the vase, opting to get Doug to help her rearrange them the following day, she took the vase to the center of the table. Then she lit a pair of tapered candles.

She saw Reggie watching her. "What do you think? It's a table set for grown-ups." She winked at him. "You sure you don't want anything harder than lemonade?"

"I'm good. I met the guys for some beers earlier today. I'm not a big drinker anyway, so I hit my limit."

She nodded. "Sounds good. Now if you would just—"

"Hold it. I realize I'm a guest, but no way am I going to sit and watch while you try to balance hot dishes with one arm."

"I was going to ask if you'd help me get the food from the oven."

"Oh." He looked embarrassed. "Okay then."

The dinner was perfect. The chicken tender and flavorful, the potatoes and green beans melt-in-your-mouth amazing. The salad was crisp, and the bread added just the right touch.

Reggie finished off his chicken and was steadily working his way through the rest of the plate. "*So good.* I don't know how you're not eight hundred pounds, eating like this all the time."

"Trust me. This is a first. Everything cooked the way I wanted it. That never happens. And to be honest, I bought the bread."

"But you heated it up and put that herb butter on it. That's amazing. I'm going to have to try that at home."

It was important to her that he like the meal, and she treasured his compliments.

"I have dessert too."

He shot her a naughty grin that froze her to her seat. "Oh, is that what you're calling it? Dessert?" He nodded. "I'm game."

She bit her lip to keep from laughing. "*I meant* I made strawberry cheesecake. And no, that is not a euphemism for anything but food."

"Damn." He looked so disappointed.

She cracked up.

He smiled with her. "I'm full right now. Do you mind if we wait on *that* dessert?"

She tried to ignore his emphasis. "Want to take a walk and let our food settle?"

"Sounds like a plan." He helped her into a light jacket, not wearing one himself. She didn't know why not, as the weather typically cooled down in the evening.

As they walked, their hands continued to brush each other's, until Reggie took her hand in his and held on. "Okay?" he asked.

More than okay. Tonight has been fantastic. So far… "Great." She smiled and squeezed his hand.

"How's the arm feeling?" he asked.

The sun had begun to set, and the pink-and-orange blanket of daylight slowly slid back to reveal an indigo sky. Puffs of white clouds turned dark gray, but the promise of a clear night came when a southerly wind blew the clouds away.

"Wow, that's pretty." She looked back at him. "But you asked about my arm. It's healing. No problems, though it's started to itch a little under the cast." And her fingers looked like sausages. But no way she wanted to bring attention to her secret uglies.

"Whatever you do, do not stick anything down there to scratch," he warned. "I've seen more infections from people using a coat hanger to reach an itch under their casts. They end up leaving a scratch. Infection sets in. And yuck. It's never pretty."

"Okay, I won't." She loved his hand in hers. He was so warm. "You're not cold, are you?"

"Nope. I have the hottest woman in Seattle by my side. How could I be cold?"

She nodded in approval. "Oh, you're good."

"I really am." He winked.

Another reference to sex. *Yes!* "Do you have to work tomorrow?"

"I do. We have changeover at seven thirty, so I'm usually there by seven, ready to go."

"And your shifts? How do they work?" She wanted to know everything about Reggie, about his job, his family, how he looked when he pushed inside her…

"…four off, like I just had. I'm on tomorrow then off for two days. It's a set of one on, two off, one on, four off. It seems like a lot of time off, but we work twenty-four hours when we're on. That's three eight-hour days if you think about it."

"Can you sleep when you're on duty?"

"You can if nothing's going on. But in this city, we're usually pretty busy if we're working the medical side. The engine is less busy, since we focus on fighting fires, but even then, we have training, cleaning, and more training."

She subtly turned them around, wanting to head back. Her legs were starting to get pretty chilly.

He must have seen her shiver because he apologized. "Oh, sorry, Maggie. We should have turned around earlier. Are you cold?"

"A little."

"Then come closer so I can warm you up."

"Reggie."

"Maggie."

She smiled. "You're pretty funny tonight, aren't you?"

"I am. But in all seriousness, thank you for such a fine meal. I don't think I've ever eaten anything so tasty. And that's including your macaroni and hot dogs."

"Oh, stop." She blushed at the compliment.

They chatted about his work and her friends, and he told her about all the ribbing he'd gotten for being such a poor liar.

"Being a bad liar is a good thing," she said as they entered her apartment.

He shut and locked the door behind them. "Oh?"

"I like honesty in a man."

"Yeah? How honest?"

"Well, if a man told me I looked pretty and he wanted to kiss me, that would be nice."

"Yeah?" His voice sounded gritty, and he watched as she carefully eased out of her jacket and toed off her sandals. "How about if a man thought you looked gorgeous and couldn't wait to take all your clothes off and fuck you? Would that be too much honesty? Or not enough?"

Chapter Thirteen

HE COULDN'T HELP IT. HE HADN'T MEANT TO BE SO CRASS, BUT staring at her all night, pretending to just enjoy the meal when he wanted nothing more than to make love to her, had been frustrating, exhausting, and hard as hell. A lot like the current state of his body.

Maggie stared at him, like a doe caught by the eye of a hungry predator, he thought, the description apt. She looked him over, from his head to his toes, and centered on his obvious erection.

"I've been like this all night, since I laid eyes on you in that tight, red shirt, with you all *perky* and beautiful." He deliberately stared at her chest, loving the tight points of her nipples stabbing at the fabric. He'd brought several condoms on the off chance she'd agree to having sex. But he kept returning to their conversation about her being safe if he did come inside her, skin to skin.

And didn't that thought make him hard enough to pound steel.

Maggie licked her lips.

He groaned.

"I'm ready if you are." Yet she sounded more nervous than excited.

"We don't have to do anything if you don't want to," he reiterated. "I still had a great time tonight." *God, please say yes.*

"Do *you* want to?"

His eyes widened. "Are you kidding?"

Her eyes warmed. "Then come with me." She took him by the hand, shot him a shy smile, and led him back to her bedroom. Inside, she stood there, watching him. "How about we start with a kiss? You're pretty good at that."

Falling on her and ripping her clothes off probably wouldn't make a good impression. Fuck, he was hurting and wanting, and she seemed to want slow. But fine. Anything for Maggie. He leaned down to kiss her, wrapping his arms around her, always conscious of that cast and to be gentle.

Maggie shocked him by turning the tables, taking charge of the kiss until they were both panting. Then the shy woman turned aggressive by pressing him to take off his shirt. He did and kicked off his shoes.

"Keep going," she urged, kissing him again. Her hand on his chest started a fire inside him, leeching away his ability to think as she ran short nails over his nipples and down his chest to his abs.

He shuddered and broke away, breathing hard. "Hey, I'm not going to be the only one naked." Exhilarated at the excitement in her breathy "*yes*," he eased her shirt and shorts off her, leaving her in matching red lace bra and panties that took his breath away.

She should have looked ridiculous in red lace with her arm in a cast, but the cast took a back seat to her trim belly, full breasts, and long, slender legs. For a small woman, she'd been built with perfect proportions.

"You know, as much as I love you in red, I want you naked. Now."

He helped her remove her bra, a front clasp that parted with ease. Then her panties, slowly edging them down her body. He knelt and kept his eyes down, seeing her pretty nail polish, doing his best to keep in control.

Slowly, he stood and really looked at her.

"You are…" He drew her closer and ran a hand over her shoulder, past her breasts and down her belly. Her breathing came faster, her lips parted as she stared at him. He felt her gaze on his mouth, but he couldn't stop watching his hand. When he slid it between her thighs, he felt her hot and wet on his fingers.

She grasped his arm with one hand and widened her feet. "Oh, Reggie."

He didn't want to wait. "I want to take my time with you, but honey, I'm not sure I can."

"Me neither." She dragged him down for a kiss, and her tongue invaded and conquered with little effort. Stroking his tongue, sucking on him the way he imagined she'd do with his cock, she broke him.

He lifted her in his arms and put her down on the bed, then removed a few condoms from his back pocket and put them on her nightstand. "I came prepared."

"Good. We're going to need those."

He smiled and took off the rest of his clothes, proud of how hard she made him.

Maggie parted her legs and put one slender hand over her sex, showing him the trimmed hair covering her mound. "I want you in me."

"Fuck, yeah." He hurried to grab a condom and put it on. Then he joined her on the bed, his dick ready, willing, and able.

Reggie watched her fingers spread her folds, and he didn't wait. Shimmying down her body, he pushed her thighs wider and planted himself. He watched her fingers move, exposing the taut, slick nub, and he kissed her there.

Her taste went straight to his head.

She moaned and clutched at his shoulder, trying to reach him as he licked and sucked, taking her to a fast, brutal climax. She keened and arched into his mouth, moaning his name.

So wet and hot, she made him crazed to have her.

Reggie couldn't wait any longer, especially seeing her writhe under him, still lost in pleasure. He rose over her and watched her face, her eyes slumberous, and pushed inside her.

"So tight," he moaned and continued to thrust, her passage like a glove, fisting him as he seated himself deep, until he couldn't move any more.

She cried out when he shifted, and he felt her squeezing him tight.

He wanted to kiss her, to suckle her breasts and whisper naughty things. But he had to *move*.

"Fuck me," she moaned, her hand on his hip, her nails biting into his ass.

He flexed inside her, withdrew, then shoved hard.

Her cries drove him, his need biting, unforgiving, as he thrust faster and deeper and harder. Until he crested that high and came.

"Maggie," he shouted as he jetted inside her. He closed his eyes and saw black, then colors, then stars, as he poured inside the condom. The orgasm was such a rush, and it seemed to last forever.

He gradually felt her stroking his chest, her hand tracing his pectorals, teasing his nipples and making him overly sensitive.

As if aware, she moved her hand to his face, cupping his cheek. "I was right. You're even sexier when you're coming."

He groaned and pulled out slowly, the sensation overwhelming. He had to stop before fully withdrawing, the loss of her warmth warring with his need to digest what the hell had just happened. But common sense prevailed. They couldn't stay connected forever.

He flopped next to her on the bed, staring without seeing at her ceiling.

"Wow. You really filled that up." She was on her side, her good hand propping up her head.

He flushed, aware he'd been pent up. But he'd never, *ever*, even after a deployment, months away from a willing woman, exploded like that before. "Be right back." He left on unsteady legs to dispose of the condom, then returned from her bathroom down the hall.

Seeing her there, naked and waiting for him, twisted something inside him. The walls guarding his heart seemed to crumble a little, but rather than worry about it, he told himself not to care. Tonight was for him. To feel close, to enjoy having sex with a beautiful woman.

He smiled down at her. "Wow."

"Yep." Her cheeks were pink. "Sorry I came so fast."

"That's my line."

She chuckled. "We're sad and lame in the sack, huh?"

"Oh, no. That was our first time. We had to get that big orgasm out of the way so we can play."

She blinked up at him. "Play?"

He smiled, feeling the need to take charge. He joined her on the bed, and they lay facing each other, both on their sides. "I didn't get nearly enough kisses. And I totally ignored your breasts, which is a crime." He cupped one smooth globe in his hand and felt his dick twitch. Oh yeah. No way he was done with her so soon.

"Can I be honest with you?" she asked, her voice soft.

He paused. "Of course."

"What we did was better than anything I've ever had."

He grinned and put pressure on her nipple, rolling the tight bud with gentle fingers.

She groaned and wriggled. So he did the same to her other breast, in lust with her body. Enamored with her smile, her thoughts, her sweet and sexy nature.

"I have all sorts of things I want to do to you," he said.

"Same, same, same," she murmured and leaned close to kiss him.

He kissed her back, slanting his mouth over hers to deepen the contact. And when it wasn't enough, he pushed her to her back and mounted her, keeping his weight off her and on his forearms.

His cock rested against her belly, and she felt so good everywhere they touched.

"You felt so tight inside me," she whispered and let him kiss his way down her throat to her chest. "So big and hard."

"And getting harder," he rasped and licked her nipple. He sucked and nipped her with his teeth, and she cupped his head, holding him closer. "I could eat you up all day long." He moved to her other breast. One nipple in his mouth, the other in his hand, covering her. Dark skin against light skin, man to woman. Lover to lover.

"Reggie, please." She shifted under him, and every time she moved, his dick got harder.

"Please what?"

"Let me...blow you."

He froze, not having expected that. But since her mouth featured in so many of his fantasies, he wanted to see her take him. He pulled back from her and knelt on the bed beside her, now fully erect and feeling that build toward climax. But then he realized she couldn't get on her hands and knees, not with her cast.

He left the bed and pulled her with him. He spread his legs wide. "On your knees, Maggie."

It was so hot ordering her around, watching her do so with pleasure. She didn't wait but opened her mouth and drew him in.

"Yes, oh, hell yeah." He cupped her head tenderly, her hair so soft and dark. And her mouth, sweet fuck, she knew what she was doing. Her tongue stroked and licked, her cheeks hollowing as she worked him. Then she rubbed his balls.

He instinctively thrust deeper and froze when he realized what he'd done, only to see Maggie take all of him and smile around his dick.

She pulled away and kissed along his shaft. "I have special skills," she confessed.

"You do, you really do," he babbled, lost in a fog of lust. He wanted to come in her mouth, to watch himself take her, see her swallow. But he wanted even more to fill her up once more, riding her while she came.

"Maggie, back to the bed." She lay down, and he kept her belly-down and spread her legs wide. It wasn't as easy as taking her doggie style, but he knew she could handle him like this without hurting her arm.

Reggie slowly slid inside her, taking her from behind, them both lying on the bed. He couldn't get as deep, but she felt like a vise around his dick. The feel of her so good, he had to focus not to come.

She moaned and pushed back against him, her ass grinding up against his belly. He shifted her hips up and settled deeper, the feeling of her warmth around him indescribable.

He started moving and belatedly realized he hadn't put on a condom.

"Maggie, I'm not wearing anything," he said when he could catch his breath.

"Come in me. I want to feel it," she said and moaned again.

On fire now, not sure how he'd gone from taking it slow to fucking her in earnest, he slid his hands beneath her and cupped her breasts while he pounded from behind.

She grew wetter as he teased her, her nipples a direct connection to her pleasure center. But he wanted her to come with him, needed it. He moved one hand down her belly and found her clit.

The minute he touched her there, she bucked against him.

He massaged her, talking but not sure what he said as the ecstasy flooded him, the teetering precipice of pleasure and pain seesawing as he grew harder, moving faster.

Just as he feared coming too soon, Maggie cried out and jerked, her hips flexing and pushing him into a state of carnal bliss.

He thrust as deep as he could go and emptied into her, the feel of Maggie's hot flesh milking him dry. She pulled his hand from her clit, and he planted it back on her breast, holding her tight while he finished spilling inside her.

His brain floated away while he lay still, Maggie and he joined as one.

Until she muttered, "You feel good, but you're heavy."

"Shoot. Sorry." He quickly withdrew and rolled over, pulling her on top of him and pushing his cock inside her once more. He was only half-hard but enough to let him slide inside.

"You're amazing," she said, blinking down at him. She kissed him, and he realized they really needed to do more of that. If he had the energy, he would have fucked her again. But his body needed to recover. "I loved you coming in me. I hate condoms."

Will you marry me? immediately came to mind, especially remembering her oral skills. He said nothing, just nodded and cupped her head as they continued to kiss, easing them both back to an excited state of normal.

At one pause, Maggie said, "In case you're worried, don't be. I'm on birth control and, like I said before, I'm clean and safe."

"Yeah, whatever. I mean, me too." He kissed her cheek and felt her smile. "Maggie, we share something special. I have never in my life come so hard or been so turned on."

"Good. I thought it was just me."

"No. Although, it is just you turning me on," he teased.

"I love a big cock, and yours is mouthwatering."

He thought he'd misheard her. "What?"

"I love cock. The bigger the better." She leaned up to wink at him. "There. Now you know my secret."

He just stared, not putting her words together with the sweetheart image he had of her in his mind. Even considering what all they'd just done. "You love cock?"

"Big cock. And no, that's not my secret. It's... I'm a dirty talker in the sack."

Seriously. Marry me. "I like it a lot."

"Yeah?" She blew out a relieved breath. "Good. Because I know that can be a turnoff, but I figured, might as well let you know now. In case something slips out."

"Well, that something ain't me. I'm keeping my dick in you forever."

"Good."

Except he'd softened and did fall out. "Damn. We're making a mess."

"I don't care." She traced the contour of muscle of his chest. "Is it wrong that I'm really attracted to you in a superficial sense? I mean, I love your brain. You're smart and caring. All that emotional stuff."

Emotional stuff. He had to smile.

"But I really, really love your body. Especially your arms and chest. And oh man, I love your cock and the way you tongued me. Reggie, I came so hard when you went down on me."

His ego was about to burst. He'd never felt better. "You taste good. We need to do that again."

"Tonight?" She flushed. "I'm not a closet nymphomaniac. I just… I still want you. I'm tired, and I came twice. *Twice.*" She kissed him again. "But it's not enough."

"No, it's not." He put her hand on his cock, wrapping her fingers around him. "I'm thick and long. But now I'm soft. And I want you touching me." He brushed his fingers through her hair. "I can't believe how hard you made me with that sweet little tongue and those soft lips. I mean, Maggie, I feel like I'm dating an Olympic gold sex-lete."

She laughed. "Or an Olympic gold cocksucker."

"Wow, do you have a dirty mouth." He kissed her again, Frenching her until that spark of want flared. "My only regret about tonight is we couldn't do it doggie style."

"My stupid arm."

"We'll have to wait until it's healed." Wait, what had he just said? It would take weeks for her arm to be on the mend enough to put some real pressure on it. But her happiness washed away any sense of caution.

"Yeah." She smiled.

He sighed, content to lie with her in bed, stroking her bare skin.

After some time had passed, she murmured, "We never did get to the strawberry cheesecake."

"We probably should. I need my energy, after all."

Maggie leaned up and nodded, looking serious. "And you should drink more water. I would hate to send you back to work dehydrated. Especially because at some point, I'm sure to suck you dry."

Yep. Definitely a jerk between his legs.

She smirked at him.

"Feed me, woman. Then I'll feed you some of that cock you like so much." He gripped himself.

She put a hand over his, slicking her fingers through his slit. She brought her fingers to her mouth, her gaze on his, and licked.

He shivered.

Maggie laughed. "Come on. Never let it be said you went home…hungry."

———

Maggie couldn't believe how freeing it had been to finally have sex with Reggie. Like the dam that breaks, relieving so much massive pressure from a buildup, Maggie's body felt both loose and energized. She couldn't believe she'd come twice in one night with a man.

She and Reggie kept looking at each other and smiling as they ate their strawberry cheesecake to the lovely sound of some jazz music Reggie played through her speaker. Something his father particularly liked, he'd told her.

He sat in just his shorts, his glorious chest bare, and spooned up his dessert. The man had an appetite for sure. And just thinking that made her libido bubble and boil deep inside. *Churned up, that's me.*

She smiled at him and licked her spoon, not trying to be suggestive, just not wanting to waste a taste of whipped cream.

His gaze darkened. "Keep teasing me and you're going to find out how I handle bad girls." He paused. "That was pretty lame, wasn't it?"

"Not bad. But your dirty talk needs more work."

"How about, after we finish, I'm going to fuck you until you can't walk straight?"

"Better."

He grinned, his expression just this side of wicked.

Maggie sensed a softening in the giant, an emotional relief that hadn't been there before. Whether, like her, he'd been pent up physically or just not sure of her in general, Reggie had been more serious when they'd started their friendship. But now he seemed so relaxed, and so freaking handsome. Beyond handsome. Gorgeous. His brown skin glowed with vigor, the sheen of light over his muscles highlighting a work of art. His smile, always lovely, now made her want to kiss him all the time, to feel that smile pressing against her lips.

She still couldn't believe she'd made love with him. A man like Reggie, handsome, a firefighter, smart, could have any woman he wanted. Yet he'd wanted her.

She hugged that nugget to her chest and tried to stop acting so dorky about her crush.

She confessed, "I'm so, *so* glad Emily had a sleepover tonight."

"*Fuck* yeah," he replied, emphatically. Then he gave her a sheepish grin. "Sorry for all the swearing. I think my brain is still rebooting. I don't like to swear so much around women, especially." He pointed his spoon at her. "But the word 'fuck' and 'Maggie' seem to go hand in hand. It's all your fault."

"I take full blame." She sighed. "I'm trying to be grounded and mature. Like this is no big deal. But it's just so…intense." Should she stop talking about it? Stop talking, period? She didn't want to freak him out, but they had shared some serious chemistry.

"I told you. My dick spikes whenever you're near. Now, that could be because it's been a while for me since I last had sex."

"How long?" Since they were on the subject.

"Nine months, actually. And I broke up close to eight months ago. We were having problems, and the desire just wasn't there."

"I'm sorry."

"I'm not." He smiled at her. To her surprise, he looked a little relieved. "I'm tired of mourning that relationship." He paused. "The hell with it. Look, Maggie. I'm into you. Way into you. And I'm sorry, but it just happened."

"Oh." *Now that is what I like to hear!*

"I'm not good at games. I don't know that I'm ready for anything serious yet. But I'm not opposed either. I only know that I can't stop thinking about you. And now, I really can't stop thinking about you naked."

She wore his polo shirt that reached just past her ass and nothing else. "I'm having a tough time not constantly touching you. I just want to run my hands over your entire body."

He blew out a breath. "Yeah." He glanced at his lap. "I'm hard again."

"Good."

He chuckled. "It must be the arm. I'm a sucker for a girl with a cast."

"Well, it does have your name on it. It must be yours."

He pushed his dessert away. "Come sit with me on the couch. Where it's safe."

"The bed isn't safe?" She joined him on the couch and tucked her feet up under her.

"Your bed is sinful. It's now the place I think about when I consider how to get balls-deep inside you."

She shivered. She liked the dirty talk. A lot.

"Or when I think about you sucking me off, taking me in your mouth, down your throat." He stood and pulled off his shorts then took the throw from the couch and put it over the cushion before he sat back down.

He took himself in hand, his thick arousal looking small, dwarfed by that large palm. "Watch me." Reggie jerked his hand up and down, spread his thighs wider, and continued to watch her while he did.

She wanted to taste him again.

"Take off your shirt, Maggie."

"Your shirt, you mean. You want it back?" she teased and cupped her breast through the fabric.

His hand moved faster. "Yeah."

She pulled it off and knelt on the floor between his legs.

"Do it," he said, his voice gritty. "I want you licking my slit."

She moaned and put her mouth over him, loving his hiss of pleasure as she licked him then sucked. Taking him all in.

He held her head in place and arched up, thrusting into her mouth. He pumped while she moved up and down, the only sounds in her apartment the instrumental jazz and Reggie's harsh breathing.

And the sound of her moan as she sucked his thick shaft.

She played with his balls, rubbing, cupping, and felt the knots harden.

But before she could make him really lose his mind, he pulled her off him and had her straddling him.

He held his cock as he urged her to sit down. "That's it. On top." They both groaned when she seated herself fully. "Oh yeah. Ride me. Up and down while I play with your tits."

He locked an arm behind her back, bringing her close so he could suck her nipples and kiss her breasts. He encouraged a rough ride, bouncing her on him so that he continued to hit deeper inside of her.

"I'm gonna come inside you, Maggie. All of me, filling you up," he rasped as he snagged a hand between them to rub her clit.

The added stimulus made her mindless, and she rode him harder and faster, seeking release.

Reggie kept whispering dirtier, naughtier things, until he moaned her name and stilled. But she kept moving, and his fingers kept prodding her clit, while he swore.

Between one breath and the next, she exploded, clutching his neck, though she hadn't been aware of hugging him to her. They kissed while she ground over him, and he moved again, giving her the push she needed as her inner walls gripped him tightly, never wanting to let go.

When the passion finally started to fade, she eased her hold and tried to move back, but Reggie kept kissing her, murmuring sweet flattery as he planted kisses all over her neck and face, finally ending with a kiss on her lips.

"Fuck me sideways, I can't move. You broke me, Maggie. I'm done." He was trying to catch his breath, his chest rising and falling in heaves.

Maggie too had to take a moment to process the pleasure. And when she did, she realized how much of a turn-on it was to be with him, bare. "I love you coming inside me," she whispered. "It's hot. So sexy."

He laid his head back on the couch and looked up at her with melting brown eyes. "It really, really is." He caressed her hips, winding his fingers over her skin. "Almost as hot as that pussy gripping me. I love how wet you get. You get me worked up, no doubt."

He tenderly pulled her closer, and she was content to lay her head on his chest forever and never move again.

After some time, he said, "I should probably head back home."

"Do you have to?" she asked, containing a sigh when moved off him, aware of the mess she needed to clean up.

"I... You want me to stay?"

She was probably pushing too fast, confusing lust with deeper affection.

"Okay," Reggie said before she could respond. "I actually brought my stuff in the car, just in case. I always pack a go bag. So I'm prepared."

She just nodded, not sure what that meant. Prepared for what? But she wanted him to stay. "We can sleep in my bed after I clean up."

"Let me help with that."

Reggie, true to his word, used a warm washcloth to clean his seed from her body. His *baby seeds*. She had an almost hysterical desire to share with him the irony of her thoughts but knew that would not go over well. No man wanted to think about possible babies with a woman he'd slept with once. Er, three times. So she kept it to herself.

He treated her so tenderly, like she mattered. And despite knowing it was probably a mistake, she waited for him to grab his bag from his car. When he returned, she let him into her bed and hugged him while they slept. The first man since her ex-husband to spend the night.

When his alarm went off at six, she groggily got up and waited for him to shower and change. While he did, she threw on a robe and fixed a pot of coffee and some cinnamon rolls, the kind from a package that Emily loved.

He entered the kitchen half an hour later, where she blinked sleepily at him, still tired and sore in some places. And so incredibly happy.

"Whoa. I smell coffee."

She held a cup for him. "I don't know how you take it." For all that she and Reggie had shared bodies, she still didn't know a lot about him, she realized.

"A little bit of cream and sugar. I'll get it." He fixed his coffee and sighed his appreciation. "You're so sweet. You didn't have to make me anything."

"I wanted to." Her cheeks felt hot. Silly, considering all they'd done last night. "You need to fuel up."

His left brow rose. "With carbs and sugar?"

"And caffeine."

He chuckled. "Time for a diet overhaul for a cute lady I know."

"Didn't we have the cute conversation?"

He cringed. "Oh, right." Yet for all his talk about a diet overhaul, he drank two cups of coffee and put away half the cinnamon rolls. She packed up the rest for him to eat later and fixed him a cup of coffee to go.

"Maggie." He shook his head as he studied her.

"What?" She put a hand in her hair, figuring she must look pretty mussed.

"You're a sweetheart." He looked like he wanted to say more, but his gaze slipped past her to the microwave. "Crap. I have to go."

He took the coffee and bag of pastries, the strap of his go bag over his shoulder. He leaned in to kiss her, and yep, there went the warm and fuzzies flitting about in her belly.

"Damn," he swore, his voice thick. "I need to go before I'm fucking you against the wall and late to work."

She palmed his erection beneath the working uniform he wore, and his eyes crossed. She laughed. "Get out of here. I'll talk to you soon, okay?"

"No. *I'll* talk to *you* soon."

"That's what I said."

"Not quite." He kissed her, his lips both firm and smooth. "Figure out when we can go out again. I'll text you my schedule." He cupped her cheek. "Bye, Maggie."

And he was gone.

Maggie wanted to dissect the night, but a yawn told her she could afford to think too hard about everything later. She went to bed with a smile, inhaling Reggie's scent on her pillow.

Chapter Fourteen

Reggie had to work to maintain a grumpy facade through changeover. It wouldn't do to look too happy about life. No one was ever that chipper first thing in the morning. Though things did seem to look up when he realized he and the guys were back on the engine for the next month while the other crew on shift got the aid detail.

Reggie didn't exactly prefer one to the other. He loved helping people regardless. Whether putting out fires in the engine or helping with medical crises in Aid 44 or 45, he was happiest when working. Because sitting around on his ass was boring.

As he and the guys settled into work, he prepared himself for the questions about his date with Maggie.

But they didn't come.

The morning passed in a blur of activity. They had the engine to clean, some training videos to go over, as well as forcible entry drills their lieutenant had them reviewing.

Later in the day, a call came in about suspicious smoke at a residence off South Webster, but it turned out to be a barbecue smoker improperly vented. After ticketing the owner since he'd had a prior warning, they drove back to the station and decided to get in some physical training.

He should have known better.

The exercise room at the station was outfitted with some stellar gear. Everything new, from ellipticals and treadmills to exercise bikes, row machines, resistance machines, and tons of free weights and benches. The place wasn't huge, but it wasn't small either, and it always had firefighters making use of the equipment. While Reggie and his crew worked out, a few stragglers from the

off-duty shifts swung by, and Washkowski and Hernandez, part of
C shift currently working in the medical vehicles, were hanging
out, chatting.

Reggie liked C shift, though he was partial to his own crew.
Hernandez was okay but had a tendency to be an asshole more
often than not. Wash, Reggie tolerated more than the others. A big
guy from Boston who hadn't yet left the accent behind, he worked
hard and played hard and could always be counted on for a good
time.

He also hung with Mack a good bit, pranking the other shift
lieutenant more often than not. Reggie wondered when Sue
would wise up to the fact that her guys were innocent of the Dora
the Explorer stickers all over her notebooks.

As Reggie lay down and readied to bench press two-fifty, Mack,
Brad, and Tex crowded him.

"Uh, guys? I only need one spotter."

"I got this," Mack said. "I am, you recall, our pull-up champ."

Reggie snorted. "You got lucky."

"Well, reigning champ. I'm still impressed." Brad nodded. "I'm
just going to watch Reggie's form."

Reggie frowned. "What?"

"Yeah, his form is off sometimes," Tex agreed. "Like today. The
big bastard has been charming and fun to be around." Tex's grin
widened. "Kinda like he might have gotten lucky last night."

Mack hooted, which drew Wash and a few others closer.

Reggie *hated* being the center of attention. "Okay, show's over.
To whatever shithead will spot me, I'd appreciate it."

Mack stood behind the bar. "Hey, I'm the shithead who said
he'd help. The rest of you shitheads, get lost."

Wash flipped him off. "Asshole. Brad, you still owe me ten
bucks for whippin' your ass after darts last week." *Your* came out
as *yawhr*.

"Yeah, yeah. You got lucky."

"I did." Wash grinned down at Reggie. "But not as lucky as Morgan over here." Which came out as *ovah heah*. "Seen you smiling all damn day. Who's the poor chick?"

"Your mother."

Everyone jeered. A few clapped.

Wash grinned. "Not bad, chowderhead. My mom, she likes a real man. So how'd you impress her? Musta brought a strap-on, since everyone knows the dicks in your crew are short on talent."

"Oh no, he didn't." Mack laughed despite the insult to their crew. "I hate to admit it, but that was pretty funny."

Tex grinned. "You think that's funny? You should see Wash's new side piece."

And it got ugly from there. Wash and his team, their mothers, sisters, brothers, fathers, anyone and anything was fair game.

The room erupted in a riot of insults, swearing, and laughter. It took the LT to come in and bark at everyone to relax.

The lieutenant snarled, "Calm the fuck down. Hell. I can't hear myself think, and the chief is due to visit in a few days." He glared at everyone, then pointed at Tex. "You, with me." Ed turned on his heel and left.

Tex groaned. "Why me?"

"Maybe because you're dating the battalion chief's daughter?" Mack offered.

Wash shrugged. "I woulda said banging her, but yeah. That."

Tex flipped him off and strutted from the room like he owned it.

Mack and Wash bumped fists before Wash left with Hernandez. The room got back to working out, finally.

Reggie cleared his throat. "Ahem. I haven't got all damn day. One of you, spot me. I'm doing three reps, ten each." He waited for Brad or Mack to help.

Mack sighed. "Fine. Go."

Reggie lifted, feeling a good tired. His mood still high from a perfect evening with Maggie, he finished with a smile on his face.

Mack stared down at him. Brad, curling thirty-five pounders, watched him as well.

Then they both smirked.

Reggie groaned and sat up. "Stop it, you two."

"Nice." Mack gave him a thumbs-up. "You had a good showing, eh?"

"My man, Reggie." Brad's smile was wide, honest. "You look good wearing some happy."

"Happy this." He showed Brad the finger.

Brad only smiled wider. Mack laughed. "Our man is back."

"You know, I didn't go anywhere. I've been with you assholes for years."

Brad nodded and kept grinning. "Had a nice date night, huh?"

"Yeah." Reggie couldn't help the sigh that left him. "She's great. Really, really great."

Mack scooted Reggie off the bench and took his place after lightening the load off the bar. "Spot me while you talk."

Reggie watched him while answering questions from Brad, prepared to step in if Mack needed the support.

Brad watched Mack lift. "Where were you?"

"Her place."

"What did you do? Besides her, I mean." Brad winked. "Kidding."

"Very funny. You know, I'd expect this kind of talk from Tex or Mack, but you're more mature. Respectful, usually."

"Hey." Mack scowled. "Pay attention, Reggie."

"I am, dumbass." He helped Mack on his second set, last rep. "Nice, Mack. Good job."

"Thanks." Mack lay there, timing his rest. After a minute passed, he went again.

Brad studied Reggie, looking for what, Reggie had no idea. "Just be careful."

Reggie rolled his eyes.

"I know. I'm annoying. But we care about you, man." Brad lowered his voice. "When do we get to meet her?"

"Nope." Reggie shut that down right away. "She and I are having fun. We just connected. Not rushing anything, and she's not my girlfriend." Though that hurt to say, putting it out there that he wasn't attached kept him safe from making a major mistake. He felt a sense of relief not committing to anything more than pleasure with Maggie, despite how much he liked her.

"Okay, okay. Calm down." Brad nodded. "Just checking. You're being smart."

"Damn straight."

Mack finished, sat up, and groaned. "Does Emily know?"

"Who's Emily?" Brad asked.

"The most adorable kid you've ever seen. Remember, I told you about her bear named Brownie, the one that she compares to Reggie. Because they are both brown and cute." And then the bastard dug a toy bear out from under the bench and tossed it to him.

Reggie wanted to slug Mack. Hard. He threw the bear at Mack's head.

"Oh, right." Brad laughed. "But Reggie, cute? I mean, he's as big as a bear. I can see the resemblance. Look at those teeth."

"Piss off." Reggie tried not to laugh. "You guys drive me nuts."

"You know you love us." Mack batted his lashes.

Brad grinned. "Now Reggie. Don't be like that."

"And no, Emily doesn't know," Reggie told them as they hit the showers. "Since Maggie and I are new, we're being careful. Not involving the little girl."

"Even smarter. You're okay, Reggie." Brad went into the stall next to him.

"And why do you sound surprised about that, Brad?" As much as he liked the guys looking out for him, it could get annoying. Reggie lathered up and washed off, appreciating the cool water over his overheating body. He'd worked up quite a sweat lifting.

"I'm not." Brad shut off the shower. "Just glad to see you're back to being you again."

"Yeah, well, I'm not always going to be this pleasant. You've been warned."

Mack strangled on laughter in the stall on the other side of Reggie.

"Oh, shut up." Reggie smacked the wall, and Mack smacked it back.

An hour later, as they relaxed and ate dinner, Reggie felt it appropriate to call Maggie. He'd texted her earlier that morning, unable to stop himself. She'd texted him back right away with a picture of the flowers he'd given her, beautifully arranged.

He was glad he'd brought them. She'd seemed delighted, and Lord knew she deserved nice things. Especially after all the *nice things* she'd done to him last night. At the thought, he sighed.

"Fuck on a frog's dick," Tex spat. "Do you have asthma or what?"

"Give him a break," Mack said. "He got laid. He deserves to sigh a lot." Mack paused. "Did you say 'fuck on a frog's dick'?"

Tex glared. "Maybe. I'm not thinking so straight. Bree's dad is coming by Saturday morning to do a walk-through. Not a formal inspection or anything. But for some reason, the LT's got the jitters about it and wants *me* to show him around."

Brad's grin showed a lot of teeth. "Ah, the future father-in-law. Should be fun."

Tex groaned. "He hates me. He acts like he doesn't in front of Bree, but when it's just him and me, he's always trying to piss me off. Can you believe he's an Eagles fan? We're in fucking Seattle. Who here loves the Eagles?" Tex muttered under his breath, "He's only anti-Cowboys to screw with me. I know it."

Mack and Reggie exchanged a look.

"Bring in a box or two from Sofa's," Mack suggested. "I guarantee that'll soften him up." A popular bakery, Sofa's could melt even the most hardened of hearts with their scones, fritters, and delectable cupcakes.

"Hmm. He does have a sweet tooth. And I am friends with the owner. Well, part owner, but still. We're buds."

Mack gaped. "You are?"

Reggie wondered why the hell Tex had been keeping something so important under his hat.

Even Brad looked startled. "Seriously?"

"What?" Tex asked.

Reggie threw his hands up. Everyone at the station loved that bakery. "How have you never mentioned that before?"

"Because I can't take advantage of the guy. Elliot's cool." He paused and smiled wide. "But Mack, I bet *you* could take advantage of him. The face of Station 44—Mack Revere. Yeah, Elliot would appreciate someone as pretty as you think you are."

"Huh?" Mack blinked.

"Flirt with him a little. See if you can get us a discount."

Mack flushed. "Dick."

"Yeah, that. Flash a little dick. Bet he throws in an eclair."

"Ha ha. I'm not pretending to be gay to get an eclair." Mack looked thoughtful. "But those apple fritters might be worth a shot."

"Idiot." Tex shook his head.

"And speaking of flashing a little dick, Alec is engaged."

"Hey, man, that's great." Reggie slapped him on the back. He'd met all of Mack's older brothers, and the three of them could be a riot, especially when piling on Mack. A tight-knit crew of cops, with Mack the oddball firefighter out, the Revere clan lived to serve.

"Alec finally came out to everyone as bi, by the way." Something the rest of them already knew, since Alec had told them a while ago at one of Mack's barbecues. "He kind of had to since he's marrying Dean."

"I thought he was dating Alyssa?" Tex frowned. "What happened to her?"

"Tex, that was a year ago. They broke up. Then he met Dean

and that was that." Mack sighed. "A little disappointing though. He was the biggest player in the family. Now he's going to settle down and be a family man. Ugh."

"Yeah, he's a real disappointment," Reggie said, his sarcasm thick.

"I know. I mean, all those men and women." Mack shook his head. "My brother had the entire field open to him. Anyone his for the asking."

"He is pretty charming," Brad agreed. "But nowhere near as smooth as you, Mack."

"Thanks, buddy. You know just how to make me feel good."

"*I'll* make you feel good," Tex cut in. "Go pick up two dozen goodies from Sofa's Saturday morning. I'll tell Elliot you're coming in and pay ahead of time."

"Why don't you do it?"

"Because I don't want Bree to think I'm schmoozing her dad. I have a reputation to uphold, you know."

Mack rolled his eyes.

"You do me this solid, I'll talk you up with a mechanic friend of mine. He's got a Shelby Mustang in his garage you really need to see."

"You get me in to check out that car, I'll pick up the goodies."

"Deal."

One crisis averted.

Reggie's hands itched to dial a certain someone's number. "Be right back."

They nodded and continued to badger Tex about the bakery.

Reggie hurried to the room he used when on duty and shut the door, ensuring some privacy. He dialed Maggie. As usual, he felt jumpy just thinking about her.

"Hello?"

He swallowed a groan. Even her voice got to him. "Hey, beautiful. It's me. Reggie?"

"Who?"

He frowned. "What?"

She laughed. "Kidding. I'm just messing with you." Her voice lowered, sounding more intimate. "How are you? Been to any fires lately?"

"Nah." He settled on his bed and smiled for no reason. "Still trying to recover from the fire that scorched me last night."

"Me too." She sighed. "Wish you were here now."

"Me too." He smiled. They both sounded a little down. "How was the sleepover?"

"It went great. But the best part about it was Dina didn't drop Emily off until one. After you left this morning, I went back to bed and slept for three more hours. I needed it. I bet you're tired."

"I'm good, actually. Energized. The guys are calling me weird because I'm happy."

She laughed.

"It's sad, and now you're laughing at me. I feel unappreciated."

"No, no. Trust me, I appreciate you more than anyone." She sounded fervent.

He allowed himself a moment of smug satisfaction.

"Emily is bugging me about your dinner invitation. Would you like to join us for pizza tomorrow night?"

"I'd love to. But *I'm* bringing dinner this time."

"You don't have to."

"I insist."

"Oh, I love it when you get all growly and bossy," she teased. "Fine. I like extra cheese. Sadly, my daughter is a major carnivore, so the more meat, the merrier."

"But not you?"

"Oh, I like meat."

The way she said that made his body tighten all over.

"I like my sausage especially juicy. And plump."

That easily, he started to sweat. "Stop it. I'm at work, woman."

She laughed, the sound of her enjoyment making his heart race. Not from arousal, but from the sheer joy in hearing her so happy. The sex they'd shared had definitely made him feel closer to her. Whether that was good or bad remained to be seen.

"What time tomorrow night?" he asked, his voice gravelly.

"How about six? Is that too early?"

"Perfect. I'll bring drinks too."

"Reggie, you don't have to. It's our invitation to dinner."

"Root beer okay?"

She sighed. "Fine. But don't think this means you can set the table too. Emily and I will do that. And you've met my daughter. If you think you can railroad her as easily as you did me, you're sadly mistaken."

"Trust me, I have no misconceptions about the dictator you live with."

He could almost hear her grinning.

"Awesome." Maggie said, "I can't wait to see you again. I miss you."

Those three words meant so much. "Me too. Missing you, I mean."

"But I'll be good when you're here. No messing around. No sly innuendos or sucking too hard on a straw. No grabbing your crotch. No licking anything or downing a whole kielbasa while you watch."

His cock was rock hard.

"No, sir. None of that. Just good, clean fun with my little girl to monitor us."

Some way, somehow, he'd get her alone and make her pay for taunting him. Whole kielbasa? *Fuck.*

"Hey, Reggie. You still there? All I hear is a lot of heavy breathing."

"You little witch. I'm so going to make you pay."

"Mommy!" he heard in the background. "Who are you talking to? Is it Frank? Is it Reggie? Can I talk to him?"

"Who?" Maggie asked. "To Frank or Reggie?" Then she chuckled and said, "It's Reggie. Reggie, can Emily talk to you?"

"Sure." He waited.

"Hi."

The bright, cheery voice made him smile. "Hi, Emily. I can't wait to hear all about your sleepover."

"Huh?"

"I'm coming over for dinner tomorrow. So I—" He winced at her shouted "*yay*," heard Maggie scold her for screaming, then had Maggie again on the phone.

"I'm so sorry. She's not supposed to do that. She's just excited."

"What? Sorry, I can't hear you. My ears are still ringing."

"Oh, Reggie. I'm sorry."

"I'm kidding. Hey, it's cool to think a little girl wants to see me again. I'll have to make sure I've got my bloodiest, scariest BLS stories ready to go."

"Please, don't."

He chuckled. "I'm kidding. I look forward to seeing you tomorrow. Especially if you down a kielbasa."

"Ha. You wish."

"Just remember something."

"Oh?"

"Payback's a bitch." He gave an evil laugh. "See you soon, Maggie."

"Bring it, Reginald." He heard her chortling with glee before she disconnected. Then he received a series of evil emojis, and of course, a bunch of eggplants, a rocket ship, and a few tongues.

It still delighted him that someone as innocent-seeming as Maggie could be so sensual and erotic. That dichotomy of sweet and sexy gave her added depth. He knew so much about her yet still had so much more to learn.

He wanted to know exactly why she and her ex hadn't worked, not minor details. He wanted to know her favorite color. Her favorite flower. Whether she wanted to travel. About her living relatives and why she didn't talk about them. And how she felt about everything from the weather and politics to sports and music.

His fixation on the woman *could* be a simple infatuation for someone new. But he didn't think so. His feelings for her went so much deeper than any he'd felt before. Even Amy, were he to be honest. Amy had been a sweet and loving single mom, and she'd looked at him as if he hung the moon. Reggie could always be counted on to help her in so many ways. She hadn't been a horrible person, no matter what his friends and family thought of her.

She'd been struggling, needing what he'd been happy to give. Sexually, they'd been compatible, but not at all to the extent he was with Maggie. And Amy had never, ever, been so frank or open about sex. Something he'd often wished she would have been.

With Amy he took care to spare her feelings. He thought hard about how he said things and when he said them. With so much already on her plate, she'd needed care. And she'd always been so grateful when he did anything that he constantly strove to make her happy.

Maggie had suffered a busted arm and a concussion. Yet she had been all about taking care of herself. *He'd* been the one to strong-arm her—no pun intended—to the hospital for her cast. It had been *his* idea to help with Frank. Not hers. And she kept feeding him when she had a kid to take care of. He had no idea what kind of child support she received, if any. How could she afford to keep feeding his big ass?

Now he felt guilty for letting her feed him before. On their date, he'd only brought flowers. He should have added a box of candy and bottle of wine, at the very least.

Hmm. Maybe he should do more than just pizza and root beer tomorrow night.

He should—

An alarm went off just as Mack popped his head in the door.

"Yo. Major accident at intersection of I5 and Swift. Car pileup, explosion. The works."

Reggie raced after him, putting Maggie at the back of his mind. But as he worked with his crew to save lives, Maggie's presence lingered, the remembered sight of her smile never quite leaving him. And it made the losses he witnessed just a little more bearable.

Chapter Fifteen

Maggie let herself relax for this dinner with Reggie. Not like the last one, where she'd practically scrubbed the kitchen floor with a toothbrush to get rid of so much as a speck of dirt. Emily bounced around the house straightening pillows and tightening the bow around the dog treat they'd bought for Frank, who would also be in attendance. Maggie had texted Reggie earlier, asking him to bring the puppy, and he'd told her he'd intended to all along.

She loved how much fun their conversation had been yesterday. She felt like an all-new person. No longer willing to pretend to be someone she was not. She'd decided that if Reggie really liked her, he'd like her for the real woman she was, not the nice, quiet one many presumed her to be.

Maybe that's why she and Doug had bonded so easily. He'd been the same way. Everyone who knew him saw him as the responsible, mature member of his family. Not someone who'd fall in love at first sight or date a semi-celebrity. Doug was quiet, introspective, and pleasant—to those who didn't know him well. Sadly, that included his parents.

She found him to be chatty, exuberant, and laugh-out-loud funny. But he only showed that side of himself with the people he cared for. Doug blossomed in his relationship with Benny.

Maggie had slowly smothered in her relationship with Stephen.

But now, with Reggie? Despite being so new to each other, she felt free to be her real self. And he seemed to like her well enough.

When she'd married Stephen, she'd been twenty-two. Young and unsure of herself, catering more to what Stephen wanted than what she wanted. And for a time, living that way had worked. Until it hadn't.

In the years since, she'd tried to be more open, as well as more sexual and adventurous. In her marriage, her husband had loved being intimate with her, but Maggie hadn't known enough about herself to ask for what she hadn't known she needed.

Her few relationships after her marriage had been a gradual effort to get to where she was today. Sexually educated, liberated, and not afraid to show it.

The lovely thing about Reggie wasn't just the sex though. She didn't feel so lonely anymore. Doug had Benny. Her teacher friends at school had partners or spouses. She often felt like a forever third wheel.

But now she had a man she really liked, who seemed to really like her. They were new, but a thrilling new. And even better, Reggie liked Emily.

So many single men didn't care for single moms. She understood, but she loved her daughter. For Maggie, Emily came first. That Reggie both agreed and wanted to do nothing to hurt Emily made him even more special. He'd been so good with her too, seeming to genuinely enjoy her company.

Okay, so I'm as excited to see him tonight as Emily is. It's Reggie. I'm entitled.

A knock on the door had Emily racing to it. Before her daughter could whip it open, Maggie ordered her to wait. Emily's hand froze on the knob. Maggie looked out through the peephole and saw Reggie waiting.

She backed up. "Okay, go for it."

Emily hastily opened the door. "Where's Frank?"

"And hello to you too," Reggie said carrying two large pizza boxes and a big paper bag.

"I mean, hi, Reggie!"

Maggie hurried to help him, only to have him maneuver around her. "Hey."

"Where do you want it?"

Men. "Okay, strong guy. Set everything on the dining table, please."

He put the pizza and bag down and scooped up Emily right behind him.

She giggled.

"Okay if I take the ninja princess to get her furry knight from the car?"

Maggie grinned. "Please do. But what are you if the knight is in the car?"

Emily huffed. "He's a super ninja, Mommy. Gosh. Everyone knows the queen has to have one of those in her court."

"I stand corrected."

Emily chatted to Reggie as he carried her out the door.

Seeing how easily her daughter perched on his arm and talked to him made her heart swell. Though Emily typically took to most people, she could also be shy with strangers, especially big men, for no reason that Maggie could fathom. It had taken a while before she'd warmed to Benny, and he was one of the gentlest people Maggie knew.

After Maggie opened the pizza boxes to some delectable smells, she rummaged through the bag Reggie had also brought and found a six-pack of root beer, vanilla ice cream, a smaller box of cupcakes, a ready-made bag of Asian chopped salad—one of her favorites—and some protein yogurt bars.

Huh. An odd assortment, but she'd take it. Reggie had been so adamant about bringing food, she would simply accept the kind gesture.

He returned with Emily and Frank, saying, "Yes, it was pretty bad. I saw the bone through the skin."

Emily watched Reggie in awe. "Did you throw up?"

Reggie looked serious. "They train us not to throw up at EMT school."

"Oh."

His lips twitched. "I'm kidding. But you learn to deal with a lot of gross stuff because the important part is helping people."

"Did the boy cry when his bone was out?"

"He did. And it really, really hurt. When your bone is broken and sticking out of your body so you can see it, that's called an open or compound fracture. And it's a bad break to get because you're at risk for your bone getting infected."

She frowned. "Infected?"

"Your bone gets sick. The doctors call it osteomyelitis. You don't want that."

Emily shook her head. "No. I don't want that."

"But something we all get that's not that serious are bruises. We medical types call them contusions."

"Contusions." She held up her knee, showcasing a lovely blue-and-purple bruise. "I have contusions."

"Yep. A nice one right there." He knelt by her and winked. "If you use 'contusion' instead of 'bruise,' you'll sound smart to all your friends."

"I'm going to use it with Sherry. Mommy, can I call Sherry?"

"How about after pizza?" Distracting Emily wasn't too difficult at this age.

"Yay, pizza!"

"Thank Reggie. He brought it."

"Thank you, Reggie."

"You're welcome."

"Now go wash your hands. Both of you," she added.

He raised a brow. "Yes, ma'am."

Emily took him by the hand, dragging him down the hall toward the bathroom. "In here," Maggie heard her say. "Don't mess with Mommy. She can be mean if you don't wash your hands."

"Right."

"And if you just pretend to eat your veggies but then flush them down the toilet, she'll find out. That's not good either." She paused. "Probably hiding them in the trash is better. We had to use the plunger on some broccoli."

"Um, okay."

Maggie did her best not to laugh. She fixed everyone a plate of pizza with a side of the salad. Root beer to drink. Just one for Emily, or she'd be bouncing off the walls. She set the cupcakes and protein bars aside.

The pair returned to the dining room, and Emily's eyes widened on the goodies, particularly, the pink-frosted ones.

Her gaze lit on the cupcakes and refused to leave. "This is the best dinner ever."

"What? No root beer floats?" Reggie said, looking for the ice cream.

"Yes." Emily danced in place.

Reggie grinned.

"No," Maggie said. "Not unless you eat all your salad. I don't mind if you don't finish the pizza though." Which she knew her daughter would. "But the veggies are a must."

"Aw, man."

Reggie parroted, "Aw, man."

Maggie shook her finger at him. "No nonsense from you, mister."

"Just kidding. I love salad. I can't wait to eat with the two smartest ladies in the city. Emily was telling me all about the solar system. I had no idea about superclusters and voids." He sounded impressed.

"Yes, we watched that on TV the other day, didn't we?"

"And then I got a book at the library about it too." Emily nodded. "I like space."

"I like having smart friends."

Emily gave him a shy smile.

Maggie's heart melted, and she worked to keep things casual and not stare at Reggie as if she wanted to kiss him senseless.

Reggie took the spot next to Emily without having to be directed. She looked to be in heaven as she glanced from Reggie to the food.

Reggie grinned. "A feast for a princess and her super ninja." He glanced at Maggie. "And queen mother. Time to chow down."

"Chow down," Emily repeated, enthused.

While they ate some ridiculously delicious pizza and a lovely salad, Reggie kept sneaking peeks at Maggie, who snuck them right back. Emily, fortunately, didn't see a thing, focused on recounting the details of her entire sleepover to Reggie and Frank, who sat at her side on the floor, desperately hoping for a stray crust to land by him.

"And then Sherry laughed so hard, milk came out of her nose. And it was funny, but also gross."

"Emily."

Reggie coughed, having been drinking.

"You know, root beer has bubbles. I bet bubbles would tickle." She looked intrigued. "Are bubbles coming out your nose?"

"Ah, not yet." Reggie caught his breath. "I'm good. Thanks."

Maggie chewed her pizza, doing her best not to laugh.

"Sherry's brother got mad and cried a lot, because he wanted to play with us."

"Really?" Maggie asked. "Because Sherry's brother is four months old."

"I could tell. He likes Barbie's dream house. I just like her car because we use it to drive to Emily Land."

"That sounds like a neat place," Reggie said and winked at Maggie. "Emily Land, huh? What's that like?"

Emily explained, in detail, about her magical land where everyone and everything bowed to the great and powerful Emily. "And everyone shares, because then we don't fight. Right, Mommy?"

"I think that sounds perfect. I want to live there."

"But I'm in charge. I'm the queen," Emily insisted. "Brownie is my protector. Reggie, you should come too."

"Okay. I will. But maybe not now, because I'm still hungry."

"You eat a lot." Emily stared at his plate, full of crusts.

"Emily, be nice." Maggie gave her daughter a look.

"But he had four pieces."

"Five." Reggie added another slice. "I have to eat a lot to make up for what I use in energy."

Emily sat, enrapt.

"See, building muscle burns calories. You need the good kind of calories though." He grinned at the pizza, soda, and cupcakes. "But sometimes you give yourself a treat. I don't eat pizza and cupcakes all the time. And root beer is only for special occasions. For when I get to visit you."

Emily's eyes grew even wider. "I'm a special occasion?"

"You sure are. Frank was so excited on the way over, he kept barking at me to hurry up. Even he knows how much fun you are."

Emily nodded. "I am."

Maggie stifled a laugh. Her daughter. So modest.

"Just like your mom. She's fun too."

"She is." Emily whispered, not so softly, "Except when she makes me clean a lot. I don't like chores."

"You think you have to clean a lot, you should try being a firefighter."

"Are girls firefighters?"

"Sure are. A long time ago there were just firemen. Now there are firefighters everywhere. My friends Natalie and Lori are on D shift. And one of our lieutenants is a girl." His grin turned naughty, and Maggie felt an unwelcome flare of jealousy that took her off guard. "She looks just like Dora the Explorer. They have the same hair and big, brown eyes. And the guys keep putting Dora stickers on her notebooks." He chuckled. "Sue doesn't think it's funny, but we do. Especially when Dora dolls keep appearing all over her desk, the kitchen, the ladies' room."

"That's terrible." But Maggie had to laugh. "That poor woman."

"I love Dora." Emily nibbled more pizza. "I wish I looked like her."

"You're fine just the way you are," Reggie said before Maggie could. "We should be who we are and not someone else."

"Oh. That's what Mommy says."

"She's right." He smiled at Maggie. She smiled back, feeling a well of something new and deep for this man.

His eyes were so warm, so caring. That wide smile, just for her. When he looked at her, he saw her. The person she was, not someone he wanted her to be, just as he'd said to Emily. And he took his time to explain things to her daughter, not talking down to her, which she truly appreciated.

"Reggie?" Emily asked.

He turned from Maggie to smile down at her. "What's up, princess?"

"Did you bring the baby seeds?"

Reggie had been expecting the question and had time to work up an answer that would hopefully satisfy the little girl. "Well, see, here's the thing. There's something called a growing season. Have you heard of that?"

The little girl shook her head, her eyes wide, innocent. She was such a cutie, a mini version of Maggie.

"Let's take my dad's tomatoes. He can't plant them in the wintertime because they'll die. They need warmth to grow. So he plants them in the summer."

"But it's summer now, Reggie. Can't you plant them in Mommy now?"

God knew he wanted to. *Nope, change that line of thinking right now.* "Right. Well, no. See, when people have babies, they have a special connection. You don't plant baby seeds with just anybody."

"That's true." Maggie finally joined the conversation. He realized her daughter was too young to know where babies really came from, but he would have thought Maggie would have talked to the girl before now, especially because Emily kept bringing up seeds. "When your daddy and I were married, we were in love. And love makes baby seeds grow. And that special love made you."

Emily's face scrunched, a comical sign of confusion. "So you need to get Dad to plant a baby seed?"

Reggie didn't like that idea at all. Fortunately, Maggie didn't either. She looked as if she'd just bitten into something sour.

"Er, no. Not at all. While I still love your dad as *a friend*, he's not my husband anymore. So I'm not, ah, harvesting babies." Her cheeks turned pink. "When two people are in love, they plant the baby seeds together. It's private and lovely and done to make a family."

A family Reggie still had yet to make. But as he sat with Maggie and Emily, watching mother and daughter interact, seeing and feeling the familial bond, Reggie yearned for what they had. And it had more to do with being a part of their family than making one with someone else.

Oh man, I am starting to seriously fall, here.

"Right, Reggie?"

He realized Maggie had asked him for backup. Like he was the dad, and she was the mom, and Emily was their daughter. The fantasy refused to leave him, and all he could do was nod, telling himself to not go down this road again.

Then he looked into Maggie's eyes, saw her appreciation and humor, and couldn't walk away.

"I'll never get a brother." Emily groaned. "It's not fair."

"Why don't you stop wishing for things you don't have and love the things you do have? Frank has been staring at you for the past ten minutes. A lot of little girls would love to have a dog. You have a cute little puppy. Be thankful for that."

"Besides, babies are stinky and yell a lot," Reggie added. "Maybe don't wish for trouble if you don't have to."

"Trouble?"

Maggie explained, "It's a phrase. Don't borrow trouble or wish for trouble. Basically, Reggie is saying you have a good home, an awesome mom, and a puppy. You have two amazing uncles, a new friend in Reggie, and Sherry, just to name a few things to be thankful for. Get it?"

But Emily was busy staring at Frank. "Yes, okay." She glanced back at her mom. "May I please be excused?"

"Impeccable manners," Reggie praised.

Emily sat up straighter.

Maggie's lips twitched. "Yes, you may. Good job."

Emily smiled and left, taking her plate to the sink. "Can I have a cupcake now?"

"After. That's for dessert."

Reggie waited for an argument. Instead, Emily nodded and left. "Come on, Frank."

After they disappeared, he said to Maggie, "You are an awesome mom."

"Thank you." She beamed with pleasure. "I do a lot of things wrong, but parenting, I want to get right. And you're pretty impressive yourself." She reached across the table to cover his hand. "Thank you for being so kind to Emily. I know she can ask a lot of questions. And her fascination with baby seeds has been driving me to distraction."

"I'll bet." He chuckled and moved his hand out from under hers, taking her hand in his. He caressed her, stroking her palm with his thumb. He hadn't meant anything by it except to be closer to her. But her eyes widened, and he felt an answering arousal building within.

She pulled her hand back, and he reluctantly let go. He still didn't understand how she could get to him so easily. He hadn't even been trying to be sexual, yet he'd aroused them both.

"Sorry," they said at the same time. And smiled.

"I, ah, I'll clean up." Maggie stood.

This time he didn't offer to help, needing a moment to calm his raging body.

When he felt more himself, he joined Emily in the back, watching and playing with her while they taught Frank how to sit. Or tried to teach him. The little guy spent more time watching Emily with adoring eyes than listening.

"Oh, I forgot." Emily darted away and returned with a dog bone wrapped in a sloppy bow. "This is for Frank. Sit, Frank."

The dog shocked them both by sitting on command.

"Yay! He sat. He sat." Emily gave Reggie a fierce hug before dancing around the room, which of course set the dog to yapping and darting around.

Unaccountably moved by the simple gesture of affection, Reggie did his best not to make a huge deal out of it in his mind and watched the girl and dog play together.

Maggie found them not long after, announcing cupcakes for anyone interested.

"It's been fifteen minutes," he said to her as they followed Emily into the kitchen. "I thought you said to wait for dessert."

"I'd planned to wait a bit but then realized I need to give my kid time to decompress after she sugars up."

"Ah."

Reggie watched Emily devour the cupcake. Damned if she didn't seem to have a little more energy afterward, but nothing he couldn't handle. They centered around the coffee table to play Uno, which seemed to be Emily's game of choice. To his surprise, she read him a book that seemed too sophisticated for a six-year-old. At least, it was more than Rachel could have handled, and she'd been eight at the time.

Maggie soon called a halt to the festivities, claiming Reggie and she needed a break. "Go get ready for bed. Frank can go with you."

She checked the clock on the wall. "You have another ten minutes until bedtime."

"Aw, Mommy."

"You heard me."

"Fine." Emily sighed. "Can Reggie tuck me in?"

Maggie glanced at him, unsure. "He might have to leave soon?" she said more as a question, giving him an out.

But he didn't need one, the idea of tucking her daughter in bed a sweet way to end the evening. "Nah. I can hang until then."

Emily brightened. "Thanks, Reggie. You're my favorite firefighter."

He chuckled. "I'm sure Mack will be crushed when I tell him."

"I liked Mack." That she remembered his partner surprised him. Mack hadn't said all that much at the library. And that day her mother had been hit had been traumatic. "But he's not as good as you."

"Thanks."

The little girl skipped down the hall, Frank in tow.

"Thanks, Reggie. You don't have to stay, you know."

Confident Emily would make her presence known before she returned, he moved closer to Maggie on the couch and stroked her cheek, taken with her softness. He leaned in for a kiss, doing his damnedest to keep it light.

But one taste of Maggie brought him back for another, and another, only her hand on his chest stopping him from taking more. He pulled back to see her lips full and slick, her pupils large and focused on his mouth.

He gave a low groan. "Sorry. I just wanted to show you that I want to stay, and I've had a terrific time tonight." He couldn't help one more tender kiss.

She sighed into his mouth, her fingers curling into his pecs. When she pulled back, she surprised him by stroking his cheek. "You are so good with her. And me." She smiled. His heart beat so hard, he knew she had to feel it. "I like you a lot, Reggie."

"I like you too, Maggie."

They heard a squeak followed by a bark and both moved away from each other, giving themselves some space.

"So is Maggie short for something?"

"That's one way to break the mood."

He grinned.

"It's short for Margaret, and no, you may not call me that."

"Margaret Swanson?"

"I was Margaret May Ellison before I married Stephen. And I only kept Swanson because of Emily. I didn't want to run into twelve years of questions when Maggie Ellison comes to pick Emily Swanson up from school."

"Huh." He watched her, sensing agitation. "Maggie May. I like it."

She groaned. "I hate it. Never call me that."

"Ah, a weakness."

"Please. You're my weakness." The minute she said it, she flushed.

Good, because you're mine too. "Am I? That's good to know." He looked her over, wondering when they might get horizontal again. Of course, one didn't always need a bed to share pleasure. "Say, Maggie?"

"Yes?"

"Do you mind if I hang out a little after Emily goes to bed? We could watch TV or something." He was counting on that *or something*. Not anything to get loud or wake her daughter. But man, he needed to touch and kiss Maggie some more. Fuck, he *craved* her.

"Or something, hmm?" No fool, Maggie saw what he'd really meant. "Sure." She paused, her eyes smiling. "Let's watch some TV together."

"I'll take it." He'd take whatever he could get, because some time with Maggie was better than no time.

Chapter Sixteen

REGGIE TUCKED EMILY IN, AND WHEN SHE INSISTED ON A KISS to her forehead, the way her mom did it, he knew he'd fallen in love with the little girl. But giving one's heart to a child wasn't selfish, and not something he could guard against. Not that he wanted to.

Despite losing Amy and her daughter, Rachel, he couldn't regret the span of time he'd been a part of their lives. The two years with them had been wonderful but not perfect. Looking back, he realized he and Amy had more than their share of ups and downs. And then they'd ended. He still missed little Rachel, but he hoped he'd made some positive impact she might remember years later.

"Good night, Emily." He left her night-light on and shut her door to keep Frank inside.

He still didn't know if he'd take the little guy with him when he left, but he'd let Maggie make that call.

He rejoined her in the living room, where the television was on and a root beer float waited for him. He chuckled. "I was kidding about dying for one of those. I brought it for Emily."

"And the protein bars?"

"An alternative to all the sugar." He grabbed one before sitting with her on the couch and enjoyed the yogurt-covered oat bar. "It's good for you and an energy boost."

"You need energy to handle me, I see. Good to know."

"Energy and a whip and chains," he murmured, wondering how she felt about wearing leather in bed, and grinned.

"I don't even want to know what just went through your mind."

"Nothing much."

"Ha. Don't play innocent with me. I live with that. Doesn't work."

He patted the spot next to him, amused at the distance she thought she could maintain. "Come closer. I don't bite." He added softly, "Hard."

When she settled next to him, everything felt right. He wrapped an arm around her shoulders and let her pick a fun sitcom to watch. Both aroused and content at the same time, he would have thought to feel unnerved. Instead he was happy. Fucking ecstatic just to be with her.

She sat on his right, her good arm tucked against his side.

"You still doing okay with the cast?"

"It's not bothering me as much. Now I just want it off."

"Hold on, Supergirl. You have another few weeks before you're anywhere near to being healed."

"Ugh."

"What?"

"How come it's Super*man* but not Super*woman*? Supergirl?" She sneered. "How about Superboy? I don't hear that often."

"Because you don't read comics. There are a few Superwoman characters, actually. And there's a Superboy. His name is Kon-El, and he goes by Conner Kent. He was cloned."

She blinked at him.

"What? I'm trying to educate you."

She rolled her eyes and said something under her breath.

"Did you just call me a nerd?" He laughed. "Because I just had a conversation with the guys on this very topic two days ago."

"If the shoe fits…"

He grinned. "Quit making fun of me. You're hurting my ego."

She snorted and cuddled close.

"And now you're distracting me from the show. Not nice, Maggie." He actually had no idea what was happening on-screen, hyperaware of everything that was Maggie Swanson.

She shifted, and her hand settled on his thigh.

His temperature rose.

"You ever watch this show?" she asked. She rolled her fingers on his thigh, tapping.

"No. I like TV, but usually I stream something. I don't have cable."

"What do you like to watch?"

You, coming. Probably not the best thing to say with her daughter down the hall. Still, what could she expect with her hand on his thigh, perilously close to his steel-hard dick? Had she noticed? His jeans were tight with a capital T. Sitting had become uncomfortable.

"I, ah, I like sci-fi shows," he said, trying not to think about tightness or tight fits. "Fantasy, adventure. I don't mind comedy, actually. But the Lifetime and Hallmark channels aren't my favorites."

"Everyone assumes if you're a woman, you have to like those channels." She stopped tapping, *finally*, but did something far worse. She rubbed her hand up and down his leg, from this knee to his pelvis, way too close to his erection. He didn't even think her aware of it, because she talked and watched the TV without looking at him. While he could focus on nothing but her scent, her touch, and how fucking close she sat.

"But I'm not into sweet romance. And some of the stuff on Lifetime isn't real enough for me. It's not dark enough."

"Dark? You?"

"Well, I like a happy ending."

Don't we all.

"But I like more serious drama than the psycho babysitter or stalker cheater guy because everyone who cheats gets a stalker in the end. Not that I mind that premise. I'm very much into fidelity."

"Good. Me too." He sucked in a breath when her hand shifted and grazed his dick.

"Oh, sorry."

"Yeah." He was only sorry he had his jeans on. She could touch him wherever she liked.

The sitcom continued as Reggie sat in his own personal hell for the next half hour, simultaneously tortured by the dick that wouldn't quit and gladdened to have Maggie near.

"I'll be right back," she said and left him.

He swallowed a groan and spread his thighs wide, needing some relief. Unfortunately, Maggie returned sooner than he expected. She saw his legs spread, and he swore she tried to bite back a grin.

"Emily's fast sleep. Frank barely twitched when I went in. He's lying next to her, and she's hugging him. It's adorable."

"Yeah. She's a cutie," he agreed, wishing his voice hadn't gone so deep. He sounded aroused while she looked unaffected and amused.

"Oh, I'm a bad hostess." Instead of offering him something to drink though, she knelt between his spread legs and reached for the snap on his jeans.

Everything inside him lit up with a *hell, yes!*

"Maggie?" he growled.

"Shh. I need you to be very quiet now." She worked the fly of his jeans open, but he was pressing so hard against the material, there wasn't much room to maneuver. "Don't you want to feel better?"

Reggie answered by easing his pants down to free his cock, now stiffly pointing at the ceiling, his underwear caught under his swollen balls. He couldn't help seeing how thick he was, the fluid beading over his cockhead a testament to his desire.

"Listen up for Emily, okay?"

"What…?" His eyes rolled to back of his head as soft lips enveloped him. He felt heat and suction as she took him in her mouth and started blowing him.

"Oh, fuck, Maggie," he whispered and pushed her hair aside, wanting to watch. "Yeah, more. *Please.*"

She licked and sucked, her tongue like magic as she stroked his shaft. Then she grazed his balls, cupping them, rubbing as she moved over him faster. She took him deep, and he did his best not to shout, keeping his appreciation to a lot of heavy breathing and whispered moans.

"I want to fuck you so hard," he admitted as she brought him closer to heaven. "So deep. Coming in you," he said, excited and close.

She rubbed his balls faster, then she grabbed the base of his shaft, pumping while she sucked, adding more friction.

"Maggie, I'm so close. Gonna come, baby. Right now."

Expecting her to move away and finish him with her hand, he instead felt her suck harder, her hand closing around the base of him with an even firmer grip.

He tried to hold back, but Reggie couldn't stop. "Coming," he warned in a strangled whisper and jetted into her mouth.

The pleasure undid him, and he jerked and moaned, his hands suddenly on the back of her head, keeping her in place as he emptied. He couldn't help himself, thrusting between her lips, her name the only thing he could say as he saw bliss.

He had no awareness of anything as he shuddered from his orgasm, lying there while Maggie finally released him. She licked him clean, and he stroked her hair, falling so hard for this woman who'd held him in place with nothing more than her mouth and one small hand.

"You taste good," she said in a low voice and smiled up at him. Gently, she tucked him back into his underwear. He straightened his jeans and refastened them with shaky hands, still seeing stars.

"I can't believe you did that. I'm so...done." He sagged back, pleased when she joined him, pressed against his side again. "Maggie. Thank you." He kissed her. "Thank you, thank you, thank you."

She laughed softly, one hand on his chest, feeling his racing heart. "You seemed pent up."

"Oh?" He cleared his throat. "You did it, teasing me with that hand on my leg. Tell me you weren't."

"So maybe I was."

He drew her into his lap, her legs lying perpendicular across his. "What about you?"

"Me?"

After all she'd done to him, he didn't want to leave her unsatisfied. Reggie kissed her, sliding his tongue into her mouth. Kissing Maggie, he expressed how he felt without words, just the press of lips and tongue.

She moaned, and he smiled and kissed his way to ear. "Did you like blowing me? Did it make you wet?" He didn't wait for her answer but slid a hand down her belly. Unlike his jeans, her shorts had an elastic waist. He continued past her shorts and panties, delving into the heat of her with satisfaction.

"So wet." He tongued her ear, leaving his hand against her but not doing more than cupping her pussy.

He could kiss her forever, and the kisses they shared soon turned more passionate. Maggie turned ravenous, which in turn stoked his fire hotter. She didn't hide her desire, and her honest need turned him *way* on.

He moved his fingers, sliding between her folds, and she shivered. Eager for every whispered moan, every muffled cry, he slid a finger inside her.

She stiffened, gripping his shoulder while arching into his hand.

"*Reggie.*" She kissed his neck, the underside of his chin. "Please."

He kissed her lips, drawing her in as he rubbed her clit and added a second finger, then he thrust deep. He curled his fingers inside her, and she moved more urgently, riding his hand while he brought her close to climax.

He shoved them hard, getting rougher at her urging, and ground his palm against her clit. Once, twice, then she moaned into his mouth, her body gripping his fingers tight, so fucking wet. He was hard again, wanting inside her like crazy. But not here, where Emily might interrupt.

"Come with me." He removed his hand and quickly drew her to her feet.

"I just did," she muttered as she moved with him on shaky legs.

"Check on Emily, would you?" he asked as they stood in front of the bathroom.

Maggie came back. "She's still out."

He tugged her into the bathroom, turned on the light, and closed the door, locking it.

"Reggie?"

"Shh. Quiet." He pulled down her shorts and underwear and turned her around. "Face the mirror."

Her hands rested against the sink, and she watched him in the mirror. "What are you doing?" she asked, her voice reedy with excitement.

"Fucking you. Shh." He stared at that perfect ass and palmed her, loving how she felt. Maggie stood a good head shorter than he did, but her presence made her seem bigger. Like now, as he stared at her ass, her toned thighs, and wondered when he'd fallen so hard under her spell. Because she'd sure as hell bewitched him.

He shoved his pants down and pulled her hips back. He crouched, staring at her wet pussy, her flesh swollen. He planted a kiss there, and she tensed all over and sighed. She melted over his tongue, and he couldn't wait any longer. Reggie rose and nudged her ankles apart. He stepped between them.

Positioning himself at her pussy, his excitement ratcheted to an unbearable level, he slowly entered her sex. He watched her in the mirror, loving her flushed cheeks, the way her full lips parted as she gasped. So slowly, he kept pushing inside, enjoying the way her slick channel gripped him with each inch.

"Oh *yes.*"

He groaned, the sheer pleasure indescribable. He didn't stop until he was balls-deep inside her. So hot and tight, her snug pussy fit as if made for him. And then he did what he'd been wanting to. Reggie *moved*.

"You're so big inside me."

"I've been dying to take you this way." From behind, where she squeezed him even tighter. Seeing her while he thrust was like every fantasy he'd ever had compressed into one perfect moment.

He looked down, watching himself slide in and out of her, seeing his dick disappear. The erotic sight undid him, and he couldn't hold back. Her breathy moans grew shorter.

The slap of his body against hers added to the intensity.

He swore he grew thicker as he slid through her wet heat, unable to stop.

"I'm coming," he warned just as he shoved one final time and stilled.

He barely held back a roar, his orgasm stealing what few brain cells he had left. He just stood there, jetting hard, filling Maggie with everything he had left.

It felt like forever and not long enough as he came back to himself. He heard nothing but them both breathing hard. As he remained inside her, he brought his hands around to caress her breasts, loving the aroused handfuls.

"Reggie. You're so deep inside me," Maggie whispered. "I think this might be my new favorite position."

Trust his Maggie to be excited to try it again and not affronted because he'd taken her like a wild man out of control. Fucking her from behind down the hall from her sleeping daughter.

"We need to try them all." He kissed her throat and continued to kiss his way to her cheek. When she turned her head, he met her mouth once more, the feel of her lips against his everything he'd ever wanted. He ended the kiss with a sigh. "Maggie, I could spend the rest of my"—*life*—"night inside you."

"I wish."

He watched her as he withdrew, loving her look of

disappointment. He cleaned her up with a washcloth, bemused when she watched him cleaning himself.

"I love looking at you. You're beautiful. Or should I say handsome?"

"Yeah, handsome. Beautiful is for chicks," he teased, his voice breaking at the end. He would have felt more embarrassed, except he was still high on his orgasm.

She took the washcloth from him and found a towel to dry him off, treating him gently. Caring for him. "Right. Handsome. And not just your cock. I mean all of you." She reluctantly let him go.

Reggie never got tired of hearing Maggie say the word "cock." He set his clothes to rights then washed his hands next to her.

They left the bathroom and headed back to the living room, where the television remained on.

Reggie wanted to strip them both down and touch and suck and lick until they came a few more times. Reality, unfortunately, dictated other plans.

"Guess I should head out."

"Yeah." She entwined her hand with his and walked him to the door.

"Do you want me to leave Frank?"

"Would you?"

He nodded. "Frank's harness and leash are in Emily's room. And I brought some extra food for him in case he needed it. He's a puppy, so you'll have to take him out at three and again at six. I've got him on a routine."

"Three? In the morning?" She cringed. "Okay. I can do that." She paused at the door and looked at him.

He looked back, his heart racing, his mind not sure what to do about all these feelings.

Maggie let go of his hand and put hers over his heart. "Thanks for coming over."

"Thanks for blowing me." He blinked, nonplussed that had

come out, but then, his brain was still rebooting. "Oh, Christ. I meant to say 'thanks for having me.'"

She laughed, and the tension that had been building faded. "Anytime. I mean that." She wiggled her brows, her joy infectious.

"Witch." He leaned down to kiss her, then set his forehead against hers. So in lust and in—like, *so much* like—for this woman, he didn't know what to do. "When can I see you again?"

She pulled back, and the look in her eyes captivated him. There was affection there, desire, and something deeper. She kind of looked the way he feared he felt. Then she smiled at him.

Oh fuck, I am so gone for her.

"Text me your schedule, okay? We'll plan on a date, and I'll get a babysitter for Emily."

He nodded. "I had a lot of fun tonight. And I don't just mean between you and me. Emily's a wonderful little girl."

"Yes, she is. I'm so glad you see that too. She likes you a lot, Reggie."

A vague remnant of past mistakes warned him to be cautious, but right now, he couldn't seem to care. "Yeah. Well, I like the Swanson girls just as much. Or, I'm sorry, the Swanson *women*."

She grinned. "There you go." She kissed him. "Now get out of here before I strip down and demand you lick me all over."

He wiped a hand over his face. "Great. Now I'll be hard all the way home. Thanks a lot."

He left hearing her laughter, and that made his night even better.

Reggie paused outside her door, the moon waning, the stars bright. He hadn't realized how much time they'd spent together because it seemed to go by so fast.

He hated to go home and sleep alone. Having held her in his arms, he was loath to go back to that lonely sphere of bachelorhood. Reggie liked his own space, and he appreciated time alone. He liked himself. But with Maggie, he started to feel like he belonged at her side.

That trickle of worry he'd been trying to ignore swelled, shattering his peace. Of course, having sex with Maggie felt good. Of course, it made sense he'd enjoy himself with a beautiful woman and her sweet kid. But none of that equated to happily ever after.

He had to avoid the same old patterns he constantly fell into. Hell, he knew that. But then, was this really a pattern?

Playing devil's advocate with himself outside his girlfriend's—no, his *friend's*—door after rip-roaring sex was nothing short of pathetic. But who else did he want to talk to about this? Brad, maybe. Tex? Not Mack, because the guy was a confirmed bachelor and didn't seem to have any problems with women. Despite their teasing, when Mack wanted a date, he got one. And he seemed to have no hang-ups when it came to relationships.

Both Brad and Tex had made some major mistakes with their girlfriends, so they could relate to Reggie's messed-up love life. But he didn't need them worrying about him, and he didn't need unasked-for advice. He just needed to unload some anxiety.

But she's not my girlfriend. Why am I worrying? Hell, can't I just enjoy my night? needy Reggie asked himself.

No, you can't. That's not how we live life, pragmatic Reggie answered.

He struggled with the need to make sense of everything now.

Why can't I just be that guy who likes getting laid and leave it at that?

Because it's a hell of a lot more than that, and you know it. Don't be a dumbass.

Maggie was no friend with benefits. Well, she was, in the sense that she gave him hotter orgasms than he'd ever had in his life. But Maggie meant something to him. Something that scared him because he knew that familiar tingle in his heart, the one that burned when the dreaded L-word emerged.

"Yo, you okay?"

Reggie turned to see a giant walking toward him, and he didn't look welcoming. Reggie tensed. The man looked familiar, likely the one he'd passed the last time he'd been to Maggie's. And then he remembered her talking about her friends. How many neighbors around here would be six foot six?

"Are you Benny?"

The man smiled, and the awful expression he'd been wearing disappeared, leaving a not-so-angry giant behind. He had brown hair threaded with gray that met his shoulders and wore a pair of jeans and a faded, blue T-shirt, showcasing sleeves of tattoos. His biceps looked like boulders, and Reggie would be hard-pressed to make his hands fit around the guy's neck. Behind him came Doug, the man who'd been with Emily at the library.

"Hi, Reggie." Doug nodded. "Remember me?"

"Yep. You're Doug. You guys are Maggie's friends."

"Yeah." Benny looked him over, but Reggie couldn't tell what he thought. "Hey, you look like you could use a beer. Want to come over?"

Reggie looked at them, then at Maggie's closed door. His mind started to clear, and he could think again without the haze of lust, needy affection, and worry clouding his thinking. "Sure, why not?"

Once inside their apartment, he noticed right away the differences between their space and Maggie's. Unlike her warm, cozy home, theirs felt like a designer showpiece. Comfortable but extremely high-end. Natural tones on the walls, beech hardwood floors, and Scandinavian-style furniture that could accommodate a man of Benny's size had been tastefully chosen to accentuate the modern feel of the space.

The living area led into a spacious dining area, complete with a long, wooden table and six chairs. The kitchen, very unlike Maggie's, would have looked at home on a cooking show. It had black granite counters, white cabinets, and a big-ass kitchen island that could seat four easily, not to mention all the stainless-steel appliances.

"Farther down the hall, we have three bedrooms and two baths," Benny explained. "And yeah, Maggie has the smallest unit in the building."

"Huh."

Doug smiled. "First time I went from our place to Maggie's, I had the same look on my face." He pulled three different kinds of beer from the fridge and offered Reggie his choice.

"Thanks." Reggie chose a tasty Peddler horchata cream ale he'd had before.

"So. You're Reggie." Benny's stare made Reggie a little uncomfortable. This guy was Maggie's friend, so Reggie didn't want to come across as antagonistic, but if the guy didn't blink soon, he'd have to say something, if only to get that serial killer expression off his face.

Doug rolled his eyes. He handed Benny the pale ale and kept for himself the imperial stout before plopping down at the island. "Ignore my husband. Please, sit."

Reggie did, then looked back at Benny and scowled. "Why do you look so familiar to me?"

"I have that kind of face."

Doug snorted.

"No. It's…" Reggie leaned toward him, searching.

Benny sighed and pulled his hair back, then put a sneer on his face. "This help?" He snarled for effect.

Reggie gaped. "*Bear Destruction!* Dude, you were my hero! How many titles did you win on the semipro circuit? Holy shit. I can't believe it's you. You're awesome." Reggie still didn't quite believe it, but why would someone try to impersonate a retired wrestler from a now-defunct league?

Benny flushed. "Surprised you recognized me."

"I didn't at first, but something kept nagging me." Reggie couldn't stop staring and knew he was acting like an idiot. But… *Bear Destruction!* "I have to get your autograph before you kick me out for fanboying you."

Benny gave a large grin. "Nah, that's cool."

"For Pete's sake. Benny, sit down. You're looming again."

Benny sat at the corner of the island, next to Doug.

The truth struck Reggie right then. "You're gay." He felt like an idiot saying the obvious. "Sorry, it's just, you had a ton of groupies back in the day. Didn't they used to call you the Titty Magnet?"

Doug snickered.

"Yeah." Benny cleared his throat. "Sadly, that was never my thing. But to please the promoters, I did what I had to do."

"That must have sucked."

"It truly did. And not in a good way."

Reggie laughed. "I'll bet."

"But man, I can tell the difference between a fake job and the real thing from half a room away. I've signed so many bare chests, you wouldn't believe it."

"That how you met Doug?"

Doug choked on his beer.

Benny laughed. "Him? Mr. Priss?"

"Benny."

"Nah. His brother, a great guy, by the way, dragged him to a match. Doug and I fell in love."

"In lust, then love." Doug shrugged. "I like to be honest."

"Oh, please. I hooked you like a largemouth bass."

"Largemouth? Really?" Doug looked peeved.

Reggie cut in, "If he knew anything about wrestling, he'd have been hooked on your backbreaker hammer claw."

Benny's grin widened. "You *are* a fan."

"To Bear Destruction," Reggie toasted.

They all drank to that.

Then Doug forestalled more wrestling talk. "Okay, enough about Benny. What's the deal with you and Maggie?"

Chapter Seventeen

Benny said with a raised brow, "You looked a little lost outside Maggie's door. Did dinner not go well?"

"How did you know about dinner?" Reggie asked.

Doug huffed. "First, we know everything. Second, Emily talked about nothing but your dinner all day."

"Emily likes you." When Benny didn't smile, he looked intimidating. Like a dark cloud blotting out the sun. Damn. Bear Destruction for sure. "She said you were pretty." Then he smiled. "I'd have to agree."

Reggie blinked. "Ah, thank you?"

"Can we keep him, Doug? Can we?"

Doug guzzled his beer. "Benny, stop it. You're scaring Reggie."

"He's not, really, I—"

"Tell us what's on your mind," Doug interrupted, his voice relaxed. "Was dinner okay?"

"Dinner was great. Emily is funny and smart. She loves the puppy and played with him. I also learned she's a demon at Uno and has a vocabulary that would put my coworkers to shame." He grinned at the thought, saw Benny and Doug exchange a look, and continued as if they hadn't. "Maggie was gracious, as always." *Holy fuck, was she.* He cleared his throat. "We ate pizza and cupcakes. And salad. It was nice."

"Uh-huh. Nice." Benny didn't seem to be believing him.

"It was." Great, now Reggie sounded defensive.

"Then why so serious outside her door?"

"Why should I tell you anything? You're her friends. You'll blab."

"We won't," Doug denied.

"We totally will." Benny nodded.

Reggie couldn't help laughing at the glare Doug shot him.

"Look, we love Maggie. We just want to make sure you're not a bad guy for her."

"And that would be...?"

"Someone who just wants an easy lay," Doug said. "She's not easy."

"Or rich or connected," Benny added. "She's a single mom with a great kid. She's like our sister. We look out for her."

"She's amazing," Reggie said bluntly. "I'm not sure why she's still single."

"Because she wants to be," Doug said, just as blunt. "She looks out for Emily first, herself second. She'll help either of us at the drop of a hat, even if it means rescheduling something for herself. That's the kind of person she is."

Reggie decided to pump them for some information since they felt entitled to question him. "So what's her deal then? Is she really over her ex?"

"Totally." Doug nodded. "What about you? Any exes rattling around in your closet?"

"A few."

"You over them?"

"Mostly."

"Hmm." Benny frowned. "Maggie is not a rebound chick."

"I know that."

"She's also not a one-night stand chick."

"I know that too."

"She's beautiful, inside and out. And funny."

"What can you tell me that I *don't* know?"

Benny and Doug studied him.

"Go ahead. Ask me anything you want. I tell you something, you tell me something."

"A fair trade," Doug agreed. "Fine. I can tell you that Maggie is a romantic. She loves flowers, milk chocolate truffles, and the language of love. So, if you're not the expressive type, she's not the girl for you."

"Okay." So his flowers had been spot-on. Words, hmm? He could do that.

Benny drank and watched him. "Question: Have you ever cheated on any of your exes?"

"Nope."

"Ever done drugs?"

"I smoked pot once back in high school."

"How old are you?" Doug asked.

"Thirty-three. How old are you?"

"How old do I *look*?"

At the glint in Doug's eye and Benny's grin, Reggie knew to err on the side of youth. "I don't know. Thirty-one?"

"Oh, I do like you."

Benny shook his head. "Suck-up."

"Ignore him, Reggie."

Reggie tried not to laugh so much, but he found himself relaxing with the pair. "My turn. Does Maggie's family not support her at all? When she was hurt, no one came to visit but you guys." He knew her parents had died, but she had no other relatives nearby?

Doug frowned. "Her parents are both deceased. I think she has a few cousins and an aunt on her mom's side, but they're all assholes she hasn't talked to since her folks' funeral. She had Stephen, but they're divorced."

"Are they still friends?"

"Yes. Stephen's not a bad guy. He's just not a great guy for Maggie."

"Hmm."

"Our turn," Benny said. "Do you have money?"

"I'm comfortable but not rich. I have my own house, my own car, and don't live with my dad. That what you want to know?"

"Pretty much, yes."

"Does Stephen help out with Emily's child support?" Reggie asked.

"Yes. He's a responsible father." Doug nodded. "Financially anyway."

"You a gym rat?" Benny asked, eyeing Reggie's arms and chest. "Not into steroids, are you? Those aren't healthy."

Reggie didn't get a prurient sense of interest from the man. "No. I like to work out. It's part of the job, but it's also a hobby."

"What do you bench?"

"My max? Three hundred, but that was a while ago. Now I do reps for max effort, not max weight."

"Nice. Three hundred isn't bad."

"Okay. I gotta know. Your max?"

Benny made a muscle, and Reggie was damn impressed. "Three seventy-five was my heaviest. But I used to lift guys in the ring who easily weighed two forty, two fifty."

"No shit." Impressive.

"But all that took a toll on his body, which is why he retired," Doug said.

"You're smart." Reggie sipped his beer and nodded. "I can't imagine the strain on your joints and muscles day after day doing those stunts. Good move to retire while you're still young. Remember Old Bob Rocket?"

"Poor bastard." Benny sighed. "I came on right as he left. Broke his neck doing a stupid chair battle. A newbie broke a chair over the back of his head instead of his middle back. Crushed his C-1 and C-2 vertebrae."

"Ended up on a ventilator and died a month later, didn't he?" Reggie remembered that.

Doug frowned. "You two are easily distracted."

Benny sighed. "Sorry."

"The question for you Reggie, is what are your intentions toward *Maggie?*"

"Is this where you whip out a shotgun and nudge us both toward the preacher to get married?"

Benny choked on his beer laughing. In a terrible Southern accent, he asked, "What are your intentions, good sir?" He turned to his husband. "Easy, Doug. Reggie's a good guy."

"You just like him because he loves Bear Destruction."

"Well, yeah. But also because he's a decent guy. Emily thinks he's the shit. And Maggie asked him to dinner on *a date*." To Reggie, he said, "That's a big deal, you know."

"Oh?"

"Maggie's pretty particular when it comes to dating. She never lets a guy come over to meet the evil little genius. I mean never."

"Well, to be fair, I met Emily first. Then Maggie."

"True." Doug nodded then turned red. "And, ah, for the record, that story Emily told about me…"

"About the nonstop pooping?" Reggie had to tease the guy.

Benny guffawed.

"I had a serious stomach bug two years ago. It's not a regular occurrence or anything."

"Good to know."

Benny's eyes narrowed. "Huh. You're really a fireman. An EMT, right?"

"I am."

"You're almost a doctor."

"Not quite," Reggie said wryly. "I'm a few letters away from that, and I have no aspirations to become one."

"But you're smart and handy to have around. And you're not puny." Benny nodded as he looked Reggie over. "Stephen's puny. I don't like him."

"Stephen's like me," Doug protested. "He's lean and fit. Nothing wrong with that."

"Not on you. You're gorgeous. Stephen. Ech. I don't like him."

Reggie liked Benny. And he had to admit, Benny had a point.

Doug was a pretty good-looking guy. Though Reggie wasn't into dating men, he wasn't one of those guys who couldn't tell if a man was attractive. He knew what women liked. And they typically liked movie-star handsome.

"Are you guys done with your questions?" he asked after a moment.

"I am. For now," Doug said.

"I'm good." Benny paused. "So... What was your favorite match?"

Excited to talk about it, he ignored Doug's groan and went back in time to Bear Destruction versus the Kobra Khan. An hour and one selfie later, he knew he needed to leave. It had grown late, and Benny needed to work in the morning.

"Great meeting you guys. Nice to have the faces to go with everything Maggie says about you." He grinned at Benny.

Doug raised a brow. "What does she say, exactly?"

"You're her best friends. And she loves you guys."

"Well, that's true." Doug smiled. "We are a big deal."

"The ego on that one." Benny rolled his eyes.

Reggie readied to leave and said to hell with it. He didn't want to talk to the guys at work and have them all over his ass. Talking to his family was as bad, if not worse. His father might share more tips on how to properly woo a lady. Great for an earlier generation; a bit out of touch in this decade.

But Benny and Doug had a warmth and shared affection Reggie wanted. "Can I ask you guys something?"

"Sure." Benny nodded.

"How do you know?"

"Know?" Doug asked.

Benny understood. "He means if you're in love. How do you know?"

"And don't read anything into that," Reggie said. "I just met Maggie not too long ago. We're friends. I was just curious, because you guys are married. Most of my friends have girlfriends, though two are nearly engaged. You went all the way. How did you know you picked the right guy?"

Benny nodded at Doug. "He's good with words. I'll let him tell you. Me? I saw a fuckin' hot guy who made my heart race. I thought about him day and night and still do. That's how I knew."

Doug gave Benny such a loving look that Reggie felt oddly out of place. And then he found himself thinking of Maggie in those exact same terms and felt a light sweat break out. His feelings for her didn't make a lick of sense, considering he didn't really know her.

"I would add to that eloquent statement that love isn't logical," Doug said. "Sometimes what makes sense to others doesn't make sense to us. No one can tell you how to feel, Reggie. And no one can tell you you're wrong for feeling what you do."

"Yeah?" He brushed a hand over his head, nervous and not sure why. "Because I got burned by an ex who has a kid, and my friends keep telling me I'm repeating a pattern with Maggie. But she's not like anyone I've ever met. And she's hot as fuck." He blinked, not sure why he'd confessed *that* to her friends.

Doug's smile made his face light up. "I have no idea what your past was like, but Maggie is unlike anyone I know. She's sweet, genuine, and loyal. And she doesn't play games. If that's someone you want in your life, you've picked the right woman."

"See? He's got all the words." Benny smiled at Doug.

"Yeah, he is pretty good at that. Well, I need to go." Reggie opened the door. "Thanks, guys."

"Anytime, Reggie." Benny stood. "And don't be afraid to use my number. Doug and I are always down for beer and sexy firemen."

Doug covered his eyes. "I can't take him anywhere."

Benny frowned. "I'm at home."

Reggie laughed and left, comforted and not sure why.

Friday morning, Maggie felt sad. Then exhilarated. Then guilty for feeling exhilarated.

Two whole weeks to herself. She had no idea what she'd do with all that time.

Stephen had returned early from a conference and wanted Emily to stay with him for two weeks. While she loved her daughter dearly and would miss her, Maggie couldn't deny she could use some downtime. Not worrying about what to make for dinner or how to occupy her little girl all day. Constantly inspecting clean teeth, a clean face, and picked-up toys could be wearing.

"Are you sure?" she asked him on the phone. She pulled it back to stare at it. Yep. Stephen Swanson's contact name and number looked back at her. She put the phone to her ear again.

"Yes. I missed the last two visits and still feel terrible about it. I want to make it up to her." He paused. "Is that okay?"

"It's okay with me." Maggie looked at her daughter. "Would you like to ask Emily?"

"Please."

Maggie handed the phone to her daughter with a smile. "It's Daddy."

"Daddy!" Emily grabbed the phone and started talking about how much she'd missed him, and Frank was so furry, and Nadia had amazing braids, and Sherry had milky burps, and Reggie had bandaged a broken ankle and brought pizza and cupcakes and root beer.

Reggie.

Oh boy. Maggie had no idea how Stephen might react to Reggie. Then again, Emily only knew him as a friend. Heck, for that matter, Stephen had no idea Maggie had broken her arm. Though they'd been divorced for three years, they remained friends. At first, the breakup had been tough, but as the months went by, both realized it had been for the best.

Stephen now pursued his dreams, and she raised Emily while doing what she wanted with her life.

"Frankenstein is his whole name. He's so cute, Daddy." Emily pulled the phone away. "Say hi to Daddy, Frank." The puppy sniffed the phone.

"Emily, Frank can't talk, but you can. Talk to your father."

She put the phone back to her ear. "Huh? Reggie? He's the EMT who does BLS and puts out fires. He has big muscles and plants baby seeds when it's summer."

Maggie groaned.

"With Mommy? No. He's my friend first. He was at the library then in the ambulance."

Before Stephen got any more vaguely troublesome details, Maggie plucked the phone from her daughter.

Emily frowned. "Hey."

"Stephen? It's me. Two weeks ago, Emily spotted Frank in the middle of the street near the grocery store. I went to scoop him up and got hit by a car."

"*Holy shit.* Are you okay? Why didn't you tell me?"

"You were in Denmark. What could you have done?"

"I'd have flown back," he blustered.

But he wouldn't have. Stephen was all about his job, and he didn't owe her anything. Not anymore. "I'm fine. I have a cool cast. Emily got a puppy. And our new friend Reggie was the EMT on duty. He helped me, and he taught a class at the library a week before that, which is how Emily first met him. He's a firefighter. A genuinely nice man who also helps with a pet charity, so he's been helping with Frank." She didn't know why she felt uncomfortable about Stephen knowing she might be interested in Reggie. *Might be? Ha.*

Then again, it was no one's business but her own. And Emily had no idea.

"And baby seeds?" Stephen asked. "What the hell is that about?" He paused. "Are you pregnant?"

She burst out laughing. "You're kidding, right?"

"Oh."

"You sound relieved. Don't worry. It's not yours." She laughed again, because that was damn funny. "Emily's been harping about baby seeds and baby pills since her friend, Sherry, got a little brother. Emily wanted a turtle, you'll remember."

"That I remember. She still talks about the turtle."

"She ended up with a puppy instead, which she absolutely loves. And now she thinks if someone gives me baby seeds, I'll have a baby. Since Reggie is a medically trained professional, our astute daughter guessed he could help me out."

"If he's seen you, he no doubt wants to," Stephen muttered.

Flattered, she nonetheless ignored the remark. "Right. Well, to recap, Reggie is a good guy. Doug and Benny helped out when I was down, and Emily's doing just fine. She's super excited to visit."

"But what about Frank?" Emily cried.

Stephen, typically kind but stern about rules—he'd been a no-pets parent for years—shocked her. "Tell her Frank can come too. I was going to get a kitten. Maybe we can see if Frank gets along with cats."

"A kitten?"

Emily's eyes grew wide. "A kitten!"

Stephen swore. "Damn it. That was supposed to be a surprise."

"You should have led with that."

"Oh well."

"A kitten?" That didn't make much sense for her world-traveling ex. "How are you going to make that work?"

"I have some things in the pipeline. Don't worry about it."

Well, okay then, Mr. Tone. "I'm not. Just making conversation."

"Sorry. I didn't mean to snap at you. I just got in, actually, and I'm feeling frazzled. Denmark was terrific. It's leading to some opportunities for a lot less travel." Stephen sighed. "I'm tired, Maggie."

"I'll bet." He spent three quarters of the year jet-setting to firms, consulting.

"It'll be nice when I can relax and start doing more remote work. It's been a long time coming, but I'm finally situated where this can be a possibility."

"I know Emily will be happy to hear that."

"Don't say anything until I'm sure."

He'd broken enough promises. She understood far too well. "No worries, Stephen. That kind of news isn't my business. It's yours. But about Emily, are you sure you want her to visit tomorrow?"

"Yes, I do, if that's okay. I'll spend today cleaning up and settling back in. And really, the house is spotless. I'll just be dusting and doing laundry."

"Tomorrow's fine. Would noon be okay?"

"Great. And if you can, maybe stick around for lunch? I haven't seen you in a while. We should talk."

Talk? What did that mean? "Sounds good. We'll be there."

"Bye."

"See you then." It had taken Maggie a while to be able to handle having a friendly relationship with Stephen. But fortunately, they did get along. And with her marauding tiny terror, that could only be a good thing.

"I'm going to Daddy's." Emily's grin stretched from ear to ear. "Mommy, I'm going to pack." Emily tore down the hallway, and Frank followed.

Maggie stood there, staring down at her phone. She felt a little unnerved that Stephen wanted to talk. But she didn't worry. They had agreed to joint custody, with Maggie as the primary caregiver, three years ago, and she'd never kept him from seeing his daughter whenever he wanted. At the time, he'd been so into his job, he hadn't protested. But what if he did now?

What if he did? The fear that threatened to rise didn't. She might not love Stephen the way she once had, but she trusted him.

And he was a good father in that he wanted the best for Emily. Maggie could and did provide a stable home, whereas he couldn't, never home long enough to provide constancy.

Unless that pipeline he was talking about proved to be a job here in Seattle, where he could see Emily all the time. And really, would that be so bad?

She needed to think on that. But in the meantime…

She dialed Reggie's number.

He answered in two rings. "Hello there. Just the person I was thinking about."

She grew giddy. "Hi, handsome." She glanced down the hallway, hoping she hadn't been too loud. Then she heard pop music from her daughter's room. Perfect.

"How are you this morning?"

"Well, after waking at three and again at six, I got an hour of blissful sleep before Emily and Frank jumped on me at seven."

"Ouch."

"Then we watched *SpongeBob* reruns, ate breakfast, and walked with Frank at Seward Park. We just got back when I got a call from my ex."

"Oh?"

"He just got back to town. Emily's going to stay with him for the next two weeks."

"*Oh.*" She could hear his smile. "Well, now. That's something, isn't it?"

"Yeah." She smacked herself in the head for sounding so breathless. *Get a grip, Maggie.* "I guess I don't need a babysitter after all."

"I am so hard right now."

Her nipples were poking through her shirt. And she wasn't cold.

He coughed. "I mean, I can't wait for us to go out on an actual date." He laughed low. "Just think, we can be as loud as we want. We can walk naked around my house. Or hell, yours.

But in all seriousness, I can't wait to spend time together with our clothes on."

"I want that too. You make me laugh. And not because you're so easy to get a rise out of. See what I did there? *A rise?*"

He laughed. "Well, aren't we…perky?"

Now she laughed.

"I'm working tomorrow. But I'm thinking that maybe when I'm done, I could swing by your place and pick you up, then take you back with me. What do you say? I might need a short nap depending on how the night goes, but I'll be up and running by noon, one tops. Then I'm off until Thursday. Yep, four free days to court Ms. Maggie May."

"I should never have told you my name."

"You really shouldn't have."

She smiled, starting to seriously fall for Reggie Morgan. "Sounds good, Studly."

"Hmm. Studly. I like that."

"You would."

"Hey, Maggie, before you go. One thing."

"Yeah?"

His voice lowered. "Tonight, when you're fingering yourself and getting off, remember how big I was when you were sucking me. Then think about what I'm going to do to you with that thick, juicy cock when I see you again."

Her breath caught and expelled in a rush.

"Yeah, me too." He sighed. "See you Sunday morning."

"Wait!"

"Huh?"

"Don't you have Sunday brunch with your family?"

She heard silence then a muttered *fuck*. "I normally would. But since I'm just getting off after a shift, they should give me a pass. But maybe we stay at your place Sunday just in case."

She smiled. "Sounds like a plan."

"And don't think I didn't hear myself say 'just getting off' because I heard it, and it *will* happen Sunday. You bet your sweet little ass."

She laughed. "See you soon."

"Oh yes, you will."

Chapter Eighteen

Maggie met Stephen the next day at noon with the puppy. She had a new bag of food that matched the stuff Reggie had sent, a few doggie treats, and of course, Emily carried her own backpack while Maggie wheeled the roller bag and carried a spare duffel for Emily's necessary toys. Her daughter did like to be prepared for anything.

They'd arrived at Stephen's home in Queen Anne, a nice neighborhood in northern Seattle. She hadn't been surprised when he'd moved from their home in Fremont to a more upscale house in an older neighborhood two years ago. The quaint cottage could easily be her dream house. It was in the Craftsman style, painted a dark blue with white and black trim, a black front door, and a wide front porch complete with a swing.

He had a spacious backyard with a playground set that didn't get much use, and the house had much more room than a single father with one little girl could use. He'd told her the two-story had twenty-four hundred square feet, and she was jealous each and every time she visited.

Stephen opened the door and welcomed them, his sandy-brown hair longer than it had been, now curling over his nape. It was a good look on him. He sported new wire-framed glasses that made him look even smarter than he was, which was no easy feat. The guy was a tech genius. His navy-blue khaki slacks and a long-sleeve button-down, not a wrinkle in sight, combated the day's sudden chill. Trust Seattle never to adhere to typical summer weather.

For that reason, she'd made sure to include both long and short layers for Emily to wear.

"Hi, Stephen." He did look tired, yet his wide smile showed he was indeed happy to see his daughter. He held out his arms and crouched, then swung Emily into his arms when she raced to him.

Maggie held on to Frank by his leash, though the little guy didn't pull or try to get away. He sat by her feet and watched Emily.

Stephen put her down, and Maggie saw little of Stephen in her daughter. Emily's looks were all Maggie, though she suspected Emily had inherited Stephen's big brain. She wondered if her daughter's resemblance ever bothered him.

"Hi, Maggie." His big, blue eyes shone with pleasure. Then he glanced at her arm. "Yikes."

"Yeah." She walked the dog toward him, carrying Emily's duffel and pulling her wheeled suitcase.

"Let me get those." Stephen quickly took the bag and suitcase from her, leaving her to hold on to Frank. When he moved away, she caught a whiff of his cologne, a subtle blend she'd bought for him years ago. Funny, she'd never smelled him wearing cologne before.

She wondered if he had a new girlfriend. She knew he dated, but he'd never been with anyone for very long, a lot like her. They didn't talk much about their personal lives, but the idea of Stephen dating didn't bother her in the slightest, and she knew, in the past, it might have.

That she didn't care brought her a relieved sense of happiness.

Once through the house, she sat with him at the farm table out back on a bench. The patio had a pergola with white lights strewn about, competing with the overhead ivy. Just one more thing to envy about her ex—his perfect backyard.

Yet, it didn't have the same charm as Reggie's place, where clusters of flowers and bushes thrived under his tender care. She missed him, and that should have alarmed her, that she kept thinking about Reggie when she needed to focus on Stephen and Emily.

A glance at the swing set showed it getting plenty of use as

Emily crawled all over it, slipping down a curving slide while Frank waited and barked impatiently below.

"I missed her," Stephen said and poured Maggie a glass of lemonade. "It's taken me a long time to figure out my priorities." Their hands touched when he passed the glass. Their eyes met.

"I'm sorry."

"Stephen, don't be." What the hell had happened in Denmark? "Are you okay? You seem kind of sad."

"Just tired." He smiled and adjusted his glasses. "And thoughtful. Leon died."

She stared at him, in shock. "Your mentor? Leon Brightwell?"

"Yeah." Stephen blew out a breath. "He was old, and it was time. Miranda let me know in time, so I took a flight from Denmark to New York and got to spend his last few days with him. We had a blast." He wiped his eyes behind his glasses, and not thinking about it, she rounded the table to give him a hug.

He stood to accept it, hugging her tight.

He pulled away and sniffed, his cheeks flushed. "Sorry."

"Don't you dare apologize." She sat next to him on the bench and held on to his hand. "I'm so sorry, Stephen. I know he meant the world to you. Was it easy for him at the end?"

"Yeah. He drifted off in his sleep. Miranda said to tell you hello."

Leon's wife had been a lovely lady Maggie had enjoyed spending time with many years ago. Then the couple had moved to New York for Leon's business, and she hadn't seen them since. Once Maggie's divorce had come through, she hadn't thought about staying in touch, as they'd been more Stephen's friends than hers.

They sat in silence watching Emily play.

"The puppy's cute," Stephen said after some time. "With a name like Frankenstein, I hadn't expected that."

She laughed. "He's got a few scars, but he's super sweet and gentle. Emily loves him."

Stephen frowned. "What are you going to do when school starts?"

"That I'm not sure about, but the more time Emily spends with him, the more I realize we'll figure it out. I talked to the landlord. When she heard how we found him and what happened to me, she waived the pet fee." Maggie smiled. "That's one thing not to worry about. Plus, look at him. He's adorable. He suckered me into belly rubs all morning during *SpongeBob*."

Stephen chuckled and looked at her, his smirk one she'd always found amusing rather than annoying.

"Laugh it up, evil genius." Her nickname for him that had stuck. "But he has to be out to potty at three and six am."

Stephen blinked. "What?"

"No takebacks. He's yours for the next two weeks." Her smile felt really wide.

Stephen watched her, his expression unreadable.

"Stephen?"

"Do you ever think about us?"

Oh boy. Hadn't seen that one coming. "Um, in what sense?"

"You know what I'm saying. About us. About our marriage. About our life together with Emily. About the amazing sex we used to have."

"*Whoa.* Really putting that out there." Yet any mention of sex and an "us" had her thinking about Reggie, not Stephen.

"I miss you, Maggie."

"Stephen, where is this coming from? You and I have been divorced for three years, and you never once, in all that time, have discussed us reconnecting." His eyes were still glassy, and she thought maybe she understood. "Oh, honey, it's Leon. You miss him, and you want to go back to the past and the way things used to be. But Stephen, we're different people now. I want different things in life. And so do you."

"But Emily—"

"Is a wonderful little girl who loves her parents. That will never change. But I've moved on. I like myself, who I am now. And I know you do too. Together, we'd be unhappy, and that would make Emily unhappy."

"Maybe." He took her hand in his, the touch familiar and comforting, but it didn't give her the same sparks Reggie did. "Sorry to get so emotional." He pulled himself back, once again together, unfazed.

And that had been a huge part of their problems. Stephen hated letting himself feel more than arousal or superficial affection. Or at least, he'd never shown it. "That's okay." She wanted to phrase her next question just right, aware he was hurting. "Does Leon's passing have to do with your decision to work remotely?"

"No. At first I loved all the travel, going overseas, all over the country. It was fun and helped my goals, broadening my network and helping my consulting. But it's too much now. Plus, I'm going into a partnership with one of my clients in Denmark. It's an opportunity for serious money and a chance to base out of Seattle. So I wouldn't have to travel nearly as much."

"That's great."

He studied her. Then he gave a slow smile. "I know you mean that."

"Why wouldn't I? You deserve it."

"Even if my being here would mean I'd want equal time with Emily?"

She looked at him. "Stephen, I love my daughter. I know you love her too. No matter what you and I have gone through, we've both always put Emily before us. I'll always respect you for that." She admitted, "I won't lie. It would be hard for me to not have her around all the time. She's my world."

He nodded, his eyes kind. "I know. I just want to be more involved in her life. You never tell me no when I ask for her. And you're always there when something comes up and I can't make it. Your support, your love for our daughter, that means the world to me."

"She's your daughter, Stephen. I would never hold her back from you."

"God, I love you, Maggie. As a friend, I mean, don't get panicked." He laughed. "I can't lie and say I'm not still attracted, but I respect you."

"Do you realize how much better friends we are now than we were when we were married?"

He sighed. "I know." He gave her a subtle once-over. "We're going to stay friends. Not just for Emily, but for me. I need you in my life in some capacity." He paused, opened his mouth to speak, then snapped it closed. "So, ready for lunch?"

She didn't know what he'd meant to say, but she didn't need to be a mind reader to realize it was probably best left unspoken. "I'm hungry. What do you have?"

"Your favorite. Chicken salad from Trader Joe's."

"Aw, you didn't cook. You really do care."

Stephen laughed. Emily and Frank joined them, and they enjoyed a family lunch together, just the four of them. And Reggie, tucked into the back of her mind, he was there too.

———————

Reggie drove to Maggie's Sunday morning, a little tired yet revved at the thought of seeing his girl again. As much as he tried to deny their attachment as serious, he couldn't stop thinking about her.

He'd revealed to the guys what a great time he'd had at dinner and that he'd met her neighbors right after, totally bypassing his sexual encounter with Maggie. Not that he normally kissed and told, but he and the guys had been known to make veiled references to their sex lives.

Reggie himself had ribbed both Brad and Tex about their girlfriends, so he tried to give them less ammunition to fire his way. However, he had no problem sharing that he'd met *the* Bear Destruction, going so far as to share his selfie.

Now Reggie had to get Benny to meet the guys. The topic of Benny had overshadowed their interest in Maggie, which was a huge bonus. It also helped that Reggie hadn't begged off the guy stuff they'd planned for their time off. Working out Monday morning at the station and a baseball game Wednesday evening.

He figured to fit those in easily, in between spending all his time with Maggie.

He shifted in his seat, erect since he'd left the station, all thoughts centered on free time with the sexiest woman he knew.

Reggie didn't want to act so sex starved, but he couldn't help it. She got to him on a primal level. And then he'd see her smile, hear her laugh, and hold her hand, and all those sweet, soppy emotions would swarm him. A plague of love and desire stabbing him in the heart.

He called his dad to try to distract himself, hitting a button on the wheel. His father's voice soon came through the car speaker.

"Hello, Son. Your sisters and I were just talking about you."

I'll bet. "Hey, Dad. I'm letting you know right now that I'm not doing brunch. I'm not sick, but I am tired. It was a long twenty-four hours."

"No problem. What? Hold on."

The phone changed hands because Nadia came on. "Hey. Where are you?"

"Driving home. My shift just ended."

"Are you going to Maggie's?"

Fucking Nadia. "It's none of your business where I'm going."

"He's going to Maggie's," she told the others.

"Damn it. I'm going to get some sleep. We had to deal with a battered wife who tried to set her spouse on fire and an explosive DUI. It was a long night."

"Sorry, bro," Nadia apologized. "I was just teasing. We'll talk to you later."

"Bye, Reggie," Lisa yelled from behind her.

Then all of them said, "Tell Maggie we said hi." They disconnected on laughter.

He groaned. Well, at least they weren't on his ass about her. Not now, but later…

He really needed to figure out what he was doing with Maggie. The sex was off the charts. That made sense. Feeling for her so soon after meeting her, fantasizing about being with her all the time, that didn't. Hell, maybe he *should* talk to Brad and Tex about her. They knew him better than Doug and Benny did.

What if Doug and Benny had told Maggie what he'd told them? He cringed. Would she think he wanted more? Did he? He kept thinking of her as his girlfriend, but neither had made a commitment to each other.

He scowled. That was stupid. They'd had unprotected sex a lot. They couldn't do that if she was going to ball other guys. And then a ray of light hit him, and he relaxed. *Of course*, they had to commit to each other, if only to continue to practice condom-free sex, something Maggie seemed keen on. And hell, he wanted nothing stopping him from filling her up.

And there went his erection once more, killing him.

He put on the radio and let some decent rap music, not that mumble crap but the old school—Tupac, Wu Tang, and yeah, some '80s Run DMC—fill his brain. And then, because he had an eclectic taste, he threw on a country station he'd never in a million years admit to Tex that he liked.

He parked at Maggie's complex, grabbed his bag with a change of clothes and some other odds and ends, and headed to Maggie's, rejuvenated.

He knocked and waited.

She answered with a smile, her hair damp and curling by her face. She wore a short, sporty skirt and a pink tank top, showing off her toned arms.

He didn't notice a bra and nearly swallowed his tongue.

"Come on in."

He stepped inside and had to stop himself from jumping when the door *snicked* closed behind him. Then she locked it.

"Are you hungry?" She motioned to the kitchen, and as he moved with her, he smelled something amazing.

"Is that French toast?" His absolute favorite when it came to breakfast foods.

"It is." She planted her hands on her hips, and he did his best to keep his gaze on her face. "I'll have you know I am the best French toast maker in the Pacific Northwest. Even Doug admits it's better than his."

Mention of Doug's name had him wondering again if the guys next door had told her about their conversation Thursday night.

Yet Maggie didn't look weird or act funny about seeing him. So maybe not?

"You look tired." She pulled him down for a brief kiss. "Do you want to shower?" She frowned. "And how come you're wearing sweatpants? I was hoping to see you in your uniform. You look so good in it." Her dimple appeared.

He needed a shower, a very cold one. "I usually take off the uniform at work, because I don't want to bring contaminants home with me."

"Oh, I hadn't thought about that."

"But I would appreciate a shower."

She bit her lip. "Come on. I'd offer to join you, but you look like you need a break."

"I need another blow job, but I'll settle for hot water."

She tripped over her own feet and muttered under her breath, but she didn't look back at him.

He grinned, glad he wasn't the only one having a tough time.

She nudged him in the bathroom and closed the door, staying outside. "Take your time," she said through it.

Disappointed yet needing space to get a handle on his out-of-control dick, he forced himself to move with deliberation and gradually started to relax. After taking off his clothes, he heated the water and got into a lovely shower. Great water pressure, surprisingly roomy tub, and hot water.

He let the water wash over him and tried not to think so hard.

Then the door opened.

His dick rose so fast, he was surprised the thing didn't slap him in the face.

"Reggie?"

"Yeah?" *That's me, the guy who sounds like he swallowed a bucket of gravel. No, don't even* think *the word "swallowed."*

The curtain moved back, and a naked Maggie stood there, staring at him. "Want some company?"

This was probably the dumbest thing, disturbing Reggie when he'd already looked disturbed enough. He seemed tense, a little unhappy, even. And Maggie wondered if she'd been deluding herself that they had something deeper between them. Yes, he was sexy, and she wanted him. Yes, she'd blown him and swallowed him down. But he might not always want to spend time with her. Maybe he'd had other plans but didn't want to hurt her feelings, and now he was trying to find a way to let her down gently.

Or he did just want to have sex with her but was pretending to act like he wanted a relationship? And that made her mad, because if he did want sex with other people, they couldn't be doing it without condoms. That wasn't safe at all.

Confronting him about it made sense. But not wearing clothes and bugging the poor guy, while he was naked and wet in the shower, that was just foolish.

Except she couldn't stop staring at Reggie, naked and wet. So wet. She wanted to be a drop of water and slide down that delicious male body.

He stared back, just as intently, but when his gaze found the bag tied around her arm, he smiled. "Get in here."

"Are you sure?"

"Do I look like I need more time to think about it?" He glanced down at his cock, which had yet to go down.

Maggie had barely stepped in the shower before Reggie lifted her in his arms, planted his mouth over hers, and plastered her against the tiled wall. He wrapped her legs around his waist while he ravaged her mouth. Maggie felt helpless and turned on, doing nothing but clutching his strong shoulders while she sucked his tongue and squirmed against the slick erection shoved against her belly.

He was so damn big. And so incredibly in the wrong place.

But she didn't have long to wait. He bent his head to suck her nipple, and she moaned his named and shifted against his groin. He sucked hard then turned to her neglected breast. "I love your tits. So much," he moaned and put a hand between them. Two fingers slid inside her, and they met no resistance. "*Fuck. Me.*"

"Reggie, stop teasing," she panted. "I want you in me."

Reggie readjusted, positioning himself between her folds, and thrust all the way inside her.

The jolt of his intrusion shocked her into an unexpected orgasm, and she screamed as he fucked her so hard, her head threatened to explode.

The rush kept coming, her body gripping him, the pleasure unending.

She didn't hear anything he said, kissing him while he took her, and then he came, his hips like a piston, hammering home.

"Oh, yeah. Fuck. *Maggie.*" He continued moving while her pussy clenched, not letting go.

They both eased the viselike hug they shared. Maggie stared

into his shocked gaze, dimly aware of water steaming around them. "Did that just happen?"

"You mean, where I fucked you until you screamed?" His slow smile scorched her. "Yeah, it did."

She sighed, running her hand over his short hair. "I took dirty, sexy advantage of you. I should be sorry."

"You should."

"I'm not." She wiggled on his semihard cock. "You're still in me."

"And I'm still hard."

"Not tired?" She slid her hand to his nape, making a note when he sighed and rested his head against her shoulder.

"Not tired. Satisfied, for now, but not tired."

"I'm not too heavy?"

"Honey, you're not heavy even soaking wet." He paused and looked at her with a wicked grin. "And you were soaked, for sure." He kissed her and murmured, "Dripping for me."

"I was," she confessed. "And last night, when I masturbated, running my fingers over my clit, I kept remembering how you tasted and how you felt when you took me from behind."

He shivered and clutched her ass tighter. "You did your homework. Good girl."

"Oh, I'm a very good girl. And I plan on showing you." She kissed him, twining her tongue with his. He twitched inside her. "But not until you've had a decent breakfast and some rest."

He started to argue, but she put a hand on his chest. "No, you need some rest." She leaned close to suck his nipple, teething the taut bud and loving how he hardened even more inside her. "Trust me, you're going to need your strength for what I have in mind."

Chapter Nineteen

REGGIE DIDN'T KNOW IF HE SHOULD FEEL MANIPULATED OR amused. She'd left him hard and hurting once more, dripping wet and watching while she finished her shower with no help from him. The little tease wouldn't let him help get her breasts clean. And they'd been so, *so* dirty.

Now he sat, clean and surprisingly refreshed, and eating the best damn French toast he'd ever had. He wore a clean pair of shorts and a T-shirt.

Maggie had put her skirt and tank back on, and he was dying to know if she wore any panties, because…damn…still no bra.

She sat across from him at the table, sipping coffee. "We need to talk."

He froze in the act of taking a bite. "What did I do?"

"That's the question." She sighed. "Reggie, I love what we have here."

Which is? Too much a coward to ask the question, not sure he could handle her answer, he ate and said nothing.

"You're awesome and I'm awesome, and together we're super awesome."

"Awesome."

She raised a brow. He forced himself not to laugh.

"But if you're going to sleep around, we can't keep doing this."

He scowled. "Whoa. Sleep around? What the hell are you talking about?"

Maggie flushed. "Look, we never made any commitments to each other, but the more I think about it, the more that doesn't make sense. We're smart people. We take our health seriously. Hell, you gave me the safe sex talk at the very beginning."

"Yeah, and?"

"And I have no plans to sleep with anyone else while we're dating." She swallowed nervously.

He watched her, in awe, as she said everything *he'd* planned on saying to *her*.

"I like you a lot. Hell, I have a huge crush. I'll admit it. But I can't have sex with you without a condom if you're going to be with other people. I'm embarrassed I haven't been clear about this before."

He blinked. "Maggie, I—"

"Wait. Before you say anything, I know it's pushy to demand you commit yourself to me. But that's who I am. A one-guy kind of woman. If you're with me, it's *only* me. And that's the only way I can be. Not just sex with other people, but no dating other girls. You date me and me alone. And if that's too much, I understand, and we'll have to go our separate ways."

She watched him, obviously nervous, but she didn't look away.

And fuck it all if he didn't feel so damn in love with her for being courageous to say what she felt, not knowing how he'd react. And for being a woman who didn't compromise her principles.

He smiled at her, feeling that warmth in his entire being. "I agree."

"You do?" She looked so hopeful.

"I agree with everything you just said. I was going to mention all that to you, but I was so worked up at the thought of being near you again, I needed time to relax. I was going to jerk off in the shower, if you want the truth, so I could think straight. You get me so hard, Maggie. Sometimes everything shuts down but my cock. And I wanted to talk to you, not sex you up."

"Oh."

"Then you came in the bathroom and ruined everything. You seduced me, and well, I'm only a guy."

"Huh. *I* seduced *you*?" Her widening grin told him they'd

weathered this storm. It hadn't been that big of a deal. Well, how about that? "Actually," she said, "*you* seduced *me*."

"Hey, you were naked."

"But you were naked and dripping wet, and that monster between your legs hypnotized me."

"You keep talking like that and you're going to get fucked before I finish my French toast."

She grinned. "So we're now officially dating?"

"Yep. I'm your boyfriend. It's official."

"Hurray, me."

He chuckled and finished his breakfast, his appetite restored.

Maggie was telling him about Emily and Frank, and her daughter's excitement to see her father again. "It was so sad, Reggie. Stephen wasn't himself. His friend and mentor died, and that man was everything to Stephen. He was a kind man, his wife equally nice. I missed them when Stephen and I divorced, but by then they'd moved to the East Coast, and I wasn't used to seeing them so often anyway."

He studied her. He knew what Doug and Benny thought. But what did Maggie really feel for her ex? "Are you and Stephen close?"

"We're friends. We share Emily, and we shared a past. But I don't confide in him, and we're not close-close." She snorted. "He asked why I didn't call him when I broke my arm. I mean, why would I?"

Hmm. So maybe she didn't feel close to him, but it sounded as if her ex might have feelings for her. Something to think about. *Great. Now I'm jealous.*

"Emily mentioned you. Stephen wanted to know who you were." She frowned. "I told him you'd helped us with Frank and that you were the EMT who helped me after the accident. But I didn't mention us as a couple."

He gauged her. "That bothers you?"

"It does, and I don't know why. We hadn't confirmed to each other that we were dating until now. So what would I have said? Stephen, I had mind-blowing sex with a man who could lift you up with one hand tied behind his back? Oh, and he's a hot firefighter, so there?"

Reggie grinned. "You totally could have said that."

"Stop it." She grinned back. "Besides, you clearly said to keep 'us' between, well, us. We aren't going to tell Emily yet."

That put a damper on things. "I think we should stick to that, for now."

She studied him, and her expression softened. "I agree. You really care about Emily, don't you?"

He nodded and forced himself to talk about the past. "I told you I dated a woman with a little girl. I was on my way home from work one morning and saw a woman whose car had broken down. I stopped to help her, and there was Rachel in the back seat. Just six and already a mini adult." He smiled at the memory, not hurting so much at reminders now. "I'll be honest. I love kids. And Rachel was—is—amazing. Amy and I connected, but Rachel was a part of that relationship from the very beginning. When it started to sour, I didn't want to let go. For Amy, but also because I really loved Rachel."

"I bet she loved you too."

"She did. I'm not going to say things were perfect between me and Amy. But we were together for two years. And then, out of the blue, Amy called us quits, and I lost them both. Rachel was devastated. She cried and cried, and then she'd call me crying, and Amy would make her hang up." He sighed. "That was tougher than losing Amy. Sounds terrible, but it's true. Knowing I unintentionally caused that little girl's tears still rips at me."

"I'm so sorry."

He cleared his throat, swallowing down the ache at Rachel's pain. "I didn't want that again. For eight months I've stayed away from relationships, especially with women with kids. You... I have no idea why I can't stay away from you. Oh, I know Emily's adorable and just snotty enough as the queen of everything that she's impossible to resist. And you, with your perfect body and beautiful face, and that smile and that dimple..." He groaned. "I can't stay away. Even worse, I haven't really tried. And I'm afraid this will end the way my last relationship did." Man, he hadn't realized he felt all that until it had poured out. He really did miss Rachel more than Amy.

"I feel exactly the same way." Maggie stared at him, wide-eyed.

"You do?"

"Yes. I've never introduced anyone I've dated to Emily. Never. No man in our lives since Stephen. Benny and Doug don't count; they're more like her uncles. I'm worried that Emily will grow attached to anyone I might date and be hurt when we break up. Or she'll see me with a man and think she's getting a new daddy. She's got a father. I don't need that for her. I want a man for *me*. And trying to convince anyone that's what I want has been hard. I wasn't looking for you when I found you. Or, you know, when you scraped me up like roadkill."

"Attractive roadkill," he corrected with a large smile, understanding Maggie because they felt the same way.

He stood and crossed to her, taking her in his arms.

She looked up into his face, and he desperately wished she felt what he imagined he saw there. "I'm just being honest with you," she said. "I don't know where you and I will end up. And I don't want Emily hurt. We're new."

"Yes to all that."

"So keeping Emily out of our dating relationship makes sense."

"Yeah."

"But at some point, if there is a forever us, she'll need to know."

"Agreed." Yet the thought of telling Emily, potentially seeing her tears and knowing he'd been a party to her pain, would eat at him. He knew himself, and Reggie could get carried away by guilt. *Just like your mother,* he could almost hear his father saying.

Maggie plucked the neckline of his T-shirt, looking up into his eyes. "Look, I have two child-free weeks to take advantage of, and you have some time off. Let's spend the time getting to know and enjoy each other and stop all the worrying about maybes."

"You're being quite reasonable about all this."

She raised a brow.

"I mean, you're a woman."

Her tone grew frosty. "And?"

"Who knew women could be rational?" He smirked.

"For that, you will pay." Her hand slid down his chest to his belly and lower.

His body responded on cue, tightening all over. Then he ruined the moment by yawning, the food and the shower orgasm doing him in.

"You poor thing. Why don't you go nap?" She started to step away.

He grabbed her by the hand. "Will you sleep with me? And I mean sleep. Holding you that night… I haven't slept so well in ages."

"Hmm. Sleeping during the daytime with a sexy man? How can I refuse?"

When Reggie next woke, he saw he'd gotten four hours of shut-eye. Just what he needed. He hadn't lied before about being up and ready to start his day by one. The clock read twelve fifty-five.

Unfortunately, Maggie was no longer in bed.

He stretched, hurriedly brushed his teeth with the toothbrush from his overnight bag, anticipating some more kissing, and looked for Maggie.

The apartment remained empty. Hmm.

He noticed a note tacked to the fridge. *Back soon. Needed next door.*

He wondered if he should go over and join them, then figured to stay right where he was. A perfect time to learn more about Maggie by snooping. And he didn't feel an ounce of guilt for it either.

Nothing in the living room he hadn't already seen before. He looked in her pantry, taking note of what she and the little dictator liked to eat. He saw an extremely—bordering on obsessive—level of organization in her refrigerator and kitchen cabinets and fell a little more in love. It was like being in his house, where everything had its place.

A perusal of Emily's room showed a girl well-loved, but nothing out of the ordinary. And then he noticed a hand-drawn picture taped to her wall. A stick figure with a big, old arm and brown hair held hands with a little girl wearing a crown. By her side stood Frank. That or an evil monkey, but Reggie was betting the creature was the puppy.

And then, to his surprise, he saw himself. A brown man with a line of black hair, looking like a giant in navy-blue pants and a shirt, holding hands with the little girl. The man had two eyes and a large smile.

He absolutely loved the picture, amazed Emily would draw him as part of her world.

He struggled with how to feel about that and spotted a photograph on her dresser of Emily sitting on a man's shoulders. The guy had to be Stephen. Emily and the man wore identical expressions of delight, a beach and ocean behind them.

And damn, but the guy was handsome. He had blue eyes, sandy hair, and from what Maggie had said, was some type of brainy business type. The complete opposite of Reggie, who would rather gnaw off his own arm than sit behind a computer all day.

"I could take him," he muttered, knowing he could easily outbrawn the dude.

He put the picture back and left for Maggie's bedroom. A

glance around showed she had a passion for the color blue, with hints of purple thrown in. Casual clothes and teacher clothes— dresses, blouses, and skirts—filled her closet.

Not too many stilettos, he thought with humor, thinking about how he'd have *loved* to have Maggie teaching him back in high school, especially in no bra or panties. Maybe they could roleplay later on. The naughty teacher disciplining her horned-up student.

Then it hit him that they had yet to do it missionary style, where he could lie on top of her and kiss her breasts, watch her while he entered her or kiss her without having to contort while they fucked.

Made love.

He blew out a breath, ready to take her right now.

Reggie had never been so sexed up for a woman before, and it was messing with his head. He wanted to shove inside her, come, and stay there, hugging her to him, forever.

His woman.

Yeah, my girlfriend, he reminded himself, gratified.

That in mind, he turned on the TV in the living room and let himself just relax, content to be near Maggie.

She returned just as, on TV, the police named the murderer.

"Hi, I—"

"Shh." He leaned forward. "Ah-ha! I knew the butcher did it."

"Oh?"

"Mystery solved."

"I like mysteries." She smiled.

"Here's one. What were you up to next door for so long?" he asked and met her by the door for a kiss.

The kiss, as usual, started light and turned passionate from one breath to the next.

"Jealous?"

"Of your gay best friends? Yes," he growled and rubbed her shoulders.

Her laugh turned in a sensual moan. "Oh, that feels good." She looked up at him through her lashes. "Do you happen to know anyone who gives a good massage?"

"Do you have any oil? Lotion?" He kept rubbing her shoulders, aroused and ready to play. "I have some all-natural stuff I can use, but it gets sticky pretty quickly once it squirts from its container."

"Reggie." She blushed.

He grinned. "Some immature guy humor for you. So what were you doing next door?"

"We were talking about you and what they think I should do for our next date."

He paused. "Do they know I'm here?"

"Maybe." She turned a deeper red. "I didn't mean to tell them, but they saw me smiling and said I had that look."

"What look?" Mystified, he tried to see it.

"They said I looked happy and that my hair was pretty much the result of a hot firefighter running his big, strong hands through it." She laughed at him. "I think the guys have a crush. They couldn't sing your praises enough."

"Nice." He would thank them later. "So nothing else?"

She looked puzzled. "Like?"

They hadn't mentioned his stopover Thursday night. He owed them. "Like sex tips on how to make your man happy? Not that you need any, but it strikes me that they would be ideal people to give you advice. Nobody knows their own equipment better, am I right?"

"I do *not* talk sex tips with Doug and Benny. That'd be like you talking to your sisters about how to go down on a woman."

"That's disgusting."

"Yep."

"Ech. I'm sorry I mentioned it."

She gripped him through his shorts, and he groaned.

"How sorry?"

"Sorry enough to give you the best massage of your life."

"Just save that special lotion for the end," she said with a wink. "I have some oil you can use."

"Just to clarify, is this massage for you or for me?" He followed her back to her room. "Because touching you with or without oil sounds like my kind of fantasy."

She laughed. "With any luck, we'll both make out."

"Oh, we'll make out. But I reserve the right to plant my kisses where they'll do the most good. Now, do you have a bunch of towels to protect your bed? I predict the outcome will be really, really messy."

―――――――――

Maggie had no idea Reggie was so good with his hands. They were large, warm, and rough from his time lifting weights and doing so much physical work at the fire station. His long, talented fingers didn't seem to miss a knot. And he had such strength in his touch. "You should do this for a living," she murmured into her pillow.

She lay facedown on her bed on top of an old blanket. Naked, relaxed, and aroused. Her three new favorite states of being.

Reggie, also naked, straddled her upper thighs. She felt his balls against the base of her ass, his cock nestled between her cheeks. Reggie seemed to be rubbing her with his dick as much as he did with his hands on her shoulders. And she wanted more.

"I wish I had a camera. You have the best ass." He continued to massage her, though his hands moved from her shoulders down to her lower back and on to her glutes.

She moaned. "That feels good."

"I know." His voice was thick. In between massaging her glutes, he'd push her butt cheeks together while sliding that giant cock between said cheeks. His breathing grew shallow. Had he reached between her legs, he'd have felt how much she wanted him.

Then he slowed down and stopped grinding, and his hands moved back up her body to her bad arm, focusing on massaging her shoulder.

"That's sore," she said and sighed. "But it feels wonderful."

"You need more movement here. You're getting too stiff."

She grinned into the pillow but left that comment alone.

He shifted across her back to her other shoulder then down her left arm, working the muscle.

"That's so good." She wanted to fall asleep, but the throbbing between her legs wouldn't let her.

Reggie continued to rub her aching muscles. After a while, he backed off her hips and knelt between her legs on the bed. She wanted to see him, but he'd insisted she lie flat, not straining herself.

He pushed her legs wider and massaged her calves. First the left leg, then the right. His hands crept steadily up from her knees to her thighs. And with every slide of his hands toward her ass, the heat within spiraled.

She had to be soaking the blanket beneath her, aroused beyond measure from his strong, driven strokes. He kept reaching higher, his thumbs gliding so close… Then he'd retreat.

"Reggie."

"Shh. Just relax."

"I can't," she wailed.

He laughed. The bastard.

He continued to rub her, and she couldn't help humping the blanket, tilting her hips so her ass lifted, showing him what she wanted. Him. Inside her.

But Reggie only deepened the caress. His thumbs finally, *finally*, slid up and over her folds, drenched in her arousal.

His breath hitched, but other than that, he didn't react.

His strokes grew faster, up and down, closer to her pussy, then farther away.

Then Reggie grasped her hips to tilt them higher and planted his face between her legs, right over her pussy.

"Yes, *please*," she begged.

He licked and sucked, and she moaned his name as she neared climax.

Talk about an expert touch and a tongue that didn't quit. He licked inside her, stroking, seeking.

And then he found her clit, and he licked her until she came all over his mouth. "Reggie, *yes, yes!*"

He moaned and sucked her harder.

When she came back to herself, she felt him lie down on top of her, his stiff erection nudging her thighs before he slid home.

All the way inside.

They both groaned. But Reggie didn't move, his thick presence just resting there.

"Fuck. Just gonna stay here a sec. Don't move." He felt huge inside her and over her. Claiming her, with Maggie unable to move, pinned in place.

And that was fucking *hot*.

"I want you again," she insisted. "Right now."

"Yeah, baby. You feel good." He kissed her shoulders, her neck, then made his way to her ear. "But I haven't done your front yet. I'm just getting my strength back."

"You feel plenty strong." She tried to grind back against him, but he stopped her by gripping her hips and holding her in place. "I love that I can't move right now. You are making me burn." She sighed his name.

"Stop moving or I'll come, and I have more I want to do to you."

She moaned when he withdrew, but then he flipped her over, and she saw how large she'd made him.

"Lick me off. I'm wet." He held his dick to her lips, and she gladly opened her mouth.

"Fuck, Maggie." He closed his eyes and tilted his head back as she nibbled his cock, what little he fed her.

She couldn't believe their chemistry. Or that she was having so much fun while being turned on. Teasing Reggie made her feel good. Knowing he wanted her made her feel beautiful, desired. And that turned her on. Heck, at this point, she figured the man could chew string cheese and she'd be aroused.

He looked like a statue, all locked muscle and a stiff definition with a face sculpted by a master artist.

When he once again glanced down at her, his gaze was intense. "Suck me," he ordered, gruff.

She did, and as he pumped more of his length into her mouth, she saw his desire deepen.

Until he pulled out.

"No," she complained and reached for him.

Reggie settled himself on top of her, his weight both welcome and tempered since he held himself on his elbows.

He kissed her, and she kissed him back. Hungry. She loved feeling his body pressed against hers.

"I haven't paid your breasts nearly enough attention." He took a nipple deeply into his mouth.

He continued to fulfill all her fantasies. He cupped her other breast while he suckled one, then turned and repeated the caress. She'd always been sensitive in her breasts, and Reggie devoted himself to bringing her nearly to orgasm with his mouth and fingers.

Writhing, lost, she was out of control, so damn needy.

"Watch me," he ordered, his voice gritty. "Look at me," he growled and caged her face between his hands. He shoved hard and fast, taking her with a thoroughness that left her breathless.

And while he rode her, he watched, not letting her look away.

"You feel so damn good inside." He thrust faster. "You get me so hard. I hurt, baby. I need to fill you up." He swore and kissed her, fucking her with his tongue and his cock, the dual penetration overstimulating.

And then she was there, coming as he seized and poured into her. The moment etched into her brain, because she'd never been taken so high, and never in the arms of someone who'd seen so thoroughly to her pleasure first.

Emotions bombarded her, and her eyes watered. Not with sadness, but from a cathartic expression of pure joy.

"Fuck, oh fuck, Maggie," he groaned as he kept jerking inside her, small thrusts until he pumped himself dry.

She brought his mouth back and kissed him.

He wiped her cheeks, pulled back, and frowned. "Hey, you okay?"

She smiled and kissed him again. "I am so incredibly satisfied."

His frown eased into a smile. "Good. I know I am." He closed his eyes and pushed deeper inside her. When he opened his eyes, she saw so much happiness. "You have no idea how good you feel. It's like you're surrounding me, and all I feel is warmth."

"You make me feel good. Thanks, baby," she said to him and kissed him again.

He moaned and kissed her back. "I like you calling me 'baby.' It's so sexy." He trailed kisses to her ear. "And when you were sucking my cock, I almost came. I love seeing your lips around me like that." He nipped her earlobe and ground into her. "You're this small sex bomb all wrapped up in me." He whispered, "All mine. And there's nothing you can do about it."

She gave him the fake struggle he seemed to want, except it wasn't exactly fake. "You know it gets me horny when you hold me down." She bit her lip and stared into his mean grin. "You're so fucking hot."

Reggie's his eyes darkened. "Talk like that will get you fucked even harder."

"I wish." She wiggled, found herself pinned with him still inside her, and watched as his arms tensed.

"Oh, Maggie, you're playing with fire."

"Good thing I know someone who can put the flames out."

"Yeah, good thing," he said before he destroyed her all over again.

Chapter Twenty

THE WORKOUT WITH THE GUYS TIRED HIM, ONLY BECAUSE Maggie had worked him out so much yesterday, he'd fallen into her bed, exhausted. When he'd blamed her for his tiredness this morning, she'd had the nerve to accuse him of being a sex maniac and said he'd been the one keeping *her* up at all hours.

He grinned just thinking about the stupid argument, because both of them had been laughing like loons by the end.

"Well, well. Look who's happy." Brad, Tex, and Mack watched him linger by the pull-up bar in the station gym.

Reggie had been going back and forth about how to deal with the new girlfriend situation, and he'd come to the realization that no matter what happened, his friends would back him. So he decided to be honest. And well, he'd already proven he couldn't lie worth a damn, but still, he decided—on his own—to be honest.

"Straight up, the woman rocks my world."

"Nice." Tex bumped fists with him. "Welcome to what we, in Texan terms, call happiness."

"It's a place where people smile with genuine pleasure because the world in a nice place," Mack added.

"This is why neither one of you has any friends." Reggie did two more pull-ups and paused, straining to keep his chin above the bar.

Brad chuckled. "And there's the real Reggie. Come on, dickhead. Get off the bar. See if you can outlift me."

Reggie let himself drop to the floor. He rotated his head on his neck and heard a crack.

"Damn, Reggie. What have you been taking? Aren't you like five times bigger than you were last week?" Suarez, one of the crew on B shift, asked.

"Hey, little guy. Don't be afraid. I won't hurt you."

Suarez flicked a hand under his chin at Reggie. "You wish. Bring your girlfriends and maybe you'd have a shot."

Reggie grinned. "Your problem is you suck at math. 'Cause what you say you're packing clearly ain't six inches." Reggie put his thumb and index finger close together.

The guys laughed.

Lori was lifting behind Suarez and nodded, putting her fingers even closer together, which had everyone laughing.

Suarez whipped his head around. "What? What's so funny?"

Brad clapped Reggie on the back. "Lori, leave him alone."

"Lori." Suarez scowled. "Why are you mocking me when you know I'm the only one you'll ever love?"

That got Lori and Suarez placing their own bets on who could out-pull-up the other.

"Hey, Reggie. Focus." Brad shoved him toward the bench. "Spot me."

While Brad lifted, Reggie told him, and by extension the eavesdropping Mack and Tex, how much fun he was having with Maggie. Without getting into sexual details, he shared that she also disliked bugs, camping, and really enjoyed a good "I told you so."

He didn't realize how enthusiastic he'd been until after they finished working out and cleaned up, all heading to breakfast at a diner by Brad's apartment. Before Reggie could get into his car, Brad took him aside.

"What?"

"I want to meet her."

Reggie rolled his eyes. "No."

"Reggie, she sounds amazing. And you're happy. Which we all love. But if she's that great, it shouldn't be a big deal to bring her over for a game night."

But what if the guys didn't like her? What if he'd overlooked something about her, as he'd done with Amy, and they pointed it out? Reggie didn't want to go back to grumping at everything. Not now that he'd seen how good life could be with a woman who seemed to like him so much. Or who gave him so much pleasure, she wore him the fuck out.

"Brad, I know you mean well. But we're new. And right now, everything is golden. Let it be, all right? I'm sure she'll see I'm a mistake soon enough."

As soon as he said it, he thought, *Huh. Apparently I still have some unresolved issues with Amy that festered. Go figure.*

Brad frowned. "You're not a mistake and you never were. Amy was lucky to have you."

Reggie sighed. "Sorry."

"No, I'm sorry for pushing you." Brad put a hand on Reggie's shoulder and squeezed. "You're cool, man. I'll back off and get the others to leave you alone. It's just… We want you to keep on smiling and laughing and, well, losing to me in the gym." Brad shot him a sly grin. "I think she's working you too hard. Tell her I said thanks."

Reggie laughed. "Asshole."

"Meet you at the diner." Brad left.

Reggie drove to meet his friends, his step light, his heart overflowing. He'd let tomorrow come when it did, and for now, he'd enjoy his new girlfriend and the joy she brought into his life.

He spent the evening playing naked Yahtzee with Maggie. When she rolled five of a kind, hot damn, did he get lucky too. *Rolling a Yahtzee* soon became a euphemism for an orgasm, which made little sense but became a fun thing for them to talk about when out and about.

Tuesday, he spent the early morning with her running errands. First hers, then his. After getting the boring stuff out of the way, they walked hand in hand downtown, taking in the farmers market.

Maggie *oohed* and *aahed* over several jewelry booths, but when Reggie offered to buy her something, she refused. When they stopped for lunch, he again tried to treat her, and she again refused.

"Damn it. You keep feeding me dinner. The least I can do is offer some lunch."

Maggie scowled, and he refused to tell her how attractive he found her when she was telling him no.

She got so adamant, a waiter swung by to see if everything was all right.

"It's not," Maggie said, glaring at Reggie. The guys at the table behind Maggie gave him the eye. "Because he keeps trying to buy my lunch."

The guys relaxed and turned back to their food.

Maggie smiled at the waiter. "Which was fabulous, by the way."

The young guy flushed. "Oh, great. Did you want dessert?"

"Only if I'm paying," she shot at Reggie.

"Oh, for fu—*fudge's*—sake, fine. Bring her the lunch bill, please. And she'll take the dessert."

The waiter grinned. "Yes, sir."

"But I'm tipping," Reggie told her. Which started another argument.

By the time they'd finished eating and "discussing," he felt as if they'd crossed a major hurdle. "Hey, was that our first fight?" They walked down the road toward the car.

She laughingly let him open the car door for her. "I guess it was. And you lost."

He got in next to her and drove them back to his place. "Yeah? How do you figure?"

"Reggie, you don't have to buy me things. I have my own money."

"What if I want to?" And he did. Maggie didn't sit and wait for him to grab the check. She didn't let him pay for her groceries he was eating. And she got prickly if he even hinted at trying to help her with anything she could do with one hand.

On the opposite spectrum from Amy.

"Reggie, what was your ex-girlfriend like?"

"Amy?" Odd to bring her up since he'd just been thinking about her. "She was like you in some ways. Kind, sweet, pretty." He smiled at her, and she smiled back. "But she had a tough time raising Rachel."

"Right. So you helped her out. Maybe buying dinner? Groceries? Some odds and ends?"

"Yeah, sometimes."

"Did you ever fix her car? Things around the house?" She put a hand on his leg. "I love spending time with you. But I don't want your money or for you to constantly do things for me."

"But what if I want to help?"

"Ask me. And if I say no, respect I said no."

He sighed. "Fine. But I still think you should have let me buy you those earrings. They can be an early birthday present."

"My birthday is next year."

"Christmas then." That was six months from now, which meant he was thinking long term. Would she understand what he meant? He felt her gaze on him.

"Okay. Christmas."

Good thing he'd bought them when she hadn't been looking.

Her hand remained on his leg.

"Ahem."

She looked out the window. "What?"

"Are you trying to get us arrested?"

"Huh?" She turned to face him, a question on her face.

"When we crash because all the blood has left my head and pooled between my legs, the cops will want to know what the hell happened. And being a civil servant, I'll have to tell the truth."

She bit her lip, but he saw her grin. She tightened her hand over his thigh, her grip nice and firm. "What will you tell them?"

"That you were distracting me with a hand job and I couldn't help myself. They'll take one look at you and know I was telling the truth. Then you'll get a ticket and go to jail. The end."

"Hand job? I'm just touching your leg. You're so full of it."

"I am. And you're making it come out."

She took her hand back and shook her head. Unfortunately, her smile faded. "Can I ask you something?"

"What?"

"Do I seem overly sexual to you?"

Talk about an unexpected question. "What are you talking about?"

He pulled into his driveway, turned off the car, and turned to face her. "Well?"

"You and I have had a lot of sex."

"Yes, we have. And I can't wait to have more. So what?"

"I've been in new relationships. I've had a few that looked like they might go somewhere and didn't. I was married. And I've *never* been so into a guy the way I am with you."

"And that's a problem?" Not from where he was sitting.

"Not for me. But do you feel pressured to perform or anything?"

"Where is this coming from?" He studied her, astonished to see her so ill at ease.

"When I was with Stephen, I wanted to have sex a lot more than he did. We had different sex drives, I guess. But it used to make me feel like something was wrong with me. For so long I've been on my own, with occasional dates but nothing that lasted. And with those guys, sex wasn't much of an issue. It was good but not great. With you, I want sex. It feels like all the time."

"You do realize I find that flattering, right?"

"You do?"

"Oh wow. You're really not kidding." He wanted to put her at ease, not having considered she might be as nervous about them as he was. She'd been so forthcoming and seemed to take their new relationship in stride. "Maggie, I won't lie. Hell, I can't." They both looked down to see him aroused. "I'm attracted to you, one hundred and ten percent. And you feel it right back. We're lucky. This physical connection between us is crazy. And I've dated enough women to know the difference between exciting and new and exciting because you're Maggie."

She smiled.

"Look, I'm a sexual guy. Like you, I've been with other partners where we didn't mesh, and it never worked out. At least, it hasn't yet for me. I'm not afraid to tell you what I feel, Maggie." Well, most of what he felt. Not the scary, emotional crap. "If I didn't want you touching me, I'd tell you."

He unzipped his fly and let the head of his dick out. She watched with greedy eyes, and he wanted nothing more than her hands all over him. "Scoot closer, Maggie. Why don't you tell me what I want?" He drew her hand to his erection and swore when she closed her fist around him. "What do I need, Maggie?"

"To come?"

"Try again. I can get myself off no problem. I need something more. Some*one* more. She makes me so happy, just being next to her. She makes me laugh and smile. And she gets me hard and hurting without trying."

She bit her lip. "You need me."

"Yeah, I do. And for more than just this." He put a hand over hers to stop her from jerking him off. "But part of what we have is this, and there's nothing wrong with desiring the partner you"— *love*—"care for." His heart raced. He'd nearly said it. Way too soon, way too much. So he did what came naturally to them and lifted his hand. "Make me happy, baby."

She watched his face while she touched him, and he found it the most erotic thing. Her eyes looked so intense, the dark brown nearly black.

He watched her watching him and spread his legs wider to give her better access. "I love when you touch me."

"Me too." She moved her hand faster, working him with enthusiasm, her breathing rushed. "I feel good when you feel good."

"Yeah." He moaned, pumping in time with her hand. "Every time with you makes a memory. I'll never look at your bed, your couch, or your bathroom the same way again." A few seconds later, he moaned her name and floated in a sea of pleasure. "Or my car. You've ruined me forever driving in here without getting uncomfortable." He drew her close for a kiss. "Trust me, Maggie. Let's not make problems where there aren't any. I can emphatically tell you that sex is not a problem I think we'll ever share."

———————

Maggie lay in Reggie's arms in his bed, enjoying his warmth in the cool night. Their closeness continued to grow. And her feelings for him only deepened. But to her shock, so did her fear of what was blossoming between them.

She had to stop trying to ruin what they had. Maggie loved him. As simple as that. Though only knowing him for a short time, she knew what she felt.

But Reggie had some baggage. His insistence that he pay for things earlier had been…*interesting*. For all that he'd admitted he and his ex-girlfriend had problems, perhaps he'd been a bigger part of them than Maggie had assumed. He'd said Amy was a taker, but Reggie seemed to be adamant, at least with Maggie, about being a giver.

While she enjoyed that he wanted to please her, she was an independent woman. Stephen paid child support. She had a job. Emily would always be cared for. What more did Maggie need?

Love with the right man.

She badly wanted to be as open with Reggie about her emotional desires as she'd been about her physical ones. But they needed more time to get to know each other. And she needed to see how he handled not always being in control.

Today it had taken him a while to realize she meant what she said. He'd given in, less than graciously, but he'd still capitulated. And he'd handled their argument with a maturity she appreciated. He'd been able to laugh it off, proud they'd made it through their first fight.

She smiled and turned toward him, feeling a surge of affection when he sighed her name and drew her closer. Pressed to his chest, she smelled nothing but Reggie and a hint of his soap. He smelled divine. A real man who knew and liked her for herself. She still couldn't believe she'd asked him if she was overly sexual.

Maggie blushed. Stephen and she hadn't been on the same page when it came to sex. Oh, he liked it well enough. But they usually did it one of two ways, never laughing so much or with such intensity. She'd had orgasms. Stephen had loved getting a blow job. But the cuddling afterward, the talking, the shared intimacy of body and soul, just hadn't been there.

Maggie wondered if Reggie felt that between them. Because even though they were physically intimate, as close as two people could be, she also felt emotionally in sync with him. But maybe that was because she'd never been able to consider sex as merely physical. Maggie didn't do one-night stands. Her sexual engagements had always been with a partner she'd been seeing for at least a few weeks and with whom she shared a measure of trust.

Reggie... He was an anomaly. A one-of-a-kind man she'd fallen for. Hard.

But he had to know she didn't *need* him, but that she *wanted* him. A vast difference.

And more, he had to allow himself to care for Emily too, not keeping a wall between Maggie and the rest of what made her the woman she was today. Emily had given Maggie patience, a sense of responsibility, and a capacity to truly love.

Reggie knew how to be responsible. But could he handle helping to parent the child of another man? Especially after giving his heart once before and getting burned in the doing?

Only time would tell.

When she woke the next morning, Reggie was behind her, his head in the crook of her neck, his arm around her middle, drawing circles on her belly.

"Hey, sleepyhead. You awake?" he asked, his voice deep, husky. Sexy.

"Mm. I must be dreaming. There's a big man in my bed hugging me."

"An amazing dream I'm sharing, because there's a curvy kitten in my arms, and she's begging for my cock."

"Oh?"

He gave her ass a firm nudge.

"*Oh.*" She smiled, resting her head on his arm.

She heard him chuckle then felt his hand slide up toward her breasts. He cupped her, toying with her nipple.

"Put your leg over mine. That's it." He shifted, moving behind her until she reached down and put his cock between her legs. "Better, but not there yet."

He stroked her breasts and kissed her neck, giving her soft bites that sent shocks though her body. He rocked against her, teasing her breasts until she couldn't stop grinding back against him, needing more. She shifted, and he notched against the slippery opening of her sex.

"Push inside me," she begged, desperate.

"Maggie May," he breathed as he slid inside her, nothing but a hot, slick welcome to bring him home. "This, baby. This is what we have." He tightened his hand over her breast, above her heart, and melted her by adding, "And this. Always this."

She let herself go as he took her, loving her with long, slow strokes until she couldn't take much more.

"Touch yourself," he ordered. "Come around me."

She reached down, feeling aroused at the thought of masturbating in front of him.

"Oh yeah. That's it." He shoved harder, still slow, but she could tell he was close.

"I'm going to come," she told him, unable to hold back.

"Do it. All over me."

She cried out as he shoved harder, faster. He gripped her breast tightly then thrust once more and released. She loved his breathy moans, the way he held her so close.

And the knowledge that she'd made him lose all control made everything better.

When they finally relaxed, he released his grip on her breast and stroked, rubbing his palms over her nipples, her belly, and easing her into a drugged, semi-aroused state.

"Good morning."

"Yeah." She sighed.

He laughed. "I could do this *every* morning."

"Me too." She kissed the arm she rested her head against. "What's the plan for today? You said something about a softball game?"

He tensed beneath her before withdrawing from her body. "Be right back." He left and returned with a towel for her. "Come on. Let's get clean."

After another half hour spent getting clean—Reggie spending a lot of time on her breasts, getting dirty again, then showering in warm, not hot, water—they finally managed to dry off and get dressed.

"Reggie, I'd like you to meet Benny and Doug," she said while they sat drinking coffee together outside at his picnic table.

"Ah, I…"

"I know it might feel too soon, but I really, really like you." She felt her cheeks heat as she said it.

He watched her and sighed. "I really, really like you too."

Maybe she wasn't wrong to continue being so honest—to an extent. "Good. I was talking to the guys yesterday, and they said they'd like to meet you."

"Oh, they did, did they?"

"Is that okay?"

His wide smile answered for him. "Yeah. Tell you what, I was going to ask you to come tonight to the game." He fidgeted, nervous. "It's with the guys. My brothers. Well, not my biological brothers, obviously. I only have sisters, but you've met them and my dad, so you know." He snapped his mouth shut. "It's the guys. They want to meet you."

"They do?" He'd told them about her?

"Yeah. They, ah, they knew Amy. We all hang a lot. We're tight, and the right girlfriend has to deal with all of us."

"All of you?" She tried to tease him, "You need a bigger bed then. Okay, I'm game."

He jerked and sloshed his coffee from his cup over the table. "*What?*"

She grinned. "I was just kidding, doofus."

He groaned. "Don't ever say that again. Mack might actually take you up on your offer."

She snickered.

"They make me nuts. We call it the Girlfriend Gauntlet. You find someone you like, the guys have to approve. It's no big deal, and I didn't even want to mention it, but I'd like you to come see me play." He looked vulnerable, and she fell even more in love with him. "But you don't have to. I just thought I'd let you know that they'll be there, and that might be more pressure than you want."

"I'd love to meet your friends. Mack has already seen me at my worst, if I remember."

"Oh, yeah. That's true." His knee bobbed. "You could bring Benny and Doug so you don't feel so alone. I'll be in the dugout with the team until the game ends."

"It sounds like fun." He didn't look any more at ease with her agreement. "Unless you would rather I didn't come?"

"Yes. No. Hell, I don't know."

Maggie stroked his hand. "Talk to me."

"I really like you. A lot. Like, a fuck ton." Reggie swearing told her he wasn't himself. Not unless they were having sex, then he dropped a ton of f-bombs. But in regular conversation, he kept it pretty clean. "I don't want anything to come between us."

"Relax, Reggie. If your friends not liking me is enough to keep us apart, then we probably weren't meant to be." She patted his arm and pressed a kiss to his cheek. "I'm not worried about it. Do you want to know why?"

"Why?" He pulled her onto his lap.

"Because you're a good person, and your best friends will be good people. Just like my friends, Benny and Doug, are good people. We don't hang with dickheads."

Reggie grinned. "Actually, my friends *are* dickheads. Wait until you talk to Mack for more than a minute."

"Nah. They'll be fine. And if they're not, I'll just threaten them with you."

He seemed to lose his tension. "Is that right?"

"That's right. My boyfriend is badass. Anyone who messes with me gets him to deal with."

"Huh. I like the way you think."

"And if that doesn't work, we'll throw Benny at them and run."

He laughed. "Even better. Now convince Benny and Doug they have to come. I just realized that if I bring Bear Destruction, everyone will bow to my amazingness."

She rolled her eyes. "You're just using me to get to Benny."

"Hell yeah. Now go get him to agree, or no sex for you later."

"Really?"

He shrugged. "Well, no. I'll still want to make love to you. But I won't go down on you. I mean it."

"Then by all means, I'll call the guys. I'm not a masochist."

Chapter Twenty-One

MACK WATCHED HIS BUDDY DANCE AROUND AS IF HE HAD spiders crawling up his ass. They were up by three runs, crushing the Top Cops, the police department's lame-ass sports team. One particular outfielder kept giving Mack the eye. She was fine as shit, but such a poor sport. Okay, so maybe he shouldn't have said anything at the coin toss to determine who would be the visiting team, and thus batting first. Like, about the losers owing the winners blow jobs, but he'd been addressing their dickhead captain, a huge homophobe, and it had been awesome to see the guy's face turn purple.

The Burning Embers, the firefighters' team, often competed with the other county teams. They typically crushed when it came to soccer and flag football, where brawn made a big difference. Although the district attorney office's Legal Eagles had some new guy on the soccer team who ran rings around them. Basketball wasn't the Burning Embers' thing either. The Parks & Wreck team had two six-five guys who could dribble. But when it came to baseball, the Burning Embers had an edge.

Wash had played a few years in college, and the guy could throw. Tex could hit anything they threw at him and was a natural. Reggie, their powerhouse home run hitter, liked baseball. When Reggie liked something, he gave it his all. Weight training, saving lives, baseball, girls.

Or one particular girl.

They'd reached the seventh inning, and he watched Reggie swinging a bat just outside the dugout, smiling up at the stands as he waited for his shot at home plate. They'd drawn quite a crowd tonight. The weather was perfect, warm with a slight breeze. The food trucks made the entire field smell like barbecue, and the Top Cops were celebrating some jackhole's promotion. Oh, right, that would be Alec, his brother.

Mack sneered at James, his oldest brother, the Top Cops' catcher, and shouted, "Suck it, Revere." Though that could have easily applied to the pitcher, Xavier, another sibling.

Mack's buddies on the bench laughed.

"Screw off, Mack." James glared at him before yelling to the pitcher, "Light him up, Xavier. He can't hit worth a shit."

Brad, standing near home plate, glared at both the pitcher and the catcher behind him then got serious.

Sadly, James was right about a no-hitter.

Xavier struck out Brad with little effort.

Honestly, the guy's head was in the clouds lately. Reggie being dopey made sense. He was getting laid again, seemed to be falling for a genuinely nice woman, and deserved all the happiness he could get. But what the hell was Brad's deal?

Though they didn't always share their feelings, Mack and the others loved one another. Hell, he felt closer to Reggie and the guys than his own brothers sometimes. But always feeling like an outsider with his family, he'd gone and done the one thing guaranteed to make him remain an outcast. Not only had he joined the Air Force in a house full of Army degenerates, but he'd gone on to become a firefighter in a house full of cops.

So, yeah, he knew all about being a square peg surrounded by round holes.

But finally, Reggie had become an insider on the fast track to *lurve*. Though Maggie seemed awfully sweet, Mack was reserving his right to judgment. She sat with two guys in the stands, and one of them happened to be Bear Destruction, only the best semipro wrestler to ever grace the ring.

Brad looked up at the guy before hanging his head in defeat as he passed Mack into the dugout.

"Brad, man, what the hell is going on with you?"

Instead of looking dejected, he wore a shit-eating grin. "I'll tell you later. Hey, did you see Bear Destruction out there?"

Tex, standing close by, held a bat over both shoulders and was stretching his trunk left and right. "We're getting autographs after. But now, let's focus on our killer avenging your honor. Seriously, Brad. You suck lately. You're making the cops look good."

"Shut up."

"Truth hurts," Mack muttered.

They all watched mighty Reggie step up to the plate. Not only did he looked ripped, as usual, but he looked happy too. And determined.

"James is going to signal Xavier to walk him," he predicted.

It was no surprise when the pitcher threw a wild pitch that Reggie had to duck.

"Hey, buddy, watch it!" called a female voice from the stands. The guys with her booed. To Mack's delight, the lady booing sounded like Maggie. He leaned out of the dugout and spotted her shaking her cast at Xavier.

"Shut it, lady," *Mack's mother* yelled back.

"Hey, Mack, isn't that your mom?" Tex asked, grinning.

He covered his eyes.

"You shut it, lady!" Maggie yelled back.

Next to her, in a deep, growly voice, Bear shouted, "The Top Cops are scared of getting burned!"

"Woo-hoo, go Burning Embers!" That was definitely Brad's girlfriend, Avery.

Then Bree, Tex's squeeze, shouted for Reggie to knock it out of the park.

The stands erupted in cheers, jeers, and much laughter. The good-natured ribbing was to be expected between rival teams who often worked together, serving the city.

The second pitch crossed the plate. A mistake on Xavier's part because Reggie didn't disappoint. He hit it out of the ballpark then took a leisurely jog around the bases, bringing two more runners in.

"See, Brad? *That's* how you do it," Tex pointed out.

"You keep talking like I want to hear you. I don't."

Mack was only glad he hadn't been up to send their runners home. He'd been averaging a .255, which wasn't too bad. But Mack excelled in defense, killing it at first base.

Reggie crossed the plate and waved at the stands. Three guesses on whom he waved to.

"I think love agrees with Reggie," Mack murmured to his friends as the home run king returned.

Hernandez, that smart-ass, overheard. "What? Reggie has a girlfriend? You blow her up before the game or after, Morgan?"

Everyone, including Reggie, laughed. "Why? You need to borrow her?"

Hernandez sneered.

Wash, the guy's best friend, chuckled. "Maybe you should, Pete. Might make you a better hitter, at least."

"Fuck off." Hernandez stepped up to the plate.

Reggie accepted congratulations and high fives. He sat, and Mack crowded him on purpose.

"My space." Reggie circled his head with his hand. "Your space." He put a hand on Mack's face and shoved. Tex snickered.

"So what's up with Maggie? Is she coming to celebrate at my place after?"

"If she wants to."

"She should."

Reggie looked worried, and Mack felt for him. "Hey, man, I'll be nice."

Reggie's eyes narrowed.

"Not *that* nice." Mack did value his life after all.

They ended up winning by five. The Top Cops refused to shake

Mack's hand after the game, for some reason. And the looker from the outfield actually flipped him off.

"And there you go, making friends again," Reggie said, taking him in a stranglehold.

Dude had rocks for biceps, and Mack was only half pretending to gasp for air.

Maggie and her friends joined the crew and their girlfriends on the field. Reggie, Mack noticed, was quick to go to her side as he introduced everyone. "Hey, gang, this is Maggie and her friend, Doug." The handsome, slender guy who'd arrived with Bear Destruction. "This, as we all know, is Bear Destruction. His name's actually Benny."

More people crowded around, staring with awe at Benny. Doug took a look and sighed. "We'll be right back."

Benny grinned. "Great to meet you guys. Nice win." Then he stepped aside with Doug and put on his Bear-Destruction, I-will-kill-you-just-for-fun expression and started signing autographs. Not surprisingly, the people clamoring for the giant's attention turned out to be aggressive cops and firefighters.

"Benny is in heaven," Maggie said, smiling.

Reggie grinned down at her and squeezed her in a hug. "No kidding."

When they continued to stare at each other, Mack cleared his throat.

"Right." Reggie coughed. "So, ah, Maggie, I'd like you to meet my friends. The living Ken doll is Brad." Brad glared at him. "Avery is his better half."

The pretty brunette smiled at Maggie. "Hi."

"Hey, aren't you on *Searching the Needle Weekly?*"

Avery nodded. "Reporter of the wacky and weird. Guilty as charged."

Reggie continued. "The tall Texan is aptly named Tex."

"How do, ma'am?" Next to him, Bree, his girlfriend, rolled her eyes.

"And Bree, his better half, is a famous photographer." And smokin' hot blond and former model, but Reggie hadn't tacked that on.

"Why yes, I am his *better* half." Bree elbowed Tex, who grinned. "Nice to meet you, Maggie."

Maggie shook her hand.

"You might remember Mack." Reggie nodded to him.

"Hi, Mack." Maggie's smile showed him what Reggie saw in her. Besides being sweet, she was surprisingly sexy, considering she had that wholesome vibe going for her. "Thank you for being so kind to my daughter." She explained to the crowd, "Mack and Reggie helped me after I got hit by a car. My daughter was with me at the time."

The ladies offered sympathy. Maggie only smiled. "I'm good now. Hey, you guys should sign my cast."

"I can't wait." Mack grinned.

Reggie smacked him in the back of the head.

Maggie, Mack noticed, tried not to laugh.

Benny and Doug turned from the small group who'd been requesting autographs, only to have Mack's friend group peppering the pair with questions and asking for autographs too. The women paid special attention to Doug, who might almost be as good-looking as Mack.

After consideration, Mack shook that thought aside. *Nah, I'm still the prettiest one here.*

Doug and Benny turned out to be both funny and engaging, but Mack paid stricter attention to Maggie, who had no problem standing back, chatting with Avery and Bree. How funny to see this, Reggie's girlfriend not trying to be the center of attention, having everyone feel sorry for her, or waiting on her hand and foot. Not at all like Reggie's ex.

Mack liked the differences he could see. A lot.

Bree and Avery seemed to approve of her right away. The guys were no doubt taking their time, like him, until they could talk to her more one-on-one.

As everyone started to wind down, Mack asked Reggie, who once again stood very close to Maggie, "Are you guys coming to the party?"

Reggie looked at Maggie.

"I'm game if you are," she told him.

"Let's go."

Doug and Benny decided to skip out with the promise to meet another time. Soon after, everyone wound up at Mack's. Pizzas had been ordered, and a cooler sat on a kitchen counter filled with a ton of drinks. Mack had made sure they had plenty of chips and snacks laid out on the dining table. He'd prepared for the festivities in advance, his turn to organize the after-party.

But as he laughed with his friends, who took their turns chatting up Reggie's girl by using their girlfriends as friendly buffers, he had no luck getting her alone. Her beefed-up boy toy wouldn't let him.

Tex saw what he was up to. "I'll herd him away."

"Nice." While Mack let the Texan do his thing, Brad kept the ladies entertained.

Finally, Mack ended up with Maggie, helping her with a soda.

"Oh, thanks." She blushed. "It's not easy to open a can with one hand."

"How are you doing?"

"Great. The broken arm is annoying, but I'm healing. Slowly."

He nodded. "Where's your little girl?"

"She's at her dad's for two weeks. Freedom," Maggie said with a sigh. "I miss her, but it's nice to be Maggie Swanson for a while. Not just Emily's mom."

"Must be tough."

"It's not, really. Uncle Doug and Uncle Benny help me out a lot. And her dad lives in the city." She smiled. "So what's it like working with Reggie?"

He turned to see the guy staring a hole through his head. "It's all good unless he thinks I'm messing with you. Then he'll kill me."

She laughed, genuinely amused. Again, different from Amy. Her amusement wasn't calculated, not an act to draw notice. She seemed pretty self-contained, not needing Reggie to be with her every second. Mack liked that Maggie didn't seem fake.

"What's it like dating Reggie?" he asked, sincerely curious.

"It's scary and wonderful at the same time. He's a special guy, and I don't want to screw it up." She laughed at herself. "Plus, he's intimidated by my muscles. So I have to be extra gentle so I don't scare him."

Mack laughed. "Is that right?" He smirked at Reggie. "Did he mention I beat all of them in a pull-up contest recently?" He flexed, knowing he was a lot less impressive than Reggie but still a powerhouse all on his own. Mack reveled in the nasty look his friend shot him. "Yeah, all this prime firefighter strength wrapped up in an attractive package. I rule our little team."

The guys overheard him, as he'd meant them to, and suddenly surrounded him and Maggie.

She was laughing and trying not to bobble her drink. Reggie saw her, and while everyone was looking at Mack, Mack was looking at him.

The lovesick look on his face told Mack to beware. Maggie Swanson was no passing fancy for his friend. She was the real deal. Mack just hoped she proved to be up to handling Reggie's neurotic ways. Because the big lug looked like a tough guy who could crush you without a care, but he had a marshmallow of a heart. And it would take a strong partner to help protect Reggie from himself.

Mack shared a glance with Brad and raised a brow at Maggie.

Brad smiled. Tex nodded.

So she was cool. Accepted. In a way Amy hadn't been.

Reggie saw them grinning at her and relaxed, covering up his dopey feelings with a grin.

Yeah, Maggie seemed lovely. But would she be there for Reggie when he did something stupid and started to ruin a good thing? The king of overcompensation had issues.

I sure the hell hope she sticks with you, buddy. You deserve to be happy.

And I deserve not *to sit by your moping side at work for months on end.*

———————————

Maggie laughed on the way back to Reggie's house. "I had so much fun. Thanks for inviting me, Reggie. Or should I call you 'slugger'? Holy crap, you're good at hitting."

He smiled with pleasure.

"Go ahead. Brag. You deserve to."

"Well, since you mention it… I'm the team hitter. I rarely get less than a double." He flexed. "It's all about the arms."

She sighed, overdoing it all on purpose. "My hero." She batted her eyelashes at him. "I was impressed. Doug and Benny were too."

"Yeah? Good." He sounded pleased and casually said, "I think the guys liked you."

"Well, I liked them. Let's see. Brad is Mr. Responsible Team Leader. A lot like you. Tex is the lanky, tall drink of water the ladies love. Sorry, but that accent is just sexy."

He frowned. "Go on."

"Mack is the real lady-killer. Laid-back, a comedian. But he's got hidden depths, I could tell."

He blinked. "Ah, right on. And me?"

"You? Why, you're the guy everyone trusts to save the day. Big, strong, and sexier than all of them put together."

He grinned. "Can I get that on the record?"

She laughed. "Anytime." She watched him drive. "I always feel safe with you."

"Good. You should."

"You're competent. A good hitter. Your smile makes me want to drop my panties."

He flashed her a wide grin. "Go for it."

"And you're a sweetheart." *I love you. Go ahead. Tell him now.*

"Man, I need to let you watch me play baseball more often."

"It wasn't that, you nerd."

He chuckled. "So do you want to swap favorite eighties sitcoms now or later?"

She blinked. "You like eighties trivia?"

"Maggie, I'm versed in all kinds of important pop culture. Try me."

So she did. They quizzed each other back and forth on the drive to his house and continued once inside, where they decided to drink a little more beer and fought about what to watch on TV.

"*The Goonies.* Come on. That's as eighties as it comes," he chided.

"Look. You're sexy and you can hit a ball, but that doesn't mean anything when it comes to *Buckaroo Banzai.*"

He froze. "What?"

"I realize it's considered a cult classic, but it came out in 1984." She didn't mention that Stephen had turned her on to it, as science-fiction films had always been a passion of his. Maggie had started with *The Adventures of Buckaroo Banzai Across the 8th Dimension* and gone through a string of '80s films while pregnant with Emily.

Reggie kept staring at her. His eyes narrowed. "Are you screwing with me?"

She took a large sip of beer, enjoying the apricot flavor. "This is good. And no, I'm not screwing with you. Yet. Why?"

"I've never met anyone who had my taste in movies." He pulled her next to him to sit on the couch. "And you have also expressed appreciation for my ability to organize, which is only slightly better than yours."

"You wish."

He grinned. "What's your favorite food?"

"Tacos."

"Hmm. I like pizza, but I like tacos too."

She asked, "How about your favorite color?"

"I don't know. What color bra are you wearing tonight?"

She grinned. "That would be red then."

"And pink. I'm secure in my masculinity. I do wear pink."

"I think you look good in anything." She thought about it. "But maybe not puce."

"What's puce?"

"It's like a dark red or purplish-brown color." She made a face. "The house I grew up in was puce. I hated it."

"The house?"

"No, the color. I loved the house. Loved my parents too." She sighed. "I still miss them sometimes, but it's been eleven years since they've been gone."

He played with a strand of her hair. "That must have been tough. Especially when you had Emily."

"Yeah. I really wanted my mom there. I know she'd love Emily."

"Who wouldn't?" He smiled. "Your daughter is just like her momma."

She stared at him, seeing a man she wanted to keep. Forever. She cleared her throat. "Ah, what about you and your family?"

"My mom passed when I was sixteen. It sucked. She was the life of any party, always with a ready smile, so giving. We all loved her so much. About killed my dad."

"I'm sorry." She leaned in to kiss him and didn't linger, wanting only to offer comfort.

He smiled, his eyes a little sad. "She would have liked you a lot." He laughed. "I could see her doing the exact same thing to my dad that you did to me in that restaurant, telling him off if he thought about paying for her when she didn't want him to. Mom was more a lover than a fighter. Unless you messed with her family." He shot her a look. "Or her pride. She could be prickly about stuff."

"Reggie, it wasn't pride keeping me from taking your money."

He raised a brow.

"Okay, so maybe it was. But I don't want to be a taker." *Like your ex-girlfriend.* "I like to think I'm more of a giving person."

"Yeah? So give me something." He downed the rest of his beer.

She did the same and wished she hadn't. "Wow, that was a bit much." She coughed.

He hugged her, his body shaking with mirth. "Maggie, you make me laugh."

She felt warm, and it wasn't just a buzz. The overflowing love she had for Reggie was inexplicable yet real.

"You want me to give you something?" she asked and took off her top.

His amusement faded.

She nodded to her bra. "Take if off for me, would you?"

"Whatever you want." He removed it and stared at her, his breathing raspy.

"I want to give you my heart." She put his hand over her breast, and her nipple beaded.

He closed his hand around her and leaned close. She had her legs pulled under her on the couch, giving her a little added height. And it made them nearly level. Perfect for kissing.

She closed her eyes when Reggie kissed her, his mouth coaxing, his seduction subtle yet packing a wallop. He put his other hand on her breast, molding her chest with hands that burned.

"So hot," he said, reading her mind, and slid his tongue inside her mouth. He showed her how much he cared by giving her so much pleasure. Reggie didn't like to rush, savoring her. Even when they came together suddenly, he always made sure to see to her pleasure first.

This lovemaking wasn't hurried, and it contained an element

of affection that overwhelmed the carnality, pulling her deeper under his spell.

He angled his mouth over hers and carefully put her cast along the back of the couch, out of the way.

"Reggie?"

"Let me." He stared into her eyes. "You're so beautiful, Maggie." He didn't smile.

She grew nervous, not sure why. But it felt like something monumental was happening between them. "I…"

He leaned forward and took her nipple in his mouth.

She sighed and held him tight, wanting to feel him everywhere. He gave her breasts careful attention, sucking her nipples into stiff points, cupping the heavy globes, learning what she liked and repeating what made her moan the loudest.

Then his mouth returned to hers, and he lifted her in his arms with ease.

They kissed as they walked down the hall, her head spinning with a heady combination of lust, love, and fascination for Reggie's sheer power.

He laid her on the bed and took his time removing her pants, leaving her pink lace panties on.

His gaze narrowed. "I know I said my favorite color was red, but now it's definitely pink." His shirt came off, followed by the rest of his clothes.

And as he stood there, a bastion of strength looming over her, she sighed and smiled at him.

"I love you, Reggie."

Chapter Twenty-Two

REGGIE HEARD THE WORDS BUT COULDN'T MAKE SENSE OF them. A gorgeous, nearly naked woman lay in his bed, staring at him as if she'd never seen anything better. And then she confessed that she loved him.

"Am I drunk?"

She smiled. "Come here."

He knelt on the bed next to her. "Am I dreaming?"

She knelt before him and put her hands, her cast included, over his chest. "I don't know. Am I dreaming? I'm in love, and he's perfect. Will he want me if I'm a bad girl?"

Reggie just stared. "I think you should be bad and find out."

She smiled against his chest. He felt her lips curl. Then they parted and closed around his nipple.

Fuck. He put his arms around her, holding her close, his cock trapped between them.

She licked and nibbled, and he thought he'd lose his mind. When she turned to his other nipple, he let his hands wander. Her breasts felt full, heavy, and he played with her, loving how she felt. With Maggie, he usually felt powerful.

But right now, trapped by her hot little mouth, he felt weak. Needy. And so damn hard.

He reached down, sliding past her slender belly, and sought her heat.

"You're wet," he whispered, in awe that she could get so aroused by being with him. Lord knew he felt the same way, but every time with her kept getting better.

She leaned into him, still kissing his chest. Her hand tickled down his abdomen and grazed his cock.

He hissed and thrust his finger inside her.

She squirmed but didn't stop kissing him, her mouth now moving lower. Knowing where she was headed, he didn't stop her. Instead, he dragged his hand from her body, paying attention to her tight, wet clit. He rubbed her and watched through shuttered eyes as she tilted her head back and moaned.

He kissed her neck, sucking hard enough to leave a mark, feeling possessive as hell. And loving. So fucking lost in love with her. He pinched her clit, rubbing then pinching again, and she rode his fingers, faster and faster.

But then she pushed his hand away and looked him in the eye. "I'm not that bad yet. Do you still want me?"

"When *don't* I want you? You kill me. You really do."

She smiled and kissed his chest. She savored each nipple, drawing out his arousal until he feared he'd snap. Then she kept moving, down and farther down.

She lowered her head so her ass waved in the air.

He closed his eyes, trying to hold on.

And then she engulfed him, working up and down, so damn slowly.

He felt a spurt leave him, his balls tight, his dick ready to blow. "I love you, Maggie," he rasped, because he had to. He pulled her off him and lay back on the bed, pulling her with him. "I love you so damn much."

Her bright smile was the answer to every question he'd ever asked.

He turned her around so she faced his cock, and he stared up at her pussy. "Now be a bad girl and show me you care."

She gave a soft laugh and bore down.

He pulled her hips down and plastered his mouth over her. She had him so lost to anything but sensation, he didn't know what he did, acting solely on instinct, wanting her to come when he did. To feel what he felt.

He licked and sucked, shoved one finger then two inside her, and ate her out with desperation as she took him to the edge of ecstasy and sucked him right over the cliff.

As he came, he sucked harder on her clit, feeling her jolt against him. He licked her cream, entranced with her sultry taste.

They finally parted, and she turned around to sit over his belly and stare down at him with bright eyes.

"Did I hear right?" She kissed him, and he tasted himself on her lips. He wondered if she tasted herself, and if she found it as sexy as he did.

"What?"

His heart was racing, and all he wanted to do was kiss her.

"Did you say you love me?"

"Hell, yeah. And I meant it."

"No takebacks." She pulled back, and tears filled her eyes.

"Aw, Maggie. Don't cry. But if you have to, I'll still love you."

She smiled through tears. "I love you too."

"I know, and I still can't believe it." He hugged her to him, blinking to clear his own eyes. "I think you were made for me."

"Yeah." She sighed and snuggled on top of him. "Can we stay here like this forever?"

"Sure. But I have to warn you. If I don't show up for duty tomorrow, the guys will come over. And knowing them, they'll stare if you're naked."

"I guess I can let you get back to work tomorrow. If I have to." She smiled against his chest. "Reggie?"

"Yeah?"

"Let's be the same as we were before tonight. Loving each other shouldn't change things."

Ah, so she did feel the same worries he did, that their perfection couldn't last and wished it would. "Sounds good to me, Maggie May." When she tugged his chest hair, he laughed. "I mean it. Love isn't something to be scared of." *Listen to yourself, dumbass.* "I love you, baby. But Maggie, I really do love you more when you're bad."

He grinned when she nipped her way to his mouth and kissed him. "Then you're going to love me tonight, Studly. I feel a Yahtzee coming on."

———

The next week passed in a haze of bliss. Maggie visited Reggie once at the station, not wanting to intrude but welcomed by him and his crew. The entire C shift swung by to say hello, all of them teasing Reggie for having such a hot girlfriend. But in a nice way, making her feel accepted.

She and he continued to debate all things '80s, though she drew the line at country music and preferred the '80s female rappers to the guys.

They saw an action-adventure movie they both loved and pigged out on popcorn and Raisinets. She went with him to a bowling match with the guys and spent her time laughing with Avery and Bree, whom she really liked. Mack provided a running commentary while the guys tried to out-macho each other. Then their girlfriends would cut them down to size. It made her laugh to see. But she especially liked being hugged and kissed and treated like she mattered by Reggie.

Since confessing how they felt, they'd grown closer, spending passion-filled nights at her house or his, sleeping together and playing together. Maggie hadn't been so happy in so long, and even Doug and Benny commented on it.

But of course, nothing lasted forever. On the Saturday when they readied to pick Emily up, Stephen called.

"Hello?"

"Hey, Maggie. It's me, Stephen."

She grinned. "Yeah, I know. Your name popped up in my contact info."

"Oh. Right. I was wondering if it would be okay to keep Emily another week. I can bring her back if you say no. I just thought I'd ask."

She hadn't considered he might want *more* time. The fact that Emily and Stephen had spent an entire two weeks together without incident had surprised her, but Emily's tweets and Stephen's pictures showing them having fun had amused her.

"Well, I guess so. Can I talk to Emily?"

"Sure. Emily, come say hi to Mommy."

"Hi, Mommy."

Maggie smiled. "Hey, Ninja Princess. How are you?"

"So good! We got a kitten named Vader. He's black and keeps pouncing on Frank. Frank's kinda scared, but I'm making them be friends."

"That's great, honey."

Reggie stood by her shoulder, waiting.

"Do you want to stay another week with Daddy? It's totally up to you."

"Can I? We're supposed to look at stars tomorrow, and Vader needs me to find his mouse for him. He lost it under my bed."

"Sure thing. I'll see you next week, okay? And you can call me whenever you want."

"Okay."

Maggie looked at Reggie as she asked her daughter, "Would you like to say hi to Reggie?"

"Reggie? Yes!"

Maggie handed him the phone.

"Hey, BLS buddy. How's it going?"

The conversation lasted several minutes, until Reggie handed the phone back.

Emily said, "Tell Reggie to wait there until I come back next week, okay? I want to talk to him again. I have more questions."

Maggie grinned. Of course she did. "Sure thing. Bye, sweetie. I love you."

"I love you too, Mommy. Bye, Reggie!"

Stephen came back on the phone. "Reggie, huh?"

Maggie blushed at Reggie's raised brow. Obviously, he could hear Stephen. "We're dating, but don't mention it to Emily yet, okay?"

Silence, then Stephen said, "No problem, and congrats. Enjoy the extra week. I'll drop her off at your place next Saturday at noon. Okay?"

"Sounds good. Have fun."

"Bye."

He disconnected.

She saw Reggie watching her. "What?"

"Emily's staying another week. Are you okay with that?"

She shrugged. "Why wouldn't I be? I love her, but Stephen loves her too. Emily is okay with it."

"Maggie."

She let out the breath she'd been holding. "Yes, no. I don't know. I love her and miss her. She's my baby girl. But you've had me so distracted." At that, he smiled. "I feel guilty that I get another uninterrupted week with you."

He pulled her to him so she stood between his spread legs while he leaned back against the couch. "You could have said no to her staying longer."

"I want her to be happy, and she wants to stay with him. He's missed so much already."

Reggie's expression hardened. "Was that his fault or yours?"

"What?"

"I know you. And I think if he ever wanted to see her, you'd say yes. So this is really him finally having the balls to be a dad."

She blinked. "Um, well, yeah. You're right."

"But you can't let him step all over you."

"Reggie? It's okay, really. I don't mind. And I get to spend extra time with you." She kissed him. "Honestly, if I thought for one minute my daughter wasn't safe or cared for, she'd be here with me."

He studied her. "You're a great mom." He sighed. "Sorry. My ex used to drop everything when her ex-husband told her to. And it hurt Rachel with all the back and forth at the end."

"What happened with them? Will you tell me about it?"

He shrugged, looking uncomfortable. "I told you I met Amy while helping her out of a jam. She was pretty. She liked me. I liked her. And we started dating. I fell for Rachel right away." He smiled in remembrance. "She's a lot like Emily but not a genius, I have to say. And not as bossy."

"My daughter, the termagant."

He chuckled. "That's what I like about her. Emily doesn't take any sass. Anyway, my relationship with Amy followed a pattern. She would need help. I'd be all too happy to give it. I like feeling needed."

She nodded. "Nothing wrong with that. I like feeling needed too."

His eyes warmed. "We're a lot alike."

"We are."

"Well, Amy always seemed to need me. At first, it was satisfying. She stroked my ego, would tell her friends how helpful and smart and strong I was. I ate it up." He looked abashed. "But I also loved her. It was real, for both of us. She's not a bad person."

Maggie nodded but said nothing.

"Rachel loved me. And I loved her. She was such an innocent, sweet little girl. I showed her how to fix things, how to exercise, how to make a fist." He grinned. "That kid could box, let me tell you. She was also shy around people she didn't know, and that was okay with me. Everyone's different, you know?

"I introduced my dad and sisters to Amy three months into our relationship. They didn't like her."

"Why?"

"She was shy. Always looking to me before answering. Letting me get her food and drinks, basically wait on her. I thought it was out of politeness because we were at my dad's, you know? I didn't try to tell her what to do or anything. She was just, well, meek."

"Not her fault."

"Exactly. But my dad thought she was all wrong for me, and she offended my sister without meaning to." He pinched the bridge of his nose. "She overheard Nadia talking to Lisa about Shannon, a date that went wrong. Amy tried to join the conversation by telling Nadia about a few friends she knew that Nadia might like. Girlfriends of hers."

"O-kay." Maggie didn't understand.

"Shannon was a dude."

Comprehension dawned.

"Yeah. Nadia's a little sensitive about being called gay because she's been stereotyped in the past."

"She has?"

"My sister has muscles bigger than Mack. She's aggressive and has no problem cutting a guy down to size. Well, she's dated some real assholes, and their clever comebacks are to tell her she should stick to lesbians and stop trying to pass for straight."

"That's rude."

"And hurtful. I mean, my sister couldn't care less about a person's sexuality. She's not biased against anyone But now she has this idea she's not feminine enough, whatever the hell that means." He sighed. "Of course, Amy had no idea and was only trying to be nice. Nadia wasn't having it."

"Oh boy. I wouldn't want to get on your sister's bad side."

"I don't either. Lisa tried to stick up for Amy, but then Amy turned on Lisa, saying how Lisa hated her and they were mean and blah, blah, blah. She never went back to visit."

"Awkward."

"You don't know the half of it." He rubbed his head. "I love my family, and we were distant for a while. I would still visit, but the topic of Amy was off-limits. Things were strained."

"That's awful."

"Yeah." He sighed. "So you have my family and Amy not getting along. Then Amy starts talking to her loser ex-husband again. The guy ran out on them both when Rachel was just six. He never contacted them, divorced her, then dumped her. Then he calls out of the blue wanting her back."

She could see the hurt had yet to leave him.

"I thought Amy and I had something, but I didn't like the way he used her. And the way she let him. We argued. She'd cry, I'd feel like shit, then we'd pretend we hadn't fought." He looked thoughtful. "That went on for the last six months of our relationship, actually. But she stopped bringing him up, and we started to get along again."

"Huh."

"But the jerk eventually convinced her Rachel needed him. So, for her daughter, she went back to him."

Maggie didn't know what she would have done. For Emily, she'd move heaven and earth. And yet, a user and a deserter wouldn't deserve her love.

"Amy wouldn't hear me out. Wouldn't take my calls or let me say goodbye to Rachel. She moved out one day, and that was that."

That put a different spin on things. "You guys lived together?"

"She had nowhere else to go." Reggie shrugged. "When Devon left her, he took everything. The rent money, the good car, all their stuff. She had a crap car and two suitcases of clothes. That was it."

"So you stepped in to help and fell in love."

"Yeah." He huffed. "She moved in right away, but we weren't a couple until a few months later. I didn't want to take advantage of her or anything."

Seemed to Maggie like Amy had been the one taking advantage, but she didn't say so.

"I've done it before. Helped women in need. I don't try to get cheated on or dumped. But it happens. My family gets pissed at me for helping. My friends tell me to not be such a sucker. But I can't help it. I want to help."

She had a bad feeling in the pit of her stomach. "Is that what it is with me?"

He shot her a shocked glance. "Hell, no. You're the prickliest, most independent woman I've ever met. Well, except for my sisters, but they don't count. You won't let me buy you anything, and you don't need me for anything but Frank. And even on that note, you'll figure things out. No, you are definitely no Amy."

"Okay, good." Still, a hint of doubt remained.

"Besides, my dad and sisters like you. So do the guys." He paused. "But I can't lie. Seeing you cave to Stephen has me seeing flashbacks of Amy all over again."

Irritated, she scowled. "I didn't *cave* to anything. My daughter's father wants extra time with his daughter I'm happy to give, because it lets me spend extra time with my boyfriend. Everyone's happy."

"Okay, yes. I'm sorry." He groaned and pulled her close for a hug. "I'm sorry."

"Reggie, I love you. I'm not Amy. And you're not Stephen."

He pulled back and frowned. "I know I'm not him. You don't have to rub it in."

"What are you talking about?" She had no idea where all this weirdness was coming from. "Stephen is the man I divorced. I don't want Stephen. I want you."

"Hell. I'm acting like an idiot. Sorry, Maggie."

Seeing this side of Reggie gave Maggie a fuller picture of him. On the one hand, she liked knowing he wasn't perfect. No one was, but up until this point, he hadn't put a foot wrong. His baseless jealousy made little sense, but at least he owned the feeling. Something Stephen had never done.

"Do you think we can start our weekend over?" he asked.

"I think you'll have to grovel."

His slow smile melted her reserve. "I can do that. And I promise all the foreplay your heart can handle tonight. I swear."

"Well then. Okay."

"Just one thing."

"What's that?"

"I have something I need to do tomorrow. And I'd like you to come. After brunch with my family, I mean."

She smiled. "That I can do."

———————

Sunday afternoon, surrounded by puppies and kittens at a pet adoption north of Fremont, Maggie helped volunteer while Reggie, Brad, Tex, and Mack wore Pets Fur Life T-shirts and flirted—ahem, *talked*—with people interested in adopting animals.

The area in West Woodland Park was crowded with children playing sports, people walking, and the sectioned-off area that Pets Fur Life had chosen to host an adoption. Several small, wire pens contained animals needing good homes. And Maggie, with only one arm to use, had been stationed with the kittens.

Watching Reggie smile and talk to others, she saw his natural charisma in effect. She loved looking at him. She only wished half the other women wandering by would stop cozying up to him with "questions." *Please. It's an animal. It has fur and whiskers. Now move along.*

Mack sidled up to her. "Hey there, Magnificent Maggie."

"Hello to you, Magnificent Mack."

A woman stood a little too close to Reggie and, laughing, put her hand on his arm. So obvious. But Maggie's *boyfriend* just smiled back and kept talking.

"Yeah, Reggie's great at these things. But he's clueless, so cut him some slack."

"Clueless?" She handed a kitten to a lady asking to see one.

She and Mack watched the lady and her two children play with the little fellow.

"Reggie's too nice," Mack said. "Not to guys, but to women. Amy used to play him like a fiddle."

"Really?"

"Reggie's decent. Has a heart bigger than anyone I know," Mack admitted. "But he never saw her working him. To him, she was sad and nice and needed a hand. But we saw right through her. She used him until she didn't need him anymore. And the big dope still thinks she was sweet but naive." Mack sneered. "Naive my"—he watched the children playing with the kitten and finished with—"butt."

An interesting perspective. But was it true? "I don't know, Mack. Reggie told me you guys didn't like her, but that she was just shy."

"Maybe that's what he thinks, but I swear she made a move on Brad. It was subtle, but I saw it."

"Really?"

"Brad doesn't think so, but I know what I saw. But Brad refused to think his buddy's girl tried anything. Hell, maybe it's just that I didn't like her much. I don't know. Reggie would never hear a word against his precious Amy, so I never mentioned it. And we still don't talk about her or Rachel because it hurts him." He looked her over and waited for the lady to hand back the kitten.

"We're going to go fill out the adoption form." The woman smiled. "Can you hold him for us?"

The little guy meowed, and Maggie set him back down with his littermates. "Sure thing."

The lady and her children left.

Mack said, "I just wanted you to know. I like you. You don't seem like the using type."

She stared at him. "I'm not."

"Then help keep an eye on him when the next sob story comes rolling in. I don't want to see him hurt again. He deserves better."

Maggie agreed. She gave Mack a kiss on the cheek, and he pulled back, startled.

"You're a good friend, Mack. And that's not me making a move, just stating a fact." She smiled. "But my daughter thinks Reggie is better."

He chuckled. "Your kid is of course wrong, but she has good taste." He left her to help someone with a dog.

The adoption went well. And two hours after arriving, Maggie and Reggie walked back to his car, the others following. But once there, Maggie yanked him down and gave him a kiss to remind him he was hers. Behind them, Tex let out a wolf whistle.

"Hot damn, girl. Best you get on home before you set his hair on fire. What little he has left." He laughed before disappearing into his truck.

Behind him, Brad and Mack hooted.

Reggie opened the door for her and quickly got in. "What the hell was that?" His crazed smile indicated he wanted more.

"I don't like everyone looking at you. You're mine."

His smile grew wider. "Yes, I am. Now let's go home so you can do that again. But maybe without so many clothes on this time. And remember, I have a lot more groveling to do."

"As if I could forget." But on the way home, she continued to harbor just a sliver of doubt. Did Reggie really love her, or did he, deep down, just need someone new to save?

Chapter Twenty-Three

By Saturday, Reggie felt as if he'd missed something. Maggie had been loving and smiling but growing more distant. He had work, and they were slammed with crazy calls, so he and the guys had assisted the other crew with medical emergencies when they could. They also had a fire to put out that could have turned serious had they not arrived when they did.

He felt good about that one.

By the time his shift ended, he was tired. Maggie had texted that she was getting Emily at noon, and he was more than welcome to wait with her.

But after their weird week, he thought it best to come over later, once Emily had settled into a familiar rhythm at home again. No matter what Maggie said, he'd seen the effects of a dysfunctional parental dynamic and didn't want to add to any trouble.

He said goodbye to the guys and sat in his car, needing a breather.

The phone rang, and he picked it up on autopilot. "Yo?"

"Reggie?"

He froze at the familiar little girl's voice. "Rachel?"

"Reggie, I miss you," she cried.

"Honey, are you okay?" Movement in his rearview pulled his attention.

To his shock, she and her mother walked behind his car. He quickly exited. "What the heck are you guys doing here?"

Rachel ran to him, and he laughed as he lifted her up and swung her around. "Hey, sweetheart."

"Reggie, I missed you." She planted a kiss smack on his cheek.

"Me too." He looked over her shoulder at Amy, who smiled at him. He didn't smile back, not sure what to feel about her. "Amy."

"Hi, Reggie."

"What the hell is this?" Mack said, sounding colder than Reggie had ever heard him.

He turned around to see Mack glaring at Amy.

"Mack, you remember Amy and *Rachel*."

Mack glanced at the little girl Reggie held and eased back on the animosity. He flashed her a charming grin. "Hello there, lovely lady. You sure got big."

She giggled. "Hi, Mack."

Reggie set her down, but she continued to stand close, wrapping an arm around his waist.

"Reggie, can I talk to you?" Amy asked, her voice soft.

Mack snorted. "Oh, *now* you want to talk? What's wrong? You need a place to stay again?"

Amy blushed. Rachel looked back and forth between her mother and Mack but said nothing.

"Mack." Reggie shook his head.

"Yeah?" Mack crossed his arms over his chest and planted himself by Reggie's car.

Reggie sighed. "Amy, let's head to the diner." A familiar spot the gang often went for breakfast after a shift, back when they'd been at their old station. Since they'd made the move to Station 44, they no longer frequented the place, preferring a diner closer, in Beacon Hill.

"I'll come with you," Mack offered.

Surprised, Reggie looked at him. "Ah, I think it would be best if I talked to Amy alone."

"Sure. But what do you think *Maggie* will think?"

"Maggie?" Amy frowned.

"His girlfriend," Mack blurted. Then he turned and left mumbling, "Stupid bastard."

Reggie let Amy drive them to the diner since he no longer had a booster seat for Rachel. Which made him wonder if he should get a new one for Emily.

"You have a girlfriend?" Amy asked.

She looked good. The same. Smiling yet resigned, her hazel eyes bright in an otherwise beautiful yet drawn face. Amy had freckles across the bridge of her nose that turned her from bombshell sexy to a mix of glamorous beautiful. Her melancholy added a hint of drama, and he'd always considered her intriguing rather than gloomy.

Rachel, on the other hand, was an exuberant girl, with her mother's riot of dark-brown curls, hazel eyes, and freckles. Fortunately, she looked more like her mother than her father. Devon was a con man with a criminal past who'd deserted his family. And this was the man Amy thought her daughter needed?

Realizing she'd asked about his new girlfriend, he answered, "Yeah. Maggie's great."

"I'm happy for you."

Yeah? So why don't you look happy?

She kept her eyes on the road as she drove and said, "Reggie, I need help."

He swallowed a sigh. They pulled into the diner. She turned off the car. "Shall we go in?"

They entered and sat in the back. After ordering breakfast, Rachel colored with crayons on the kiddie menu while Reggie and Amy watched each other.

"I've missed you," she said.

He wanted to yell at her for coming back now, hug her because he still cared, and shake her while asking why the hell she'd broken his heart. *Why didn't you at least try to make it work? Why leave me for that jerk?*

Instead, he said, "I missed you too. For a while." He smiled at Rachel. "But I never stopped missing this one."

Rachel smiled up at him.

Amy sighed and fiddled with her fork. "Devon and I aren't together."

"I'm sorry."

"No, you're not."

"Amy, I don't think this is the place to talk about Devon." He nodded at Rachel.

Amy shrugged. "She knows."

"Daddy's coming back soon." The little girl didn't look up from the menu, busy coloring. "He has to do a job, but he's coming back for us."

"In six to ten, earlier if good behavior?" Reggie asked Amy, his brow raised.

She frowned. "He's really working. He does construction now. He's becoming an electrician."

"Good for him." Reggie studied her, seeing the past in her face. He remembered them laughing, being a family. The way they'd play games or go for walks by the water. Festivals and dinners spent as a unit.

And he remembered Amy always needing more. Attention, money, hope. Propping her up to keep her from falling had been a chore, but one he'd done to the best of his ability because he'd loved her. And she'd loved him back, taking care of the house, being there whenever he'd needed her. Loving him gently in the dark, taking them to places where only pleasure existed.

Did he love her still? A month ago he would have said yes and probably taken her back without question. But now…?

"Amy, what do you want?"

"I missed you, and I realized I made a mistake."

"It's been eight months. I've moved on." *With a woman who loves me.*

"I haven't." She reached across the table to grab his hand. "I'm sorry for barging in on you like this. You're probably tired from work. But we have nowhere else to go."

"Again?" He stared in disbelief. "Amy, you had a job. You had a house. Rachel's got school in another month."

"I *had* a job. We had to move for Devon's work. And Rachel will still go back to school. We have time."

"And the house?"

"Devon can't afford school and renting a place here in the city. His school is in Tacoma."

"They why aren't you there with him?"

"We had a fight." She sighed.

The waitress brought their food, so they tabled the discussion and ate.

Once their plates had been cleaned, Amy asked, "Look, can we talk about this at your place?" She watched him take the check from the waitress and go up to pay. As usual, she didn't try to grab the check or protest his paying.

Not wanting to embarrass her by asking if she had money, he settled the bill without question.

Maggie had loudly fought with him in a restaurant to pay for her own meal. Maggie would never talk about things that might hurt her daughter in front of her. And Maggie would never ask him for something without doing everything in her power to get it herself.

He stood with Amy outside, waiting by the passenger side, studying her.

"I'm sorry, Reggie, but we have nowhere else to go."

He looked at her then at Rachel, who gave him a tentative smile. His heart literally hurt for the little girl. And he knew he couldn't not help. Or at least, not hear Amy out.

He sighed. "Drop me at my car and follow me back to my place."

"Thank you."

Once back in his car, he stared at his phone. He had to call Maggie and tell her about Amy. But he didn't want to. The situation had *danger* written all over it. Sucking it up, he dialed and pulled away toward his house.

"Hello?"

"Hey, Maggie. How are you? Ready for Emily to come back?"

She laughed. "Oh yeah. I stocked up on macaroni and yogurt bars. Can you believe Emily took a bunch with her to her dad's and actually likes them now?"

That made him smile. "I told you those were good." He paused. "Hey, ah, something came up. Why don't you and Emily hang today? Have some mother-daughter bonding time. I'll pop over tomorrow afternoon, and we can make a day of it." Which reminded him. He had to see his father and sisters for brunch since he'd skipped last week.

"Is everything okay?"

"I hope so." He sighed. "I'll tell you about it tomorrow. And wish me luck at family brunch."

She laughed. "Good luck. And Reggie, call me if you need me, okay?"

"I will." He hung up and continued to the house, wondering why he felt so guilty for not coming clean. *It's not like I'm cheating or anything.*

Once at home, he parked and let himself inside.

Amy and Rachel soon followed, and it was as if they'd never left.

For all of a split second.

The hurt, the feelings of betrayal, and his broken heart rushed back. "Rachel, honey, can you play outside? Or would you rather watch TV while I talk to your mom?"

She smiled, so sweet. Still innocent, no matter what her mother had done. "Can I watch TV?"

"Sure." He kissed the top of her head and handed her the remote. "Go for it. Amy? Let's talk outside."

She sat with him at the patio table and looked around. "The house still looks great. I love the flowers." She nodded to the rose bushes. "The maple looks amazing."

He studied her, wishing he didn't have such conflicting feelings. "Can you please just answer me? Why are you here?"

She ran a hand through her hair, the sunlight glinting off the auburn highlights. That hadn't changed, that Amy could still captivate sheerly on looks. But he no longer found them mesmerizing. "Devon and I were doing well. He's changed, I know you won't believe it, but it's true. He was working over in Renton with a construction crew, but then they cut back when they lost a few bids. So he looked around and found a course he can take in Tacoma. He learned that becoming an electrician would provide steady income. But it's too expensive for him to commute. We'd have to live there. I'd lose my job."

"The job you no longer have."

She sighed. "I had it until we moved to Tacoma, but he couldn't start right away. I was looking for work. Our savings were stretching thin."

"Savings? That's new."

She glared. "Look, we were trying. I wanted to do right for Rachel, to show her that everyone deserves a second chance."

He couldn't argue with that. And though at the time he'd wanted to, he knew he couldn't argue that a child should be able to see her father. He might consider Devon scum, but the guy had never physically harmed his family. And he'd admitted his mistakes and asked for a second chance. While still screwing the neighbor, but Amy had bought into his apologies.

"In Tacoma, we started fresh. But the lack of money caused problems. I got a job cleaning office buildings, but we couldn't afford the rent. Devon moved in with a roommate. I had to talk to my sister." She grimaced.

Reggie shook his head. "That roommate wouldn't happen to be an attractive woman, would it?"

She looked away. "It's just until he's done the course he's taking. Till he can get us a good house. He's doing what he has to to provide for his family."

By fucking another woman? Oh, Amy.

She glanced up, tears glimmering on her long lashes, and he felt so bad for her and the poor choices she continued to make.

"Denise forgave me for our past arguments. But she can't help me right now. I had to go apologize to Mom and Dad and play by their rules." She started crying. "They kicked us out."

He hated to see her cry and fetched her some tissues. "Here."

She wiped her eyes.

"How does Devon feel about you coming to me for help?"

"He doesn't know." She grabbed him before he could sit, clutching his wrist with both hands. "Please, Reggie. I know I didn't handle our breakup the right way. But I wouldn't have asked for help if it wasn't for Rachel. Can't you just let us stay here for another month or two? That should be enough time for me to find work and a place to live."

"Seriously?" He stared at her. "You break my heart, rip Rachel away without even letting me say goodbye, and expect me to let you move right back in here? Oh, and while you're still with Devon?" He frowned at her. "I used to wonder if you and he were getting together while we were dating. But I never asked, because I guess I didn't want to know."

She cried silent tears and looked at him, so sad. "I didn't want to come here. I'm so sorry, Reggie. But I need your help. No one else will help me."

A feeling of, not compassion, but pity for her filled him.

Yet…he'd read the guilt in what she didn't deny—that she had been cheating on him with Devon when they'd been dating. And that fucking hurt. He wanted to say no to her moving in and would have, but she called for Rachel.

The little girl came out. "What, Mom?"

"How would you like it if we stayed here with Reggie for a while?"

Rachel lit up. "Oh, could we? I missed you so much, Reggie."

He wavered.

"Devon and I aren't in a good place. I want Rachel to be stable, just for a little while."

Rachel, the innocent in all of this. "One week," he said and wondered how much of a mistake he was making. "Enough time for you to find another place to live. Sorry, but that's the best I can do."

"Thank—"

"You know where everything is. I have someplace to be." He kissed Rachel on the head and left before he started talking to Amy, laughing with her, forgetting what she'd done while they reminisced about the old times and how great they'd been. Back when she'd been cheating on him and he'd been so in love and wanting a family, he'd ignored the signs.

And he'd known. Idiot that he was, he'd pretended they'd been tight for the two years they'd dated. It hurt to know that about himself now, something he'd never before admitted.

The more he thought about their "glory days," the more he realized that anytime in the past that he'd thought about breaking off with her, she'd make love to him or get him to spend more time with Rachel. Sweet, innocent Rachel and sexy, lovely, fragile Amy. They'd needed him, she'd say. And they needed him again now.

But he had Maggie. And Emily. He couldn't mess that up.

One week shouldn't matter though. If Maggie broke up with him over helping someone who needed it, was she really the right woman for him in the long run?

He sighed, wishing life were simple again.

Monday afternoon, Reggie came to visit, and Maggie felt the same butterflies inside that she always did around him. She and Reggie had decided to tell Emily together that they were dating, to gently feel her out and field any questions as a united front.

But after he'd chatted with Emily, who left to get something from her room, he turned to Maggie and with a too-wide smile and too-happy tone, asked, "Maggie, do you think Emily could hang with Doug and Benny while we talk for a bit?"

The smile stayed in place but didn't reach his eyes. He looked serious. Nervous. Maybe even scared.

Anxious, she sent Benny a quick text. "Let me see." A minute later, she heard a knock on the door. "Come in."

Benny entered, saw Reggie, and grinned. "If it isn't the home run slugger. What's up, man?" He clapped Reggie on the back.

"Doing great. How about you?"

"Same old, same old." He yelled for Emily.

Maggie shook her head and cupped an ear, as if in pain. "Thanks for that."

He laughed. "It works." He pointed to the little girl and her dog. "Just you, with two feet. The girl child. Come on. Uncle Doug wants your help making play dough."

"Oh. Okay." She ran to Reggie and kissed his hand. "Don't leave before I come back."

Reggie nodded. "I'll try not to."

After they left, Maggie gave in to her urge and gave Reggie a big hug. "You look like you need this. I sure do."

He hugged her back so tightly, she let out an *oomph*. "Oh, sorry." He pulled back to kiss her. "I missed you."

"You look tired."

"I am. So fucking tired."

"What's going on? You look worried."

"Oh man. Where do I start?"

When she had time to process his story, beginning with seeing Amy again outside the station and ending with the woman now ensconced in his home, Maggie could do nothing but repeat what he'd said. "She's in your house. Sleeping in your bedroom."

"In the *guest room*," he was quick to correct. "Sleeping with her daughter in the spare bed. Not mine. They have no place else to go." He scowled. "I'm so angry. Then I'm sad. Then I'm pissed off again. Why am I cleaning up her mess?"

"Why are you?"

He sighed. "Because I don't want Rachel to suffer for her mom's bad decisions. You'd love her, Maggie. She reminds me of Emily."

Maggie felt for him. But she didn't like any of this. Not at all. "Let me see if I can understand this better."

"Good luck," he muttered. "I sure as hell can't."

"She has a husband. Or is it an ex-husband?"

"According to Amy, they're still divorced but living together. Or they *were* living together." He shrugged.

"Right. So your ex-girlfriend tells you her daughter's father is working in Tacoma and can't afford more rent. So where is he living?"

"With some woman. I don't know specifics. But I got the impression Devon's sleeping with his roommate to pay his rent. Amy's hurting. She can't go to her sister because Denise is having a hard time herself, and Amy's parents kicked Amy out after a few weeks living with them."

"Her parents kicked out their daughter and grandchild. What happened? Do they not get along?"

He frowned. "Her mother dotes on Rachel."

"Yet she kicked her out. Why?"

"Probably because they hate Devon. I don't know."

"Don't get mad at me. I'm just asking questions because this doesn't make sense."

"I know that," he snapped. "And I'm sorry for being angry. I just… I feel like she's using me, and it's happening again."

"She is using you." Maggie saw that clearly. "But you're letting it happen."

"No. I'm trying to help Rachel. I can't let a little girl go homeless. Just like if you and Emily needed my help. I'd do everything I could for you."

She softened. A little. "I know, Reggie. That's who you are." She looked at him, seeing the mixture of misery and confusion hurting him. "But Amy isn't telling you everything, and you obviously know that. I think maybe you're willing to overlook it because you want to help Rachel. And maybe if you know the truth, you won't."

"Maybe." He groaned. "I didn't want to let her stay."

"Then she used Rachel against you."

"I don't think she meant to."

I do. Mack's words came rushing back about the woman. "Reggie, I love you, but I can't make your decisions for you. If you feel having her at your house is the right thing to do, then it's the right thing to do."

He sagged, relieved. "You're not leaving me?"

"Do you want me to?"

"Hell, no. I love you."

"And I love you. I don't like her being there. She's taking advantage of you. But you are who you are. And your generosity is one of the things I love about you." Yet she worried for him.

"Thanks, Maggie. You don't know how worried I've been. It's only for a week that she's going to be there. She asked for a few months, and I said no. Trust me. I'm over her. I love *you*. You don't need to worry about anything happening with her. I did this for Rachel, not Amy." He snorted. "She's still pining for Devon anyway."

"Does that bother you?"

"Huh? No way."

Maggie saw a hint of uncertainty, and it hurt. A lot. But Reggie had a right to his feelings, and only he could process them. She couldn't do it for him. "Okay. Let's spend today together. But maybe we'll wait on announcing our dating status to Emily until after things settle down."

He agreed too quickly for her peace of mind, but then, what choice did she have?

A week later, Maggie had seen Reggie a total of once. He'd come to dinner Monday night and they'd had a wonderful time playing with Emily and going for a walk together, the three of them trying to see who could make Frank fetch.

Reggie worked Tuesday, and she didn't hear from him. But that wasn't unusual. She knew how busy work could get and didn't want to distract him. She didn't hear from him on Wednesday or Thursday either. And she started to worry, but she didn't want to come across as needy or mistrustful.

By Friday though, she started to fear the worst. She texted Mack, having gotten his number at the pet adoption. He confirmed Reggie was physically okay and added, HE'S ALSO A FUCKING IDIOT. All in caps. Then he wished her good luck.

Troubled, Maggie called Reggie once more. This time, a woman answered.

Maggie frowned. "Hello?"

"Hi. Who's this?" The woman sounded pleasant, her voice husky.

"This is Maggie. Can I please speak with Reggie?"

A pause. "Oh, you're Reggie's girlfriend. Hi. I'm Amy."

Her tone sounded friendly, but Maggie sensed not to trust it and, in a superpolite voice, said, "Hello. I've heard about you as well." *Ha. I can be bitchy nice too.* "Can I talk to Reggie, please?"

"He's in the shower. But I can leave him a message."

The shower? "Thanks. Have him call me back if you would."

"He has your number, right? Oh, of course he does." Amy gave a light laugh. "You guys are dating. Never mind me."

"Thanks."

"Right. Bye."

So chipper. Maggie wanted to pop her one. She had no idea what Amy looked like or acted like except for a phone call, Reggie's memories, and Mack's sheer dislike. At the moment, Maggie was siding with Mack. But hey, she could tolerate Reggie's ex for one more day. According to Reggie, Amy and Rachel were to be leaving tomorrow—Saturday.

Yet none of that explained why he had been avoiding her.

She found out the next morning when Reggie showed up at her door to explain Amy would be staying another week.

Chapter Twenty-Four

REGGIE WAS PISSED. "LOOK, I CAN'T HELP THAT AMY NEEDS TO stay longer. But why won't you talk to me?"

"Excuse me?"

Reggie had never been so uneasy about his relationship with Maggie. She seemed annoyed. No, hostile. And there he was, trapped in the middle of doing what was right with what was popular. His family was on his ass to get far away from Amy and her problems. Mack wasn't talking to him, and Brad and Tex had expressed concern so gently, he wondered if they thought he'd lost his fucking mind. Maybe he had.

But Amy had sworn she needed just one more week to get herself together. And she'd been such a help, doing his laundry, making dinner. Listening as he complained about how everyone seemed against him lately.

"Maggie, we've been open and honest with each other from the beginning. Why are you avoiding me now?"

"Reggie, I don't like to text you when you're at work because I'm afraid I'll interfere with your job. But I always answer you when you text me. I waited, but you hadn't texted me in three days. I finally called *again* yesterday and left two messages. The last time I called you, I got Amy, who told me you were in *the shower.*"

She tapped her foot.

He didn't understand. "I didn't get any calls. I might have been in the shower when you called yesterday, but so what? I worked out and needed to clean up. It's not like she was in there with me." *Okay, bad joke.*

Maggie was steaming. "How are you not seeing the clear manipulation here?" She bit her lip, took in a deep breath, then let it out. "No. I will be calm, collected." She did her breathing thing again. And if Emily hadn't been so close, in her room with Frank while her mom and Reggie had a grown-up talk, he would have gathered Maggie to him and made love to her.

It had been a week, and he missed her like crazy.

"Reggie, I'd like you to imagine that this situation was reversed. Pretend that instead of you and Amy, I'm living with Stephen for a week. Just the two of us. And you called to talk to me, but I never called you back. Three times. Oh, and he answered the phone when you called and told you I was in the shower. How do you think you'd feel?"

"I'd want to rip his nuts off," came the immediate answer. He knew she had a right to be angry, but he still didn't understand the misconnect. "Damn. I'm sorry, honey." He shook his head. "I feel like I keep failing, and I'm only trying to help."

"I know. But Reggie, you're a grown man. A lot of what Amy has said doesn't make sense. For one, I have a hard time accepting she has no one to help her but you. She left you a long time ago for her ex-husband. He's not abusive or cruel, right?"

"No."

"But he's busy and working in Tacoma. And the family who absolutely loves Rachel kicked them both out? My bet is they wanted Rachel to stay and for Amy to leave. But Amy won't leave without Rachel because Rachel is her way of getting around you."

"That's not true."

"Isn't it? You were going to kick her out until she asked Rachel how she felt about staying with you. You said it yourself. And I'm sorry, but the only way you didn't get my messages is if someone deleted them from your phone. Why is she answering for you, anyway? Did she tell you I'd called?"

"Well, no. But she might have written it down and I missed it."

"You said you didn't call me because I'm avoiding you."

He could see her growing more upset.

"You did." Maggie was adamant.

"Did I?" He thought about it. "Actually, Rachel told me I had a message. She was playing with my phone. And she said some lady named Maggie told me not to call her for a while."

"And you believed her without even talking to me about it."

"I thought you were mad."

She nodded. "Why would I be mad? Just because my boyfriend is living with his ex for the foreseeable future? Maybe because I'm not sure why he's with me?"

"Hold on." Where the hell had that come from? "I love you."

"Do you? Or do you just want someone who needs you again? But now that Amy's here filling that void, who needs Maggie?"

"Damn it. That's not true." Her eyes watered, and he felt like shit. "Maggie, you know that's not true."

"I don't know anything anymore. Reggie, go figure out what you want in life. Not what I want for you. Not what Amy needs from you. And do some research. Talk to her parents or sister. Get at the truth. Then make some decisions. I love you, but if you don't truly love me, if you're only going through the same patterns as the past, then I'm not good for you either. And you're not good for me."

"Are we breaking up?" He couldn't understand how his life was spiraling when just two weeks ago, he'd been the happiest he'd ever been in his life.

"I know how *I* feel. It's you who's the problem." She gently helped him to his feet and walked him to the door. "You're a smart man. So why do you let others step all over you? Why are you so drawn to saving others when you really need to be saving yourself? Figure it out and let me know. And please, don't have her answering your phone anymore. It bothers me. A lot."

She shut the door behind him.

He just stood there, feeling stupid. And then the rage hit. He stormed away from her apartment and jumped into his car.

Next stop—Amy's sister.

An hour later, he pulled into her sister's driveway, walked to the door, and knocked. Denise opened the door, took a long drag of her cigarette as she looked at him, and laughed. "Now I get it. She went running back to you."

"Hi, Denise." They'd never gotten along when he'd been dating Amy. He'd thought at the time it was due to Denise's jealousy issues, since she and Amy had never been best of friends. Now he wondered… "What's going on with Amy?"

"You here for the truth or to confirm the lies she's been spinning?"

"The truth."

"Your girl is on again, off again with Devon. This must be an off period. He's in Tacoma interning as an electrician. But that shit takes time, and he's too busy to deal with a needy ex-wife. Plus, his girlfriend doesn't like Amy around all the time. She's gorgeous and distracts Devon."

Reggie felt a headache coming on. "What about Rachel?"

Denise puffed away. "That poor kid has no idea she's being used by her mother to get everyone to jump to her bidding. My folks took her in, you know."

"She said. Then she said they kicked her and Rachel out."

"No. They kicked Amy out because she keeps hanging on to Devon. They want her to keep her distance and take care of Rachel. But Amy follows that creep around. One thing that seems to be true is he's off the drugs and supposedly done running scams. I don't know."

"Wait." He had to be hearing wrong. "Amy can stay with your parents if she leaves Devon?"

"Yep. But she loves him and won't leave him. He wants little to do with Rachel, sadly. So she's not sticking around for my niece." Denise sneered, "Hell, I even bounced Devon a few times. He's great in the sack but such a loser when he's not fucking."

Reggie blew out a breath.

"She loved you, you know. She wasn't faking that," Denise said kindly. "From everything she said, you're a decent guy. She just can't quit Devon. He's like a drug." Denise shrugged. "She makes bad choices, but no one ever holds her accountable. Frankly, I'm surprised my folks threatened to kick her out and actually followed through. The problem is, it's Rachel who's suffering."

Reggie, disturbed, thanked her before driving to Amy's parents. Once there, he got the same story. He invited her folks to come to his house and get Rachel, and they agreed to come the very next morning.

He drove home, not sure what to think. But before veering toward his house, he made a detour. Someone he needed to talk to.

He knocked on Mack's door and waited.

Mack opened it, saw him, and closed it again.

Reggie banged again. "Damn it. Mack, I need to talk."

Mack opened up and stepped back with a bow. "Your Royal Fuckhead, please, come in."

Reggie sighed. "Can just one person get off my dick?"

Mack looked him over and shook his head. "Beer?"

"Got any lemonade?"

"Actually, yes."

They sat outside on Mack's porch. "You should never have taken Amy back."

Reggie drank and waited. "I didn't take her back."

"Didn't you?"

"No." Hell no. Not really. At least, he didn't think he had.

"I'll tell you what I saw when Amy and Rachel walked up to you outside the station. I saw you staring in shock and then with longing. Yeah, I said it. *Longing.* And it wasn't just when you looked at Rachel. It was seeing Amy too."

"But I don't love her. I love Maggie."

"Then why the fuck did you let your ex-girlfriend and her

kid move back in with you? Amy's a user, man, and she seriously messed you up less than a year ago. You're smart, Reggie. Why are you doing this?"

"I don't know." He felt such a burden, trying to do the right thing and getting screwed everywhere he turned because of it. "Do you know why I came here instead of going to Brad, Tex, or even my dad?"

"Because I'll tell it to you straight," Mack said plainly. "I never liked her for you, and it had nothing to do with Amy being quiet or too pretty or even that she went back to her ex. Do you know why I hated her?"

"Why?"

"Because she took the best parts about you and twisted them." Mack shook his head. "You're one of the nicest guys I know. Oh, you pretend you're a big old bastard, but we both know you'll do anything for your friends or for someone who genuinely needs help. In Amy, you had a chance to be the hero who saves the day, and then you never got off that horse. She kept you on it by hooking you on her daughter, because we all know what a sucker you are for a kid."

"Thanks a lot."

"Don't you see? That's who you are. A protector. A helper. Being a firefighter and EMT suits you down to the bone."

Reggie stared at his friend in surprise. "Thanks."

"Yeah, well, those traits also make you a major fuckhead. You're so scared to hurt a girl's feelings, you keep your mouth shut and turn into a doormat."

"Hey."

"See? Where's that attitude when dealing with Amy?"

He sighed. "I think she cheated on me with her ex when we were together. Hell, I know she did. And I knew then, I think. I just didn't want to know, mostly because I'd hate myself for loving her. Who loves someone who disrespects them?" Certainly not big, strong Reggie. He told Mack about all he'd learned. Then he went back to the very beginning and told him about everything that worked and didn't work with Maggie.

"I knew Amy was a bitch, and I can totally believe she cheated on you." Mack grimaced. "But messing with your relationship with Maggie is just wrong. Are you going to let her get away with it?"

Reggie automatically defended her. "We don't know she actually did anything. Rachel could have accidentally mistaken a message or deleted the messages."

"Open your eyes, asshole. Amy's sabotaging you! If you're happy with Maggie, you don't have time to help poor Amy. And no way Maggie lets that shit with Amy continue. So fascinating how your line in the sand—*one week, tops*—turned into another week. Another line. Then there will be another and another until Amy is back living with you until she leaves you for Devon again."

Reggie sat there with his head in his hands. "I know."

"What is wrong with you?"

Reggie felt an equal mix of guilt, shame, and disgust with himself. "I don't know. If anyone treated you guys the way she's treating me, I'd gut them. But for some reason, the women in my life get away with shit. I don't know. I guess I'm just a great big shithead."

Mack slugged him, and he put some power behind the punch to Reggie's shoulder.

"Hey."

"You *are* being a great big shithead. Now what are you going to do about it? And what are you going to do about Maggie? She's really cool, Reggie. Guaranteed, if you drag your feet and keep making her feel second-best, you'll lose her. If you won't have enough self-respect to stand up for yourself with Amy, then do it for Maggie. You remember, the woman you supposedly love?"

"I do love her." Oddly enough, putting Maggie first made it easier to think about pushing Amy, and possibly Rachel, away.

He needed to stop worrying about hurting their feelings and start worrying more about killing his relationship with Maggie.

"I believe you. And I think Maggie loves you back." Mack paused. "But didn't you say her ex-husband is spending more time here in the city? Gee. I wonder what that's about."

———

The next morning, Reggie watched the drama unfold. Amy's parents had come to pick Rachel up, and the little girl was ecstatic to go away with Grandma and Grandpa. Amy was livid and blaming Reggie for her mistakes. Which should have made him feel lower than scum. He used to feel terrible whenever he'd disappoint her. But now, he just felt numb.

Her parents took Rachel away, but before she left, she turned and ran back to hug him. "Thanks for helping, Reggie. I'll miss you."

"I'll miss you too." He felt better about her leaving this time. Her grandparents would look out for her.

They waved and left.

Reggie took a deep breath, centering himself, and let it go. He needed to do the right thing here. Not for Amy, the guys, his family, or even Maggie. But for himself. "Amy, you need to leave. Now."

"What?"

"I said get out. You lied to me. You manipulated me. I'm done."

She cried, and he knew the tears were real. "Where will I go? I can't go back home."

"You can. You choose not to. But you know, it's your choice. I won't clean up your messes anymore."

"But Reggie, I love you."

Looking into her eyes physically pained him because he could almost feel her despair. "I think you did once, but you don't now. Not really. You love the idea of what Devon should be for you.

But he's not a good person, and you know that. You just don't love yourself enough to expect you deserve better." He'd lived with her long enough to know that was true.

Amy kept crying. He couldn't handle it. So he hugged her and dried her tears. But when she tried to kiss him, he gently pushed her back. "No."

"Why?"

Her fragility and helplessness, what used to urge him to solve all her problems, now just made him sad for her. "Because I love someone else. And you need help I can't give."

"Can't or won't?"

He never got to answer the question, because that someone he loved stood there in the doorway, looking shocked.

With Mack grinning from ear to ear behind her. *Oh, shit.*

———————

Maggie stared at a woman who looked unnaturally beautiful. Like someone stepping out of a seashell, all legs and goddess-like grace. She was everything Maggie was not. And a big, fat liar to boot.

After clearing her throat, Maggie said, "Hi, Reggie. Hello. You must be Amy."

Amy of the timeless beauty wiped a tear from her cheek, the act perfection itself. "Hi."

"Yeah, you're the bitch who lied and tried to get me to break up with my boyfriend."

Amy blinked. "I don't know what you're talking about."

"Save it. Get your skinny ass out. Now. You have manipulated him for the last time. You're done."

Reggie gaped. "Maggie, I—"

"*Shut. Up.*" She glared at Reggie, so mad, she wanted to hit something. "Well, Cinderella? Your prince is waiting in Tacoma. Better hurry up before he shoves a glass slipper on someone else's foot."

Amy angrily wiped her tears. "You're mean."

"Yep. And you're so pretty. And sad. And helpless." Maggie sneered. "Give me a break. That worked last time. It's not working now."

"I don't have to leave," she tried again, looking pleadingly at Reggie. "Reggie? I need your help. If you kick me out, I could be in serious trouble. You'll never forgive yourself if I end up dead."

"You're right." Maggie moved past the woman toward the hallway, conscious of her following close behind. "You could be in serious trouble. But you're not a little girl. You can make your own decisions and live with them." Maggie grabbed a bunch of girlie things from the spare room and found a suitcase to throw it all in. At this point, she didn't care who it belonged to. Once she'd gone through the spare room, she did a cursory inspection of Reggie's and removed a picture of the two of them, tucked among several photos of friends and family, from a table in the hallway. Fuck it. It had to go.

She found toiletries in both bathrooms that she added to the suitcase, dimly aware of Reggie and Mack arguing and Amy crying big buckets of tears as the woman trailed Maggie like a fading shadow.

Returning to the living room, Maggie shoved the suitcase at Amy, who grabbed it reflexively. Then Maggie pushed her toward the front door.

"Wait," Amy wailed. "Stop it. Reggie! Help me."

Mack hurried around them and opened the door. "Here you go."

"Mack, you never liked me."

Heck, even Maggie had to admit she was starting to feel sorry for the woman. So she forced herself to say, "*I* don't like you. So add me to the list." She hauled the fragile beauty down the steps, opened the door to the woman's car, and tossed in the suitcase. "Get out of here. If you come back, I will seriously punch you in the face." Maggie was angry enough to do it too. Compassion or no compassion. "With this." She held up her cast.

"Fine. I'm leaving. I don't belong here." She looked back at Reggie, who stood on the porch next to Mack, watching. Waiting for him to stop her?

"No shit," Maggie agreed. She waited for the woman to leave. Once Amy left, Maggie stormed back to her car.

Reggie rushed up to her. "Maggie, that was amazing. I—"

"Get out of the way. I'm done with her, and you know, I might just be done with you too." She poked him in the chest, so hurt and angry, she couldn't contain it. "I'm worth ten of her. I love you for you. But *that's* what makes you happy? Getting your rocks off playing Mr. Fix-It?"

Reggie scowled but didn't argue.

"I understand your need to help everyone. But what happens when the next sob story asks to borrow money? To move in? To help pay the child support the kid's crappy father won't pay? Will you let them live with you and empty your bank account?"

"No. Of course not." He looked both angry and disgusted, with himself, she hoped.

"And what about me?"

"What about you?"

"Do you love me at all? Or are you still trying to fix a poor woman down on her luck? Because if that's all we really had, then I don't need you. No sex is that spectacular that I should settle for a man who thinks I can't handle my own problems." She got in the car and slammed the door shut. After turning the key, she rolled down the window. "Let me know what you decide to do with your life, and feel free to text me your answer. Now if you need me, I'll be at Stephen's with Emily."

She pulled away, letting the tears fall once out of sight. All in all, she'd been confrontational, but the fight that hadn't happened with Amy had been anticlimactic. Amy's cards collapsed the moment someone told her no.

How hard would that have been a week ago? How tough to ferret the truth without having to be *told* to figure things out? Was Reggie that pathetic, he couldn't see the manipulation for what it was? Or worse, had he known but done nothing about it? Because at heart, he *did* need to be needed?

How silly to fall in love without knowing the person you fell in love with.

She cried all the way to Stephen's.

When she parked, she dried her eyes and tried to pretend she hadn't been upset.

But when Stephen opened the door, he took one look at her and pulled her aside. Over his shoulder, he said loudly, "Keep playing, Emily. We'll be out soon."

She waved from the swings in the backyard, visible through the wide-open back doors. "Okay, Dad. Tell Mommy I said hi."

Stephen walked to Maggie's side and wiped a tear from her cheek. "Oh, Maggie. What's wrong?"

She cried into his chest, comforted when his arms settled around her.

When she'd cried out all her tears, she pulled back and accepted the hankie he offered.

"Thanks." She blew her nose. "I needed that. I'll wash this and get it back to you."

"Don't worry about it. What happened?"

"It's messy."

Stephen watched her carefully. "Reggie?"

"Yes. I think he's with me because he thinks I need him. But I don't. I'm not needy."

"No kidding." Stephen tugged her to sit next to him on the wide wooden stairs leading to the second floor. "Let me tell you a story. A man meets a beautiful girl and falls in love. They marry. But she doesn't seem to need him, and at times, not even like him much, and he can't figure out how to impress her. He's not very good at emotional cues, and she's the type that needs to hear the words. They have a baby, whom he loves to distraction. But he doesn't understand babies the way he understands work, so he takes comfort in doing what he does best—his job.

"The woman realizes their marriage isn't helping either of them. So they split up. And the man understands he lost his heart, and he has to figure out a way to put it back together again."

He watched her carefully, leaned close, and gave her a tender kiss on the lips. The kind from one friend to another, offering comfort.

Her breath hitched, and for a brief moment, she wished they had been able to make it work. "Did he figure out how to put it back?"

Stephen sighed. "He's very smart, but feelings aren't his specialty. And just when he thinks he's getting closer to understanding how to undo all his mistakes, the woman falls in love with someone else. The man thinks that maybe she was right. He did try to cling to the past. And that for him and the lady to be happy, they need to find happily ever after with other people. For the woman, it's someone who has the words of love and who shows her how he feels. Someone kind and generous and affectionate."

"Reggie is all those things."

"Is he, now?"

Maggie sighed. "Am I being too demanding?"

"Sweet Maggie Swanson, demanding?" He laughed. "I know you think Emily takes after me, and yes, in part she does. But that way of bulldozing through obstacles is all you. You're just nicer about tearing through the tough stuff than Emily is."

She leaned her head on his shoulder. "How'd you get to be such a good listener?"

He hugged her and kissed her on top of the head. "I had a good role model. And I'm not talking about Leon."

"See? We are better as friends."

"Yeah." He sighed. "I still miss the sex though."

"Stephen."

He chuckled. "But I—"

Banging on the door interrupted them.

Stephen went to answer it and said loudly, "You must be Reggie. She's on the stairs." He paused. "Maggie, get your clothes on. You have a visitor."

Chapter Twenty-Five

REGGIE HELD STEPHEN UP BY THE COLLAR OF HIS SHIRT, NO doubt prepared to pound him into tomorrow. "No way was Maggie in any state to have sex with anybody. She's upset. What did you do to her, asshole?"

Maggie entered the large foyer and stopped.

Reggie's gaze shot to her face. She could only imagine what she looked like. She'd been crying, so her eyes were red and puffy, her nose pink, and she held a crumpled handkerchief.

"What are you doing here?" Her eyes narrowed. "Put him down."

He did, and Stephen took a healthy step back, his gaze dismissive as he looked Reggie over. "*This* is who you fall for? A huge cretin who acts first and thinks later?"

Reggie bared his teeth at the guy.

Stephen rolled his eyes, apparently too stupid to realize Reggie could destroy him. Easily.

"He's a firefighter," Emily piped up from behind Maggie. "Hi, Reggie."

His entire demeanor changed, and he crouched as Emily ran to greet him.

Her gentle giant, Maggie thought with bemusement. She couldn't change him. And honestly, should she want to? She'd wanted Stephen to be something he wasn't, and they divorced. If she really loved Reggie, she had to accept that he would always want to look out for the little guy, to the point of maybe sometimes giving too much.

But she needed to know if what he felt for her was real.

He gave Emily a high five. She gave him back a kiss on the cheek that put a big grin on his face. "Hey, Ninja Princess."

Stephen just watched him then sighed.

And just like that, as if they were still married, he annoyed her.

"Come on, Emily. Let's give your mom and Reggie some talking time. We'll go in my office and learn more about the planets. I just got a terrific atlas of the universe with great pictures. You can ask any questions you want."

They left together, closing themselves in Stephen's office.

Maggie watched Reggie straighten. He looked tired and unhappy but hopeful.

"I want to apologize," he began, "not for helping Amy, but for not taking your feelings into account. It was selfish, and I'm sorry."

She nodded, liking how this was going.

"I am who I am, Maggie. I help people. And I like helping people. I liked helping you." He stepped closer. "But that's not why I love you."

"Well, then, why do you?" She sniffed. "I'm not tall and willowy with super pretty hair and legs to here." She put a hand above her head. "I can't be a stand-in for Amy."

"You aren't."

"How do I know that? You couldn't even get her to leave."

"I was making that happen when you arrived. And though I wouldn't have put my hands on her to get her ass out, the way you did…" He paused for a brief grin. "I would have handled it."

"Yeah? How?"

"Two words. Nadia and Lisa."

"I…oh."

"Yep. You think you were tough on her? Imagine either of my sisters, who can't stand her, escorting her to the door." He snorted. "Nadia would have put Amy's head through the wall on the way out."

"I can see that happening." Frankly, she'd *like* to see that happen.

"Amy isn't a bad person. I'm not making excuses for her. She's weak. I know that. I also realize that just because I'm strong doesn't mean I should involve myself in everyone's problems. But I know you, Maggie. There's no way you would have turned a little girl away, knowing her mother couldn't care for her."

"But she's back with Amy now."

"No. Amy's parents are trying to get custody of Rachel. And if they can't work it, maybe her sister can help. But it's their problem to handle. Not mine."

She huffed. "Reggie, I wasn't asking you to not help a child in need. I was upset because you let yourself be used. And you liked it."

He tilted his head. "I did. I admit it. That's part of what makes me tick—being needed. Is that so bad?"

"No, unless that's the only thing attracting you to me." She teared up again, damn it. "It isn't, is it?" She hoped against hope that wasn't true.

"Oh, Maggie." He stepped close and hugged her, and everything felt right again. "I love you for you. You're the only person I've ever been with who's stood up for me. And I'm not talking about my family and friends. You make me whole, baby. I was jealous when I thought of you with Stephen. But I never worried you'd cheat on me. I trust you completely, and I don't say that about many people. Even with Amy, I never really trusted her, even before she hurt me, deeply. Emotional wounds take longer to heal."

"I know." She looked up at him. "Are you sure you want me? I'm going to be healed in another few weeks, you know."

"But you're still short, so you'll still need me to grab the vase from the top shelf."

"Funny." But she needed to know. "Why, Reggie? Why did you let Amy step all over you? Why do I worry you'll do that again? You seem to have no problem arguing with *me*. Heck, we've argued with each other a bunch of times."

"Because I know you're strong." He sighed. "I should probably get counseling."

"You should."

"And I'll go. I swear. With you, if you want. I don't know why I tend to take forever to have a backbone with the women in my life. My sisters have always been strong. My mom, well, not so much. But she always had my dad helping her." He looked at her with love in his eyes. "The way you help me. I was so fucking proud of how you dealt with Amy earlier. And how you're such an independent woman. But I want you to need me too."

"I do, but not for what you can do for me. I need you to love me. That's all."

"I do. More than anything or anyone. I love you, Maggie May. And if you leave me, I'll never be the same. I don't deserve you. But baby, I'll do anything to make you happy."

"But not at your own expense," she reminded him, exasperated.

He chuckled. "Right. See? You should go to therapy with me, to make sure I'm getting the help I need."

She smiled. "Are you sure about this? About me? I'm talking forever, Reggie."

He nodded, solemn, and kissed her so tenderly, she wanted to cry. "Forever. You, me, Emily, and Frank. And the guys, my family, Benny and Doug, and…" He sneered. "Stephen, if you insist on remaining friends."

She laughed and wrapped her arms around him, loving him so much. "We should tell Emily we're together now."

"Ah, I think she knows."

"How?"

He showed her the text Benny had sent him. A photo of a hand-drawn picture. Two sticks that looked suspiciously like Maggie and Reggie held hands with a big heart above them. A little girl and her dog sat in front of them with a flower. The flower had a smiling face and a baby bottle near it. "She drew this last Saturday at Doug and Benny's, apparently, when you and I were talking."

"Huh."

"According to Benny, Emily said you and I make a lot of googly eyes at each other when we're together."

She blushed. "She saw that?"

"Yep." He smiled. "Now do you forgive me or what? Because I have nothing but time, and I can tell my being here is annoying Stephen, so I'm happy to wait all day to hear you tell me you love me again."

"I do, but I'm still mad."

"Excellent. I'm pretty damn good at groveling."

"Are we talking about Yahtzee groveling?"

"Oh yeah. Double score, for sure."

She traced a line across his chest, missing how it felt to be skin to skin, pressed up against his heart. "Well, I could be persuaded to discuss the matter. But first we have Emily to deal with."

"After you."

They walked to the closed door of Stephen's office and knocked.

Emily opened the door. She glanced from Maggie to Reggie. "Did you do the kissy stuff yet?"

"Yes, want to see?" Reggie asked.

Stephen looked pained.

"Yeah."

Reggie planted a solid kiss on Maggie's lips then took her good hand and raised it to his lips. Another kiss, and they remained holding hands. "See?"

Emily grinned. "Are we going home now?"

Stephen sighed. *So much* sighing. "Emily and I are planning to spend tonight here. We're going to watch a movie, okay? I'll bring her by tomorrow."

"Thank you, Stephen." Maggie kissed him on the cheek, and Emily clapped.

"So much kissing!"

Then Maggie, Stephen, and Reggie took their turns kissing Emily on the cheek. Delighted, Emily kissed Frank, who woofed and yipped when Vader hissed then ran away, waiting for Frank to play chase. When he didn't, she flopped on her back and pawed at the air.

Maggie grinned. "I love your kitten, Stephen."

"She is cute." He smiled. "Have fun you two. And Reggie, treat her well or I'll destroy you financially. And that's not an idle threat. Ciao."

Maggie hustled her boyfriend away before his frown grew any darker. "He's kidding." *I think.*

They made it back to his house in record time. Inside, Maggie looked around, still feeling Amy's presence, a miasma of guilt and shame and greed that coated everything. Reggie took her by the hand and led her down the hall to his room. "I swear, nothing happened between Amy and me. I love *you*, Maggie."

"I believe you. But I still hate that she was here."

"Which is why we have to work very hard to exorcise her from the house." He wiggled his brows, and she laughed at herself.

"I'm jealous."

"And I'm sorry, but I love that you are." He stripped her naked and placed her on the bed.

"Why do I feel like an offering?" She watched him get naked, hungry for him since it had been several days.

He didn't waste any time. Reggie moved her legs apart and dove in, his mouth whispering such sweet things while he sucked her into an explosive orgasm.

He turned on his back and pulled her over him.

But she had a tough time focusing, still lost in pleasure.

"Fuck. I'm so hard, Maggie." He drew her down for a kiss, grinding up against her.

She shifted, and the head of his shaft slid inside her. They both paused, panting.

Reggie watched her, and she watched him as she sank down, taking him all the way inside her.

"Yeah, baby. Fuck." Reggie gripped her hips, urging her to move.

And she did. Maggie rode him hard, up and down, feeling such fullness, she never wanted to stop.

Reggie's moans and hands on her breast and hip urged her to move faster. He touched her so deeply, hitting that special place inside her that pushed her toward another climax. He soon had her slamming down on top of him, shouting her name as he came.

Which set her off, both of them moaning while they shared in the perfect union of their love.

When she'd finished, she slumped over him, her hand on his chest, the fingers of her bad hand gently exploring his warm skin. "I can't wait until I have two good hands to touch you."

"Hmm. Neither can I." He drew her down for a lazy kiss that turned into a marathon kissing session.

Which lead to more sex and more positions, until, finally sated, she collapsed on top of him.

"I have a confession to make," he said.

"Oh no. No more drama."

"It's harmless."

"Tell me." She looked down at him, so in love, especially when he smiled.

"I have been coming in you for a solid month. Each and every time, a part of me envisions a baby with your looks and my strength."

"Or your looks and my strength," she said as she made a tiny muscle that made him laugh.

"I love you, Maggie May."

She smiled and kissed him. "And I love you, but if you say that name again, I will brain you with my cast."

"Sorry." He snickered and looked up at her with a wondrous expression on his face. "Let me ask you something… How would you feel about getting some magic baby beans so I can get to planting? I hear it's the growing season."

A baby with Reggie. She couldn't wait. "Is that what you hear?"

"I surely do."

She bit her lip. "You realize if we do this, we're talking major commitment first. Moving in together. Co-parenting with Stephen. No other women running the gauntlet with your friends. Just me. And Emily, of course."

"I can't wait. Will you marry me, Maggie?"

"You're still inside me," she gasped. "You can't propose when you're inside someone!"

"I can and did. Besides. You have to marry me to save me from myself. I need you. No, let me rephrase that. I love and adore you."

She stared at him, seeing a future she wanted badly enough to take a chance on love, and on a man who never stopped giving.

"Well, okay then. Yes, I'll marry you."

He stirred inside her and blinked in surprise. "I think that's my dick telling you how happy he is."

She laughed. "I'll marry you on one condition—you have to propose on bended knee at a later date. And I don't need a big ring or lots of nonsense. Just you loving me. But not while *inside* me."

He grinned. "Talk about rolling a Yahtzee."

Two months later

Mack watched from Reggie's dad's kitchen. The guy threw a hell of a pre-Halloween brunch.

"Yo, Nadia, who's the dude?" He pointed to the out-of-place academic standing in the living room by himself. Around him, Brad, Tex, and Reggie were laughing at something Doug said. Benny stood with Harry, talking vegetables and swapping romance tips.

Maggie and Emily were playing with Frank and Bree while Avery watched with a cautious eye on the dog.

Nadia slung an arm around Mack's shoulders. "That cutie is Maggie's ex-husband. He's not a bad guy. I met him earlier. Why do you ask?"

He nodded to Lisa, who stood, looking flabbergasted, in the front doorway. She closed the door behind her and walked straight to Stephen.

"Hello."

Stephen blinked. His smile warmed by several degrees. "Why, hello. I'm Stephen Swanson. Emily's dad."

She shook his hand and got the strangest look on her face. "I'm Lisa." She just stood there for a moment, then, flustered, pulled back her hand.

Mack looked around, but he didn't see anyone but himself and Nadia noticing Lisa's odd behavior.

"How do you know everyone here?" Stephen asked.

"I'm Reggie's older sister." Lisa smiled.

Stephen looked as if he'd been knocked sideways.

Mack chuckled. "Is it just me, or are we watching cupid's arrows sink into two lame-asses who can't seem to find love?"

Nadia snickered and kissed him on the cheek. "Don't ever change." She left him to join her sister and Stephen, no doubt to screw with the pair.

Mack shook his head, in no rush to find love. But with all his friends falling, he worried he just might be next.

As the party wrapped up, Reggie made an announcement. "Everyone, I just wanted to say that…" The big bastard got down on one knee in front of Maggie, who smirked down at him.

Damn, but Mack loved that woman. She was exactly what Reggie had been missing in his life.

Emily giggled and hurried to hand him a small box.

He kissed her on the cheek, and everyone smiled.

"Aw." Harry beamed.

"Maggie," Reggie said, his voice thick with emotion. "Will you marry me?"

"Yes, I think I will."

They kissed. Everyone cheered. Congratulations and hugs were shared.

Reggie stood and dragged Brad and Avery close. "And something else needs to be said."

Brad looked at Avery, who grinned and nodded. "Tell them."

Brad sucked in a breath and said, "We're pregnant."

More cheers and hugs, and Emily congratulated the pair for planting their seeds during the right growing season, which had everyone laughing.

Then Mack got the hell out of there before he caught the love bug. *No way. Not for this single stud.* Letting the car take him home on a beautiful, crisp fall day, he lost track of his speed. Until flashing lights drew him over.

"Well, shit."

He waited, his driver's license and registration at the ready.

"Well, well, well. If it isn't the blow job king."

He did a double take and swore under his breath. "And if it isn't one of the losers, I mean, the Top Cops." He wished she looked hard and not like the fake cop in one of his overwatched X-rated movies. His favorite outfielder looked trim, dangerous, and sexy as hell as she wrote him up for speeding.

"So you're the Revere who lost his way." She handed him the ticket and looked him over, peering over her mirrored glasses.

Damn if his body didn't react to that gray-eyed stare. "You mean, the only Revere to follow his passion for saving people as opposed to writing speeding tickets."

She sneered at him.

He sneered back.

"Have a nice day." She started walking back to her car.

"Oh, you too, officer. I'm sure we'll see each other again."

"Soccer on Saturday, as a matter of fact." She turned and grinned, walking backward. "We're up against the Burning Embers."

"Great. See you then, Officer Sexy."

She stopped. "What did you call me?"

"Officer Carmichael. That is your name on the ticket you handed me."

She frowned. "Yeah, and it's a warning, slick. Go easy on the speed around here or the next ticket's for real."

He smiled again.

She got in her car and left.

Mack considered the ticket. "Officer Cassandra Carmichael. A beautiful woman and sexy cop. A chance meeting while she's on duty with a hunk in a cool car. The exact scenario that gets me off in two seconds flat." He heard his words out loud and laughed himself silly. A coincidental sexy plot that turned into a happy ending—pun intended.

Now wouldn't that be a kick, cupid shooting Mack in the ass the next time he ran into the angry Cassandra?

He crumpled the ticket—make that *warning*—and sped home, wishing he could stop himself from wanting to fast-forward to Saturday's soccer game. Did she know the effect her icy-gray eyes had on him? Was she as mean in bed as she was on the playing field?

And why the hell do I care?

Read on for a sneak peek at book 4
in the Turn Up the Heat series
Turn Up the Heat
Available March 2022 from Sourcebooks Casablanca

Chapter 1

MACK REVERE WANTED TO BELIEVE THAT THE WOMAN HAD hit him by accident. He couldn't chalk up the incident to alcohol, a joke gone wrong, or the fact he'd been flaunting the rules. He hadn't. For once, he'd been playing clean and fair.

Yeah, and look where that got you.

Winded and flat on his back, he blinked up at the clear November sky. Seattle remained cloudless yet cold. The forecast predicted clear skies for the next week, but with the way the weather could turn on a dime, he hadn't put aside his umbrella just yet. Too bad the rain from the past week had turned the soccer field into a mud bowl.

He grimaced as the cold, wet muck seeped into the back of his jersey and shorts. Ew. Talk about a wet start to his Saturday morning.

A head interrupted his field of vision. Bright-gray eyes dominated an unforgiving face that smirked down at him. A dark ponytail swung over the woman's shoulder as she tilted her head, studying him like a cockroach. Police officer Cassandra Carmichael, in the flesh.

She stared. "That tumble you took must have hurt."

"Ya think?" he snarled, trying to ignore the ache in his tailbone. Her slide tackle had done most of the work, but the mud sure the hell hadn't helped. "Totally unnecessary."

"Yet we have the ball, so maybe it *was* necessary." She glanced over at her teammate, who kicked a goal, then turned back to him and shook her head. "No wonder your team is losing. If they're smart, they'll move you from midfield to offense. Put you out where the ball *isn't*."

Before he could say something cutting, witty, and God-willing sarcastic, she flounced away to congratulate her teammates.

He wanted to grab her by that ponytail and roll *her* around in the mud. Then, maybe, the ref would call a time-out for a mud fight. Everyone would get involved. Carmichael would get wet and dirty. *Oh, so dirty*. Then she'd have to take off that nasty uniform to showcase that tight, toned body…

He glanced over at her. She didn't look back, completely ignoring him. Or maybe she'd forgotten she'd nearly broken him on the soccer field.

So much for a family-friendly game.

"I could use a little help here," he yelled out to her, annoyed to still be so attracted to the woman who just a week ago had given him a speeding ticket. Well, a warning, but still.

"Sorry, can't," she yelled back without looking at him and said something he couldn't make out that caused her nearest teammates to laugh.

"You don't sound sorry," he muttered and flipped off her buddies, who promptly sneered and sent the gesture right on back.

The bastards. He absolutely loathed playing against the Top Cops, no matter what the sport.

Tex, fellow firefighter, teammate, and one of Mack's best friends, helped him to his feet.

"She did that on purpose," Mack said.

"Of course she did. Duh." Tex raised a brow, his Texan accent thick as he responded, "If your brains were leather, you wouldn't have enough to saddle a june bug."

"What the hell does that mean?"

"Well, my uncle likes to say it every now and again to the stupid cousin everyone hates."

"Not helping, Tex."

But Tex had already turned to yell, "Nice illegal tackle, Officer." To Mack he said, "Gotta say, though, that tackle was totally bitchy. She added an evil laugh there at the end."

"Agreed." Mack wiped gobs of mud from his legs and backside and glared at the woman who should have been penalized with a red card. Or at least a yellow warning. He raised his voice. "Maybe if the refs would quit leering at a certain someone they'd make the right call!"

The tall referee who couldn't seem to take his gaze from Carmichael's ass ignored him.

"I feel for you." Tex shook his head. "Our fans are giving you a pity clap just for standing up."

Mack glanced to the stands to see Tex was right. A thumbs-up from Tex's girlfriend. And a "You can do it, Mack!" from… Oh God. His mother.

Mack seethed with embarrassment. For all of five seconds. Then he decided to get even.

On the Top Cops' next breakaway down the field, Mack switched with the left halfback. "I got this." He proceeded to steal the ball from one of the Top Cops' lead scorers and sent it down-field to Tex.

"Lucky break," the scorer sneered.

Mack waited until the refs turned away before shoving him aside. Talk about annoying.

"Hey!"

"Whatever."

"Prick."

"Momma's boy."

Mack dodged when the guy took a half-hearted swing at him. Which brought several comments from the stands: pro-tests from the Burning Embers' fans and cheers from the Top Cops' side.

The idiot Mack had just shoved eyed Mack with clear derision. "*I'm* a momma's boy? Really?" He nodded to the stands.

"You can do it, Mack!" Their mother frowned. "Xavier, be nice to your brother."

Xavier smiled wide. "Sure thing, Ma." Then he punched Mack in the arm.

Mack frowned, punched him back, and narrowly avoided a soccer ball to the face. Xavier wasn't so lucky. He took the ball to the side of his head.

"Gee, that must have hurt." Mack grinned at his brother swearing and shaking his head, no doubt to clear the ringing between his ears.

"Sorry, Xavier," Carmichael called.

Mack chuckled, took the ball, and dribbled down the field. He pretended to pass to the center and juked Carmichael into tripping over her own feet. She went down in the mud.

Still laughing, Mack yelled over his shoulder, "Officer down!"

"Jackass!"

He passed to an open player and cheered his delight when their team scored, evening the game.

Turning, he found himself surrounded by muddy, burly police officers, Carmichael among them.

"What?"

"That was cheap," she argued.

"Was it the 'Officer down' part or the part when you fell over your own feet? And wow, are you dirty."

Out of the corner of his eye he saw one of the cops grab a handful of mud. Mack ducked behind Carmichael just as the guy slung it. He heard her gasp and saw she'd been hit in the chest. And what a sorry sight that was, obscuring anything so fine.

She glared at the offender, who startled whistling and quickly walked away.

Deciding that would be the smart move, Mack followed. But

not before his brother tackled him to the ground and shoved his face in wet dirt and grass.

Mack retaliated. The rest of his team joined him, and the soccer game turned into a real free-for-all. Laughter, swearing, and a lot of mudslinging went both ways. Unfortunately, both teams ended up being disqualified for unsportsmanlike behavior—but only because some smartass had decked both refs with mud as well.

———————————

"What a great game," Mack said as he and the guys joined their friends at the bleachers.

"Great but messy." Brad, his buddy and part of their tight, four-man firefighting crew, looked down at himself with a frown.

His girlfriend rolled her eyes. "It's just dirt, Brad."

Brad blinked. "Oh?" Then he chased her around the field laughing maniacally.

"Don't even think about it," Tex's girlfriend warned.

"Darlin', I have half a brain. Not much, but it's the half that works." He didn't even try touching her as the pair made their goodbyes.

Reggie, the last member of their four-man fire crew, stood next to Mack's mother in jeans and a jacket. He sniffled a few more times for effect. "This cold is just awful. Too bad I couldn't have joined you."

Considering the guy had been just fine the night prior over beers and darts, he wasn't earning any loyalty points for not playing this morning.

"I'm so disappointed in your weak lies." Mack shook his head.

Reggie apparently felt no such upset because he just grinned. "Gotta go. I promised Maggie and Emily doughnuts this morning."

"Fine. Go. Not like we could have used you or anything."

"Great. Bye."

Reggie left.

And then there was one…

"Oh, Mackenzie. Monkey-face, you're a mess."

He cringed. "Ma, not here." Where too many witnesses might overhear and use that name against him at work.

She huffed. "Please. It's a fine name. After your great-grandfather."

"Not Mackenzie. That nickname." He lowered his voice. "You have no idea what the guys—"

"Oh, Mon-key-face…" Xavier, older by two years but always so much more immature than Mack, called in a singsong voice. "There you are." He walked up to his brother and mother and grinned. "Buddy, you look awful."

"Right back at ya, moron." Mack couldn't help grinning back. The youngest of four, Mack loved his family. Even if they didn't always seem to understand him. Or like him. But today, Xavier appeared in a decent mood, and their mother had cheered for Mack, the lone firefighter in a family of cops.

Perhaps soon he'd see pigs fly.

Mack made small talk, watching as the crowd dispersed while subtly looking for one particular dirty player—pun intended. There. He saw Carmichael wringing the bottom of her shirt by the parking lot.

"Be right back." He left before his family could corner him. "Hey, Carmichael."

She flipped her head back, slapping herself in the face with a wet ponytail, and glared at him. "Well, if it isn't Mr. Pushy."

"Oh please. You pushed me first. I didn't even touch you. It was my fast moves and amazingly handsome face that caused you to go down, hard."

Her lips twitched, but to her credit, she didn't laugh. "You are so full of it."

"I really am."

Ha. There. She smiled. Her expression turned sour once more, and she said in a crisp, cold tone, "What do you want, Revere?"

Excited she remembered his name, he nevertheless tried to play it cool. "Just wanted to let you know I was okay, that my tailbone is still in one piece, you know, in case you were wondering."

"I wasn't."

"Yeah, I'm feeling loose." He rolled his neck and pulled a knee to his chest, carefully balancing as he stretched his glutes. "Everything still works." He set his foot down before he fell over and ruined all his careful posturing.

"Am I supposed to be happy for you?"

"Yes, you are." He smiled. "So, you busy tonight?"

"Seriously?" She spread her arms wide, bringing unintended attention to her full breasts. "I'll be spending the next week washing the mud from my body."

As soon as she said it, she stilled, blinked, and watched him.

Don't say it. Don't say it.

Her eyes narrowed, as if reading his mind.

"So…you want any help with that?"

"Unbelievable," she muttered, turned on her heel, and stalked away from him.

But Mack would swear he saw a grin on her face before she left.

Amused and granting himself permission to treat today as a victory, he rejoined his mom and brother, in the mood for a family breakfast after all.

Cass stomped back to her car, glad she'd had the foresight to bring a towel with her. At least she'd keep her car seat fairly clean while she drove home.

"Yo, you coming over later?" her partner asked.

She turned to see Jed standing by his car, his wife and the twins already inside and no doubt buckled up. "Who's cooking? You or Shannon?"

Jed frowned. "Why the hell does that matter?"

She just looked at him.

He sighed. "Shannon's cooking, okay?"

"I'll be there." She gave him a thumbs-up.

He glowered before entering his car and driving away.

Cass chuckled. Her amusement lingered on the drive home. Though she'd never admit it, she thoroughly enjoyed the competitive games she played as a Top Cops team member. Challenging—and usually beating—the other teams in their countywide sports league was so satisfying. Cass played to win. Why else bother playing?

The Burning Embers, those arrogant no-neck men and women firefighters, always gave as good as they got. She could respect that. Even though they'd both lost today, they'd put up a heck of a fight.

She particularly liked the very handsome, sarcastic, and frustrating Mackenzie Revere, though she'd deny it 'til her last breath. From the first time she'd seen the guy, she'd been dumbstruck.

Short, dark-brown hair framed an unforgettable face. He had amazing cheekbones, a straight nose, a square chin, and bright-blue eyes. And when he smiled...*good night*, but he could stop a girl in her tracks. He'd surely stopped hers. That was to say nothing of his perfectly proportioned, muscular, long-legged body. Or of his seasoned tan that said he liked the sun. She'd once seen him with his shirt off during softball season in the summer... *Whoa, momma.*

Even the fire department agreed. They'd used him as their poster boy for Station 44. She'd seen Mack on public service advertisements and in the paper and on TV, informing everyone about the new fire station that had opened earlier in the year.

Unfortunately, he was a Revere, one of the many cop families working for the city. His father, mother, and three brothers had all worked or continued to work in law enforcement. Heck, Xavier Revere worked in her precinct. Since Cass never mixed business with pleasure, she'd had to strike the sexy, firefighting Mack off her hottie list. She didn't date friends of work friends—something she continually told her partner's tenacious wife.

As much as Cass genuinely loved Shannon, Jed's wife could be pushy. For some reason, a year ago, she'd decided to put her matchmaking skills to work finding Cass a boyfriend.

At first, Cass had wondered if Shannon might be jealous of all the time Cass spent with Jed on the job. But after a frank conversation with the woman, she'd learned that, no, Shannon trusted both Cass and her husband. She had every right to, but Cass had dealt with many spouses of fellow officers on the job, and none of them seemed to like her much. Just Shannon with her wacky sense of humor and adorable, troublemaking twins.

So why was Shannon so keen on setting Cass up for a love connection?

A question that still plagued her, but Cass knew better than to bring up the subject. Lately, Shannon had been laying off, so Cass said nothing about being dateless. Or about how she'd started to feel as if she might actually be missing out on a part of life. Loneliness could be a real bitch.

As Cass pulled into her driveway, she tried to forget about the path her dating life hadn't taken and focused instead of what she needed to get done on her days off. She worked a four-on, two-off rotation with her partner. So she had one more day until she went back to work.

And that laundry wasn't going to do itself.

Seven hours later, she arrived at Jed and Shannon's wearing a nice pair of jeans, a warm navy sweater, and her favorite boots. She parked in the back, per Jed's orders, and raised her hand to knock on the door, startled to hear several people inside, along with music and laughter.

That sounded like a party.

Oh, hell no. Time to go.

As she turned, the door opened.

"No, you don't. Get your ass in here." Faster than should be humanly possible, Jed grabbed her by the shoulder and spun her around. He pulled her inside and shut the door behind her. Then he shifted places with her, blocking her from exiting.

"You asshole," she swore in a low voice, conscious of the twins, who always seemed to appear out of thin air. "What the hell is this?"

Noise from several adults, alternative rock music, and children's laughter promised a cacophony of trouble.

Cass hated crowds, parties, and, according to her father, fun.

"Not my idea." He held up his hands in surrender. "Shannon told me nothing until about an hour before she forced me to change into 'company clothes.'" He grimaced and plucked at his button-down shirt.

"And you couldn't text me?"

"She hid my phone."

That did sound like something Shannon might do. "Oh, come on." Cass took a look around at the clean kitchen, decorated dining space, and mingling adults. "Your house is never this clean. Not one pair of shoes for anyone to trip over in the doorway, and you didn't notice until she told you to expect company an hour ago?"

"It's cleaning day." He groaned. "I know. I swear, though, I had no idea. And I'm a little concerned. Shannon really wanted you at this party. I hope she's not—"

"Cass! There you are." Shannon shot Jed a death glare and put on a wide smile for Cass. Despite Shannon's petite stature, beauty, and dainty appearance, the woman had a death grip when she wanted something. The hold she had on Cass's forearm actually hurt.

Cass shoved the six-pack she'd brought at Jed and reluctantly followed—*was dragged by*—Shannon into the crowded living room. "What the hell—"

"Quiet, you." Shannon pulled her toward a tall, handsome guy who looked familiar.

"Hey, Carmichael. What's up?" the man asked, his smile widening as he looked her over.

Josh Newcastle. The new guy. Her groan turned into a cough when Shannon elbowed her. "Sorry, Newcastle. Something in my throat. Ah, not much going on with me. Great party, Shannon," Cass said with feigned enthusiasm.

"Isn't it?" Shannon chirped. "So, you two know each other from work, I take it?"

Newcastle nodded with enthusiasm. "I started last week. Transferred from Spokane."

"I love Spokane." Shannon smiled.

Cass stood there, dying for a beer and pretending to be unaware of Newcastle stripping her naked with his gaze while Shannon and he chatted like besties. Over her shoulder, she spotted Jed fast approaching with a beer in each hand. He mouthed, *Hold on, I'm coming*, or something to that effect.

But just as he neared, Shannon cut him off by taking the beer meant for Cass. "Oh, thanks, honey. I was just coming to get you. Cass, can you and Josh talk while I take care of something?"

"Er, ah…"

"Sure," Josh said, beaming.

Shannon yanked Jed with her, leaving Cass at the mercy of Officer My Eyes Are Up Here.

"I hear you're single." Josh sipped from his drink. "Me too. We should go out some time."

Who? Me or my breasts? Cass sighed, waiting for him to make eye contact.

It promised to be a long, long night.

Acknowledgments

Thanks to my sensitivity readers, Donna W.B. and Lisa R., for making sure I did justice to my characters. To Cat and Donovan for giving me solid details about firefighting and lifesaving. And to my agent, Nicole, for always backing me up.

About the Author

Caffeine addict, boy referee, and romance aficionado, *New York Times* and *USA Today* bestseller Marie Harte is a confessed bibliophile and devotee of action movies. Whether biking around town, hiking, or hanging at the local tea shop, she's constantly plotting to give everyone a happily ever after. Visit marieharte.com and fall in love.

THE KISSING GAME

"I bet you a kiss you can't resist me."
Game on.

Rena Jackson has worked her tail off to open her own hair salon, and she's almost ready to quit her job at the local bar. Rena's also a diehard romantic, and she's had her eye on bar regular Axel Heller for a while. He's got that tall, brooding, and handsome thing going on big-time. Problem is, he's got that buttoned-up ice-man thing going as well. With Valentine's Day just around the corner, Rena's about ready to give up on Axel and find her own Mr. Right. But Axel has a plan of his own when he makes one crazy, desperate play to get her attention...

"Sexy, sweet, and thoroughly satisfying."

—Lauren Layne, *New York Times* bestselling author

For more info about Sourcebooks's
books and authors, visit:

sourcebooks.com

FEARLESS

These highly competitive racers are torn between the glitz of the international stage and the ranches they call home.

Billy King may be smiling under his black Stetson, but the plain truth is this cowboy-turned-racer is hurting. The moment he's free from the press circuit, Billy bolts home—resolved to heal, and ready to win Taryn's heart a second time. Hopefully, before the love of his life is gone for good.

Taryn Ledell never wanted to fall for sweet blue eyes and a deep southern drawl. As a World Superbike racer, she had plans, and none of them involved playing second fiddle to any man. But now he's back, and she's forced to make some hard choices. But broken bones and broken hearts don't heal overnight, and the cost of forgiveness can be sky high: unless Billy can prove that his heart never left the ranch...or her.

"Vivid and fearless."

—Kari Lynn Dell

For more info about Sourcebooks's books and authors, visit:

sourcebooks.com